The Lucky Eight

Sheila Bugler grew up in a small town in the west of Ireland. After studying Psychology at University College Galway (now called NUI Galway) she left Ireland and worked as an EFL teacher, travelling to Italy, Spain, Germany, Holland and Argentina.

She is the author of a series of crime novels featuring DI Ellen Kelly. The novels are set in South East London, an area she knows and loves.

She now lives in Eastbourne, on the beautiful East Sussex coast. Eastbourne is the location for her series of crime novels featuring investigative journalist Dee Doran.

When she's not writing, Sheila does corporate writing and storytelling, she runs creative writing courses, is a tutor for the Writers Bureau and is a mentor on the WoMentoring programme. She reviews crime fiction for crimesquad.com and she is a regular guest on BBC Radio Sussex.

She is married with two children.

Also by Sheila Bugler

The Lucky Eight

An Eastbourne Murder Mystery

I Could Be You
When the Dead Speak
Before You Were Gone

THE LUCKY EIGHT

SHEILA BUGLER

CANELO CRIME

First published in the United Kingdom in 2021 by

Canelo
31 Helen Road
Oxford OX2 0DF
United Kingdom

A CIP catalogue record for this book is available from the British Library.

Print ISBN 978 1 80032 362 9
Ebook ISBN 978 1 80032 166 3

Look for more great books at www.canelo.co

Printed and bound in Great Britain by Clays Ltd, Elcograf S.p.A.

1

To my parents, Harry and Adrienne, for everything they've done for me. Love you both so much and have missed seeing you over the last year!

Prologue

The Lucky Eight

One week after a passenger plane crashed at Gatwick airport, the nation is still coming to terms with the event that has devastated so many lives. One hundred and sixty people died when Air Euro flight 975 tumbled during landing. After touching down too far along the runway, the pilots pulled up to attempt a second landing but the plane quickly lost speed and crashed back down, with devastating consequences. In aviation terms, this second attempt to land a plane is known as 'go-around'.

Air Euro issued a statement earlier this week in which they said:

> *A go-around is a standard aircraft manoeuvre which simply discontinues an approach to landing. Go-arounds ensure passengers and aircraft are not placed in potentially dangerous situations. At this stage, we do not have further information about what caused the crash.*

The dead consist of 153 passengers and seven airline staff. Three of the flight attendants were ejected from the plane's tail section when the aircraft hit the ground. The remaining flight attendant, Shelly Clarkson, repeatedly risked her life as she attempted to evacuate the surviving passengers from the burning wreckage. Air Euro have described Ms Clarkson's work to free trapped passengers and help them to safety as 'heroic'.

Among the dead are Irish actress Vivienne Kinsella, whose sister, Clodagh, is one of only eight people who survived the crash. She remains in hospital in a critical condition. Celebrity chef, Nick Gilbert, is another one of the 'lucky eight'. He had been returning to the UK from a week-long holiday in Crete with a group of friends who included the pilot, Gary Wakefield. The Gilbert family released a statement earlier this week in which they thanked Shelly Clarkson for saving Nick's life. The chef sustained serious injuries in the crash. His family described his condition as 'serious but stable'.

The troubled flight had already run into a string of difficulties before it ever took off from Heraklion airport. Prior to take-off, it was delayed for over ten hours because of a technical issue. During this time, the captain fell ill with food poisoning. Air Euro have confirmed that they then asked Mr Wakefield, due to be on the flight as a passenger, to take over as captain. It's not yet clear if this last-minute replacement had anything to do with the crash.

For all the latest news on this and other stories, visit our website or follow us over on Twitter. If you read something you like, don't forget to leave a comment and tell us what you think!

Five Years Later

One

Day One

Clodagh squeezed her eyes shut and breathed slowly, counting each breath the way she'd been taught. Forcing her mind to focus on nothing except the rise and fall of her diaphragm.

'It's okay,' she whispered.

But it wasn't okay. Because when she opened her eyes, the body was still there. Exactly where it had been when she first saw it. His head twisted sideways, at an odd angle from the rest of his body. Black blood pooled beneath his crushed skull. More blood splattered over the shingle beach. Too much blood.

A sound came out of her mouth, somewhere between a moan and a wail as it hit her, finally, that he was dead.

'No. No, no, no.'

She ran towards him, then stopped. She remembered enough from crime novels and TV programmes to know she shouldn't touch a dead body. She scanned the beach, desperate to see another person out here. Someone strong and reliable, like Clodagh herself had once been, who would take over and make cups of tea and tell her that everything was going to be all right. But apart from Clodagh, the dead man and a squalling squabble of seagulls skimming the surface of the water, the beach was empty.

So still and silent it was easy to believe no one else would ever come here and disrupt the quiet of this lonely place.

A pink line on the horizon, where the sky met the water, announced the start of a new day. This was the reason she'd come onto the beach: to watch the sunrise. Now, she barely noticed it as her mind went back over the previous day and evening. They'd had the memorial service in the afternoon. Sad and moving, but uplifting too. The feeling of community she only felt when they came together as a group. The sharp reminder of the fragility of life. Knowing how lucky they were to be here. The pain and guilt, as they remembered the 160 people who had died.

Then later, dinner and drinks and more drinks. A single memory standing out from the blur of the others. The dizzying lurch of fear when she'd read his text message:

> Meet me outside now. We need to talk.

Was that why he'd died? Because he'd been out here, waiting for her?

He'd been drunk. Falling over drunk. She tried to picture him, coming out here in the dark, stumbling over the stones and falling backwards. Except there was something about that image that didn't work. In her mind, every time he stumbled, he fell forward. But he was lying on his back, his dead eyes staring up at her. The scar on his left cheek, pale and silver in the early morning light.

It didn't seem right, after everything he'd been through, that he was dead. He was a survivor. Like her. Eight of them, in total. Everyone else on the plane that day had died.

Clodagh remembered the moment she'd realised she wasn't the only one. She'd woken up in hospital. Dazed and disorientated, no idea where she was or how she'd got there. When she tried to remember, her mind was blank. She knew something bad had happened, but the memory of it was gone. Along with so much else, although she didn't realise that until much later.

There was a TV on the wall opposite her bed. Eight photos on the screen and a man's voice, low and serious, speaking about 'the terrible tragedy'. A shock of recognition, tinged with fear, when she saw her own face, some letters beneath. At first, they didn't mean anything but gradually her brain worked out that the letters spelled her name. There were names beneath each of the photos, including the one next to hers. His face on the TV nothing like his face now – he looked happy and bursting with life. Running across the bottom of the screen was the headline that would come to define them:

The Lucky Eight: the survivors of 975.

She had no idea, back then, that the phrase would become so widespread that the only people who never used it when talking about the crash were the survivors themselves. And after today, no one else would be using it either. Because now there were only seven of them.

Two

Detective Inspector Rachel Lewis parked in one of the spaces outside the front of the Blue Dolphin villa. Climbing out of the car, she paused a moment to appreciate the architecture of the classic Art Deco building. Built in the early Thirties, the exclusive East Sussex property had originally been a getaway for some of the country's richest and most powerful people. Legendary parties had been held here; rumour had it that the hotel had once been a favourite with Edward, Prince of Wales, and his mistress Wallis Simpson. In those days, it had been called the Sandcastle. Following a complete renovation a few years ago, it now had a new name and a new reputation as one of the finest holiday properties on the south coast.

Rachel and her wife, Grace, had spent a weekend here a few months ago. Two nights of unadulterated luxury. If she'd been able to afford it, she would have stayed for two months, not two nights. But they were saving for their future. A future that included children and a house in the Preston Park area of Brighton. As Grace was keen to point out, children and houses were expensive. Which meant that, for now, indulgent weekends in fancy hotels were on hold.

'Wow.' Ade Benjamin slammed the car door shut and came to stand beside Rachel. 'I didn't think there was anywhere like this in Seaford. It's something else, isn't it?'

'Wait until you see the rest of it,' Rachel said. 'There's a stunning roof garden and direct access to the villa's own private section of the beach. Which is where we're going now because that's where the body is.'

Together, the two women walked around to the back of the villa, past the hot tub and the tear-shaped swimming pool, following the path that led onto the beach.

'How do you know so much about this place?' Ade said.

'I've stayed here with Grace,' Rachel said.

'See, that right there is why lesbians have it better than straight people,' Ade said. 'I've never once dated a guy who would take me somewhere this fancy.'

'You're dating the wrong sort of guys, then.'

'Nah. The only guy who ever thinks of coming to a place like this is when he's nagged into doing it by his wife or girlfriend. I bet you didn't have to nag Grace to take you here, did you?'

'Actually,' Rachel said, 'she did take a bit of persuading. Even now, she still talks about that weekend as if it was a luxury we couldn't really afford.'

'Was she right?'

'Probably. But what's the point of working as hard as we do if we can't treat ourselves from time to time?'

Without waiting for a reply, she pushed open the gate to the beach. Black and yellow police tape cordoned off an area around the same size as the hotel garden. A team of crime scene investigators, dressed head to toe in white and wearing purple disposable gloves, were methodically scouring the beach for anything that might help identify how the victim had died.

On any other day, this would have been a glorious place to be. Sunlight reflected off a flat, still sea. Waves of heat rose off the white shingle, blurring the yellow ferry that was pulling out of Newhaven harbour two miles further along the coast. Rachel knew if she looked in the other direction, she'd see the white cliffs of Seaford Head. But she wasn't here for the view.

She pulled a pair of plastic shoe covers out of her bag and put them on, waiting while Ade did the same thing.

'There's Brian,' Rachel said, nodding at Brian Higgins, the uniformed sergeant who'd responded to the call about the body. Rachel knew that Brian and two uniformed officers had already been here for several hours. It would have been Brian who made the decision to pass this particular case on to CID, assigning one of his officers to start a log book, logging all attendees at the scene and their reason for being there.

'Morning, Rachel and Ade,' Brian said, crossing the beach to greet them.

'What have you got for me, Brian?' Rachel asked.

'It's not a drowning. The body's well above the tide line, no sign of water damage. There's injury to the back of the head, but he's lying on his back so I can't see how bad that is. The on-call doctor has attended the scene and confirmed ROLE.'

Rachel knew that ROLE stood for Recognition of Life Extinct. In other words, the on-call doctor had confirmed what the uniformed sergeant would have already worked out. The person lying on the beach was dead.

'Pathologist?' Rachel asked.

'With the body now.'

'What made you call us?' Rachel asked.

'Because of who the victim is,' Brian said. 'Nick Gilbert, the celebrity chef. You've heard of him?'

'Shit.' Rachel's mind was already running ahead as she thought through the implications of this piece of information. A dead body was one thing, a famous dead body quite another.

'One of the other guests found him,' Brian said. 'She came out to catch the sunrise, apparently.'

'Where is she now?'

'I've arranged for all the guests to stay in their rooms until we've had a chance to talk to them. Meantime, the pathologist is ready to speak to you. Here he comes.'

Sure enough, Rachel could see Raj Mallick walking towards her across the shingle. Silhouetted in the bright sunlight, Raj's tall, gangly frame reminded her of one of L. S. Lowry's matchstick men. Rachel knew sod all about art, but Grace had dragged her around a Lowry exhibition at London's Tate Modern a few years earlier and the artist's work had stayed with her.

'Rachel,' Raj said, as he reached her. 'Good to see you.' He turned his full wattage smile on Ade. 'Raj Mallick, forensic pathologist. You must be the new Ed.'

'Ade Benjamin. Not the new Ed or anyone else. Just me.'

Raj's smile widened, something Rachel wouldn't have thought was possible.

'Well, very pleased to meet you, Ade Benjamin. You ever seen a dead body before?'

'I was based in Lewisham before I moved out here to the sticks,' Ade said. 'So, yeah. I've seen more than one dead body in my time. Why? You afraid my little womanly stomach won't be able to cope?'

Raj laughed, clearly enchanted. Rachel couldn't blame him. At five foot ten, with mahogany skin, eyes the size of plates and cheekbones you could ski down, Ade Benjamin was stunning. Rachel was used to being ignored. Her wife, Grace, drew people to her like a magnet. Unlike Rachel, who never seemed to make a lasting impression on anyone apart from the people she arrested and charged for the crimes they'd committed. Most of the time, the lack of interest was something she saw as a blessing. Except when it delayed getting work done.

'Are you going to let us see him?' she said. 'Or are you going to stand here all day trying – and failing – to impress my partner?'

'How do you know I'll fail?' Raj asked.

'Because I know Ade has taste.'

'Ouch.' Raj put a hand on his chest. 'Straight to the heart, Rachel. Come on, then. He's over here.'

He held the tape up while the two women slipped under it, before leading them across the shingle to the body.

'Won't know exact time of death until after I've done the PM,' Raj said. 'But if you wanted me to guess, I'd say he's been dead at least eight hours.'

The victim was lying on his back. When Rachel saw his face, she realised why Raj had asked Ade if she'd seen a dead body before. Because it was different when you recognised the victim. Your initial reaction was stronger. There was a feeling that the person you were looking at couldn't really be dead.

Nick Gilbert was a restaurateur turned celebrity chef whose career had gone from strength to strength after surviving a notorious plane crash five years ago. His face was familiar from any number of TV shows, celebrity profiles in newspapers and magazines, and the several cookbooks that came out each year with his name and face on the cover. The blue-grey eyes, the dimple in the centre of his chin, and the distinctive scar from the injuries he'd sustained in the crash.

'Is that what killed him?' Ade asked, crouching down and pointing to the blood beneath the victim's head.

'Possibly,' Raj said, 'although…'

'I know,' Ade interrupted, 'you won't be able to tell us for sure until after you've done the PM. Looks like someone pushed him.'

'How do you work that out?' Rachel said.

'Because people don't fall backwards,' Ade said. 'If you trip, you fall forward not back.'

'He could easily have stumbled backwards,' Raj said. 'It does happen, you know. Although I don't think that's what happened here. If I was to put money on it, I'd say someone killed him.'

'Why?' Rachel asked.

'I won't be able to see the full extent of the injury while he's in situ,' Raj said. 'But from what I can see it looks too severe to have been caused by a simple fall. I think someone smashed in the back of his head, possibly using one of the stones here on the beach.'

'Why's he lying on his back, then?' Rachel asked.

'My guess is whoever did this to him rolled him over when they'd finished,' Raj said.

Still crouched over the body, Ade looked up at Rachel. 'If it's murder, this is going to be a huge story, isn't it?'

'I'm afraid so,' Rachel said.

'My mum's going to be gutted,' Ade said, standing back up. 'She loved this guy.'

Grace too, Rachel thought. But clearly not everyone else felt the same way. In all the years Rachel had worked with Raj Mallick, she'd never known him to call it wrong at a crime scene. If Raj thought Nick Gilbert had been murdered, then that's what had happened. Ade was right. They were about to face the mother of all media storms.

Three

The Blue Dolphin interior was every bit as beautifully elegant as the exterior. Crossing the entrance hall, Rachel remembered the pure pleasure of being a guest here. Knowing that, for two precious days, her every need would be catered for.

'Police?'

A stout man with a completely bald head hurried towards her, skidding to a halt in front of her.

Rachel's M&S trouser suit and cheap haircut clearly marked her out, she thought glumly. Putting her professional face on, she held her hand out and introduced herself.

'Detective Inspector Rachel Lewis. This is my colleague, Detective Constable Ade Benjamin.'

'Ah, I see. Marcus Chevalier. Manager.'

'We've met before,' Rachel said. 'Although I wouldn't expect you to remember. You must see so many people every day.'

The frown on his face cleared, replaced by a big smile.

'Of course! You stayed with your wife. Not long married, as I recall. How is Ms Cotton?'

'She's fine, thank you.'

'Marvellous news,' Marcus said, still beaming. 'Please pass on my very best regards, won't you?'

'I'll do that.'

'Such a shame this visit is under different circumstances.' Marcus lowered his voice so that she had to strain her ears to hear him. 'Perhaps we should continue this conversation in my office?'

'Good idea,' Rachel said. 'Why don't you take me there? In the meantime, are you okay if my colleague speaks to your staff?'

'I'm sure that will be fine. I doubt there's very much they can tell you that will help, but I know they'll co-operate in whatever way they can.'

Rachel told Ade they'd reconvene ahead of speaking to the guests, before following Marcus Chevalier to his office. The bedrooms in the villa were all on the ground floor; each room had French doors with direct access to the gardens. As Rachel passed the room she'd stayed in with Grace, she felt a pang of nostalgia. When she'd first got together with Grace, they'd had lots of weekends away. Now, those weekends were nothing but a distant memory. Saving for a house apparently meant giving up all the fun things in life and eating at home night after night, instead of ever going out and letting your hair down.

Despite the luxury of the public areas, Marcus Chevalier's office was a remarkably modest room. A single small window looked out over an enclosed concrete car park and nothing else.

'I prefer to leave the views for our guests,' Marcus said, when Rachel glanced out of the window. 'Please, take a seat. Can I get you something to drink?'

Rachel shook her head, keen to get to business.

'I'll need you to tell me everything you can about the victim,' she said, taking out her notebook and the Cross fountain pen that had been a birthday present from Grace. 'Why he was staying here, who was with him, when he arrived and how long he was planning to stay. Let's start there.'

'You already know who he is I assume?'

'Nick Gilbert, the celebrity chef. Who, from what I recall, now has two restaurants in East Sussex alongside the flagship one in Soho. He also had his own reality TV show, following the lives of ten young people from deprived backgrounds as they tried to make their way in the hospitality industry.'

Again, when she pictured his body, Rachel had the strange sense that none of this was real.

'You're a fan, then?'

'My wife is. If it wasn't for her, I probably wouldn't have a clue who he was.'

'Of course, his celebrity status isn't the only reason people know him,' Marcus said. 'It seems impossible to think he survived that terrible plane crash only to end up dead five years later.'

Like everyone else working for Sussex Police, Rachel knew all about the crash of Air Euro 975. Officers from forces across the south-east had been called to the airport to help in the hours following the tragedy. Rachel had been on holiday when the crash happened. But in the days and weeks that followed, she'd got caught up in the aftermath. The horror of it would never leave her. Bodies stripped of clothes, many of them impossible to identify. The baggage handler who couldn't be identified because the force of the crash had pushed his body through fencing like a grater, cutting him into small pieces of unrecognisable bits. The cargo scattered over the ground, reminders of all those lost lives. Worse than all of that, though, was the sight of those devastated families, shocked and grieving, as they tried to understand what had happened to their loved ones.

Only eight people had survived the crash. Nick Gilbert was one of them. In the years since, he had cleverly used his new-found notoriety to reinvent himself as a TV personality while, at the same time, expanding his restaurant business.

'Some of the others are here too,' Marcus said. 'Four of them, in fact.'

'Excuse me?'

'The lucky eight.' He frowned. 'Well, I suppose there's only seven of them now.'

One week after the crash, a tabloid newspaper had gone with the headline 'the lucky eight' and the name had stuck. Although Rachel was pretty sure the people who'd survived such a terrible incident would rather their experience wasn't summed up in such a trite and over-simplistic way.

'Yesterday was the five-year anniversary,' Marcus continued. 'You must have seen the stories in the press?'

Rachel nodded. She'd heard something about it on the radio during the week. But Ade had been in the car with her, talking about a man she'd been on a date with the previous evening, and Rachel hadn't paid too much attention to what was on the radio.

'Apparently the survivors get together every year to remember those poor people who died. This year, they came here. Not all of them. Two of them live in Greece and, understandably, they chose not to fly to the UK for the anniversary.

'We were hugely honoured to host the event. Mr Murray is an absolute pleasure to deal with. He organised the whole thing. As the head of the foundation, I suppose he feels it's his duty to organise these events every year.'

'Hang on.' Rachel held a hand up, needing him to slow down. 'Can we go back a bit? Who is Mr Murray?'

'Adam Murray, the man behind Vivienne Kinsella Foundation.'

Rachel recognised the name. Adam Murray was an author and inspirational speaker whose wife had died in the crash. He'd set up a foundation, in her name, to support all those affected by the tragedy.

'He wrote the book about his wife,' Marcus said. 'You must know the one I'm talking about?'

Rachel nodded. She knew the book, all right. *Vivienne: a memoir.* She'd bought it after seeing multiple copies in Waterstones soon after it was published. Rows of hardbacks lined up with the covers facing out at her. The title in white print beneath a photo of the dead actress. Dozens of identical images of Vivienne Kinsella's face smiling from the shelves. The book, when Rachel finally got around to reading it, had been such a saccharine account of Adam Murray's 'perfect marriage to my perfect wife' Rachel hadn't been able to get past the first few chapters.

'My neighbour went to see him speak last year and described it as a transformational experience.' Marcus stopped speaking and smiled. 'Sorry. I'm going on a bit, aren't I? It's the shock, you see. One simply doesn't expect something like this to happen here. It's one of the reasons I took this job. I spent most of my career in LA, managing a luxury hotel in Malibu. Beautiful location, but it was a big operation. I got burned out after a few years. So I moved back to England and looked for a smaller job, something a little less stressful. Running this place was just the ticket. Until now.'

Resisting the urge to grab him by the shoulders and shake him until he pulled himself together, Rachel asked him – as gently as she could – to go back to the events leading up to the discovery of Nick Gilbert's body on the beach.

'They had a beautiful service in the grounds yesterday afternoon,' Marcus said. 'Followed by drinks in the bar, then dinner. They'd booked out the whole house so they had complete privacy. It was all very lovely. Although Mr Gilbert did get rather the worse for wear.'

'Drunk, you mean?'

'Yes. Understandable given the circumstances. I can't imagine what it must be like to be one of the few who survived. The guilt would be terrible.'

'Any idea how he ended up on the beach?' Rachel asked.

'None whatsoever.'

'I understand one of the other guests discovered his body,' Rachel said. 'Which one?'

'Another survivor called Clodagh Kinsella.'

Also a name Rachel recognised. Vivienne Kinsella's younger, less famous sister.

'I'd like to speak to her.'

'Of course. I knew you'd want to interview all the guests. We've got a reading room on the first floor. You can use that. I'll take you there now.'

'Before we go,' Rachel said, 'what can you tell me about Clodagh Kinsella?'

'She looks a lot like her sister,' Marcus said. 'It was a little unnerving when I first saw them together, if I'm honest. It felt, for a moment, as if the great actress was still alive.'

'Saw who together?' Rachel said. 'I'm afraid you've lost me.'

'My word.' Marcus smiled. 'You're really not up on local gossip, are you? Clodagh Kinsella and Adam Murray are a couple. Last month's *Sussex Life* did a big piece about them. They're living together in the house Adam used to share with his wife.'

A chill ran down the centre of Rachel's back. A series of images flashed through her mind. The rows of books lined up on the shelves in Waterstones. Vivienne Kinsella's face smiling out from each one. TV footage of some of the victims' funerals. A black and white newspaper photo of Adam Murray laying flowers on his dead wife's grave. A tearful TV interview Adam had given two years after the crash, professing his undying love for his dead wife. Something about those images jarred with the idea of him moving on with his life by moving in with Vivienne's sister. Rachel didn't know why the idea bothered her so much. All she knew was that it did.

She pushed her chair back, stood up and beamed at Marcus Chevalier.

'Time for me to meet Clodagh Kinsella.'

Four

Clodagh was glad they'd been told to stay in their rooms. She couldn't bear having to face the others, knowing they'd want to interrogate her about what she'd found on the beach. From the noises in the corridor, she knew they were going in and out of each other's rooms. She imagined the conversations that were taking place, the facts around Nick's death swollen and distorted with each retelling and embellishment. Words hanging in the air long after they'd been spoken: *murder, foul play, suspicious.* The current of fear running through every sidelong glance and whispered insinuation.

Because they were all scared. Terrified at the prospect of their personal lives being raked over in the press again, each one of them potential targets for a smear campaign. They already knew what it felt like to be part of a big news story, the harassment and intrusion and the constant sense of being watched and judged. None of them wanted that to start up again.

Like the other rooms in the villa, this one had French doors leading onto the garden. She had seen Ivan out there earlier, chain-smoking his way through a packet of cigarettes. She longed to go outside and join him, but she didn't want to leave Adam, who was growing more wound up by the minute.

'I can't stand this much longer,' he muttered now, looking up from his phone which he'd been scrolling through obsessively for the last half hour. 'When is someone going to come and tell us what the hell is going on?'

So far, he'd divided his time pacing around outside, trying to peer over the garden wall at the activity on the beach and pacing around in here, complaining about the way they'd been treated.

'There's nothing we can do about it,' Clodagh said. 'Nick's dead, Adam. The police have a job to do. Getting stressed isn't going to speed things up.'

'I know.' Adam put his arm around Clodagh and hugged her tight. 'I'm sorry. It's just… I guess I can't believe this has happened.'

Before Clodagh could reply, someone knocked on the door, making them both jump.

'Adam? Are you in there? I need to speak to you.'

'Tara,' Clodagh said, recognising the voice. 'What do you think she wants?'

'Maybe a shoulder to cry on.' Adam stood up. 'I've been wondering how she's doing. I'm glad she feels she can come to us.'

But when he opened the door, it was immediately clear that Tara hadn't come looking for comfort.

'This is your fault,' she said, her voice low and angry as she pushed past Adam into the room.

Clodagh swallowed before answering, her hand instinctively patting the outline of the phone in her pocket as she remembered reading Nick's text message last night.

'Excuse me?' she said.

'Not you.' Tara pointed at Adam. 'Him.'

Adam frowned. 'What are you talking about? How is any of this my fault?'

'I saw you.' Tara prodded Adam's chest with her finger. 'You and Nick had one hell of an argument last night. You didn't think anyone saw you, but I did. And I heard you threatening him. I've been sitting here all morning, trying to keep quiet, waiting until I could tell the police what I saw. But I can't keep it in. I need to know, Adam. What happened in the smoking area last night?'

'Oh that.' Adam's face cleared, causing some of the tension to leave Clodagh's body. The relief was short-lived, rapidly replaced by guilt at allowing herself to think, even for a second, that Adam might have had something to do with Nick's death. The very idea was ludicrous.

'It wasn't anything important,' Adam said. 'Nick was drunk and trying to stir up trouble. You know the mood he was in yesterday. He was having a go at me about Bella.'

'Bella?' The confusion on Tara's face mirrored how Clodagh felt. 'Why was Nick talking to you about Bella?'

'He thought the foundation should have done more to help her.'

'Bullshit.' Tara pushed her face close to Adam's. 'We both know Nick has never cared about any of that. You can lie to me all you like, Adam Murray. But I'm going to make sure the police know what happened.' Tears started rolling down Tara's face, but she didn't seem to notice. 'I keep waiting for him to walk in and ask me what all the fuss is about. But that's never going to happen, is it?'

She looked at Clodagh.

'Is that why you went out there this morning? Did Adam send you out to check on the body and make sure Nick was really dead?'

'Of course not.'

Clodagh's mind raced as she tried to work out what Adam was playing at. He hadn't mentioned anything about an argument with Nick. Not even when she'd run back into the room this morning and woken him up to tell him Nick was dead. Something cold lodged itself in the pit of her stomach, refusing to shift.

'You need to calm down, Tara,' Adam said.

There was a hard edge to his voice that Clodagh recognised. He spoke like that when he was struggling to keep his temper under control.

'Don't you dare tell me what to do,' Tara said. 'Nick's lying out there on that beach. Dead. And you know what I've worked out? All those people are out there because they're searching for clues. They think Nick was killed. And if you've got anything to do with what happened to him, I'm going to make sure you pay.'

'I don't need to put up with this shit,' Adam said. 'I'm sorry about Nick, Tara. Truly sorry. But if you think I had anything to do with what happened to him, you're more messed up than I thought. And that's saying something, believe me. Now if you'll excuse me, I'm going to do something constructive and find out how much longer the police are planning to keep us cooped up in here.'

He pushed past Tara and stormed out of the room.

'I'm going to make sure he's not trying to wriggle out of this,' Tara muttered, hurrying after him.

Finally alone, Clodagh took her phone out and opened her text messages, scrolling to the one she'd received last night from Nick.

> Meet me outside now. We need to talk.

They'd only spoken about it once. Six months after the crash, when the rumours first started. She'd gone to visit him, desperate to hold on to the tiny pieces of her life she could still have some control over. She'd needed to know if any of it had been her fault. Because she'd lost all her memories from the day of the crash. All she had instead was a persistent feeling of dread. The sense that something bad had happened in the airport that afternoon. The creeping fear that all those deaths were because of her. But he'd told her that wasn't what had happened. They'd never spoken of it again and, in the intervening years, she'd let herself believe he'd forgotten that conversation had ever taken place. Until last night.

She read the text message again. Sent at 9:47 p.m. Was that before or after Adam had rowed with Nick? She needed to know what Nick had really said. Because Tara was right. Whatever they'd rowed about, it wasn't Bella.

She opened the door and looked along the corridor. Adam was on his way back. As he drew closer, she saw that he was looking calmer now, back in control.

'The manager's going to see if he can get one of the detectives to tell Tara what's going on,' Adam said. 'Poor thing's in a bit of a state. I didn't realise things with her and Nick were that serious.'

'I think she was trying to make a proper go of it this time,' Clodagh said. 'But you know Tara, she changes her mind so often. Who knows what was really going on between them?'

'Do you think he was killed?' Adam asked.

'I don't know what to think, Adam.'

'I'm sorry, darling.' He wrapped his arm around her shoulders and pulled her towards him. Clodagh knew he was trying to comfort her, but the weight of his arm made her feel hot and uncomfortable. 'I didn't mean to imply you knew anything. I know this is terrible for you.'

'I'm fine.' She stepped back, putting some space between them. 'Adam, what was the row with Nick really about?'

'Jesus, that again?'

'Yes, that again. I know Nick and he didn't care enough about Bella to start a row with you or anyone else.'

'You're right.' Adam sighed. 'He was being nasty about Vivienne. He said some horrible stuff that I don't want to repeat and I certainly didn't want Tara to hear.'

'And that's it? He didn't say anything else?'

'That's not enough?'

'Of course it is.' Relief washed through her. The row hadn't had anything to do with her. Which still didn't explain the text message but maybe that didn't matter now. 'It's difficult to think straight. I still can't believe Nick's dead.'

'We can't let this drive a wedge between us, Clodagh.' Adam kissed her cheek. 'It's horrible what's happened, but the best way to get through it is by staying strong together.'

She opened her mouth to tell him about the text message. At the same time, his phone started ringing.

'It's Jake,' he said, looking at the screen. 'I need to get this.'

She wanted to tell him that Jake Harris could wait. That, by rights, the man shouldn't even be here this weekend. He was only here because, as Adam's agent, he'd somehow managed to inveigle his way into every corner of Adam's life.

But it was too late to say any of this because Adam had already answered the phone and was on his way to Jake's room. Sure enough, a few seconds later she heard Jake's voice, booming down the corridor as he welcomed Adam into his room. Biting back the familiar feeling of irritation she always got with anything involving Adam's agent, Clodagh took advantage of Adam's absence to go outside.

Breathing in deep mouthfuls of warm sea air, she closed her eyes and lifted her face to the sun, warm and soothing after the artificial air-conditioned cool of her room. It felt good to finally be alone, away from Adam. More than once this morning, she'd had to dig her fingers into the palms of her hands to stop herself screaming: *How the hell do you think I'm doing? I feel as if I'm losing my mind.* But she hadn't screamed because none of this was Adam's fault. All he was doing was being his usual, caring self. If she'd been irritated by his solicitousness, that was her problem, not his.

'Over here, lady!'

Ivan was calling to her from the other side of the garden. Clodagh walked over to him, her heart swelling with love for the chubby Croatian who'd become one of her closest friends. As she drew nearer to him, the bitter smell of nicotine hit her. She wrinkled her nose in disgust, nodding at the cigarette clasped between his thumb and forefinger.

'How many of those have you smoked already?'

'As many as my body has told me I need. You should try smoking, you know. It might help chill you out a bit.'

'I'm perfectly chilled, thank you.'

He threw his head back and laughed. Despite everything, Clodagh couldn't help smiling. Ivan's big-belly laugh was contagious. Partly because he had so much belly to put into it.

'You, lady, are the least chilled person I know. Actually, that is not true. Your boyfriend is worse than you are.'

'Adam? Most people say how laid-back he is.'

'Most people don't know shit. Your boyfriend reminds me of Sandra.'

'Who's Sandra?'

'My boss. The headmistress of the school I'm working at. I told you about her last night. Keep up, lady.'

'Ah yes. How could I forget?'

Ivan had spent a large chunk of last night regaling her with tales of his new job, teaching cookery at an exclusive private school in Worthing. Not the most obvious job choice, and Clodagh still had no clue how he'd persuaded the school to hire him. There was nothing vaguely teacher-like about Ivan. A big man with a seventies-style, drooping moustache and a round stomach, he looked like a retired porn star. The floral shirt he was wearing this morning, open to reveal a hugely hairy chest and a gold medallion, only added to the impression.

'Sandra practises her meditation every morning and tells everyone how transformative it is. Which is a load of crap, I can tell you. Because if her meditation is so transformative, why does she lose her shit at the smallest thing?'

While he talked, Clodagh felt some of the tension leaving her body. Ivan always had that effect on her. No matter how bad things were, and there had been plenty of bad times over the last five years, he'd always been able to make her smile.

'So, enough about my crazy boss,' Ivan said, flicking the cigarette butt onto the ground and stubbing it out with the toe of his leather loafer. 'How are you doing?'

'Hunky-dory,' she said, 'how do you think?'

'Sorry. That was a stupid question.'

'No less than I expected.'

'Watch it, lady. It's too early to start into me. I need my hangover to clear first. Seriously, it must have been horrible for you.'

So horrible, Clodagh knew she'd never forget it.

'Do you know how he died?' Ivan asked.

She shook her head, not trusting herself to speak without breaking down.

'Poor Nicky,' Ivan said. 'He was a bastard but I am still sad he is dead. I'm sad for Tara too, because even though she didn't really love him this is going to be terrible for her.'

'You think she didn't love him?'

'I think she loved his money,' Ivan said. 'But I'm not so sure she felt the same way about him.'

Despite the warm sunshine, Clodagh shivered.

'It's all going to start again,' she said, 'isn't it? The intrusive journalists and the speculative news stories. Our lives plastered all over the newspapers and TV for everyone to see and have an opinion about.'

'I think maybe I will go into hiding until it's over,' Ivan said.

'Can I come with you?'

'Of course.' Ivan smiled. 'But only if you tell me what really happened last night.'

'What do you mean?'

'You and Nicky. What did he tell you?'

'How do you know he wanted to speak to me?'

'I was there when you got the text, remember?'

'I didn't find him.'

'But you know why he wanted to speak to you, don't you?'

'No.' Clodagh shook her head. 'Not a clue.'

'Well,' Ivan said, after a moment. 'If you that's what you say, then I believe you.'

She wished she could tell him the truth. But if she told him, then he wouldn't want anything more to do with her. Ivan was her friend and, ever since the crash, her list of close friends had steadily got shorter. She'd already lost so much; she didn't think she could bear losing Ivan too.

Five

Marcus Chevalier had given Rachel and Ade use of what he called the 'reading room' on the first floor. Like all the other public areas in the property, this was a stunning space. Two walls lined from floor to ceiling with books. Sweeping views of the ocean and Newhaven harbour from the large, curved window cut into the side of the building in classic Deco style.

Ade and Rachel sat at the oversized glass and chrome table in the middle of the room, making notes on what they knew so far and preparing for the series of interviews they had lined up.

'Sixteen people were here yesterday,' Ade said. 'Ten guests and six staff, including the manager who you've already spoken to. The guests consisted of five of the survivors and the people they'd invited to be here with them, including Nick's brother Simon. One of the guests didn't stay the night.'

'Which one?' Rachel asked.

'Shelly Clarkson. No room booked under her name so presumably she hadn't planned to spend the night.'

'Wasn't she the flight attendant who helped the others off the plane?'

'That's right.' Ade nodded. 'A brave woman.'

'Any idea why she didn't stay?'

'Not yet,' Ade said. 'But I'm working on it. According to the staff I've spoken to, most of the guests were very pleasant. The one exception was our victim, who seemed to have pissed off pretty much everyone he spoke to last night.'

'Let's assume for now that Raj is right and Nick was murdered,' Rachel said. 'We don't have time of death yet. But we know all the guest bedrooms are on the ground floor with direct access to the garden and, beyond that, the beach. The dining room and bar also have direct access to the garden and beach. We'll need to get statements from the staff at some point but let's start with the guests. I've asked Marcus to get Clodagh Kinsella.'

As if on cue, there was a knock on the door and Chevalier's head peeked in at them.

'One of the guests is asking to see you,' he said. 'She says it's important.'

'Which guest?' Rachel asked.

'Tara Coleman,' Marcus replied. 'Says she was Nick's girlfriend and she deserves to know what's going on.'

Girlfriend? Rachel glanced at Ade. This was new information to both of them.

'Well then,' Rachel said, 'you'd better ask her to come in.'

She'd already gone onto the internet and looked up all the survivors. When Tara Coleman came into the room, Rachel recognised her from the photos she'd seen online. Tall and willowy, with a wispy fringe of brown hair and big brown eyes. Even today, dressed in a crumpled linen shirt and jeans that had clearly seen better days, there was an elegance about her that Rachel could only dream of possessing. According to a profile piece Rachel found online, Tara worked for a luxury fashion brand in Mayfair and lived in an apartment near the river on London's South Bank. She was single but was regularly pictured in the tabloid press on the arm of various C-list celebrities.

'What happened to him?' Tara said, as soon as she'd sat down. 'You've got to tell me because I've been sitting downstairs in my room going out of my mind. Please. I deserve to know the truth, no matter how bad it is.'

'We don't know yet how Nick died,' Rachel said. 'Our priority for now is building up a timeline of what happened last night. I'm glad you're here because I'm sure you'll be able to help with this. When was the last time you saw Nick?'

'Yesterday evening,' Tara said. 'Sometime after dinner. I don't know the time exactly. I was tired and wanted to go to bed. I went looking for him and found him outside with Adam.'

'Adam Murray, you mean?'

Tara nodded.

'They were having a row. I asked Adam earlier what they rowed about but he wouldn't tell me the truth. Which makes me wonder if he had something to do with Nick's death. Because he was killed, wasn't he? If he'd died of natural causes you wouldn't have kept us in our rooms for so long and there wouldn't be so many people out on the beach. I know who they are. They're the CSI guys. They're out there looking for clues, trying to find out who killed him.'

Tara's voice was rising as she spoke, becoming borderline hysterical.

'Take some deep breaths,' Ade said softly. 'I can see you're getting upset, Tara. I don't blame you. But right now the best thing you can do for Nick is slow down and tell us everything you know. We need to work together if we want to find out what really happened. You said you're Nick's girlfriend? How long have you two been together?'

'About a year,' Tara said. 'We were deeply in love.'

Rachel doubted that was true. She'd already checked the room bookings for this weekend. Nick Gilbert and Tara Coleman had booked separate rooms. Which didn't strike her as the act of a couple 'deeply in love'.

'I imagine it was a very emotional day yesterday,' Rachel said, keen to move the conversation along. 'The five-year anniversary. It can't have been easy for any of you.'

'It was very sad,' Tara said.

'Is that why some people drank too much?' Rachel said.

'You mean Nick.' Tara scowled. 'He was suffering, that's what no one seems to understand. He wasn't even going to come, you know. But I persuaded him and he changed his mind at the last minute. And because he did what I asked him to, he's dead.'

'How would you describe Nick's state of mind last night?' Ade asked.

'I've already told you,' Tara said sulkily. 'He was upset. These sort of events are traumatic for him. I don't know what Adam said to him, but it made things worse. I wanted to go over, but Nick saw me and waved me away. I didn't see him after that.'

She started crying, her body shaking as she sobbed, tears rolling unchecked down her face.

'I just want to know what happened to him,' she said between sobs. 'My Nick didn't deserve this. Not after everything he's been through.'

She seemed genuinely upset, Rachel thought. But there could be all sorts of reasons she was telling them about the row with Adam Murray. Including the possibility that she was trying to deflect police attention away from herself. Except if that was the case, why would she have come forward and told them about the affair?

'How about this?' she said. 'I'll ask Ade here to take you back to your room so you two can have a proper chat. You can tell Ade everything you know, including how long you and Nick have been seeing each other and anything else you think might be relevant.'

'Good idea.' Ade stood up, smiling at Tara. 'And while we're there, maybe you could tell me how I can find Nick's brother as well.'

'Simon?' Tara said. 'He doesn't know anything. He went to bed straight after dinner. None of us saw him for the rest of the night.'

'I'd still like to speak to him,' Ade said, as the two women left the room. 'His wife too. But let's get you back to your room first, shall we?'

Once Ade and Tara were gone, Rachel went to the door and looked out. There was a woman sitting on a chair that, presumably, had been placed there by Marcus Chevalier. No detail too small for the meticulous manager.

'Clodagh?'

The woman looked up and Rachel was instantly transported back to her early twenties. She'd had the mother of all crushes on Vivienne Kinsella, the sassy Irish actress with the volatile personality and incredible screen presence. Marcus Chevalier was right: Clodagh looked remarkably like her dead sister.

'Detective Inspector Rachel Lewis. Do you want to come in?'

She held the door open, trying to maintain an air of professionalism when all she really wanted to do was gush.

'Please.' Rachel gestured in the direction of the table. 'Take a seat.'

She remembered reading a number of newspaper articles about Clodagh. The press had zoomed in on her relentlessly in the weeks and months following the crash. Clodagh's personal life made her more interesting than some of the other survivors. Because Clodagh hadn't just lost her sister. Four years before the plane crash both her parents had died as well. In a strange twist of fate, Clodagh's mother and father had both succumbed to different forms of cancer that had killed them within six months of each other. And now this. Rachel felt a pang of compassion for the haunted-looking young woman sitting opposite her.

'Do you know how he died yet?' Clodagh asked as she sat down.

'It's too early for that,' Rachel said. 'I realise this must be very difficult, but do you think you could talk me through exactly what happened this morning when you found Nick's body?'

'I went out for a walk,' Clodagh said. 'And he was just lying there. What else do you need to know?'

She looked tense, on edge. Twisting her hands together in her lap, chewing the inside of her cheek as she waited for Rachel to answer her questions.

'Can you remember what time this was?'

She already knew the 999 call had come in at five twenty-five that morning. Which meant Clodagh had been on the beach earlier than that.

'I don't know exactly,' Clodagh said. 'But it was early. Sunrise, whatever time that is. I hadn't been able to sleep so I decided to get up and go for a walk. Having the beach right outside, it seemed a shame not to make the most of it.' She gave Rachel a small smile. 'It was beautiful. The sea was so calm and everything was very silent and peaceful. I remember feeling… happy, I guess. It sort of surprised me. These last few years haven't been easy. Well, you know what happened, right?'

'I can't imagine how you get past something like that,' Rachel said. 'It must be tough.'

'Some of the others have been better at it,' Clodagh said. 'We've all had counselling. The airline provided lots of support in the first few years. And Adam's been amazing, of course. He's been the glue that's held us all together. He's helped everyone, especially the victims' families. Because it's so much worse for them. People talk about how lucky we were to survive. And they're right. We are lucky. None of us ever take that for granted.'

'But you lost someone too,' Rachel said.

'Most of us lost people we love,' Clodagh said. 'I'm no different to the others in that respect.'

She stopped speaking, as if the shared loss experienced by all of them was impossible to explain to someone who hadn't experienced it.

'You mentioned counselling,' Rachel said. 'Did it help?'

'A little, I guess. But the thing is, it never goes away. It gets stuck inside your head and becomes a part of you. Even though I don't remember anything about the crash itself, I have flashbacks and nightmares. I dream my sister's screaming, begging me to save her. And I want to do that, more than anything, but there's nothing I can do.'

Rachel was starting to regret sending Ade away. She had a way with people that Rachel could only envy. In a situation like this, questioning a potential suspect who was also traumatised and needed careful handling, Ade always knew what questions to ask to get the best results. Rachel, on the other hand, found these interviews excruciating, constantly worrying she would say or do the wrong thing.

'I'm sorry,' Clodagh said. 'Most days I try not to think about it. But after seeing Nick this morning, I can't help it.'

'You said it was sunrise when you found him,' Rachel said. 'Are you sure about that?'

'Positive.' Clodagh frowned. 'Why do you ask?'

'The 999 call came through at twenty-five past five,' Rachel said. 'That's – what? – half an hour after sunrise. What did you do between finding the body and making the call?'

'I did nothing at first. I was in shock, I guess. Then I went back to my room and woke up Adam, told him what happened. I don't think I did anything else.'

'You don't think?'

'I get confused, you see. Not as often as I used to. But when I saw Nick and I realised he was dead, everything sort of fell apart.'

'How long had you been on the beach when you found the body?' Rachel asked.

'Fifteen minutes, maybe? I almost didn't see him. There's a row of concrete buildings, like little huts? I think they're for the fishermen. He was lying between two of those. I saw his feet and thought it was a homeless person, or maybe someone camping on the beach. But he wasn't moving and there was something… I don't know. I moved closer to get a better look and then I saw who it was. I thought I was seeing things. I know that sounds crazy but I was so tired. I've had cognitive processing issues since the crash which make me get muddled up sometimes.'

'What does that mean?'

'It manifests itself in different ways,' Clodagh said. 'I'm not allowed to drive, for example. Which is a pain because I have to get taxis everywhere or rely on Adam for lifts. It gets bad when I'm following instructions. Like, I'll be cooking dinner and I'll suddenly forget, midway through, what I'm cooking. I can see all the ingredients but, no matter how hard I try, I don't know what I'm meant to do with them. It's not as bad as it sounds. There are things I can do to get around it. I make sure I always have the recipe in front of me so if I forget what I'm doing, I do some breathing exercises to stop myself panicking and then I make myself follow the recipe step by step, until the memory comes back.

'But there are other problems as well. Like this morning? When I saw the body, I thought it was there for a reason. That I'd known he was there all along and that's why I'd got up and gone to the beach in the first place.'

'Do you think that's possible?'

A silence, so long Rachel thought she might have to repeat her question. But eventually Clodagh spoke.

'Not now. No.'

'Why would you have thought it in the first place?' Rachel asked.

'Because last night, Nick sent a text asking to speak to me. He said he had something important to tell me. But when I went looking for him, I couldn't find him.'

'Have you got your phone with you?'

Clodagh took a mobile phone out of the pocket of her jeans, pressed the screen a few times and slid it across the table to Rachel.

'Meet me outside,' Rachel said, reading the message. 'Any idea what he wanted to speak to you about?'

'Not a clue.'

'You sure about that?'

'Positive.'

But Clodagh's eyes slid to the side and Rachel knew she was lying. The problem was, she didn't know which bit Clodagh was lying about – not finding Nick when she'd gone looking for him, or not knowing what he'd wanted to speak to her about.

'Which one of you wasn't here yesterday?' As she asked the question, Rachel wondered why it hadn't occurred to her until now.

'What do you mean?'

'There are – were – eight of you,' Rachel said. 'Two survivors living in Greece, who chose not to fly over for the anniversary. Which leaves six. But according to the hotel manager, only five of you were here yesterday. Who's the missing person?'

'Robbie Fuson.'

Rachel ran back through what she'd read about the survivors. Robbie Fuson. Thirty-eight years old, living in Winchester at the time of the plane crash. He was one of the trustees of the Vivienne Kinsella Foundation set up to support those whose lives had been destroyed by the tragedy.

'Why wasn't he here?' Rachel asked.

'He's disappeared.'

'Excuse me?'

'He stepped down from his role as a trustee three months ago,' Clodagh said. 'None of us have seen or heard from him since.'

A spike of panic as Rachel absorbed this new information. The investigation had just stepped up a notch. Eight survivors. One dead. Another one missing. She'd been hoping the case would be closed quickly. But she knew, already, that wasn't going to happen. This case was going to be messy and complex and drawn out. All of it conducted beneath the unforgiving glare of the tabloid press.

Six

Clodagh walked barefoot across the perfect lawn to the wild garden. This, down here, was where she liked to come when she wanted to be alone. Out of sight from the house, she could sit here for hours, listening to the hum of honeybees and breathing in the perfume from the flowers that bloomed in glorious abundance at this time of the year. Evenings were the best time to be here. Dappled dots of light and shade where the sun flowed between the gaps in the leaves and branches of the tall trees that bordered the garden. Seagulls screaming, dashes of white against the clear blue sky. A row of blue and lilac delphiniums, bobbing and swaying to their own private music. All of it exactly what she needed after the emotional rollercoaster of today. She was drained and exhausted, every remaining bit of her energy focused on not falling apart.

The police had kept them at the hotel until late afternoon. While they'd interviewed each guest, the others had been forced to wait in their rooms. The interview with Adam had dragged on for over an hour. During that time, Clodagh had sat in her room, obsessively going back over everything that had happened. Several times, Ivan had knocked on her door to ask if she wanted to hang out with him. Each time, she'd sent him away saying she was too tired. The truth was she couldn't face being with

Ivan, knowing she'd have to continue lying if he asked her again about the text message from Nick.

When Adam had eventually come back to the room, he hadn't wanted to talk about what the police had asked him. At the time, she hadn't pushed him, telling herself it wasn't fair, that he would talk to her when he was ready. Now, she couldn't stop wondering if the real reason was that she didn't want to know the truth. Because the more she thought about it, the more convinced she had become that Adam hadn't told her the full story about the argument he'd had with Nick.

She might have asked him about it now they were back home, except Jake had insisted on coming back with them. Thankfully, he hadn't brought his airhead girlfriend with him. That would have been the final straw for Clodagh.

He'd been here for two hours so far and was showing no sign of leaving any time soon. Clodagh had come out here to get away from them both, sick of their endless examination of the different ways Nick's death could impact Adam's career. Jake was already looking at how to capitalise on what had happened, cynically using it as another way of making money. As if they didn't both already have more wealth than most people could ever dream of. *Fakey Jakey* was the name Ivan had given to Adam's agent, a name so appropriate Clodagh sometimes worried she'd say it to Jake's face one day by mistake.

She sat down on the deckchair that she'd forgotten to put away the last time she'd been here. Adam didn't like it when she left the chairs out overnight, although he rarely came down to this part of the garden so mostly didn't realise when she had. The chair was part of a set he'd bought at the Towner Gallery last year; each one had a print of the South Downs on its canvas cover. Clodagh loved them all, but this was her favourite – a print of Beachy Head with its white cliffs, red and white striped lighthouse and clear blue sea.

She closed her eyes and focused on her breathing the way her counsellor had taught her, trying to calm her restless mind and keep the anxious thoughts under control. She'd spent the day ricocheting between fear and anger. One moment terrified the police were going to arrest her for murder, the next raging at the injustice of what had happened. She hadn't been close to Nick, hadn't even liked him very much, but she couldn't shake the sense of outrage at his death. After everything he'd been through, it didn't seem right that his life would be cut short so suddenly and brutally. Forty-five years of living. He deserved another thirty, at least.

A wave of grief rose from deep inside her, hitting hard and fast the way it always did. Memories raced towards her, an endless torture that she had no choice but to endure. Because she knew the alternative, to forget those happy times and the people she'd loved and lost, was infinitely worse.

Gradually, the rush of emotion subsided. It didn't disappear, because the sadness never left her entirely, but it eased until she could bear it. The roaring inside her head was replaced by other sounds – birds singing in the trees, the rustling of leaves on branches swaying in the gentle breeze. The booming voices and braying laughter drifting from the kitchen, where Adam and Jake sat plotting and planning.

Clodagh had long suspected it was Jake, not Adam, who was behind the relentless drive to build Adam's career. Constantly pursuing the endless TV appearances, roadshows and publishing contracts. In Clodagh's opinion, Adam's agent was a charmless, shallow man who had weaselled his way into Adam's life after the roaring success of *Vivienne*. Uncertain of how to handle his new-found celebrity, Adam had let Jake take over. Today was a perfect example of the way Jake operated. He'd stuck to Adam like a limpet all day, insisting on coming back to the house with them, when they were finally allowed to leave the hotel.

'You okay?'

Adam's voice made her jump. She hadn't heard him approaching.

'I'm fine,' she said. 'I just needed a bit of space.'

'I know it's a pain having Jake here,' Adam said. 'But we've got a busy few weeks ahead of us. It makes sense to get our heads together today and work out what we're doing.'

'How can you think about work after what's happened?'

Times like this, it was difficult to see the Adam she'd first fallen in love with. She knew, deep down, he was still the same person. She wouldn't be with him, otherwise. But recently, whenever he spoke about his work, he sounded like someone else. And Clodagh wasn't sure she liked that person very much.

'I don't have a choice,' Adam said. 'Talking about the bad stuff is how I make a living. People expect me to share my experiences with them. I know you don't like it, but I have a responsibility. I can't avoid that, no matter how much I might like to.'

She felt bad, then, for judging him so harshly. Adam believed in what he was doing, and there was nothing wrong with that. It crossed her mind that maybe she was jealous because her own life lacked any sort of focus and drive.

'You're doing what you feel is right.' Clodagh reached out and took his hand. 'It's one of the reasons I love you, because you care so much.'

'I love you too.' Adam leaned down and brushed his lips against her cheek. 'If it's any consolation, Jake will be gone soon.'

'Good.' Clodagh squeezed Adam's hand before letting it go.

'I don't deserve you,' Adam said. 'You put up with so much.'

'You know flattery doesn't work with me, don't you?'

'That's a pity,' Adam said. 'I was hoping I could persuade you to join us for a bit?'

Clodagh groaned.

'Please, Clo? I don't know how I'm going to get rid of him by myself.'

Try standing up to him for once, she wanted to say.

'Come on,' she said instead, pushing herself out of the deckchair. 'Let's get this over and done with.'

'Clodagh,' Jake boomed as she walked through the folding glass doors into the open plan kitchen. 'So glad you could join us. Here.' He pulled out one of the stools at the island, gesturing for her to sit down. As if, Clodagh thought sourly, this was his home, not hers.

Ignoring the stool, she sat down on the sofa, which had the dual advantage of being more comfortable than a stool and significantly further away from Jake. She'd hoped Adam might sit beside her so they would present a united front. Instead, Adam sat on the stool meant for her and smiled at Jake as if he was genuinely pleased he was still here, taking up space in their kitchen.

'We've got a slot on *Good Morning Britain* tomorrow morning.' Jake looked at Clodagh. 'The producer's asked if you'd think about going on with Adam. I've told her you don't like doing stuff like that, but she's very keen. She's done me a big favour squeezing Adam in at the last minute. It would help a lot if I could say yes. You wouldn't have to talk about anything you didn't want to. I'd make sure of that. What do you think?'

'Seriously?' Clodagh looked at the two men, incredulous. 'You already know what I think of that, Jake. You too, Adam. I've told you that I will never, under any circumstances, speak in public about the crash or anything that's happened after that.'

'Even if it helps Adam?' Jake said.

'It doesn't help me if it's not something Clodagh wants to do,' Adam said. 'I'm sorry, Clodagh. I told Jake you wouldn't want to do it, but he insisted on asking you himself. I understand why you don't want to do it, and I respect that.'

'What's respect got to do with anything?' Jake said. 'The production company offered to double your fee if you appear together. Your public profile has taken a big hit these last few months. We need to be taking any opportunity we can to get you back out there.' He scowled at Clodagh. 'After everything he's done for you, I didn't think it was too much asking you to do this one small thing in return. Clearly I got that wrong.'

A surge of rage burned through her, hot and fierce. She didn't know which one of them she was angrier with – Jake for being an overbearing boor, or Adam for dragging her in here under false pretences.

'Fuck you, Jake,' she said, when she was able to speak without shouting. 'How dare you come into my home and speak to me like that?'

'Sorry.' Jake held his hands up, clearly not sorry at all but knowing he'd pushed her too far. 'I didn't mean to upset you, but this business with Nick is going to be big news whether we like it or not. Which means that no matter how unpalatable you find it, I've got to try to find a way to turn it into an opportunity for your fella here. I need to get him speaking to the media, getting his side of the story out there before they start making stuff up. Surely you can see how important that is?'

'Not really,' Clodagh said. 'Adam hasn't done anything wrong.'

'I was thinking more about you than Adam,' Jake said. 'This could turn pretty nasty for you if you're not careful.'

'Nasty how?'

She shouldn't listen to him, knowing he'd do and say anything to get his own way. Yet part of her already knew he was right. In the years following the accident, she'd become accustomed to the intrusiveness into every aspect of her private life.

'You're Vivienne's sister,' Jake said, 'who's recently moved in with her ex-husband. And now this business with Nick? Have you even thought about how that's going to play out in the press over the coming weeks? One of the lucky eight is murdered. That's a big enough story in its own right. Add to that the fact that the victim sent a text to one of the other eight right before he was killed. And that same person – you – found his dead body the following morning.' Jake paused, puffing out his cheeks and shaking his head. 'They're going to slaughter you, Clodagh.'

Clodagh looked at Adam.

'You told him about the text?'

'You're jealous,' Jake said, before Adam could reply. 'Took me a while but I've finally worked it out. It makes you sick that after all this time, Adam's still grieving for his dead wife. That's why you're always so reluctant to support his career, isn't it?'

'That's enough,' Adam said, crossing the room to sit down beside her. He took her hand and held it as he spoke to Jake.

'I think you should go now.'

'I thought you were coming back to London with me. You'll need to be at the TV studios first thing tomorrow morning.'

'I'm not sure,' Adam said, looking at Clodagh. 'It might be better if I stay here tonight and go to London early tomorrow morning.'

'No,' Clodagh said. 'You should go tonight. Get a good night's sleep before the show tomorrow morning.'

'I don't like leaving you alone,' Adam said. 'Not after today. Jake, you can arrange a car to pick me up in the morning?'

'I'm not a child who needs looking after,' Clodagh said. 'I'll be fine. You go pack a bag and Jake will drive you back to London.'

Her body ached with tension. She wanted them both gone so she could be by herself.

'Okay,' Adam said, after a moment.

'And you can wait for him in the car,' Clodagh said, looking at Jake. 'I assume you can find your own way out?'

Twenty minutes later, Adam was packed and ready to go.

'You sure you're okay about this?' he asked, as they said goodbye in the front garden.

'Fine,' Clodagh said. 'Although I wish you hadn't told Jake about the text. You shouldn't have done that, Adam.'

'I wasn't thinking,' he said. 'Sorry. I'd never have said a word if I'd realised you wanted it kept a secret.'

'It's not that,' she said. 'It's just not any of his business, that's all.'

'I can see that now,' Adam said. 'I'll have a word in the car, make sure he knows not to tell anyone else.'

'Thanks. Now go. Call me in the morning after the show and let me know how it went.'

'I'll speak to him about his behaviour earlier as well,' Adam said. 'I had no idea he was going to kick off like that.'

'Don't worry about it,' Clodagh said, deciding it would be petty to pick a row with him as he was about to leave.

'Thanks.' Adam put his hands on her shoulders and looked into her eyes. 'I don't know what I'd do without you, Clodagh. I love you. I hope you know that.'

'I know.'

She tried to smile but she couldn't get her mouth to work. Over the last few months, she'd allowed herself to believe she could be happy again. She had forgotten, for a brief period of time, that happiness wasn't something she deserved. Today, all that hope and cautious optimism had disappeared. As she stood here with the man she loved, in the golden light of the warm evening sunshine, all she could see ahead of her was darkness and despair.

Seven

Rachel pushed her chair away from the desk and stood up. She'd spent the last hour writing her report on the body found on the beach earlier. Writing was a key part of any detective's job but it would never be something Rachel enjoyed doing. Mildly dyslexic, she'd always struggled to get the words from her head onto the page. But the report was finally done, and now she needed a break.

'Fancy a walk around the block?' she asked Ade.

'Damn right.' Ade stood up and stretched. 'I'd kill for a bag of chips.'

'Best get a move on, then. Chippy closes in half an hour.'

'Another reason no one should ever move out of London,' Ade said.

'What do you mean?'

'What sort of place has a chippy that closes *before* the pubs? That is messed up. No way you can tell me it isn't.'

'Well, messed up or not,' Rachel said, 'if we don't go now there'll be no chips for you tonight.'

'You know we're going to get the scaggy bits at the bottom of the tray?' Ade said. 'It was the same last time we went just before they closed.'

As part of the Surrey and Sussex Major Crime Team, Rachel and Ade worked out of the East Sussex headquarters in Lewes. The complex of buildings, on the outskirts of Lewes town, was a twenty-minute walk to the nearest chippy. Enough time for Rachel and Ade to run back over Nick Gilbert's death.

'What are you thinking so far, Ade?'

'I'm thinking that, apart from his brother and girlfriend, no one seems very sad that Nick Gilbert is dead.'

Nick's brother, Simon, and his wife had both been staying at the hotel with the rest of the party. During his interview, Simon explained that Nick had invited them because he wanted them with him to mark the five-year anniversary of the crash.

'Eight survivors,' Ade said. 'Five of them were at the villa yesterday. With them were Adam Murray, Simon and Bella Gilbert, Jake Harris and his girlfriend.'

'I still don't understand what Jake Harris was doing there,' Rachel said.

'I got the impression Adam was the only one who wanted him there,' Ade said. 'Didn't Jake tell us he does some work for the foundation, as well as being Adam's agent? Maybe that's how Adam justified inviting him along. You ask me, though, the guy's a dick. You know, one of those who tells a woman he fancies that they remind him of someone famous? Adam wasn't too bad. Less obnoxious than I expected. But I still don't buy that crap about his marriage to Vivienne being perfect. He saw an opportunity to cash in on the tragedy and went for it.'

'Is there anyone you're not cynical about?' Rachel asked.

'It's not being cynical,' Ade said. 'It's being honest. There's a difference.'

Not for the first time, Rachel congratulated herself on taking a gamble when newly qualified Detective Constable Adesanya Benjamin had contacted her about transferring to Serious Crime for a six-month secondment. Ade's email had coincided with Rachel's long-term partner going on sabbatical, and she'd decided to take a punt on Ade. So far, the new partnership was working out pretty well.

'What about Ivan Babić?' Rachel said. 'Are we being cynical about him too?'

'I sort of liked him, actually. He certainly has the measure of all the others. At the same time, I thought there was something slightly off-kilter about him. I can't describe it, but I felt it. You ever get that, Rach?'

'Gut instinct,' Rachel said. 'Your predecessor was a big believer in it.'

'Sounds like a sensible guy.'

'He is.'

They were near the South Street Fish Bar now, the smell of chips and vinegar making Rachel's mouth water and her stomach rumble. She hadn't realised how hungry she was.

'My treat,' she said, pushing open the door and inhaling a mouthful of deep-fried aromas. 'Cod and chips okay for you?'

'And a Diet Coke,' Ade said, as if Rachel needed reminding. She had never known anyone to drink as much Diet Coke as Ade.

Once they'd got their food, they sat on the bench across the road from the chippy to eat it.

'Do you remember the day of the crash?' Rachel asked.

'Course I remember,' Ade said. 'You don't forget something that big.'

'I was on holiday when it happened.' Rachel bit into a chip, savouring the tangy heat of vinegar and deep-fried potato. 'But I heard all about it from my colleagues who were there. Some of them are still getting counselling because of it, even now. And, of course, I was roped in to help when I got back. Along with every other officer in Sussex and Surrey. It's not something I'll ever forget.

'It's never one reason when a plane crashes. I didn't know that before. In this case, there were two causes: a strong wind that made landing conditions really challenging; and the pilot had been drinking.'

The rumours about the pilot had started a few weeks after the crash. A particularly scurrilous piece in one of the tabloids, followed by several more newspaper articles and then an hour-long documentary on Channel 4. All of them exploring whether or not Gary Wakefield had caused the plane to crash. Finally, two and a half years later, the Department of Transport's Air Accidents Investigation Branch announced the outcome of their investigation. The AAIB's statement, widely welcomed, confirmed what many people already knew to be true. If Gary Wakefield hadn't been drinking, there was every chance that 160 people would never have died.

Rachel's brain snagged on something. The pilot.

'The press blamed his wife,' she said. 'He'd recently got divorced. There were a lot of stories saying that's why he'd been drinking.'

'Ooh hang on,' Ade said, taking her phone out of her pocket. 'Let me take a look.'

'I wonder how that made her feel afterwards,' Rachel said, 'knowing people were saying all those deaths could have been avoided if her marriage had never broken up?'

'I hope she didn't dwell on it too much.' Ade's eyes were glued to her phone as she answered. 'You could drive yourself mad thinking about what might have been.'

'It's hard not to,' Rachel said. 'Hard too, not to feel sorry for those poor people who've got to deal with this after everything else they've been through. It doesn't seem fair.'

'It's life,' Ade said. 'When is it ever fair when someone dies before their time? Shit, Rach. Look at this.'

She handed her phone to Rachel. The screen was open on an archived news story, written about six weeks after the crash. Rachel scanned the text, trying to find what Ade wanted her to see. It was a piece about the pilot, Gary Wakefield. From what Rachel read, it seemed to be nothing more than a rehash of the same stuff written elsewhere. The journalist who'd written the piece claimed Gary's divorce had left him 'broken and bereft' and drink had become 'his only solace during those lonely months.' It sounded like a load of old tosh to Rachel, and she didn't know why Ade had got so worked up about it.

'The photo,' Ade said.

A grainy black and white image accompanied the piece. Gary Wakefield and his wife, Arabella, on their wedding day. Using her thumb and index finger, Rachel enlarged the image. And suddenly she understood the connection her mind had been trying to make.

'It's her,' Ade said. 'Arabella Wakefield and Bella Gilbert. They're the same person. Nick's brother is married to the wife of the pilot flying the plane that caused the accident.'

Eight

After Adam left, Clodagh sat in the garden until the sun went down. As night started to creep in, darkening the edges of the sky, she went upstairs and ran a bath. Submerging in the deep, hot water, the tension in her body slowly eased. She closed her eyes, her mind focusing on the gentle movement of water and her breathing. Letting go of her anxious thoughts, one by one.

Twenty minutes later, her mind was calmer, and she was able to see that one bad day didn't mean she was inevitably sliding back to the darkness that had consumed her in the months following the crash. She was going to be okay.

For most of her life, Clodagh had taken her brain for granted. She had sailed through school and university, always one of the brightest students who consistently got good grades. It was no surprise to anyone, including Clodagh, when she qualified as a solicitor and was offered a training contract in one of the best firms in London. Then the crash happened and Clodagh's mind suddenly became something she didn't understand and couldn't trust.

It was easy, sometimes, not to acknowledge how far she'd come since then. Five years later and her short-term memory was almost back to normal. She still struggled from time to time, but things could have turned out a hell of a lot worse. She was lucky and would do well to remember that. It had been difficult to accept she would never go back to her old job. But she had money and a beautiful home, and she was in a relationship with a man she'd been in love with for years. Unlike Vivienne and all the others who'd died that day, Clodagh had a life.

The water had gone from steaming hot to lukewarm. She got out of the bath and was leaning down to pull out the plug when she heard something. Footsteps crunching on gravel outside, as if someone was walking along the side of the house right beneath her. Wrapping a towel around herself, she pushed open the window and looked outside.

'Hello?' she called. 'Who's out there?'

No response. She strained her ears, listening for any further sounds, but there was nothing. She went into the bedroom and looked out of the window there as well. Again, she couldn't see anyone.

The sudden sound of her phone ringing broke the silence, making her shout out with shock. She ran into the bedroom, half-expecting to find she'd imagined this too. But when she picked up the phone it was still ringing and the screen was lit up, showing Adam's name.

'Just checking to see how you're doing,' he said, when she answered.

'You've been gone less than two hours,' Clodagh said. 'I haven't fallen apart yet, if that's what you're worried about.'

'Of course not. I know you're strong, but it didn't stop me spending the entire journey wondering if I'd made a mistake. What happened today was terrible. I should have stayed and made sure you were okay.'

Part of her wished he'd had the guts to put her first and tell Jake to stuff the TV interview. At the same time, she was irritated at the assumption that she needed looking after.

'You don't need to worry about me,' she said. 'I'm going to have something to eat and get an early night.'

'I keep thinking about the text message Nick sent you,' Adam said. 'Are you sure you don't have any idea why he wanted to speak to you?'

There had been times in the past, when he was annoyed about something, that he would ask a question he already knew the answer to. Like the last time she'd left one of the deck chairs out overnight and he'd asked her if she knew how it had ended up in the garden. Acting as if he honestly didn't know how it had got there. Usually, she was able to tell immediately when that's what he was doing. Now, she didn't have a clue if he knew more than he was letting on or if he was genuinely trying to understand what had happened.

'I've already told you,' she said. 'I don't know.'

'Right. Well, I think I've worked it out.'

Her chest tightened. This was the real reason for his phone call. Not to check if she was okay. To tell her he knew.

'Nick told you.' Her voice sounded flat, almost like it was someone else speaking.

'I didn't tell you the whole truth earlier,' he continued, talking over her, 'about my row with Nick.'

Clodagh closed her eyes, braced herself for what was about to come.

'I told you Nick was saying some nasty stuff about Vivienne. It's what I said to the police as well. But the truth is, it was you he was being nasty about. He said I'd only got together with you because you reminded me of

Vivienne. He tried to get me to admit that being with you could never match up to what I'd had with her.'

The words were so different to the ones she'd expected him to say that she thought, at first, she'd misheard him.

'I'm not sure I understand,' she said.

'It's nothing for you to worry about,' Adam said. 'You know I've never once compared our relationship to my marriage. You and Vivienne, you're completely different people. And I'm happier with you than I could ever have imagined being again. You do know that, Clodagh, don't you?'

'Of course,' she said, when she could trust herself to speak. 'But are you saying that's why Nick wanted to speak to me? To… what? What did he want to say to me, Adam?'

'He wanted to humiliate you,' Adam said. 'Remind you of all the ways you're not like Vivienne and make you feel really shit about yourself.'

A lump had lodged in her throat. She had to swallow several times to clear it.

'I don't need Nick to make me feel any more shit about myself than I already feel,' she said, when she was finally able to speak.

'Don't say that, darling. You're the world to me. I've never been happier in my life than I've been with you these past few months.'

The lie was so blatant it hung in the air long after he'd said it. It was true that Adam was happy now, Clodagh could see that for herself. But happier than he'd been when Vivienne was still alive? No way.

'Thank you,' she said, hating herself for sounding so pathetically grateful.

'I feel bad even telling you about Nick,' Adam said. 'But I knew you'd be worrying all night about why he'd sent that text message. I thought it was better you knew the truth.'

Maybe he was right, Clodagh thought, after they'd said an awkward good night to each other and ended the call. It wasn't nice hearing that Nick had viewed her as nothing but a poor substitute for her dead sister. At the same time, she'd spent most of the day worrying about what Nick had really said to Adam. Now, at least, she knew.

Doing all she could to put the conversation to one side, she got dressed and went downstairs to get something to eat. There was some leftover chickpea soup in the fridge. Pouring this into a saucepan, she put it on low heat, while she set the kitchen table. As she opened the cupboard to get out some plates, she saw a movement out of the corner of her eye. A reflection in the glass doors that led into the garden. Someone was in the kitchen, standing behind her. She froze, keeping her eyes trained on the glass, watching as the reflection in the glass started walking towards her.

Nine

Rachel looked at the photo of Gary and Arabella Wakefield a while longer before handing the phone back to Ade.

'Maybe it's not as odd as we think,' she said. 'Adam told us he arranges regular meetings for all those whose lives were affected by the crash. Her life was as much affected as anyone else's. It's probably how they met.'

'Why didn't either of them say anything when we spoke to them earlier?' Ade said.

'Arabella was the subject of a lot of press scrutiny at the time,' Rachel said. 'You can't blame her for wanting to put all that behind her.'

But even as she said this, Rachel couldn't shake off the sense that she was missing something important.

'I know we have to wait until the post-mortem's done,' she said, 'but I'd bet my last pound that this is going to turn into a murder investigation. If that happens, it will be my first case as SIO. I'm bloody terrified, Ade. Although if you dare say that to anyone else I'll get you taken off this case faster than you can finish those chips.'

'My lips are sealed.' Ade grinned. 'Besides, I'm too scared of you to ever say or do anything you've told me not to.'

'Good,' Rachel said, knowing Ade wasn't being serious. In the two months since they'd been working together, Ade Benjamin had never once shown the slightest sign of being scared of anyone or anything.

'They must have hated being called *lucky*,' Ade said. 'I mean, sure, they were lucky they didn't die. But it's hardly luck to be involved in a plane crash, is it? They were injured too. Clodagh suffered serious brain injuries. Nick Gilbert had to learn to walk again, and he was left with that terrible scar. There's nothing lucky about that.'

'I'm sure they do hate it,' Rachel said, remembering her conversation with Clodagh earlier.

'I read a newspaper article about them last year,' Ade said. 'It must have been the four-year anniversary of the crash, I guess. It was all about the psychological effects of surviving something like that.'

'PTSD?'

'Yeah, but not just that. Post-traumatic stress disorder is common, as you'd expect. But something called post-traumatic growth is equally common although you never hear people talking about that. It's when people experience positive change that comes from struggling with a major life crisis or traumatic event. Apparently, after a trauma some people develop a new understanding of themselves and the world they live in, and they're better able to work out how to live their life to the full.

'This article I read profiled Nick Gilbert and Adam Murray, saying they were both examples of this post-traumatic growth. Over the last few years, Nick became hugely successful. He expanded his restaurant business and made a name for himself as a celebrity chef. Adam wasn't in the crash but he still experienced the trauma of losing his wife. And he's used that trauma to turn his life around in a hugely positive way.'

Rachel was impressed by this insight, but not surprised. Ade was a constant source of fascinating information about all sorts of things Rachel had never heard of.

'It hasn't happened with all of them,' she said. 'Clodagh didn't strike me as someone who's managed to turn her life around.'

Rachel had read that, before the crash, Clodagh had been a high-flying corporate lawyer working for a prestigious international law firm. Since the accident, she'd had to give up her law career and seemed to have spent the rest of her time doing not very much at all.

'Maybe her luck's changed too,' Ade said. 'Now she's found love with Adam Murray.'

'Maybe.' Rachel wasn't convinced. There was a sadness, an emptiness, that she'd seen when she'd spoken with Clodagh earlier today.

She felt exhausted suddenly. She'd barely touched her food but couldn't face eating any more.

'You want this?' She held the leftover fish and chips out to Ade who shook her head.

'Absolutely full, thanks.'

'We should get back.' Rachel crumpled up the paper and the remains of her food and stood up. As she threw the bundle in a nearby bin, her phone started to ring. There was a number she didn't recognise on the screen.

'Hello?'

'Oh, hello. Is this Detective Lewis? It's Shelly Clarkson. You've been trying to contact me.'

The guest who'd been at the villa yesterday but hadn't spent the night. Rachel had left two messages for Shelly earlier today. Finally, the woman had decided to call her back.

'Indeed I have,' Rachel said. 'I was starting to think I was never going to hear from you.'

'I'm sorry I'm so late getting back to you,' Shelly said. 'I've been out walking all day. I didn't take my phone as I wanted a day of complete peace. I need days like that sometimes, especially after yesterday.'

'You know why I'm calling?'

'Nick,' Shelly said, after a short pause. 'You're not the only person who's left messages, detective. I've had so many that my voicemail is full. He died last night and you think he might have been killed? I've just come off the phone with Tara. The poor thing is devastated.'

'We don't know yet how Nick died,' Rachel said. 'We'll know more after the post-mortem's been done. For now, I simply need to ask you some questions about yesterday. We can do that now if it's okay with you?'

'Of course,' Shelly said. 'Ask away.'

'You didn't stay at the villa last night,' Rachel said. 'Why not?'

'I can find that group a bit claustrophobic sometimes,' Shelly said. 'Don't get me wrong. It's wonderful that we all have each other. We're incredibly lucky to have that support and mutual understanding. But it can all get a bit much sometimes. The crash was terrible. The worst day of my life, bar none. But I'm a pragmatist, detective. After it had happened, all I wanted was to move on with my life. Put it behind me. I knew I couldn't go back to my old job, so I focused instead on what I could do. I sold my home in London and I used the money from that, and what I got from the airline, to buy a small pub in Surrey. These days, I'm a pub landlady and I love it. But I don't drink, you see. I never have done. These sorts of reunions can get a bit boozy. When people are drunk, they become maudlin and I can't stand that. So I'd decided early on that I wasn't going to stay.'

Rachel had already formed a good impression of Shelly from what she'd read about her. Speaking to her now, she was starting to like her even more. Rachel got the impression Shelly would make a bloody good pub landlady.

'What time did you leave?' she asked.

'Just after nine thirty,' Shelly said. 'I would have left earlier but I got caught up in a conversation with Tara and was finding it difficult to… oh dear.'

'What's wrong?'

'I'm sure it's not relevant,' Shelly said. 'And I wouldn't like you to think I'm stirring up trouble.'

'If you've got something to tell me, just spit it out,' Rachel said. 'It may not be important, I understand that. But it's better you let me know so I can decide for myself.'

'You're right,' Shelly said. 'Sorry. Tara was upset. She'd had another row with Nick. They had what you'd call a tempestuous relationship. One minute, they'd be all over each other then, before you knew what was happening, they'd be at each other's throats. From what I could make out, last night's row seemed particularly bad. Tara was in a terrible state. I did my best to console her but, after a while, I realised she was too angry to listen to reason so I left her to it.'

'What was the row about?'

'They were due to go on holiday shortly,' Shelly said. 'Then last night, out of the blue, Nick announced he'd cancelled the whole thing. Tara was very upset about it.'

This was news to Rachel. Between herself and Ade, they had spoken to all the guests and staff who'd been at the villa yesterday evening. Not one of them had mentioned anything about a row between Nick and Tara.

The only row Rachel knew about was the one later that evening between Nick and Adam.

'Did Nick seem drunk to you by the time you left?' Rachel asked.

'Definitely,' Shelly said. 'Drunk and nasty. A tired old pattern that we'd all seen too often over the past few years. I think because Gary was his friend, he's found it harder to deal with what happened than some of the others. I mean, we all struggled to come to terms with what Gary had done. But as Gary's friend, it was harder for Nick.'

'How did Gary get away with it?' Rachel asked. 'Surely his co-pilot would have smelled the booze on his breath?'

'None of us smelled anything,' Shelly said. 'And he didn't seem drunk. Not that we were looking for it. Gary was a professional. I don't think I'd ever seen him drink alcohol, even at social events. I've no idea what happened to make him drink that day. It was completely out of character.

'The thing I found most difficult to accept is that he should never have been flying that plane. He was on holiday with his friends. He only had his uniform with him because his last rostered duty was being on standby. When he wasn't required to fly, he joined his pals on the flight to Crete. On the flight back, the captain who was due to fly the plane fell ill with food poisoning; the airline asked Gary to step in at the last moment. Normally, he'd have met the first officer at the airport crew room, but because it was all so last-minute, they didn't meet up until they were both on the aircraft.'

'It must have made it even harder for you all to come to terms with what happened afterwards,' Rachel said, 'knowing how close you'd come to avoiding the disaster.'

'Like I said, Nick found it harder than some of the others. It was sad, really. He'd made this big show of inviting his brother, said he wanted Simon with him to mark this important landmark in Nick's life. But Nick got so drunk that poor Simon went to bed soon after dinner. It was clear he found Nick's behaviour embarrassing.'

This pretty much matched Simon Gilbert's own account when Rachel had spoken to him earlier.

'Sounds as if Nick upset quite a few people last night,' Rachel said.

'I've always thought one of Nick's problems was his determination to put it behind him and move on with his life. I know he's done very well for himself, but it takes time and hard work to get past something like that.'

'I can't even begin to imagine,' Rachel said.

'Of course you can't.'

There was silence and Rachel guessed Shelly was reliving the horror of what had happened that day five years ago.

'What can you tell me about Nick's relationship with Tara?' Rachel asked, after what she hoped was a suitable pause.

'Tara's a mess too,' Shelly said. 'In her case, it's more obvious than it was with Nick. And, I'm afraid to say this, I doubt she'd ever have ended up with someone like Nick if it wasn't for his fame and his money. Tara's a sweet girl, but she's foolish too.'

'What do you think happened to Nick?' Rachel asked.

'I'm hoping it will turn out to be an accident,' Shelly said. 'I'm sure Nick upset lots of people last night. But enough for one of them to murder him? I doubt that very much. We were all used to him and, no matter how bad he got, we never forgot that he's one of us. There's a bond between the eight of us that's difficult to explain to anyone who wasn't on that plane. We're like a family. We may drive each other mad, but we'll always be there for each other too.'

Soon after that, Rachel thanked Shelly for her time and asked her to get back in touch if she thought of anything else.

'Did anyone mention a row between Tara and Nick?' she asked Ade, after hanging up from Shelly.

'First I've heard of it,' Ade said. 'Who was that on the phone?'

'Shelly Clarkson returning my call. She says Tara and Nick were always arguing and they had a particularly bad one last night.'

'But according to Tara, the row was between Nick and Adam,' Ade said. 'And for the record, I'm still not sure Adam told us the truth about that. He said they argued about his dead wife, but I think there's more to it. I did a bit of reading up on him earlier. He was a nobody when he married Vivienne. A struggling crime writer who'd only ever had one book published. Two months before the crash, he was dumped by his publisher. Everything changed for him after he wrote the memoir.'

'None of it would have happened if his wife hadn't died.' Rachel sighed. 'Tara did her level best to make sure we knew about the argument between Nick and Adam, but never mentioned anything about the row she'd had with him.'

'You want us to go and speak to her again?' Ade said.

'No.' Rachel shook her head. 'Let's wait until we know for sure how Nick died. If the PM clearly shows his death was an accident, then maybe it doesn't matter who Nick rowed with last night.'

On the walk back to the station, she felt edgy, impatient. The need to take action was tempered by the knowledge that there wasn't anything constructive they could do until they had the post-mortem results. Until then, they would have to sit tight and wait. But Rachel wasn't good at waiting. Especially not when her gut was telling her, loudly and repeatedly, that Nick Gilbert's death was no accident. Someone had wanted him dead.

Ten

The knife rack was on the worktop to her left. As quietly as she could, Clodagh sneaked her hand forward and removed Adam's beloved Miyabi chef's knife. Eight inches of ice-hardened carbide steel. Gripping the handle tightly, she turned and lunged forward, knife out, screaming.

'Clodagh! It's me. Stop!'

The moment of recognition almost came too late. She stopped with the blade centimetres from the woman standing in front of her.

'Jesus, Bella. What the hell are you doing here?'

'I needed to see you.' Bella took several steps back, her hands up as if to protect herself.

The surge of adrenaline that had given Clodagh the courage to grab the knife and face the intruder was gone, leaving her empty and exhausted. She dropped the knife onto the worktop. The sound of metal on marble made Bella flinch, causing the familiar feelings of guilt clawing at Clodagh's insides. She didn't have the strength to put on the front she always needed when dealing with Bella.

'How did you get into the house?' she asked, remembering the footsteps she'd heard earlier when she was upstairs.

'The front door was open,' Bella said. 'I should have rung the doorbell, I know. But I was worried Adam would answer and it's you I'm here to see, not him.'

'I heard someone outside,' Clodagh said, 'walking around the side of the house. Was that you?'

'Guilty as charged. I wanted to avoid Adam, so I thought I'd try the garden first. I know you often like to sit out there in the evenings. When I couldn't find you, I came back around to the front of the house. Then I saw the door wasn't fully closed and, before I knew what I was doing, I'd pushed it open and come inside. I can see now how stupid that was, but you've got to understand, my head's all over the place. I'm sorry. I probably shouldn't have come. I just really needed to see you.'

Bella's voice cracked and Clodagh's guilt expanded until she could taste it at the back of her throat – bitter and raw and impossible to get rid of.

'It's okay,' she said. 'I'm glad you're here.'

'Really?'

'Yes.' Clodagh hoped she sounded convincing.

'Oh, thank you.' Bella smiled and leaned in a little closer, like she was about to whisper in Clodagh's ear.

Something about the movement triggered a memory, so small and indistinct Clodagh couldn't hold onto it. Out of mind, out of sight.

'The thing is, Clodagh, I need to ask you a favour.'

'Of course,' Clodagh said. 'Anything. Let's sit down. Can I get you something to drink? Or eat? I'm heating up some soup if you'd like some. Or I could make something else, if you'd rather.'

She stopped, realising she was babbling. She was always like this with Bella, anxious and too eager to please. Somehow, Bella never seemed to notice or, if she did, was too polite to ever say anything.

'I'm fine,' Bella said, pulling out a chair and sitting down at the kitchen table. 'But you go ahead and have your soup. Please.'

'I'll have it later,' Clodagh said, switching off the hob. The very idea of food made her want to throw up. She sat down opposite Bella.

'I haven't even asked about Simon. How's he holding up?'

She hadn't seen Simon at the villa earlier. He'd stayed holed up in his room with Bella, presumably trying to come to terms with the fact that his only sibling had just died. More than once, Clodagh had thought about knocking on their door and asking if there was anything she could do. But each time she'd stood up to go and see him, Adam had talked her out of it.

'He'll let you know when he's ready to talk,' Adam had said, pulling Clodagh into an embrace that was meant to be comforting but made her feel stifled instead. 'Until then, it's better you leave him be.'

At the time, she'd done what Adam suggested and left Bella and Simon alone. Now, sitting opposite Bella, she felt bad for not having made more of an effort.

'He's not doing too good,' Bella said. 'It's too much to take in. For both of us. Losing Nick brings it all back. The pain and the grief and the bloody awfulness of what happened.'

'You haven't left him alone, have you?'

'He's at his parents' house in London,' Bella said. 'We drove straight there when we were finally allowed to leave the villa. I've been with them all evening, but I think they want some time together just the three of them. I was going to head directly home but I couldn't face it. So I came here instead.'

With something approaching dread, Clodagh realised she should ask Bella if she wanted to stay for the night. She wondered, in fact, if that's why Bella was here in the first place. Because she couldn't face going back to her own house alone.

'Is there anything I can do?' she asked, pushing down the dread and forcing herself to do the right thing, even it wasn't what she wanted.

'You're such a good friend,' Bella said. 'I don't think I'd have got through these past years without you. I know it's different because I wasn't on the plane…'

'You don't need to explain,' Clodagh said quickly. 'I know how hard it's been for you, Bella.'

She hadn't planned this friendship. In the weeks and months following the crash, she'd done all she could to avoid contact with any of the people whose lives had been devasted by the crash. The person she wanted to avoid more than anyone was Bella Wakefield, the ex-wife of the pilot who'd been flying the plane that day. But a year after the accident, Bella turned up at Clodagh's London apartment asking for help. And because, by then, Clodagh would have done anything to alleviate the crippling guilt that was with her every waking moment, she told Bella she'd help in whatever way she could.

'You were the only one who didn't turn me away,' Bella said now. 'You'll never know how much that means to me. It was such a terrible time. All those rumours and speculation about whether or not the crash was Gary's fault. The fact we were already divorced by then didn't seem to make a blind bit of difference. Everyone still tried to find a way to blame me for what he'd done. I'm sure that's why none of the others wanted to help me. Because they thought the crash was my fault.'

A dull ache at the back of Clodagh's throat that wouldn't disappear no matter how many times she swallowed.

'No one ever blamed you,' she said, meaning it.

'I still find it hard to accept he did what they said,' Bella said. 'He loved his job. I can't imagine he'd ever have taken a risk like that. I keep thinking something must have happened to him during that week in Crete to make him do what he did. What do you think, Clodagh? You were staying at the same resort. Did you notice anything?'

'No.' Clodagh pushed her chair back and stood up, unable to bear the intensity of Bella's stare. 'I'm going to make myself a chamomile tea. Do you want something to drink?'

'I didn't mean to upset you,' Bella said. 'I'm sorry, Clodagh. Nick's death has stirred up a whole load of stuff I thought I'd put behind me.'

Clodagh filled the kettle, giving herself time to choose her words carefully before she spoke.

'I can understand that,' she said. 'But the truth is, none of us will ever know why Gary was drinking that day. You could drive yourself crazy trying to work it out.'

Clodagh didn't add she knew just how difficult it was to try to move on from what had happened that day. She'd spent most of the last five years trying to make sense of it. The fact that she couldn't remember anything in the hours before she got on the plane didn't help. She could never shake off the sense that she'd forgotten something important. Something that might explain why Gary's blood alcohol was five times above the legal limit.

'You're with Simon now,' she continued. 'He's who you need to focus on, not Gary.'

'You're right,' Bella said. 'In fact, that's why I'm here. I need you to talk to him.'

'Sorry?'

'Simon. He's really struggling to get his head around what's happened. I think it would help if you tell him your version of things.'

'What do you mean – my version?'

'Just tell him what you saw on the beach this morning. Whether it looked like he'd been killed or…'

'He was dead,' Clodagh said. 'That's all I saw. I don't think there's anything else I can tell Simon that he doesn't already know.'

'Please?'

She wanted to tell Bella to go home and leave her in peace. But Simon had lost his only sibling and Clodagh knew, better than anyone, how painful that was. Besides, this was Bella asking. Clodagh couldn't say no.

'Of course I'll talk to him,' she said. 'I can give him a ring now if you'd like?'

'Not tonight. We'll be back home tomorrow afternoon. Are you okay coming to ours?'

Clodagh wasn't allowed to drive because of her brain injuries. But there were regular trains from Bramhurst, the village she lived in, to Brighton where Simon and Bella lived.

'Of course. Tomorrow's fine.'

'You're a star.' Bella stood up. 'Thank you so much, Clodagh. You've no idea how much this means to me. I'm going to head home now and get some sleep. I'll see you tomorrow.'

After she left, Clodagh drank her tea while her mind went back to the same place it always did – that last holiday before her sister died.

She'd gone to Crete with Vivienne. The holiday had been Vivienne's idea, part of her ongoing attempts to make up for marrying Adam. She'd booked and paid for everything, insisting this holiday was her treat. Seven nights in an adult-only, all-inclusive resort in Analipsi, a quiet village on the north-east of the island. It should have been the perfect break. Except it wasn't. By the end of the week, Clodagh was desperate to get back home.

In the weeks following the crash, Clodagh had barely any memories of that last week with Vivienne. Gradually, however, the memories started coming back. Slowly, at first, then a sudden rush of them all together. Until today, she'd believed the only memories still missing were those from the hours preceding the crash. Suddenly, she wasn't so sure. She replayed Bella's words in her mind – *something must have happened during that week in Crete to make him do what he did*.

What if Bella was right and something had happened – something so bad that Clodagh's damaged mind had chosen to forget because remembering it would be too painful?

Eleven

Day Two

Tara Coleman lived in a modern, glass-fronted building overlooking the river Thames in London's South Bank area. Rachel and Ade navigated their way through the throngs of people enjoying the city in the shimmering heat of summer, eventually reaching the apartment block precisely two and a half hours since they'd got the news that Nick Gilbert's death wasn't accidental. Someone had killed him. Blunt force trauma to the head was the official cause of death. The back of his head had been hit, repeatedly, with something round and hard. After he was dead, the killer had rolled him onto his back in what looked like a cack-handed attempt to make his injuries look accidental.

Rachel's boss, Detective Superintendent Sharon Spalding, had arranged for two officers to go to Nick's parents to break the news that their son's death was now being treated as a murder investigation. While they were doing that, Rachel and Ade had driven to London to ask Tara some more questions. As his girlfriend, she was top of their list of potential murder suspects.

'Fancy pad,' Ade said, looking up at the tall building.

'I don't like it myself.' Rachel pointed at the way the building curved out in the middle. 'Reminds me of my dad's beer belly.'

She scanned the list of names on the intercom system, found Tara's name and pressed the buzzer for apartment.

'Let's hope she's in,' she said.

They hadn't called ahead, wanting the element of surprise when they spoke to her. A good strategy when it worked, but it meant if Tara wasn't at home, Ade and Rachel might have to hang around outside the apartment building until she finally showed up.

'Hello?' Tara's voice through the intercom meant their gamble had paid off. Giving Ade the thumbs up, Rachel told Tara they had a few more questions for her and asked to be let into the apartment.

'Oh my God,' Tara whispered. 'Is it Nick? Do you know how he died?'

'Just let us in and we can chat then,' Rachel said.

'Of course. I'm on the top floor. You'll need to take the lift.'

A beeping sound preceded the click of the front door unlocking. Rachel pushed it open and stepped inside. The entrance lobby was huge, its size exaggerated even further by the mirrored walls which reflected multiple images of Rachel and Ade as they crossed over to the row of lifts.

'That is well spooky,' Ade said. 'Imagine a world with that many Rachels in it. Doesn't bear thinking about.'

'You think seeing multiple versions of your face is any better?'

Ade grinned.

'You got to admit, Rach. My face is a hell of a lot more pleasing to the eye than yours.'

Rachel had no answer to that, mainly because she agreed, although hell would freeze over before she'd ever give Ade any ammunition to boost her already very robust ego.

The building had six floors. Rachel pressed the button for the top floor and the lift started its smooth ascent up through the building. When they walked out of the lift a few seconds later, Tara was waiting for them in the doorway of her apartment at the far end of the corridor. She looked like she'd barely slept. Dark patches, like bruises, under her eyes; her hair, so glossy yesterday, lacked any sort of lustre and looked as if she'd forgotten to brush it.

As the two detectives drew closer, she put a hand over her mouth and started shaking her head.

'No,' she moaned. 'No, no, no.'

'Let's get inside, Tara.' Rachel put a hand on Tara's arm and managed to steer her into the apartment.

After propping Tara up on the sofa, Rachel moved into the open plan kitchen to make cups of tea for the three of them. She left Ade with Tara, knowing she'd do a better job at consoling her than Rachel ever could.

'He was killed,' Tara said. 'That's why you're here, isn't it?'

'We're here because we need to ask you a few questions,' Ade said gently. 'Do you think you're up to that, Tara?'

'Only if you tell me the truth.' Tara looked across at Rachel. 'You said you wouldn't know how he died until after the post-mortem's been done. I spoke to Nick's parents earlier and they said that was happening today. Oh God. Do they know? I haven't spoken to them since this morning. Why wouldn't they call me if they knew how he'd died? Unless you've told them you think I killed him?'

'They don't know anything yet,' Rachel said. 'We wanted to speak to you first.'

There was a row of glass jars on the worktop, herbal teabags in each one. She couldn't see any normal tea and guessed there probably wasn't any. Preferring not to drink anything, she asked Ade and Tara what they wanted and prepared them each a cup of their choice.

'We've got some more questions about Saturday night,' she said, when the tea was finally made and she was sitting down.

'I've already told you everything I know,' Tara said.

'You told us that you saw Nick and Adam having an argument,' Ade said. 'And you didn't see him again after that?'

'That's right.'

Ade took a sip of her tea and glanced across at Rachel, who nodded. She was more than happy for Ade to lead the questioning.

'You also told us Nick found the day really difficult,' she said. 'Which is understandable. From the conversations we've had with the other guests, it seems that Nick's behaviour got a bit out of hand after he'd had a few drinks.'

'It wasn't his fault,' Tara said. 'He sometimes lashed out when he was drunk. He was always really sorry afterwards.'

'Did he sometimes lash out at you too?' Ade asked.

'What do you mean?' Tara was visibly startled, and Rachel felt her own body tensing in response, ready to grab Tara if she tried to make a run for it.

'I'm just wondering what it was like for you when he got like that,' Ade said. 'It can't have been easy. Especially as I imagine the day was just as difficult for you.'

'I lost my two best friends in the crash,' Tara said. 'Monica and Jessie. It would have been Jess's birthday in a few weeks. Weirdly, that's when it gets to me the most each year. Not the anniversary of the crash but their birthdays. Twenty-eighth of March and twelfth of August.'

She shook her head, looking from Ade to Rachel.

'I still have nightmares. We all do. I dream I'm back there on the plane with all the chaos and the noise, the smoke and the fear. Everyone screaming in the dark. Because it was pitch black. We couldn't see anything. The lights had gone out, and the cabin was full of this thick smoke. I thought that's what would kill me, the smoke. Because I couldn't breathe.

'The counselling has helped, but there are days when I can't even get out of bed. I wake up and there's this blackness that blocks out everything. All I want to do then is die. But that's the one thing we can't do. No matter how bad it gets. Because we're meant to think of ourselves as lucky.'

She stopped speaking and looked down at her lap, as if embarrassed for revealing so much. For the first time, Rachel felt a pang of real sympathy for her. But Rachel was here to do a job, which meant asking questions, regardless of whether they upset Tara even further.

'You mentioned the twelfth of August,' she said. 'Jessie's birthday, right? Had you planned anything special for that day?'

'We were going to go away,' Tara said. 'Nick had booked us into Chewton Glen for a week. It's a spa hotel in Hampshire. Really gorgeous.' She gave Rachel a small smile. 'I don't fly any more. Nick does – sorry, he did – but I'll never get on a plane ever again.'

'A week in a spa hotel sounds glorious,' Rachel said.

'It's not going to happen now though, is it? Nick's dead.'

'Chewton Glen,' Rachel said. 'Is that the name of the hotel?'

'Does it matter?'

'Tara, I'm afraid you were right about the reason we came here today,' Ade said. 'I can't confirm any details of how Nick died, but I can tell you that we are treating his death as suspicious. As part of our investigation, Rachel and I will be looking into every aspect of Nick's life. That includes his plans over the coming months.'

'I knew it,' Tara whispered. 'I knew from the moment I heard he was dead that it wasn't an accident. Is that why you're here now? Because you think it was me? I wouldn't ever have hurt him, I swear to you. Nick was the only good thing in my life. He was the one who kept me going, even when things got really bad. I loved him and I don't know how I'm going to get through this. I feel as if I've lost the only person left in the world I ever cared about. I know what people said about him. They thought he was a bastard, but he could be so kind as well. And he took care of me. He really did. Who's going to do that now?'

'Is there anyone you can call?' Ade asked. 'It doesn't sound as if you should be by yourself at the moment.'

'You mean you're not going to arrest me?'

'We just want to understand what happened on Saturday night,' Rachel said. 'All of it, not just the bits you want us to know about.'

'You mean the row.' Tara sighed and the tension Rachel had noticed earlier seemed to leave her body as she slumped forward. 'I didn't tell you about it because I knew you'd think it was something it wasn't.'

Rachel could have pointed out that Tara hadn't had the same concerns when she'd told them about the argument between Nick and Adam. But she didn't because she didn't want to interrupt Tara now she was finally opening up to them.

'He told me he'd cancelled our week away,' she said. 'When I asked him why, he said he couldn't afford it. Which was a lie because he's got, like, loads of money. I was so upset because that week away was, like, the only thing I had to look forward to. My mood's been really low for a few weeks now. It gets like that around this time of the year. Nick knew that and he knew how important it was for me to get away. Yet he still cancelled. And he did it without even telling me first. Which meant he let me carry on looking forward to it, and talking with him about it, after he'd cancelled. He only told me about it on Saturday night because he was in a bad mood and he wanted to bring me down too.'

'I can understand why you were upset about it,' Ade said. 'I'd be very angry if a fella I was dating pulled a stunt like that.'

'You're right,' Tara said. 'I was upset. And angry. But not enough to kill him. What can I tell you? Our relationship was fiery. We loved each other, but we drove each other mad as well. Yet no matter how many rows we had, we always made it up afterwards. And you'll never know what I'd give to have had the chance to make up with him this time too.'

'You had separate rooms at the villa,' Rachel said. 'Why was that?'

'Nick refused to come at first. When he changed his mind, I made him book his own room. I wasn't going to let him think he could just share with me. He had to prove to me that he really wanted to be there.' She looked defiantly at Rachel and Ade. 'You've got to make men work at a relationship. Otherwise they'll walk all over you.'

They left soon after that, both of them convinced they'd got as much information as they could from Tara for now.

'I feel a bit more sympathy for Nick than I did before coming here,' Ade said, as they once more passed the multiple reflections of themselves in the mirrored walls on the ground floor. 'She wouldn't be an easy woman to go out with.'

'Maybe not,' Rachel said, 'but I'm still worried about leaving her by herself.'

'Is it worth arranging for a liaison officer to stay with her?' Ade asked. 'She doesn't seem to have anyone else.'

'Good idea,' Rachel said. 'Apart from anything else, until we know a bit more about what happened on Saturday, she's still our number one suspect.'

'Even though we both know she didn't kill him?'

'How do you know what I think?' Rachel said.

'Because it's obvious,' Ade said. 'Tara Coleman's a mixed-up mess but she's not a killer. Whoever smashed Nick Gilbert's head in, it wasn't her.'

'So if it wasn't Tara, who was it then?'

'Well that's what we're going to find out,' Ade said. 'You and me, Rach. The dream team. Your first case as SIO and my first murder enquiry. We've got this one.'

They walked away from the river, back to where they'd parked their car. Rachel felt rejuvenated, her energy rising with every step. Until this moment, she'd been worried she wasn't up to this. That she would mess up the investigation and everyone would see her for the imposter she really was. Suddenly, that insecurity was replaced by a sense of purpose. Ade was right. They had this one. Rachel was going to stop at nothing until she'd found out who had killed Nick Gilbert, and why.

Twelve

On Monday afternoon, Clodagh took a train from Bramhurst to Brighton. She hadn't watched Adam's appearance on TV earlier, but she downloaded the show to her phone so she could watch it on the train. After watching it, she wished she hadn't bothered. Adam came across as caring more about his latest book than he did about Nick's death. Each time the presenter started to ask about Nick, Adam managed to bring the conversation back to his book and the different ways it could help people who'd lost someone they loved. By the time the clip had finished, Clodagh felt more depressed than ever.

She didn't help herself by going straight from the video to the internet, once again scrolling through the different news sites checking for updates on Nick's death. It had been the top story on every site she'd visited earlier, and still was. She scanned all the stories again, her eyes skipping over the endless accounts of the plane crash and the eight people who'd survived it. A whole host of badly worded headlines that made her head hurt. *Tragedy strikes again. Last supper for celebrity chef. Unlucky eight now down to seven.*

Disgusted, she switched her phone off and put it away, knowing if it was switched on she wouldn't be able to resist taking another a look a few minutes later. The prospect of spending the afternoon with Simon and Bella wasn't doing anything to improve her mood. Several times this morning she'd thought about cancelling. Twice, she'd actually taken her phone out and started typing a text to tell Bella she couldn't make it. Both times, she'd deleted the text before sending it. Cancelling wouldn't help. Sooner or later, she'd have to do this. She might as well get it over and done with.

Bella was waiting for Clodagh as she came through the ticket barrier at Brighton train station.

'Clodagh! Over here.'

As the two women embraced, Clodagh swallowed down the complex feelings that came every time she was with Bella.

'My car's this way,' Bella said, leading Clodagh out of the station to a silver Vauxhall that had seen better days.

'Sorry about the car,' she said, opening the door and motioning for Clodagh to jump in. 'It's a bit of a mess. We'd like to afford something better, but you know how things are for us.'

Clodagh didn't say anything, looking out of the car window at the hustle and bustle of Brighton seafront. She wondered how many of those people were aware that every single decision they made this afternoon – which restaurant to eat in, whether to stop off for a drink on the way home, what part of the beach to sit on – had the potential to change the course of their lives forever.

'I've tried so hard to focus on the positives in my life,' Bella said. 'But there are times when I can't help wishing Gary and I never got divorced.'

This was a topic Bella came back to again and again. Because her marriage to Gary was officially over when the plane crashed, it meant she hadn't been entitled to any of the compensation money paid out to the survivors and the victims' families.

'I'm sure I'd feel the same,' Clodagh said.

'Exactly!' Bella smiled. 'You're the only person I can say this stuff to, you know. Anyone else would think I'm being mercenary. But you've always really got it. And I'm so grateful to you for that. How are you doing, anyway? I never even asked how you were yesterday. I was so caught up worrying about Simon.'

'I'm fine,' Clodagh said. 'It was horrible. But I know it's so much worse for Simon and his poor parents.'

'It's destroyed them,' Bella said. 'I don't think they'll ever come back from this. They've already been through so much, almost losing Nick after the crash. For this to happen now, at their time of life, it doesn't seem fair.'

Bella continued driving along the seafront, past the elegant grandeur of Brighton and Hove, towards the industrial port at Portslade-by-Sea. Huge freighter ships and factories lined the shore. The place had a run-down feeling about it, that intensified when Bella turned off the coast road and navigated her way through a warren of suburban streets.

'Here we are,' she said, pulling up outside a row of small, terraced houses. 'It's small, but it's ours.'

'It's lovely,' Clodagh said, the lie coming easily because she could see how much it mattered to Bella. 'How long have you guys been living here?'

'Seven months,' Bella said. 'We moved in right after we got married. Amazing how fast it's gone. It needs a lot of work, as you'll see. I want to extend out the back so we've got a big, open plan kitchen. The problem is, getting work like that done is expensive. We've saving like mad, but it'll be years before we'll have enough.'

'Why don't you let me help you?'

The words were out before Clodagh could stop them. Her instant, knee-jerk response to Bella. Always looking for ways to make things better. She had tried, several times, to give Bella money in the past. Bella had always flatly refused and they'd eventually agreed that Clodagh wouldn't offer again.

'Sorry.' She held her hands up. 'I shouldn't have said that.'

'Actually,' Bella said, 'it might not be such a bad idea. Normally, I'd say no way but it might give Simon something to look forward to? I'm not saying we should start the work tomorrow or anything. But maybe in a few months. If you're sure you wouldn't mind? You know I'd pay you back.'

'Of course I know that.' Clodagh smiled, relieved. 'I'm so glad, Bella. It makes perfect sense and it would mean a lot.'

'Why are you always so keen to help me, Clodagh? I don't get it. I mean, it's lovely of you but why is it so important to you?'

'We're friends,' Clodagh said. 'And friends help each other out. There's nothing wrong with that, is there?'

'I guess not.' Bella's face cleared and she returned Clodagh's smile. 'Come on then. Let's go inside.'

At the front door, Bella paused before putting the key in the lock and turned to Clodagh.

'Simon's not in a good place,' she said. 'This has hit him really hard. If he's a bit off with you, try not to take it personally.'

'Maybe this isn't such a good idea,' Clodagh said. 'The last thing I want to do is upset him any more than he already is.'

'It'll be fine,' Bella said, 'I promise. Just don't expect a big welcome party, okay?'

Clodagh followed her into the house, surprised to see how much nicer it was inside. Freshly painted walls, a vase of fresh flowers on a small table, the air sweet with the smell of baking.

'I made some biscuits earlier,' Bella said, leading Clodagh along the narrow hallway to a small kitchen at the back of the house. 'I like to bake most mornings, even if it means getting up early. There's something so therapeutic about it.'

Like the rest of the interior, the kitchen looked as if it had been newly painted. The units were old-fashioned and ugly, but it was clear someone had gone to a lot of trouble to make the place as pleasant as it was possible to do without spending money.

Simon was sitting at the kitchen table, hunched over his mobile phone. He looked up, nodding at Bella before looking at Clodagh.

'You came, then.'

'Bella said you wanted to see me,' Clodagh said. 'I'm so sorry about Nick. I can't imagine how awful this must be for you both.'

Simon grunted, but didn't expand beyond that.

Clodagh remembered the first time she'd met Nick's brother. Adam had organised a memorial service to mark the one-year anniversary of the crash. Hundreds of people turned up, relatives of those who'd lost loved ones mingling with the handful of people who'd survived. Nick had been there, still in his wheelchair back then, accompanied by a man Clodagh couldn't take her eyes off. Because while Nick had a certain thuggish attractiveness about him, his younger brother was nothing short of beautiful.

Ink-blue eyes framed with long, dark lashes, lean and long-limbed and, when he smiled, there was nothing you could do except smile back.

The sudden rush of attraction had taken her aback. She'd spent most of the previous months feeling nothing at all. Empty days that she endured through a grey fog that left her feeling isolated and alone. Driven by the need to keep the feeling alive, she had crossed the room to speak to him. And discovered, to her disappointment, that there was very little going on behind that perfect face.

'Sit down,' Bella told Clodagh. 'I'll put the kettle on. What would you like to drink?'

'Coffee would be lovely,' Clodagh said, choosing the chair furthest from Simon and sitting down. Bella hadn't exaggerated when she said Simon wasn't in a good place. He was wound up so tight, Clodagh got the impression one wrong word and he'd explode.

'I saw Adam on the TV this morning,' Simon said. 'I bet he's enjoying all this, isn't he?'

'Of course he's not enjoying it,' Clodagh said. 'He's very upset by what's happened. We both are.'

'Didn't look that upset this morning, did he? It should have been me in that studio speaking about my brother. Not Adam bloody Murray. But I don't have a new book to promote, do I? So no one wants to hear what I've got to say.'

'It's not Clodagh's fault,' Bella said, putting a cafetiere of coffee on the table, along with three mugs and a plate of homemade biscuits. 'Milk and sugar, Clo?'

'No thanks.' Clodagh's head had started to throb. The house was too hot and too small. She had no idea how to respond to Simon's seething anger that seemed to swell and fill the little available space.

'I'm not saying it's your fault.' Simon looked at Clodagh. 'But even you've got to admit it's a pretty crass thing to do.'

'Simon.' Bella put her hand on her husband's arm. 'Don't speak to Clodagh like that. She was kind enough to come here today to see you. It's not fair to have a go at her for something Adam's done.'

'He used my brother's death to promote his fucking book.' Simon looked at Clodagh. 'How on earth can you be with a man who'd do something like that?'

Clodagh stood up; she couldn't stay here.

'I'm sorry about Nick,' she said. 'I really am. But I didn't come all the way over here today just so you could tell me what you think about Adam. If you've got a problem with what he's doing, then you need to have that conversation with him, not me.'

She was halfway down the corridor when Simon caught her, grabbing hold of her arm.

'Hang on,' he said. 'Don't go, Clodagh. Please. You're right. I shouldn't take it out on you. I'm just trying to understand what's happened.'

He was standing too close to her, his hand still on her arm, holding her too tight.

'Let me go.'

He dropped his hand and took a step back.

'I'm sorry,' he repeated. 'Come back to the kitchen. Please?'

Then, when she shook her head, 'Okay, not the kitchen. How about we go outside? Into the front garden. I won't come near you and I won't get angry again. I just want you to tell me what happened.'

Behind him, Bella had appeared in the kitchen doorway and was watching them.

'Five minutes,' Clodagh said, seeing the pleading look on Bella's face. 'After that I'm leaving.'

'Five minutes is all I need. Thank you.'

Opening the front door, Clodagh breathed in mouthfuls of fresh air, a relief after the heavy sweetness inside the house. She sat on the wall that separated the square of front garden from the street.

'They did the post-mortem earlier today,' Simon said, sitting beside her. 'Which means we'll know soon enough how he died.'

'He looked very peaceful,' Clodagh said. 'It didn't look as if he'd suffered.'

It wasn't true. The only thing she'd really noticed was the one thing that mattered: the absence of life. The sudden, shocking knowledge that the man she was looking at was, beyond any doubt, dead.

'Thanks,' Simon said. 'That means a lot.'

'I don't know if you wanted more,' Clodagh said, 'but there's really nothing else I can tell you. I'm sorry.'

'Is it true he sent you a text saying he wanted to speak to you about something?'

'Excuse me?'

'You heard me.'

'How did you…?' She paused, already knowing the answer. Their little network was tight. Everyone at the villa would have spent the last twenty-four hours poring over everything they knew about Nick's death, sharing information as they tried to make sense of what had happened.

'Yes, it's true. But I never found out why he wanted to speak to me. When I went looking for him, I couldn't find him. So I went to bed instead.'

'You must have some idea what it was about,' Simon said.

'Not a clue,' Clodagh said.

'You knew him before, didn't you?'

Clodagh tensed.

'I wouldn't say I knew him. Not really. I went to his restaurant a few times, that's all.'

'And yet you ended up staying in the same resort in Crete. A bit of a coincidence, wouldn't you say?'

Clodagh was trying to work out how to respond to that when she heard Bella calling Simon's name.

'You need to come inside,' Bella said, from the front door. She said something else, but Clodagh didn't catch it because her phone had started to ring, the noise blocking out Bella's voice. She saw Adam's name on the screen and took the call as Simon stood up and went to speak to Bella.

'Hi,' Clodagh said. 'Everything okay?'

'Not really,' Adam said. 'Tara's just called, screaming down the phone at me. The post-mortem results are back. Nick was murdered. No doubt, apparently. We're all suspects in a murder investigation.'

At the front door, Bella had wrapped her arms around Simon and was holding him as he cried. She caught Clodagh's eye and shook her head.

Then, before Clodagh could do anything else, Bella led her husband inside the house and slammed the door shut, leaving Clodagh outside.

Thirteen

It was six o'clock on Monday evening. Rachel was sitting in the office of Detective Superintendent Sharon Spalding, waiting for Sharon to finish reading the information Rachel had emailed to her earlier.

She had been sitting here for fifteen minutes. So far, apart from greeting her when she'd first walked in, Sharon hadn't spoken a word. Rachel crossed her legs, then uncrossed them again.

'A problem, Rachel?' Sharon asked, without looking up from her computer screen.

'No.'

'Then stop fidgeting like you've got ants in your bloody pants.'

After another excruciating ten minutes, Sharon closed down her laptop and smiled.

'Good work, Rachel. Very comprehensive summary. How's the team shaping up?'

'Fine,' Rachel said. 'We're pulling in resources from across the county. I'm meeting Chris Young from the media team tomorrow morning to discuss how we handle this externally. The press have gone into overdrive now that we've confirmed this is a murder investigation.'

It was going to be Rachel's first case as Senior Investigating Officer. She was excited and terrified in equal measures.

'You think Ade's up to something like this?' Sharon asked.

'Absolutely,' Rachel said. 'She's very competent.'

'It's going to be a shitstorm, you do realise that? You'll need to make sure all your team are aware of the importance of not speaking to anyone outside the police about this case.'

'Absolutely.' Rachel sat up straighter in her chair and maintained eye contact with her superior, even though it felt as if Sharon was using her eyes to try to scoop out Rachel's soul.

'Okay, Rachel. I've read the file. Now, I want you to give me a summary of where you are, what your next steps are and how quickly you think you can get this one done and dusted.'

Done and dusted? Rachel's mouth fell open, but she closed it again when she realised the stunned fish reaction wasn't what her boss was asking for.

'Nick and the other guests were at the villa to mark the five-year anniversary of the crash. There was a bigger event the previous weekend for the victims' families. The weekend at the villa was just about the eight survivors, although only five of them were there. Two others live in Crete and, understandably, chose not to fly over. We're still trying to track down the missing survivor, Robbie Fuson. Along with the five survivors, the other guests were Adam Murray, who heads up the Vivienne Kinsella Foundation, Simon and Bella Gilbert, and Adam's agent, Jake Harris with his girlfriend Felicity Sparks.'

'What sort of tosspot brings his agent along to something like that?' Sharon said. 'Never mind, continue.'

'Clodagh Kinsella discovered Nick's body at approximately 4:45 a.m. on Sunday. Pathologist has put time of death at around five or six hours earlier, between ten forty-five and midnight. Cause of death was blunt trauma injury to the back of the head. He was hit, repeatedly, possibly with one of the stones on the beach. He'd been drinking quite heavily. His blood alcohol level was just below 0.15 per cent. We know he rowed with at least two of the guests, Adam Murray and Tara Coleman. He also sent a text message to Clodagh Kinsella at 9:47 p.m., asking to speak to her. Although she claims that conversation never happened.'

'Forensics?'

'Nothing of note on the area around his body. Some strands of hair found on his jacket, which we've sent off for testing. We've taken DNA samples from everyone who was at the villa, so we may get a match. For now, everyone who was at the villa on Saturday night is a suspect. The villa had CCTV. One camera at the front of the building, another at the back facing the garden and the beach. I've got two officers going through all the CCTV footage from that today.

'Oh, and the foundation paid for everyone's accommodation except Simon and Bella. They came as Nick's guests. He paid for their room, the meal, everything.'

'You think that's relevant?' Sharon asked.

'At the moment,' Rachel said, 'everything's relevant.'

That got a smile from her boss.

'Quoting the great Ed Mitchell. Well, you could do a lot worse.'

Ed Mitchell had been Rachel's partner for most of her career as a detective. Until he'd taken a sabbatical while he tried to work out whether he wanted to take early retirement like so many other detectives had done.

'We'll be speaking to Simon Gilbert later today,' Rachel said. 'I want to get a better idea of his relationship with his brother. And I'd like to know why neither he nor his wife thought to tell us that she used to be married to Gary Wakefield.'

Rachel stopped speaking. She hadn't referred to her notes once and sincerely hoped Sharon had noticed and might even be impressed.

'What about the one who's missing?' Sharon said. 'Robbie Fuson. Tell me a bit more about him.'

'Until three months ago, he was a trustee for the foundation. He stepped down from that, apparently refusing to give any reason, and no one seems to have heard from him since. We've got an address for him in Chiswick, west London. Someone from the local force is going there this morning to see if they can track him down.'

'Let's hope they manage to find him before the press do,' Sharon said. 'Speaking of which, I hope we won't see any further debacles like this morning?'

'Definitely not.' Rachel knew Sharon was referring to Adam Murray's appearance on *Good Morning Britain*. A badly timed interview that did nothing to help the investigation, and everything to bring more unwanted press attention on Rachel and her team.

'I spoke to his agent this afternoon and made it clear there were to be no more interactions with the press unless we specifically approved them. He didn't like it, but I think he got the message.'

Didn't like it was an understatement. Rachel's instructions had, at first, been met with flat-out refusal. It was only when she'd threatened to charge Jake Harris and his client with perverting the course of justice, that he grudgingly agreed there would be no further TV or newspaper interviews.

'I've arranged a press conference for eleven thirty tomorrow morning. I can handle that myself, obviously.'

Obviously. Rachel bit her lip to stop herself smiling. Unlike most detectives she knew, Sharon was at her most animated when she was taking centre stage at any public event. She seemed to draw energy from being in front of a crowd and handled questions from the press with charm and wit, always giving away just the right amount of information.

'I've had my hair done,' Sharon said, beaming at Rachel. 'And I'm wearing my special pants that make your body look curvy instead of flabby. Not that I need them, of course, but they do say the camera adds half a stone. You ought to try them, Rachel. They'd do wonders for your backside in those trousers. I'll send you a link, if you'd like?'

'Um, that would be great. Thank you.'

Rachel pushed her chair back and stood up, relieved she'd made it through the encounter relatively unscathed. Even the comment about her bum hadn't bothered her. She knew that, in her own way, Sharon had been trying to be helpful not insulting.

'Rachel?' Sharon called as she opened the door.

'Yes?'

'I forgot to ask for timescales on when we can get this one cleared up. I'm meeting the Chief Constable later this morning. How about I tell her we'll have someone charged by close of play Friday?'

'I'm not sure...'

'No need to be so modest.' Sharon smiled. 'I have every faith in you. CPS will drag their heels. Their backlog is getting bigger as every week passes. No need for us to do the same. Let's set a good example and show the rest of the county how good we are.' The smile disappeared. 'If you think that's going to be a problem, I can always get someone else in to work alongside you on this?'

'No,' Rachel said quickly. 'That won't be necessary.'

'Excellent. I look forward to seeing how you get on.'

Rachel managed a smile that she kept plastered onto her face until she was out of the office with the door closed behind her. Only then did she let the smile turn into a frown as she flicked two fingers at the closed door, before hurrying away just in case Sharon's laser eyes could see through wood.

Fourteen

Adam lifted the bottle of wine and refilled his glass. When he tried to do the same for Clodagh, she covered her glass with her hand.

'Not for me, thanks.'

Her head had been aching ever since leaving Brighton earlier. She'd taken some painkillers but they hadn't made much impact on the dull throbbing behind her eyes, made worse by the constant noise in her brain.

'You've been very quiet this evening,' Adam said. 'Are you okay?'

It was such a ridiculous question. Clodagh didn't know what to say so she said nothing.

'I still can't get my head around it,' Adam said. 'I keep thinking the police are going to call to say they made a mistake and he wasn't killed, after all. Or that they've found the person who killed him and it was some random stranger who happened to be on the beach that night.'

Clodagh hadn't told him about her trip to Brighton, or Simon's odd question about why Nick had been at the same resort as her in Crete. But she hadn't been able to stop thinking about it, going back over the details of those seven days wondering what she'd missed. Because Simon was right. It was strange they'd all ended up at the same resort. And the more Clodagh thought about it, the more convinced she became it wasn't simply coincidence.

'I've been fielding calls from journalists all day,' Adam said. 'All asking questions about Nick. Not one of them wants to talk about my book.'

'It's all going to start again,' Clodagh said. 'I don't know if I can stand it, Adam.'

He frowned, and she assumed he was thinking about how they were going to deal with the inevitable intrusion over the coming days and weeks. But when he spoke, it seemed he was worrying about something else entirely.

'You told me earlier you were here all day.'

'That's right.'

'So why were there so many messages on the answerphone? I would have thought you'd answer the phone if you were here.'

'A journalist called Stephen Hughes kept calling,' Clodagh said. 'I couldn't face speaking to him so I stopped answering the phone.'

Adam seemed to weigh this up for a moment. But then he smiled and the tension across Clodagh's shoulders relaxed.

'I'd probably have done the same thing,' he said. 'I know Hughes. He's the worst sort of muck-raking hack. Let me speak to Jake, see if he can get Hughes to ease off a bit.'

'You think he'll be able to do that?'

'It's his job,' Adam said. 'Listen, Clodagh. You sure you're okay with me going to London again tomorrow? I know the timing's not ideal with everything else that's going on right now. It's just that I'm scared to reschedule in case they lose interest. I can't risk that.'

'Of course I'm okay with it,' she said. 'Why wouldn't I be?'

The truth was, she couldn't wait for him to go. Apart from the occasional reference to Nick's murder, Adam had spoken about little else except this meeting about his forthcoming TV series. Normally, Clodagh found his enthusiasm endearing. This evening, in the light of what had happened to Nick, it was offensive. More than once, she'd almost snapped and told him how selfish he sounded. But she didn't snap, because she knew he deserved whatever success he was enjoying these days. He'd worked so hard to get where he was.

She'd met Adam during her final year at university in Dublin. Through some mutual friends, they ended up in the same shared house and had struck up an easy friendship. Back then, Adam was a struggling crime fiction writer supplementing his meagre writer's income by teaching some creative writing modules at the university. Unable to find work in the UK, a friend had put him touch with someone at the university and he'd moved to Ireland. He was funny, unassuming and passionate about crime fiction. Clodagh had had the mother of all crushes on him and, for a time, had thought her feelings might be reciprocated. But then she'd introduced him to her sister and those illusions were well and truly shattered.

'They sound really keen to press ahead with the show.' Adam paused to take a sip of wine. He was drinking more than usual tonight, Clodagh noted, wondering if that was due to excitement about the new TV show or shock at finding out Nick had been murdered. 'It's going to be huge, Clodagh. A proper game-changer.'

The TV series was to be a new Saturday night chat show. Hosted by Adam, the series would feature in-depth interviews with all sorts of famous people about their lives. According to Adam, the programme's USP (which, he'd had to explain to Clodagh, stood for 'unique selling point') was that it would only feature a single guest each week.

'A bit like Piers Morgan's *Life Stories*,' Adam had explained, 'but without all the arse-licking. Not just the same tired old celebrities they roll out on every chat show, either. I'm going to make sure we include writers, politicians, thought leaders, a whole range of people you don't normally see on mainstream TV but who really should be there.'

Clodagh had never watched Piers Morgan's *Life Stories* and doubted she ever would. She wished she could share Adam's enthusiasm, but she'd never been able to understand the allure of fame. She'd seen with Vivienne how intrusive it was to live your life in the public eye. Clodagh couldn't imagine anything more dreadful than never knowing who was watching you or having people secretly taking photos of you when you least expected it.

But if it was what Adam wanted, she should try, at least, to be pleased for him.

'You know what?' she said. 'Maybe I will have another glass of wine.'

She reached for the bottle and poured a small amount into her glass.

'Here's to you.' She clinked her glass against his and took a sip. The wine – an expensive Merlot from Adam's extensive cellar – tasted sour, but she swallowed it anyway.

'That's the same wine we drank the night we got together,' Adam said. 'Do you remember?'

'How could I forget?'

She smiled at the memory. Adam had called to tell her he was in London, doing a book signing. They'd arranged to meet for dinner. He'd changed; that was the first thing she noticed when he greeted her in the restaurant. There was a lightness about his mood that reminded her of who he'd been when she first met him. Unlike the other times they'd met since the crash, their conversation didn't focus on their memories of Vivienne. Instead, they spoke about films they'd seen recently, countries they wanted to visit one day, their plans for the future. At the end of dinner, when Adam asked if she wanted to join him in his hotel for a nightcap, she hadn't hesitated.

'One year next week,' Adam said.

'Is it really?'

'You haven't got a romantic bone in your body,' he said. 'How could you forget the date we first got together?'

'I might have forgotten the date,' she said, 'but not anything else about that night.'

The best sex of her life. She was unlikely to forget it anytime soon. It was one of the reasons she'd agreed to move in with him three months later. Mistaking sex for love like she'd done too many times before. Telling herself this time would be different, because this was Adam.

She closed her eyes, exhausted. Adam wasn't the problem; she was. If she wasn't careful, she would spend the rest of her life repeating the same, tired old pattern – running away from every relationship as soon as it got complicated.

'Hey.' Adam squeezed her hand. 'Penny for whatever dark thoughts are making you look like that.'

Tell him, the voice inside her head insisted. *Tell him you're having doubts. It's normal. What's not normal is not talking about them*.

'Adam, we need to talk.'

But the landline started to ring at the same time as she spoke, and he jumped up to answer it.

'I'm expecting a call from Keith Mason,' he said. 'He called earlier, but I couldn't speak to him. I told him to call the landline if he couldn't get through on my mobile. You know what the signal's like here.'

Keith Mason was one of the many people affected by the plane crash that Adam kept in regular contact with. A surgeon from Maidstone in Kent, Keith had lost his wife and his three teenage daughters in the plane crash. They'd been returning from a fortnight's holiday in Crete.

'A girls-only holiday,' he'd told Clodagh the first time she met him. 'I drove them to the airport to catch their flight out. It was the last time I ever saw them. My whole life taken from me, just like that.'

Knowing it would be a long phone call, Clodagh leaned back in her chair after Adam left and tried to relax some of the tension in her body. She lifted her glass to take a sip of wine. But the smell of alcohol was repugnant, making her retch. Disgusted, she put the glass back down. And then it hit her; with such sudden and shocking certainty, she felt the room starting to spin as it sunk in. Twelve weeks since her last period. Vaguely, she'd been aware she was late, but hadn't worried too much. Her periods had never been regular. But not like this. Twelve weeks was a record. She was pregnant. The knowledge was pure instinct. Apart from her late period and a sudden distaste for alcohol, she had no evidence. But she knew, as certainly as she knew her own name. She was pregnant with Adam's child.

'Clodagh.'

At some point he had come back into the room and was standing in front of her, frowning. For a moment, she thought he'd worked it out. Until she realised that was impossible.

'What's wrong?'

She thought of the tiny cells inside her. Not a baby yet, but on their way to becoming one. The miracle of life. Or a monumental cock-up. All depending on what way you chose to look at it. Right now, both perspectives felt about right.

'That wasn't Keith,' Adam said. 'It was Rachel Lewis. She wants to see us both again. Says she has more questions for us.'

'What sort of questions?'

'I don't know. I've told her I'm going to London tomorrow, so I've arranged to meet her the following day. But she asked if you'll go and see her tomorrow morning. Is that okay?'

No, Clodagh wanted to scream, it was not okay. But she didn't say that, because she knew she didn't have a choice. She was a suspect in a murder enquiry, which meant doing whatever the police told her to do. Even if it wasn't what she wanted.

Fifteen

Simon Gilbert and his wife lived in a terraced house on a narrow street behind Southwick train station.

'Not quite what I expected,' Rachel said as Ade pulled up outside the house. 'You sure this is the right place?'

'Positive.' Ade switched the engine off and looked through the window at the house. 'You think he was jealous of his brother's wealth?'

'I'm hoping we'll find out.' Rachel opened the door and stepped out of the car. The sun had gone down, and a round white moon hung low at the end of the street. It was still warm, the air sticky with residual heat as she walked up to the house and rang the bell. A few seconds later, the door opened and Simon Gilbert peered out at her.

'Oh, it's you.' He frowned. 'Has something happened?'

'We've got a few more questions if that's okay,' Rachel said. 'Any chance we could come inside?'

'You want to ask me questions at this time of night? Couldn't you have waited until tomorrow?'

'Not really,' Rachel said. 'We're conducting a murder investigation, Mr Gilbert. Which means working non-stop to find your brother's killer. If that's inconvenient, then I'm afraid there's not much I can do about that.'

'You're not going to find the killer by talking to me, are you?' Simon leaned forward and Rachel caught the stink of body odour and stale booze. He was a handsome man but, right now, he was a mess. His hair was standing on end, like he hadn't brushed or washed it and there were several stains on his too-tight T-shirt that strained across his toned six-pack.

'You'd be surprised what information people know that can help us solve a case,' she said. 'Our best chance of finding out who killed your brother is to keep asking questions. We're speaking to everyone who was at the villa on Saturday night, not just you. The more questions we ask, the better chance we've got of finding the answers we need.'

She waited for him to argue back at her. But after a moment, he shrugged and stepped back into the house.

'You'd best come in, then.'

They followed him along a narrow hallway to the kitchen at the back of the house.

'Is Bella here?' Ade asked, as the three of them sat around the kitchen table.

'She's at work,' Simon said. 'It's a busy week for her. I've hardly seen her.'

'I thought she worked as a computer technician,' Ade said. 'Do they work nights?'

'Sometimes,' Simon said. 'Depends what they're working on. They're rolling out a new IT system and they can only do that at nights when the staff aren't working.'

'We didn't realise when we spoke to you both yesterday that Bella used to be married to Gary Wakefield,' Rachel said.

'So what?' Simon scowled. 'They'd already got divorced when the crash happened. Unfortunately for Bella. If she'd still been married to him, she'd have been entitled to some money. Instead, she didn't get a penny.

You ask me, it's a bloody disgrace. She suffered just as much as any of the rest of them.'

Rachel thought of a woman she'd spoken to in the weeks following the crash whose twin teenage daughters had been killed. It seemed remarkably insensitive to suggest Bella's loss was as bad as that.

'She isn't even entitled to help from the foundation,' Simon said. 'All the rest of them, they get free counselling and holidays and a legal team that's still fighting to get them more compensation. Not my Bella, though.'

'As a registered charity,' Ade said, 'they probably have to make sure everything meets the requirements of the Charity Commission. My sister tried to set up a charity a couple of years ago. She had to go through so much red tape she gave up in the end.'

'Whatever.' Simon shrugged. There was a can of beer on the table. While he lifted it and took a drink, Rachel looked around the kitchen. The units were outdated and scuffed but someone had made an effort to make the place look homely. The surfaces were spotlessly clean and there was a vase of fresh flowers on the windowsill over the sink.

'How are you doing?' Ade said, when Simon put the can back down.

'How do you think? He was my only brother. I'm trying to support my parents, who are understandably devastated. They already came close to losing him once. To have to go through this now is unbearable.'

'Simon.' Rachel put her elbows on the table. 'Do you have any idea why Nick was killed?'

'Of course not.' He slumped down in his chair, as if the effort of sitting upright was too much. 'Nick could be a right wanker sometimes, but you don't kill someone just because they're a wanker. He was well out of order on

Saturday night, stirring up any sort of shit he could with anyone who was stupid enough to give him the time of day. I knew what he could be like, so once I realised how drunk he was, I steered well clear. Some of the others weren't so lucky.'

'Anyone in particular?'

'Adam, I guess. But I'm sure he wasn't the only one.'

'It can't have been easy for you,' Ade said, 'knowing he could get like that.'

'I learned to get used to it,' Simon said. 'It was a lot worse when we were younger. By the time of the crash, we'd more or less stopped speaking to each other.'

'So what changed?' Ade asked gently.

'He nearly died.' Simon ran a hand through his hair. 'That makes you reassess a lot of stuff. The first year, after the accident, we spent a lot of time together. We agreed to put the past behind us and try to rebuild our relationship.'

'Seems as if you did a good job of that,' Ade said.

'I guess,' Simon said. 'Wasn't always easy.'

'Why not?' Rachel asked.

'His money sometimes put distance between us,' Simon said. 'Our lives are very different, as you can imagine. But we did our best to put our differences to one side and find a way of getting on with each other.' Simon started to smile, but his face crumpled midway through. 'He was complicated. Half the time I hated him, the rest of the time I loved him. And now he's gone and I'm absolutely gutted.'

'How do you think things were between Nick and Tara?' Rachel said, after a suitable pause to allow him to compose himself.

Simon shook his head, looking miserable.

'Tara's a nice enough girl, but she's messed up. Some of the others, they've made a better job of picking themselves up after what happened. Tara hasn't been able to do that. She's hard work. Very needy. And I know this is a God-awful thing to say, but I'm convinced Nick's money is the main reason she was with him.'

'I've been to Tara's apartment,' Rachel said. 'She doesn't strike me as someone who needs anyone else's money.'

'She put every last penny she had towards buying the place,' Simon said. 'Her parents give her handouts from time to time, but she spends it all the moment she gets it.'

'Doesn't she work?' Rachel was sure she'd read something online about Tara being employed at a fashion house in Mayfair.

'She hasn't really had a job since the crash,' Simon said. 'She gets a bit of work from time to time but the jobs never last. Bella says she's lazy, which feels a bit harsh given what the poor girl's been through. On the other hand, Bella's way more switched on about people than I am.'

'Did things seem okay between them on Saturday?' Ade asked.

'I didn't notice,' Simon said. 'Bella said she thought Tara was a bit off with Nick but the truth is, I wasn't paying that much attention to them. I was too busy making the most of staying in a fancy place.' He held his hands up. 'I know that sounds insensitive. We were there for a sad reason, but Bella and I never get the chance to stay somewhere like that. It's the only reason we agreed to go.'

'What do you mean?' Rachel asked.

'Well, spending the weekend with Adam Murray was always going to be awkward for Bella. When Nick first invited us, I said no. I thought there was no way she'd be up for something like that. But when I mentioned it to her, she said we should go.'

'She didn't want to be with Adam because of the lack of support she's got from the foundation?' Rachel guessed.

'Exactly.' Then, after a brief pause, Simon asked suddenly, 'Have you spoken with Clodagh yet?' Simon asked suddenly.

'Why do you ask?' Rachel said.

'There's something I keep thinking about. It might not mean anything. I spoke to Bella about it and she said it wasn't important.' He smiled. 'She's usually right about stuff, see. I'm the one who gets things wrong all the time.'

'Why don't you let us decide what's important?' Rachel said.

'I probably wouldn't ever have thought about it,' Simon said, 'if it wasn't for the text message. You know he sent her a text on Saturday night, right?' Then, when Rachel nodded, 'Well she's telling everyone she doesn't know what Nick wanted to speak to her about. But I think she's lying. Because she knew him, you see. Her and Nick knew each other before the crash.'

'Knew each other how?' Ade asked.

'She used to go to his restaurant a lot,' Simon said. 'Her and her sister. It was where they always went whenever Vivienne visited Clodagh in London. And I know you're probably thinking so what? But isn't it a bit of a coincidence that all three of them ended up staying in the same resort in Crete as well as being on the same flight back home?'

Rachel glanced at Ade, saw her frown and knew Ade was thinking the same thing she was. Simon was right. It was indeed 'a bit of a coincidence'. Rachel had called Adam and Clodagh's house earlier and arranged times to question both of them over the coming days. Top of her list of questions for Clodagh would be asking her about the exact nature of her relationship with Nick Gilbert.

Sixteen

Day Three

'Are you sure you don't want a hot drink as well?' Rachel asked, putting a plastic cup of water on the table in front of Clodagh.

'This is fine,' Clodagh said, 'thank you.'

When she lifted the cup, Rachel noted the tremor in her hand. The only sign so far that Clodagh wasn't entirely comfortable being interviewed.

She'd already been here for two hours. First, giving a formal statement, going back over how she'd found Nick's body. After that, Rachel had explained they would be asking Clodagh some more questions about Nick's murder. As this interview would be done under caution, Rachel had arranged for the duty solicitor to be present. The solicitor and Clodagh had already had an initial meeting and were now ready for the interview to take place.

'As I've already explained,' Rachel said, 'we'll be interviewing you under caution, and recording the interview as we go along. Any questions before we begin?'

Clodagh shook her head. 'Let's get it over and done with.'

Rachel hit the record button and started speaking.

'Interview commencing at 11:15 hours. Present in the room are Detective Inspector Rachel Lewis and Detective Constable Ade Benjamin, along with Ms Clodagh Kinsella and her legal representative, John Goodall.

'Clodagh, we've brought you in this morning to ask you a few more questions about the murder of Nick Gilbert. When we spoke to you on Sunday, you told us that you weren't particularly close with the victim.'

'I wasn't,' Clodagh said. 'It's why his text message didn't make any sense. I didn't even know Nick had my number. Actually, that's not true. There's a WhatsApp group so we all have each other's phone numbers, but he'd never contacted me before.'

'You didn't tell us that you knew Nick before the plane crash,' Rachel said.

Clodagh took another sip from her glass before replying.

'I didn't know him well,' she said. 'I ate at his restaurant a few times, that's all.'

'Yet you ended up staying in the same resort in Crete?' Ade asked.

'How is this relevant?' Clodagh's solicitor asked.

'We think Clodagh might not have been entirely honest with us about how well she knew the victim,' Rachel said.

'That's not true,' Clodagh said. 'I've told you the truth. I knew Nick a little bit because I'd been to his restaurant. But it was a complete shock to me when he turned up at the same resort.'

'So you hadn't planned it like that?' Rachel asked.

'Of course not.'

'It doesn't make sense.' Ade frowned, like she was struggling to understand what Clodagh was telling her.

'You knew Nick before the crash. You both stayed in the same resort in Crete. And then you remained in touch with Nick after the crash. In fact, you both share an experience that no one – apart from the eight of you who survived that crash – can even begin to understand. Yet you're still saying you barely knew each other and you've no idea why he wanted to speak to you on Saturday night?'

'It's the truth.' Clodagh's eyes slid to the side. 'I've no clue why he sent that text message.'

Rachel sensed Clodagh was holding something back and didn't want to end this interview without finding out what that was. She pretended to consult the slim folder of papers on the table in front of her, shuffling through them for a few seconds, hoping the pause would make Clodagh uncomfortable.

'You stayed in the San Antonio Beach Resort,' she said, looking back up at Clodagh.

'What about it?'

'I looked it up on the internet last night,' Rachel said. 'Gorgeous place. Boutique accommodation, adults only. And small. Thirty suites in total? I imagine you'd get to know most of the other guests who were staying there at the same time, wouldn't you? Especially if you were already acquaintances.'

'It wasn't like that,' Clodagh said. 'Everyone had their own suite, with a private terrace and direct access to the beach. There was an option to eat all your meals in your room if you wanted to. You could easily spend the week there and not see anyone at all.'

'Where did you eat your meals?' Rachel said.

'There was a little restaurant near the resort,' Clodagh said. 'I went there most evenings. You can ask me all you want about how well I knew the other guests, but I'm telling you, I didn't want to mix with any of them. I spent most of the week alone, if you must know.'

'Not with your sister?'

'She liked being by the pool, I preferred being on the beach. We ate together some evenings, but not all of them. She didn't like the restaurant I went to; and I didn't like the one in the hotel.'

'Why not?'

'It was too pretentious for me,' Clodagh said. 'I preferred the other one. It was more traditional. And a hell of a lot quieter.'

'When we first met,' Rachel said, 'you told me you still experience some cognitive processing issues. The way you explained it to me, you said that means you sometimes forget things. Isn't it possible you did actually go outside and speak with Nick on Saturday night and you've simply forgotten that conversation ever took place?'

'No.' Clodagh shook her head. 'I would have remembered something like that.'

By now, Clodagh was looking utterly miserable and Rachel felt a pang of sympathy for this young woman who'd already endured so much loss.

'I'm sorry we have to put you through all this,' Ade said softly, playing good cop to Rachel's bad cop. 'I know this must be very hard for you.'

'It's like the crash all over again,' Clodagh said.

'What do you mean?' Rachel asked.

'I keep thinking if I'd found him on Saturday night, he'd still be alive,' Clodagh said. 'I feel as if it's my fault he was killed.'

'How is that like the crash?' Rachel said.

'Oh God.' Clodagh slumped further down in her chair. 'If you knew what it's like, to keep thinking over and over what you could have done differently. I've got this constant voice inside my head telling me I messed up. But because I can't remember, I don't know how I messed up. There's this huge gap in my memory and I can't shake off the feeling that if I could just remember it would help me understand why my sister and so many other people died that day.'

'But you already know why,' Rachel said. 'The investigation into the crash was very comprehensive, wasn't it?'

'It doesn't stop me obsessing about what could have been done to prevent the crash,' Clodagh said. 'I'm not the only one who feels like this, you know. Survivors' guilt. We all have it. It was unbearable, at first. It still is, a lot of the time.'

She sounded sincere. Except Rachel couldn't help thinking that whatever guilt Clodagh was living with, it hadn't stopped her having a relationship with Vivienne's husband or moving into the house Vivienne had lived in before her death. A cynical person might think that Clodagh Kinsella had, effectively, stolen her dead sister's life.

'You've all done remarkably well,' Ade said, 'considering what you've been through.'

Outside interviews, Ade Benjamin was loud and opinionated. But in situations like this, she was gentle and softly spoken. Rachel had seen her employing this technique several times now. She never failed to be impressed. Ade's softly-softly approach meant the people she was interviewing didn't expect the question that always followed.

'Some of us have done better than others,' Clodagh said. 'You learn to take things day by day. It's the only way to keep going.'

Beside Clodagh, John Goodall cleared his throat.

'My client has been here for almost two hours now. I think it's time we finished up, don't you?'

'Just one more question,' Ade said. 'If that's all right with you, Clodagh?'

'Sure.'

Ade smiled.

'Thank you. You've been so helpful, we really appreciate it. I wanted to quickly ask about Robbie Fuson.'

Clodagh had looked tense, as if she'd expected a different question. But at the mention of Robbie's name, she visibly relaxed. Which meant two things, Rachel realised. One: Clodagh didn't know anything about why Robbie Fuson had disappeared. Two: there was something else she did know that she didn't want the police to find out about.

–

Clodagh felt like punching the air. They wanted to know about Robbie, not anything else. Her jaw ached from the tension of grinding her teeth together while the two detectives had asked their questions. She could feel her anxiety rising as each moment passed. Her mind repeatedly going back to that moment, five years ago at the hotel, when she'd walked into the lobby and seen Nick, Gary and their friends. The shock and the outrage as she'd slowly realised their being at the hotel was more than just a coincidence.

'I don't think I can tell you anything you don't already know,' she said, answering the detective's question. 'Robbie helped set up the foundation with Adam. He was the treasurer, responsible for the finances. As the foundation got bigger, Robbie's role got bigger. Then three months ago, completely out of the blue, he stepped down from his role and dropped all contact with the rest of us. Adam's tried to contact him, but he hasn't returned any of his calls or emails. The only family he has is a mother who lives in Spain. She doesn't know where Robbie is, either. Although when Adam spoke to her, she didn't seem too worried about the fact that her only child has disappeared. We've reported him missing to the police there, but they don't seem to be taking it very seriously.'

'Was there some sort of disagreement between himself and Adam?' Ade asked.

'I don't think so. Adam would have talked to me about it.'

But as Clodagh said this, she remembered the whispered conversations between Adam and Jake in the weeks following Robbie's abrupt departure. She'd asked Adam about it at the time, and he'd brushed off her questions, telling her the talks with Jake were about work. Nothing to do with Robbie.

'Why are you asking about Robbie?' she said. 'You can't think he had something to do with what happened to Nick?'

'One survivor missing, another killed,' Rachel said. 'You don't think there's anything strange about that?'

Yes, Clodagh thought. There was definitely something strange about it.

'Have you tried Robbie's mother?' she asked. 'If anyone knows where he is, it'll be her. She wasn't very forthcoming with Adam, but she might be more willing to talk to the police.'

'We spoke to her yesterday,' Rachel said. 'She claims she hasn't heard from her son in months. Not since he left the foundation.'

Did they think Robbie was dead as well, Clodagh wondered. Or, worse, that Clodagh might have killed him?

'I don't know what else to say.' Clodagh looked to the duty solicitor for guidance.

'You don't have to say anything else.' The solicitor looked at Rachel and Ade. 'I think we're done, aren't we?'

'Unless there's anything else Clodagh wants to tell us?' Rachel said.

'No.' Clodagh shook her head. She could feel the anxiety creeping up the longer she was in here. The effort it took to monitor everything she said, make sure she didn't tell them everything, was exhausting. She knew if she had to stay in here much longer it would only be a matter of time before she let something slip.

Five years had passed without anyone finding out. It was unbearable to think that now, after all this time, it wouldn't be a secret any longer. She thought of the friendships she'd made during this time and the people she'd grown close to. This little group of people whose lives had been devastated by the plane crash, they were her community now. Her friends and her support network. If they knew the truth, if they knew the sort of person she really was, then all of that would be lost to her. Because not one of them would want anything to do with her ever again.

Seventeen

Rachel stood at the front of the Major Incident Room, looking at the timeline on the interactive whiteboard.

'Penny for them,' Ade said, walking over and joining her.

'He was killed some time between ten forty-five and midnight,' Rachel said. 'Most of the other guests were still up at that time. Although Clodagh and Tara both claim they'd gone to bed by then. Ivan Babić remembers saying good night to Clodagh, but she could easily have slipped outside to the beach when she left him instead of going to her room.'

'So any one of them could have killed Nick,' Ade said. 'We already know that, Rach. What's your point?'

'We're missing something. The problem is, I can't see it. Those people,' Rachel pointed at the names of the five survivors who'd been staying at the villa, 'they all went through something extraordinary together. That must have created a special bond between them, no matter how different they are from each other.'

'And?'

'I keep thinking, if you experienced something like that, would it be possible for you to then kill one of the few people in the world who understood what that was like? Clodagh spoke about survivors' guilt. She said they all had it. They must have been a great support to each other, don't you think?'

'You're saying that whoever killed Nick, it wasn't one of the survivors,' Ade said. 'Which leaves Bella, Simon, Adam and Jake.'

'And Jake's girlfriend.'

'Felicity Sparks? Nah. She hasn't got the brains to pull off something like that and get away with it. Anyway, Rach, I thought you'd like to know we've finished going through Nick's bank records.'

'Oh yeah?' Rachel turned away from the timeline. She could tell from Ade's voice they'd found something interesting.

'First of all, he had debts. A lot of debts. Bank loans, credit cards and a second mortgage on his London home.'

'Shit.' Rachel's brain went into overdrive as she tried to work out the implications of this new information. If Nick's bank records showed he had serious money problems, it was possible he had other debts too that they didn't yet know about.

'There's something else,' Ade said. 'There are also several payments over the last three years to his brother's bank account.'

'Why was he giving money to his brother if he didn't have any himself?'

'Until a year and a half ago, Nick's finances were in a healthy state,' Ade said. 'Whatever money problems he's had have only started since then.'

'Maybe Bella can tell us why Nick gave so much money to Simon,' Ade said. 'We're going to see her today, right?'

'No time like the present,' Rachel said. 'I've already rung her work to check she's there. Let's go.'

Bella worked for a pharmaceutical company located in a business park just north of Brighton. Rachel told Ade to drive so that she could call Tara along the way.

'Did Nick ever mention problems with money?' she asked, when Tara answered.

'I don't think so,' Tara said. 'He could be a bit tight sometimes, I guess. That's why he cancelled our trip to Chewton Glen. He said the hotel was too expensive, which was a load of rubbish because it's actually quite reasonable for such an amazing place. But Nick didn't see it like that. He said why waste money when we could stay somewhere just as lovely for half the price?'

Rachel had looked up Chewton Glen on the internet the other evening, half thinking she would surprise Grace with a weekend away when this case was over. One look at the eye-watering costs and she'd changed her mind.

'But you never thought he'd cancelled because he had money worries?'

'No. Because he didn't. He was, like, really famous. A proper celebrity, you know? He had loads of money. I'm telling you Rachel, he was just a bit mean. He was like that with Simon too. He had a real thing about Simon always wanting money from him. I tried to get him to understand how hard it must be for Simon and Bella. I mean, they're not exactly rolling in it. But Nick didn't see it like that.'

'Was it your impression too that Simon was always asking his brother for money?' Rachel asked.

'Maybe,' Tara said. 'I'm pretty sure Simon owed him some money that he hadn't paid back. I overheard Nick speaking to Simon on the phone about it.'

'When was this?'

'Maybe a month ago?' Tara said. 'The thing is, Simon was jealous of Nick. You can't blame him, I suppose. Nick was so successful at everything he did, whereas poor Simon's never really achieved anything. Hang on, are you saying you think Simon had something to do with what happened to Nick?'

'I'm certainly not saying that, Tara.'

'But it makes sense, doesn't it? Nick was everything Simon wanted to be. I'm right, aren't I? They had one of their stupid arguments about money and Simon flipped. He's got a temper, you know. It wouldn't take much for him to lose it.'

Rachel ended the conversation soon after that, thanking Tara for her time and promising she'd be in touch soon.

'I heard most of that conversation,' Ade said. 'Sounds as if she was in serious denial about her boyfriend's finances.'

'Maybe Bella can shed more light on things.' Rachel nodded at the sign for the business park. 'Looks like we're here.'

Unlike the other properties on the business park, Max-Roysten Pharmaceuticals had its own gated entrance.

'Fancy-looking premises,' Ade said, driving through the open gates and parking the car near the building's entrance.

'Max-Roysten is a fancy organisation,' Rachel said. 'They're one of the UK's leading researchers into cures and treatments for insomnia. I read about them on my phone on the drive over.'

'If Bella works in a place like this, wouldn't she be bringing in a big salary?' Ade said.

'Depends what job she does,' Rachel said. 'She told us she was a computer technician. That's a frontline support job. I don't think they make much money, even working for big pharma companies like this one.'

Rachel opened the door and motioned for Ade to go first. They were greeted inside by a gated barrier and a security guard who insisted on checking their IDs before allowing them to pass through the barrier to the entrance lobby. A woman with cropped silver hair, wearing an immaculate silk blouse, was sitting behind a curved, dark wood reception desk. She beamed at Ade and Rachel as they walked towards her.

'Good morning, ladies. How can I help you?'

'We're looking for Bella Gilbert.' Rachel took out her ID and laid it on the desk. 'She works in your IT department?'

'Is this about her brother-in-law?' The woman's eyes widened. 'I've been following the story on the news. Me and my hubby used to love his TV show. Such a shame there's not going to be any more programmes.'

'Would you mind calling Mrs Gilbert and telling her we'd like a word?' Rachel said.

'Of course.' The woman blushed. 'Take a seat. I'll call her right away.'

She lifted the phone, but Rachel didn't move.

'It's Theresa from reception,' the woman said, glancing up at Rachel. 'Two policewomen are here to see you.'

Bella said something Rachel couldn't hear.

'Detective Inspector Lewis,' Theresa said, reading the information on Rachel's card. Then, a few seconds later, 'Okay, thanks Bella. I'll let them know.'

She put the phone down and smiled at Rachel.

'She'll be here in a few minutes.'

While they waited, Rachel walked across to the TV screen on the wall above the seating area. A series of promotional videos were playing, all highlighting the different areas of Max-Roysten's work. Image after image of smiling men and women, with lab coats and improbably white teeth, extolling the virtues of the important work they were doing. After a few seconds, Rachel started to feel nauseated so she looked away.

'If Nick was cross because Simon owed him money,' she said to Ade, 'why did he insist on having Simon and Bella with him last weekend?'

'Good question,' Ade said. 'Here's Bella now. Maybe she can tell us.'

'Hello,' Bella said, giving a tentative smile as she approached the two detectives. 'Is everything okay?'

'We wanted to ask you a few questions,' Rachel said. 'Is there somewhere we can speak in private?'

'We could go outside,' Bella said. 'There's a grassed area around the side with some seating and lovely views. Would that do?'

'Sounds great,' Rachel said. 'Lead the way.'

It was another warm day, and Rachel was glad Bella had suggested coming outside. They sat at a wooden table situated on a hill with views across rolling green fields to the English Channel. With the sun reflecting on its surface, the sea sparkled and shimmered as if someone had scattered thousands of diamonds across it.

'It's lovely here,' Ade said, smiling at Bella as if they were two friends enjoying a spot of sunshine.

'Isn't it?' Bella returned Ade's smile, visibly relaxing. 'I come out here to have my lunch every day. Even in winter. Unless it's raining, obviously.'

'Obviously,' Ade said.

'I've been expecting you to get in touch,' Bella said, looking at Rachel. 'Simon said you'd been asking about me when you spoke to him the other night. How can I help?'

'When we spoke to you on Sunday,' Rachel said, 'you never mentioned you were Gary Wakefield's widow.'

'We were divorced when the plane crashed,' Bella said. 'So I'm not officially his widow.'

'I'm sure that didn't make what happened any easier to bear,' Ade said.

'Of course not,' Bella said. 'I was devastated when I heard about the crash. But I don't understand how Gary has got anything to do with what happened to Nick. Am I missing something?'

'It must have been difficult,' Ade said, 'watching everyone else get their share of the compensation money, knowing you weren't entitled to any of it.'

'There was nothing I could do about it,' Bella said. 'I had to find a way to accept it, or it would have ruined my life. I wasn't willing to let that happen.'

'Simon told us Adam Murray also stopped you getting any support from the foundation as well,' Rachel said.

'Sort of,' Bella said. 'But the thing is, it's not really Adam's decision. There's a board of trustees and all of them voted to stop me getting anything. It was frustrating at first, but I can see why Adam and the trustees made the decision they did. The foundation was set up to support the survivors and the victims' families. That doesn't include me because Gary and I were divorced. If they bent the rules for me, they'd have to do that for other people too. It drives Simon mad, but only because he wants what's best for me.'

'Would you say Simon and his brother were close?' Rachel asked.

Bella paused, as if she was considering the question carefully.

'Yes, I would. They hadn't always seen eye to eye, as I'm sure Simon's already told you. But over the last few years, they'd both made a real effort. And it paid off, I think. That's the only reason we were there last weekend, because it was what Nick wanted.'

'That's not what we've heard,' Rachel said.

'What's that supposed to mean?' Bella said.

'We've been told that Nick and Simon hadn't been getting on too well recently,' Rachel said.

'Who told you that?' Bella's face flushed. 'Tara, I bet. She was always trying to stir up trouble between those two. She couldn't stand Nick paying attention to anyone except her. He found her suffocating, you know. I'm sure that's the only reason he wanted us at the villa. To avoid having to spend all his time with her.'

'So, you're not aware of any issues between the two brothers then?'

'There weren't any issues.'

'Do you know if Nick ever lent any money to his brother?'

'Did Tara tell you that too?' Bella sounded properly angry now. 'Why would she say something like that? Simon and I tell each other everything. If he'd borrowed money from Nick, I'd be the first to know about it.'

She said this with such confidence, Rachel was pretty sure she was telling the truth. But if she was, then someone else was lying. Either Simon Gilbert had hidden the loan from his wife, or Tara had deliberately lied when she'd told Rachel that there was tension between the two brothers.

Eighteen

Day Four

Clodagh had barely slept on Tuesday night. Her mind wouldn't switch off. She kept going back over the interview in the police station, wondering if she could have handled things better. She had lied to the police. What the hell had she been thinking? She hadn't been thinking, that was the problem. She had been utterly unprepared going into that interview. The person she'd been before the crash wouldn't have let herself get tripped up like that.

It hadn't helped that Adam had come back from London in an ebullient mood yesterday evening. His new TV programme had been given the green light. Filming was due to start over the coming weeks. He'd droned on about it for hours, Clodagh doing her best to pretend to share his excitement until it was late enough for her to feign tiredness and slip away to bed. She'd lain awake most of the night, drifting into an uneasy sleep as the first fingers of daylight started trickling through the curtains. She dreamed of being in a plane that was falling to the ground, people screaming all around her and Vivienne's face, white with fear, as she tried to tell Clodagh something. But Clodagh couldn't hear her, and when she tried to reach out for Vivienne, her sister's face disappeared.

She woke up, confused and disorientated, forgetting for a moment where she was. Gradually, the familiar shapes and shadows of the room came into focus, birdsong in the garden replacing the nightmare sounds from the dream. She lay in bed, waiting for the last of the dream to fade before throwing the quilt back and getting up.

Standing under the pounding water, she put her hands across her stomach, imagining the baby growing there. Trying to work out how she felt about it. She'd never given much thought to having children, apart from assuming – in a vague way – that it would probably happen one day. When she was ready for it.

As she dried herself after the shower, she wondered if now might not be the right time. The decision to leave her old life behind and move in with Adam had seemed so easy at first. But recently, she'd started to feel something was missing. She was bored. She'd tried to rationalise it. Told herself it was natural to be bored when she didn't have a job and mostly spent her days waiting for Adam to finish work so they could spend some time together. But deep down, she knew it wasn't that simple. She was starting to suspect there was something fundamentally wrong with their relationship.

For so many years, she'd believed she was in love with Adam. When he'd first got together with Vivienne, it had been painful but Clodagh had found a way to accept that her feelings weren't reciprocated. In the months and years that followed the crash, her friendship with Adam had taken on special significance. He was the only part of her old life that she had left; she didn't want to lose that. Then, when they finally got together, she'd never stopped to ask herself if this was still what she wanted.

The longer she spent with him, the more she realised there were aspects of his personality she didn't like. He was still the kind, funny and clever person he'd been when she first got to know him. But he was also self-centred, and giddily excited about his new celebrity status. His obsession with book sales, reviews, and appearing on TV and radio was wearing her down. It had crossed Clodagh's mind, more than once, to wonder if Vivienne's fame was the real reason Adam had been so drawn to her.

He was awake when she came out of the en suite. Sitting up in bed, scrolling through his phone, updating his social media accounts and no doubt looking for favourable mentions of his latest project.

'See this?' He held the phone out while she got dressed. 'Johnny Marsden in the bloody *Telegraph* this morning, describing my new TV show as *a pointless platform for a pointless celebrity.* Arsehole. Just because his own Arts programme flunked so badly last year. He's jealous, plain and simple.'

'I thought you never let negative comments get to you?' Clodagh said, recalling what he'd said in a radio interview last week.

'You're right.' He put the phone down. 'Sorry. I shouldn't get upset. But I work so hard at this, Clodagh. I wouldn't mind a bit of recognition every now and then. People like Marsden, they think I get all this stuff handed to me on a plate, which simply isn't fair.'

He was right about the amount of work he did. Clodagh hadn't realised, until they moved in together, just how hard he worked at being a celebrity. The sheer amount of effort it took was a complete eye-opener. She finished getting dressed, desperate to get into the kitchen to make a pot of coffee. Until she remembered you weren't meant to drink caffeine when you were pregnant. Which left her wondering how on earth she was going to drag her exhausted mind and body through the day without it.

'Are you okay?' Adam asked.

'Fine. A bit tired, that's all. I didn't sleep very well last night so I'm feeling grumpy this morning.'

He threw the quilt back and got out of bed, coming over and wrapping his arms around her.

'It's more than that,' he said, his breath tickling the top of her head. 'You've been distant for a while now, Clodagh. Do we need to have a chat?'

'I'm not sure.' She pulled back slightly so she could look up at his face. 'Can you give me a few days to get my head straight? This thing with Nick has left me feeling like I barely know who I am.'

'A few days is fine.' Adam reached up and stroked her cheek, so softly her heart twisted and it was all she could do not to cry. 'You make me so happy. I hope you know that. I'll do whatever I can to make this work. If that means giving you a bit more space while you work out what you want, then I can do that. Okay?'

She had a sudden urge to tell him she was pregnant. Even though she hadn't done a test yet, and she needed to work out what she wanted first. Instead, she swallowed down the words and told him to jump in the shower while she went downstairs to make breakfast.

Nineteen

Tara sat on the balcony of her sixth floor, riverfront apartment, drinking wine and watching the tourists milling along the riverbank. Men and women and children, carrying on with their lives, unaware how precious every single moment was. None of them knowing that it could all end at any moment.

She loved this apartment. Situated on London's South Bank, it had views of the river or Tate Modern from every room. Nick had helped her move in. They'd spoken about him maybe living here too one day so they could be together properly. Tara's chest tightened. The grief was all-consuming, filling up every part of her until she felt as if she was going to explode with it. Worst of all, was knowing there was nothing she could do, not a single thing, that would make this go away.

On Sunday evening, coming back here alone, she'd worried she wouldn't be able to get through this. The temptation to hurt herself, or worse, had been stronger than any time since her suicide attempt three years ago. She thought she had moved past all that. Foolishly, she'd let herself believe the worst was behind her. These last few days had taught her it would never be behind her. She could have times in her life when things would be close to normal. Or as close to normal as possible, because there was no comparing her 'new normal' with the life she'd had before the crash.

After the detectives left on Monday, she'd fallen apart. When the police liaison officer had turned up later that afternoon, Tara had been relieved to see her. But the next day, she couldn't stand having her in the apartment and she'd sent her away. The last thing she'd needed was some nosy police officer watching her while she sobbed and ranted.

The trauma never left her. The fear and anxiety and suffocating guilt was always there, lying beneath the surface, waiting. As soon as she let her guard down and started to believe she could move forward with her life, it resurfaced. Instinctively, her fingers trailed the scar that ran from her knee to midway up her thigh. A legacy of the crash that had also left her with a slight limp. The only outward sign of what had happened.

There'd been no warning, no sign at all that the plane was about to crash. As they were coming in to land, there was the normal announcement from the cockpit: 'cabin crew prepare to land.' The seatbelt lights came on and the plane started its descent. The first moment of uncertainty came when it rose abruptly, instead of landing. Tara remembered looking at the other passengers, wondering if any of them had noticed something was wrong. But none of them seemed too bothered. Then the plane circled and came back into land a second time. And the screaming began.

Tara had been on holiday with her two best friends, Monica and Jessie. Three privileged girls from wealthy families with good genes and wealth and a lifetime of privilege to look forward to. Then, suddenly, all of it was gone in the blink of an eye.

She lifted her glass, the wine golden and green in the afternoon sunshine. She'd been drinking solidly for the last hour. So far, the alcohol had done nothing to take away the emptiness of her grief or the burning heat of her anger. All of it underpinned with fear. She'd got used to having someone in her life to take care of her. With Nick gone, she was alone again and the idea terrified her. She didn't have a job, and the little bit of money she had saved up wouldn't last more than a few months. Her parents had made it clear that she couldn't live off them forever. It wasn't fair. All this unnecessary anxiety because someone had killed the one person who really loved her and wanted to look after her.

Again, she went through the list of people who'd been at the villa at the weekend. It was three days now since his body had been found on the beach. So far, the police didn't seem to have got any closer to finding out who'd killed him. Tara was sick of sitting around waiting for them to do their job properly. She had to do something to push the investigation along. The problem was, she didn't know what else she could do. She'd already told the police about Adam and Nick arguing. And she'd made it clear that Simon, too, had a motive for killing his brother. Simon had a short fuse at the best of times. Tara had noticed how annoyed he'd got on Saturday night when Nick was drunk. It wouldn't have taken much to tip him over the edge.

She picked up her phone, scrolling through her call log and reading the names of the people she'd called earlier. Not one of them had phoned her back yet. Bastards. She hovered over Adam's name, considering whether or not to try him again before eventually deciding there was no point.

Moving away from the call log, she looked at the names of the three people she hadn't called yet: Shelly, Robbie, Clodagh. Her eyes hovered over that final name, remembering what Nick had told her last week. He'd made Tara promise not to tell anyone. Once she'd got over her annoyance at him for never having said anything until now, Tara had sworn – on the memory of her dead friends – that she wouldn't tell a soul. But that was before Nick had been murdered. Clodagh was probably glad he was dead, Tara realised. With Nick out of the way, she would think her sordid little secret was safe.

Her glass was empty. When she lifted the bottle out of the wine cooler, she saw that was empty too. She stood up to get some more wine. The balcony swayed, triggering a fluttery panic in her chest. Until she realised it was her, not the balcony, that was swaying.

On her way inside to get a new bottle, she stopped at the mirror in the living room to look at her reflection. Even now, drunk and grief-ravaged, she had to admit she didn't look too bad. It baffled Tara that some women chose to ignore what age did to their faces and bodies. There was no excuse for it. Especially these days when a simple procedure could knock a decade off your face. Another reason to get her hands on some money, so she'd be able to afford whatever work she'd need to get done when the time came.

An idea started to form at the back of her mind. Clodagh had money. Lots of it. And now she was living with Adam, she'd have even more. If Clodagh wanted Tara to keep quiet about what she knew, maybe she'd be willing to pay for it.

She found Clodagh's number and called it before she could change her mind. As she waited for Clodagh to answer, she felt her heart racing hard and fast and her skin tingling with anticipation. It was a disappointment when she got Clodagh's voicemail.

'It's me,' she said, 'Tara. I need to see you. Nick told me—'

She was interrupted by a buzzing sound, so loud it made her jump.

She stumbled back, against the arm of the sofa. The bottle of wine slipped from her hand, smashing onto the marble-tiled floor. Shards of glass scattered across the white marble, cool wine splashed against her bare ankles.

Her face in the mirror looked confused and scared. Until the buzzing sounded again and this time she recognised it. The intercom system. Someone was here to see her. She stepped over the broken glass and crossed the room. Peering into the video screen that showed her who was at the front door, she saw a familiar face looking back at her.

'You?' she gasped.

Her mind was racing, trying to piece it all together. Nick's murder, Clodagh's secret, the phone call she'd just made. Now this. Was it a coincidence, or something more than that? Something more, she decided, her heart lifting as she understood. It was a sign; Nick reaching out from beyond the grave, telling her what she needed to do.

'I'm so glad to see you,' she said, pressing the buzzer that released the outside front door. 'There's something important I need to tell you.'

Twenty

After breakfast, Adam had packed his overnight bag. He was spending the night in London. A day of meetings, followed by dinner in a fancy restaurant with the TV executives behind his new programme. He'd tried to persuade Clodagh to come with him, but she'd held firm. She couldn't think of anything worse than dinner with Jake and a whole load of media people, all telling Adam what a great talent he was.

When he'd gone, Clodagh went for a long walk across the downs. She'd been planning to get a taxi to the beach for a swim, but she'd spotted two journalists loitering at the end of the driveway and she hadn't been able to face having to pass them. Instead, she'd slipped out the back gate and started walking. By early afternoon, she had covered over ten miles and could easily have done another ten. The countryside here was stunning. She had explored little parts of it when Vivienne was alive, but she'd got to know it a lot better since moving here. The area never failed to surprise her. Rolling green fields with far-reaching views across the English Channel; ancient woodland and picture-postcard villages untouched by time. Because Adam worked so hard, she spent a lot of time alone. Over the last nine months, Clodagh had learned to love these solitary walks across the downs to the different villages nestled between the hills.

Walking helped her to think and today, more than ever, she needed to get her thoughts in order. The fear of having lied to the police was physical, a tightness in her chest and stomach that no amount of walking could ease.

She wished she could talk to Adam, but she'd never told him what she'd done and it was too late to do that now. There was someone she could talk to, though. Pulling her phone out of her bag, she called Ivan. When she got his voicemail, she frowned. This was the third time she'd called him over the last few days. Each time, the call had gone straight to voicemail. So far, he hadn't returned any of her calls.

'Me again,' she said. 'Sorry if it seems like I'm harassing you. I just want to make sure you're okay. I was interviewed by the police yesterday and… oh never mind. Just call me, Ivan, would you?'

'Stupid Croat,' she muttered, hanging up. Where the hell was he? She wanted to see him and hug him and smack his big, moustached face and make him tell her why he wasn't returning her calls. More than anything, she wanted to hear his laugh, because there were few things in this world that made her feel as good as the sound of that belly laugh.

She noticed the new voicemail message on her screen. The irritatingly chirpy recorded voice told her she had two new messages. The first was from Bella, asking if Clodagh was still okay to meet up tomorrow. She'd called yesterday, full of apologies for the way Simon had behaved on Monday. Clodagh had told her there was no need to apologise, and they'd arranged for Bella to come over to Clodagh's for a proper catch-up. Clodagh sent a quick text now, telling Bella she was looking forward to seeing her. Then she moved onto the second message.

'It's me, Tara. I need to see you. Nick told me—'

The voice was cut off by the cacophony of a loud buzzing and something that sounded like smashing glass, before the call abruptly ended. She'd sounded drunk, Clodagh thought, her chest tightening as she replayed the message in her head. What the hell had Nick told Tara?

She put her phone into her jeans pocket and continued walking, needing to move while she sorted out the different thoughts swirling around inside her head. As she'd done so many times before, she forced her mind to go back to the day of the crash, carefully examining every memory. Breakfast in the restaurant. Fruit and yoghurt, honey and sunshine. Coffee and freshly squeezed orange juice. Something off about Vivienne. An edgy energy about her that Clodagh knew was a sign her sister was about to do something reckless.

Clodagh stopped walking. This memory was new. She closed her eyes, focused on the image of her sister's face, sitting opposite her.

Vivienne took a sip of her coffee, her eyes scanning the restaurant like she was trying to find something. Or someone.

'Is everything okay?' Clodagh asked.

'Fine.'

But Clodagh knew she wasn't fine. She was jittery, distracted. Her red-painted fingernails were tapping the table, the sound so loud the couple at the next table kept looking over.

'Can you stop that, Vee?'

'Stop what? Oh. That.' She curled her hand into a fist. 'Sorry. Listen, Clo, I'm going to head off for a bit after breakfast. You'll be okay without me?'

'I've spent most of this holiday without you. I think I can manage one more day.'

The memory faded, replaced by the image of Nick's dead body. Clodagh opened her eyes. Why had her brain made the connection between that final morning in Crete and Nick? Because he'd been staying at the same hotel, or was there another reason?

The holiday hadn't turned out the way Clodagh had imagined. The week away was meant to be a chance for the two sisters to spend quality time together. Instead, Clodagh had spent most of it alone while Vivienne disappeared on walks or trips into town or wherever else she went when she wasn't at the hotel.

'Oh Vivienne,' she said softly, 'what were you up to?'

Luckily, Vivienne didn't answer. If she had, Clodagh would have worried more than she already did about her own state of mind. Pushing down the memories of that last day in Crete, she took her phone out again and called Tara. When she got Tara's voicemail, she left a short message:

'It's Clodagh returning your call. Can you call me back as soon as you can? Thanks.'

She hung up, frustrated. Tara had said she needed to speak to her urgently. If it was that urgent, why hadn't she picked up? On the way back to the house, she tried Tara three more times but continued to get her voicemail. Listening to Tara's recorded message a third time, Clodagh made a decision. She was going to get a taxi to Lewes station and take a train to London. If she hurried, she could be at Tara's apartment within three hours. One way or another, she was going to find out why Tara wanted to speak to her.

Twenty-one

It was late afternoon by the time Clodagh arrived in London. She walked from London Bridge station, along the South Bank towards Tara's riverfront apartment. This was her favourite part of the city. When she'd first moved to London, she'd rented a small flat near Borough Market. She'd spent her weekends exploring the area, walking down the narrow streets and lingering at the food stalls in the market, before going to meet a friend or see some art at Tate Modern.

There was an air of gentrification about the place that had been absent when Clodagh lived here, and the market seemed to have doubled in size since then. But it felt familiar enough to trigger a wave of nostalgia as she walked amongst the tourists and street artists and buskers and the groups of people drinking outside the riverfront pubs. It was a million miles away from the sleepy village she lived in now.

She'd tried calling Tara again from the train but kept getting her voicemail. Now, she was starting to think coming up here was a stupid idea. Tara could be anywhere. She could see Tara's apartment building up ahead. A curved glass construction, wider in the centre than at the top and bottom. She'd been here once before for Tara's birthday, two weeks ago. A drab affair despite the canapes and the free champagne and the sweeping views of the

Thames. Clodagh remembered now, how the shape of the building had reminded her of a pregnant woman. The impression was stronger today, possibly because the whole idea of pregnancy was at the forefront of her mind these days.

Properties in this part of London sold for exorbitant prices. Thanks to Adam, and the law firm he'd hired, all those affected by the plane crash had received substantial compensation money. But Clodagh doubted even that would cover the cost of an apartment here. She knew Tara didn't work and wondered, now, how she managed to afford living somewhere this fancy.

At the entrance to the building, Clodagh rang the buzzer for Tara's apartment, and waited. When nothing happened, she tried again. Pulling out her phone, she called Tara's number but hung up without leaving a message when she got Tara's voicemail.

'Damn.'

She was a bloody fool, coming all the way to London without checking first that Tara would actually be able to see her. She pressed the buzzer a few more times, pointlessly because she knew by now that Tara wasn't at home, and was about to give up and walk back to the train station when an elderly woman came out of the building.

'Can I help you, dear?'

She was tiny, like a fragile bird, wearing a wide-brimmed white hat, a face of make-up and a vibrant silk shift dress that shimmered when she moved.

'I'm trying to get in touch with a friend of mine,' Clodagh said. 'She lives in this building.'

The woman peered at Clodagh for several seconds, before smiling.

'I knew I recognised you,' she said. 'You're Vivienne Kinsella's sister. I've read all about you. I knew Vivienne, you see. I was a costume designer until I retired three years ago. I worked with Vivienne when she was in *Streetcar* at the National.' The woman frowned. 'Dear me, how long ago was that now? Must be seven years.'

'Eight,' Clodagh said, swallowing the lump that had appeared at the back of her throat. Playing Blanche DuBois had been the high point of Vivienne's career. Alongside the inevitable comparisons with Vivien Leigh, the performance had been widely praised by critics and the public. Clodagh had seen the play four times and been moved to tears at every performance.

'Such a tragedy.' The woman sighed. 'You look a lot like her, don't you? I'm sure you're sick of people telling you that. Anyway, don't let me stop you. I assume you know where you're going?'

She stepped back, holding the door open so Clodagh could pass into the building.

'Thank you,' Clodagh said.

'My pleasure.' The woman put her hand on Clodagh's arm. 'I remember Vivienne telling me all about you. She was very proud of you – her sister, the hot shot City lawyer. You must miss her terribly.'

'I do.'

The woman squeezed Clodagh's arm before letting it go.

'I'm on my way to meet my girlfriends. I can't wait to tell them I've just been talking to Vivienne's sister. I'm sure they won't believe me when I tell them you're even prettier than she was.'

With that she was gone, leaving Clodagh alone in the vast entrance lobby. The walls on either side were made up entirely of mirrored glass that reflected back on each other. The overall effect was disconcerting. Multiple images of Clodagh followed her as she made her way across the tiled floor to the row of lifts. It was a relief, to step inside one of the lifts and escape herself.

Tara's apartment, she remembered, was on the top floor. It was quiet up here, the sounds of the city silenced by concrete walls and triple-glazed glass. As she walked towards Tara's apartment at the end of the corridor, her footsteps sounded too loud, echoing against the hard edges of the building.

She was halfway down the corridor when she felt it: a crawling sensation at the back of her neck. The sudden realisation that something was wrong. A series of images flashed through her mind, too vivid and bright. Nick's body motionless on the grey and white shingle beach; his eyes, open and staring. Tara's face, pale and haunted later that same morning.

Every part of Clodagh's body wanted to turn around. To step back into the lift and get as far away as she could from whatever lay on the other side of that door. Yet somehow, she kept moving forward. Gradually getting closer, until she was standing directly outside Tara's front door, pressing the doorbell then banging on the door with her fist when Tara didn't answer.

'Tara! Are you there? It's me, Clodagh. Open the door.'

'Can I help you?'

The door to the apartment next door opened, and a woman's face peered out. Heavy-framed glasses, long blonde hair and a surprised expression on her face that Clodagh suspected was caused by extensive cosmetic surgery.

'I'm looking for Tara.'

The woman somehow managed to frown without a single line appearing on her face.

'Were you the person who was here earlier?'

'No.' Clodagh shook her head. 'I've just got here.'

'So you're not here because of the row?'

The feeling of dread intensified.

'I don't know what you're talking about,' she said.

The woman looked her up and down, as if assessing how much she could trust her. Clodagh guessed the woman was in her early fifties, although the surgery made it hard to say exactly how old she was.

'I've been wondering what to do,' she said. 'Someone was in with her earlier. There was a fair bit of shouting. I came out and knocked on her door, asked if she was okay and she said she was fine. Told me to go away, so that's what I did. The walls in these apartments are pretty thick. You don't normally hear any sound from your neighbours. But the shouting was pretty intense, you know?'

She spoke with a whispering, little girl voice that grated Clodagh's nerves.

'You didn't try to help her?' Clodagh said.

'I waited outside for a bit, then I knocked on the door again, told her to call if she needed me. Again, she said she was okay so I went away.'

'How long ago was this?'

'A couple of hours ago?' She shrugged. 'Maybe more than that. It's not as I've been watching the clock all afternoon.'

'If she's okay, why isn't she answering her door?' Clodagh said.

'How would I know? I'm her neighbour, darling, not her guardian. If she's not opening the door, maybe you should take the hint and leave her in peace.'

'Or maybe something's wrong.'

'Now you mention it, after what happened to her boyfriend I should have considered she might be in some sort of danger. I've actually got a key to her apartment. She's always losing her stuff, so she keeps a spare key at mine in case she loses hers. Although, she's a pretty private person. I'm not sure she'd like it if we went in there poking through her things, you know?'

'We don't have to tell her.'

'No. I suppose we don't.' The woman gave Clodagh the hint of a smile. 'Hang on a second, then.'

She disappeared, before returning a few seconds later with a key dangling from her index finger.

'It's probably best if you go in first,' she said, holding the key out. 'Tara can be a bit tempestuous sometimes. I don't want to get on the wrong side of her.'

Grabbing the key, Clodagh shoved it into the lock, twisted it, pushed the door open and stepped inside the apartment. Several things hit her at the same time. The open glass door that led onto the balcony. The putrid smell of faeces. Shards of green glass scattered across the white marble tiles. The soles of Tara's bare feet, white and vulnerable. Her body, sprawled across the cream leather sofa that wasn't cream any more, but had turned a dirty brown colour from the dead woman's blood.

Twenty-two

Rachel and Ade sat across the table from Simon Gilbert and the duty solicitor. It was Wednesday evening. Rachel was meeting Grace for dinner later and was willing the interview to end soon so she could get away. Date nights had become a rarity since they'd started saving to buy a house. She wanted to make the most of every moment of this evening.

'These are copies of your bank statement over the last year,' she said, laying sheets of paper on the table so Simon could see what was on them. 'You'll see several payments – I've highlighted the ones I'm talking about – all from the same bank account. You want to tell me who these are from?'

She already knew the payments had come from Nick, but she wanted to see how much Simon would tell her.

'I'm guessing you already know,' he said, after a moment. 'The money was from Nick. So what? He was my brother and he was loaded. He helped me out from time to time. There's no law against that, is there?'

'No,' Rachel said. 'But it is a crime to pervert the course of justice, which is what you're doing if you lie to us during a murder investigation.'

'How am I lying?' Simon looked so ridiculously outraged at the suggestion, Rachel knew they'd done the right thing bringing him in for this interview.

'The last time we spoke,' she said, 'you told us that Nick's money sometimes caused issues between you.'

'So?'

'But you didn't mention that your brother had given you substantial amounts of money over the last year.'

'I didn't think it was important.'

'It's our job to decide what's important or not,' Rachel said.

Simon opened his mouth, but before he could speak, the solicitor put his hand on Simon's arm.

'Detectives, could you give me a few minutes with my client, please?'

'Five minutes.' Rachel switched the tape off and stood up.

'What do you think?' she asked Ade once they were both outside.

'He doesn't seem to have any clue his brother's finances were a mess,' Ade said. 'I'm starting to wonder if anyone knew how much trouble Nick was in.'

'We've got an appointment with his business partner tomorrow,' Rachel said. 'Maybe she'll be able to tell us what was going on with Nick's money.'

While she was speaking, Rachel took her phone out to check for new messages. Seeing the voicemail symbol on her screen, she stepped aside from Ade and dialled the service.

One new message.

'Jake Harris here. I need to speak to you urgently. I'd be grateful if you could call me back as soon as possible. Thanks.'

Rachel scrolled back through her call log, found Jake's number and phoned him back.

'This is DI Lewis,' she said, when he answered. 'You called earlier?'

'I want to make a complaint,' Jake said. His words merged together slightly and Rachel guessed he'd had a few drinks.

'A complaint about what?' she said.

'The tabloid press. They have done nothing but harass and harangue my client ever since we announced the news about his new TV series. If they continue like this, there's a real chance the TV company will pull out. Which would be a disaster for his career.'

Rachel held the phone away from her ear and looked at it, as if she might see something that would explain this bizarre phone call.

'Hello?' Jake shouted. 'Are you still there?'

'Indeed I am,' Rachel said, putting the phone back to her ear. 'But I'm afraid I can't help you, Mr Harris. Besides, I seem to recall you were more than happy to use the press yourself earlier this week.'

'What's that supposed to mean?'

'Adam Murray on *Good Morning Britain*?'

'That was different. No one deserves to be treated this way. These journalists are nothing better than vermin and you need to do something to stop them.'

'If you're finding it that difficult,' Rachel said, 'you could try taking out an injunction against them. Although I'm not sure what grounds you'd have for it, quite frankly.'

'Which is why I need your help,' Jake said. 'If you refuse to take action, I'll have no choice but to go above your head and speak to your superiors. I'm sure they won't be happy when I tell them how unhelpful you've been.'

'Well good luck with that,' Rachel said, hanging up before he could say anything else.

'What the hell was that?' Ade asked.

'A drunk Jake Harris asked me to tell the naughty tabloid journalists to stop harassing his precious client.'

'He really thinks you can control the press?' Ade grinned. 'The man must be very drunk indeed.'

Rachel knew she should be able to smile it off too. But the truth was, the phone call had shaken her. What sort of impression did she give if people like Jake Harris thought it was acceptable to phone her up and issue orders? She was pretty sure he'd never try that trick on Ed, if he was still here. And definitely not on Sharon.

'He's a knob,' Ade said. 'You do know that, right?'

'Yeah.' Rachel put her phone back in her jacket pocket. 'I know.'

It was part and parcel of the job. People thinking they could call you any time of the day or night with outlandish requests that they expected you to respond to immediately. Most of the time, she was able to see the funny side. But right now she was so tired, fed up leading an investigation that was going absolutely nowhere, she wasn't able to do that.

The door to the interview room opened and the solicitor's head peered out.

'We're ready,' he said.

Rachel straightened her shoulders, pushed down her feelings of frustration and inadequacy and nodded.

'Good. Let's get this over and done with.'

'Simon has something he'd like to tell you,' the solicitor said, once Rachel and Ade had sat back down and Rachel had re-started the recording.

'Nick lent me the money for a deposit on the house,' Simon said. 'But that's the only transaction on those bank statements that was a loan. All the rest were gifts.'

'Even this payment?' Ade pointed a purple painted fingernail at a payment of fifteen thousand pounds from nine months ago.

'He paid for our wedding,' Simon said. 'He could be generous when the mood took him. Which is why, when he gave me the money for the house, I assumed he was joking when he said it was only a loan.'

'Is that the payment for ten thousand pounds?' Ade asked.

'That's right.'

'A lot of money for a gift,' Rachel said. 'Especially when he'd already given you quite a lot already.'

She'd counted six payments from Nick's account to Simon over the last three years. And knew there were at least three further payments he'd made in the years before that.

'It is a lot,' Simon said. 'But he had so much. I didn't understand why he was making such a big deal about it. Ten grand was nothing to him. I'd have thought he'd want to help me out, get me onto the property ladder with a place of my own. But he didn't give a damn about that. After all the work I'd done to build bridges between us, have a good relationship with him, and he just threw it all back in my face over a bit of money.'

'Quite a lot of money, actually,' Rachel said.

'For me and you, yeah. Not for him.'

He sounded like a petulant child, Rachel thought. She had an older sister, Debs, who she loved dearly. But Debs would never have considered handing over large sums of money to Rachel on a regular basis without ever expecting the money to be paid back. Rachel wouldn't have wanted it, either. That sort of financial dependency could only damage their relationship over time. Which is exactly what seemed to have happened between Nick and Simon.

'It wasn't fair,' Simon said. 'He had so much and I've always had to work hard, scrimping and saving for every penny. But he wouldn't stop going on about that bloody loan. Pestering me about it every opportunity he got.'

'Is that what happened on Saturday night?' Rachel asked.

'Saturday?' Simon frowned. 'No. I already told you. I kept well out of his way on Saturday. I saw the mood he was in and I knew if I went anywhere near him he'd start on at me. I was worried Bella would hear him. She didn't know about the loan and I wanted to keep it that way. Of course, thanks to you she now knows something's up.'

'She asked you about it then?' Ade said.

'She was really upset,' Simon said. 'Wanted to know why I hadn't told her about it.'

'What did you say?' Rachel said.

'What could I say? I told her there never had been a loan and there was obviously some sort of misunderstanding.'

'So you lied to her again,' Rachel said.

'I can't see that my client's relationship with his wife is relevant to this conversation,' the solicitor said.

'It proves he's a liar,' Rachel said, 'and that is certainly relevant to this conversation.'

She was starting to strongly dislike Simon Gilbert and was wondering just how far he might be willing to go to make sure his wife didn't ever learn that he'd been taking handouts from his brother.

'I'm guessing the weekend must have been difficult for Bella too,' Ade said, looking for all the world like this idea had just occurred to her. 'It must have been tough, knowing everyone else there had the money to stay in places like that any time they wanted.'

'It was horrible for her,' Simon said. 'But like I told you already, we weren't about to turn down a free weekend.'

'I don't blame you,' Ade said. 'It must have made you quite angry, knowing the others all got so much while your wife got nothing at all.'

'Where's this line of questioning going?' the solicitor interrupted.

'I'm just trying to put myself in Simon's shoes.' Ade smiled sweetly. 'Simon, we've already heard how badly Nick behaved that night. I find it hard to believe he didn't take the opportunity to rub your nose in things.'

'He would have done,' Simon said. 'But I didn't give him the chance, did I?'

'What about Bella?' Ade pressed.

'No.' Simon shook his head, adamant. 'Nick didn't speak to Bella. I'd have known if he did. The first she knew about that money was when you told her about it yesterday.'

He was telling the truth, Rachel thought glumly, remembering how confused Bella had seemed when they'd asked her about the loan.

They continued questioning Simon for a while longer. When it was clear they weren't going to get anything more from him, they let him go. By now, Rachel was already running late for her dinner date. She thought about calling Grace to cancel but decided against it. The case would still be here waiting for her when she got back into work tomorrow. Tonight was about her and Grace. Nothing else.

She was at the station, waiting for the Brighton train, when the call came through. A London number on her screen, one she didn't recognise.

'Hello?'

Later, she would think how carelessly she took the call. Not pausing, even for a second, to consider it might be bad news. She was watching the departures board, trying to work out how quickly she could be at the restaurant, when she heard a man's voice.

'Is this DI Rachel Lewis?'

'That's me.'

Ten minutes before her train arrived. Twenty minutes to Brighton. Then a ten-minute walk to the restaurant. She'd be about fifteen minutes late. Not too shoddy.

'This is DC Sonny McLeod, Charing Cross CID. We've had a murder, which I think might be relevant to a case you're currently investigating.'

As Rachel listened, with growing disbelief, the information on the departures board had changed. Her train was running five minutes late.

Not that it mattered now. By the time the phone call had ended, Rachel had already crossed over to the other platform and jumped on the London-bound train that had just pulled into the station.

Twenty-three

It was almost midnight by the time Clodagh was allowed to leave the police station. The hours since finding Tara's body had passed in a blur of shock and fear and activity. Tara's neighbour had called the police. Two uniformed police officers had turned up, firing a barrage of questions at Clodagh. At some point, they'd bundled her into the back of their car and driving her to Charing Cross police station. She'd spent the next few hours sitting across a table from two police detectives, answering the same questions again and again. Finally, when she was on the verge of breaking down and begging them to stop, they'd told her she was free to go for now.

Clodagh stood on the quiet street, breathing in deep mouthfuls of dank city air, trying to work out what she was meant to do now. It was too late to take a train back home. Even if the trains were still running, which she doubted, she didn't think she had the energy to do that journey tonight. And she didn't want to be alone.

She took her phone out to call Adam, but when she tried to switch it on nothing happened. The battery had died. Her own fault, as usual. She couldn't remember when she'd last charged the damn thing. Luckily, she knew Adam was staying in Soho House, so she decided that's where she'd go now.

She walked to Charing Cross train station and climbed gratefully into one of the black cabs waiting outside.

'Soho House,' she said.

'Which one, love?'

The question flummoxed her. She hadn't realised there was more than one Soho House in London.

'Shoreditch or Dean Street?' the driver said, when Clodagh didn't answer.

'Dean Street,' she said, vaguely remembering Adam giving the address to someone over the phone a while back.

Midway through the journey, the taxi driver asked Clodagh if she was someone famous.

'I get a lot of celebrities in my cab,' he said. 'Usually, I spot them easily. But not you. I recognise your face, but I can't work out where I've seen you. You're Irish, right? My old man's from a place called Clonmel. You ever heard of it?'

Clodagh told him she'd heard of Clonmel but had never been there. Despite insisting she wasn't a celebrity, the driver spent the rest of the journey trying to work out where he'd seen her before. By the time she'd paid him and said goodbye, she was relieved to see the back of him.

At Soho House, she gave her name to the doorman and asked if he'd pass a message to Adam Murray. She'd expected to be waiting for a while, but within five minutes, she saw Adam coming out of the lift and hurrying towards her across the lobby.

'Clodagh.' The smile on his face turned into a frown as he drew closer to her. 'My God. What's happened?'

She fell into his arms, never more grateful to see him.

'Come on,' he said, keeping his arms wrapped around her. 'Let's get you upstairs.'

She let him lead her into the lift, leaning against him as he pressed the button for the top floor.

'I've been so worried about you,' he said. 'I've called you loads of times, but I kept getting your voicemail. I was starting to think something bad had happened. Or that you were ignoring me.'

She didn't answer, didn't say a word until they were inside the room. She sat on the side of the bed watching Adam. He switched on the small lamp by the bed, before lifting a half-empty bottle of wine off the table and pouring some into the glass beside it.

He hadn't been asleep, she realised. Adam usually went to bed early, but tonight he'd been sitting here in his room drinking red wine. Normally, she would have asked him if something was wrong, but she didn't have the energy for that tonight.

'Will you have some?' he asked, holding up the bottle.

She shook her head. Right now, she felt as if she'd never be able to eat or drink ever again. It kept hitting her, over and over, that this was the second dead body she'd seen in less than a week. She knew, if she wasn't very careful, she might never get beyond this. Something inside her was close to breaking, and if that happened, she didn't think she'd have the strength to fix it.

'Tara's dead.'

Adam stood stock still, staring at her.

'Tara? What time did this happen?'

There was something odd about the question, but Clodagh was too tired to work out what that was.

'Someone killed her,' she said, speaking faster now, the words tumbling out of her mouth as if she had no control over them. 'She called me earlier, left a message. Except I couldn't call her back because I kept getting her voicemail.

So I came to London. Her neighbour had a key and she let me in and we found her. There was blood everywhere. It was like something from a horror film, except far worse. I'll never forget it. I've spent the last few hours in a police station answering questions. They think I killed her. They didn't say that, but I could see it in their faces and all the time I sat there, trying not to fall apart, I kept thinking what if this is my fault, somehow?'

'Clodagh, stop it.' Adam sat beside her on the bed and took her hand in his. 'You're not making any sense. How could any of this be your fault?'

She blinked. Had she really said that out loud?

'I don't know.'

But it wasn't true. Because no matter how hard she tried, Clodagh couldn't shake off the feeling that all of it – the plane crash, the murders of Nick and Tara – was because of something she'd done. Something bad, that her damaged brain had hidden away so she wouldn't have to ever face up to it. But she couldn't go on hiding forever. It was time to find out what had happened that day at the airport, and who else knew about it.

Twenty-four

Day Five

Rachel's eyes felt dry and gritty from too much time spent staring at a screen. Her brain had stopped processing information several hours earlier, her body was sluggish and heavy. All she wanted to do was rest her head on her arms and fall asleep. It had been the early hours of Thursday morning by the time she'd got home from London. She'd managed to grab three hours' sleep before being woken again by the alarm. So far this morning, she'd led the team briefing at eight thirty; she'd driven to Brighton to speak with Bella and Simon Gilbert; and she'd spent the last three hours at her desk working solidly.

Tara's murder had changed everything. Until yesterday, Rachel had been working on the assumption that Nick's murder had most likely been caused by an argument that had spiralled out of control with devastating consequences. Now, it was starting to look as if both murders might have been pre-meditated.

Adam Murray had called her first thing, asking for guarantees that the other survivors weren't in any danger. Rachel had assured him she and her team were doing all they could, but her reassurances sounded hollow even to her own ears. The simple truth was that four days after Clodagh Kinsella had discovered Nick's body on the beach, Rachel was no closer to working out who had killed him, or why. And with another one of the survivors killed, she had no idea which one of them might be next.

For now, the investigation into Tara's murder was being handled by the Major Investigations Team in Charing Cross police station. As far as Rachel was concerned, this was ridiculous. In her mind, the two murders were clearly connected and Tara's killing should be part of Rachel's investigation. So far, however, she hadn't been able to make that happen.

In the meantime, Rachel had started making her own notes on Tara's murder, adding what she knew to the existing investigation's timeline. Because no matter what the powers that be had decided, Rachel knew her best chance of tracking down Nick's killer was by finding the connection between both murders. She picked up her phone and called Sonny McLeod, the detective heading up the London investigation.

'I've been expecting your call,' Sonny said. 'I know this situation isn't ideal, Rachel. But until someone tells me otherwise, I'm SIO on this investigation.'

'But you agree it makes sense for us to share information, right?'

'Absolutely. I'm a hundred per cent with you in thinking the two cases are connected. And given you've got a four-day head start, it's only going to help me if I can pick your brains about what you've got so far.'

'Give me the name of your OIC,' she said, using the common acronym for Officer In Charge of Case, the detective typically responsible for preparing the case file during an investigation. Rachel had already assigned this task to Ade in her team, and knew Sonny would have someone too, even at this early stage in his investigation. 'I'll speak to mine and ask her to contact yours.'

'That would be really helpful,' Sonny said. 'Thanks. In the meantime, what can I do for you?'

'An update on your investigation would be great,' Rachel said.

'Not much to tell you so far. Clodagh discovered the body at 4:45. The victim had been dead for at least five hours prior to that. Probable cause of death is stab wounds to the abdomen. She was stabbed twice. No sign of the weapon and we won't know what sort of knife until the PM has been done. No concierge in the building. A dodgy CCTV means we've no way of tracking people going in and out of the building.'

'Dodgy how?' Rachel asked.

'Dodgy as in broken,' Sonny said. 'It's been down for a few days, apparently. The residents have reported it and an engineer has been booked to come out and fix it. But whenever that happens, it'll be too late for us, I'm afraid.'

'What about the intercom system?' Rachel said, recalling the time she'd visited Tara's apartment and shown Tara her warrant card through the intercom screen.

'A basic system,' Sonny said. 'The cameras don't record. But it's a busy part of London. Plenty of CCTV in the surrounding area. I've got people going through all the footage, but you know how these things work. It could take us days to find anything. Our crime scene investigators found strands of hair on the victim's clothing that are too long to be hers.'

'Another woman then,' Rachel said.

'Most likely. We'll have to wait to see what Forensics can tell us. Tara's neighbour heard some sort of argument earlier that afternoon, but she wasn't able to tell us who Tara was arguing with.'

They spoke for a few more minutes, but it was clear there was nothing else Sonny could tell Rachel for now. Promising to stay in touch, Rachel hung up and looked around the room, checking what her team was up to.

She spotted Sam Latimer at his desk. A detective on the graduate fast-track scheme, Sam was young, ambitious, bright and, according to Ade, sex on legs. Rachel thought he was a cocky git who needed bringing down a peg or two, an opinion she had – so far – kept to herself.

'Sam!'

'What can I do for you, Rach?'

It's Rachel, she almost snapped, before realising she couldn't tell him it was okay for Ade to call her that but not anyone else.

'Any update on finding our missing survivors?'

At the briefing earlier, she'd told Sam his priority this morning was to find Ivan Babić and Robbie Fuson. It was ridiculous they'd come no closer to tracking them down yet. The back of Rachel's neck prickled with irritation as she waited for Sam's update.

'I've chased Border Force,' he said. 'There's no record of either man leaving the country over the last week. So I've asked them to go back over the last three months and check the system for Robbie Fuson's name. It shouldn't take them too long to get back to me. In the meantime, I've got something else for you. I've been going back over the backgrounds of each of the survivors, trying to see if there's anything else that connects them. Apart from the obvious, of course.'

'And?'

'Well, we already know that Clodagh and Nick stayed in the same resort in Crete, right? At first, I couldn't find anything connecting the other survivors. Until now. It might not mean anything, but I think you'll find it interesting.'

Sam grinned, clearly pleased with himself.

'Go on then, spit it out.'

'At the time of the crash, Ivan was working in a restaurant on the south of the island in a small village called Mirtos. Which also happens to be the same village Robbie Fuson was staying in when he went on holiday to Crete. A bit of a coincidence that he spent two weeks in Mirtos and ended up flying back with Ivan, don't you think?'

'You think they flew back together,' Rachel said. 'Which means they're much better friends than we realised.'

'It also means Ivan might be the only person who knows where Robbie has gone,' Sam said.

Rachel ran her mind back over everything she knew so far about Ivan Babić and Robbie Fuson, trying to work out how she'd missed it. Not one person they'd spoken to had mentioned anything about Ivan and Robbie having a connection outside the plane crash. Yet it seemed the two men must have known each other, were possibly even in a relationship. A potentially important piece of information that she had somehow missed.

Twenty-five

Clodagh sat inside the house, curtains closed and her phone switched off, trying to keep the outside world at bay. She'd left London first thing this morning, keen to escape both the city and Adam's cloying concern. At some point during the day, news of Tara's death had trickled out. Since then, Clodagh had been besieged by journalists phoning her, sending emails and – over the last two hours – incessantly ringing the intercom system at the gates.

Luckily, she had something to distract herself from all that. She'd bought a pregnancy test at London Bridge station and taken the test as soon as she got home. Two blue lines confirmed what she'd already suspected: she was pregnant. No doubt about it. Now she had the evidence to prove it, she suddenly wanted to tell someone. But there was no one to tell. Adam was still in London and wouldn't be home until much later. And Ivan, the only other person she would have shared the news with, had disappeared.

She switched her phone on and dialled his number, allowing herself a moment's hope that he might pick up. But after two rings, she got the same recorded message she'd been getting all week.

> Hey this is Ivan. Leave your message. If I like you, I'll call you back.

'Your voicemail is a lie,' Clodagh said after the beep. 'I've been calling you for days now and you still haven't called back. Where are you, Ivan? I'm worried.'

Normally, they were in regular contact. He was always texting her about random things that had happened to him, like the supermarket running out of his favourite brand of breakfast cereal, or some hot guy he'd met in a bar. Until this week, whenever Clodagh left him a message, he always phoned her back.

She saw she had new voice and text messages, and switched the phone back off without checking them. She was on her way to the kitchen to get some water when someone started banging on the front door. The noise triggered a sudden surge of anger. She'd assumed the locked gates would stop anyone coming into the garden. But it seemed as if one of the bastards had somehow managed to do just that. The thought of someone going to such lengths just to get a photo or a quote they could use for the evening news sickened her.

When there was another bang, followed by someone pressing down on the doorbell, Clodagh stormed through the house, ready to tell whoever was out there exactly what she thought of them.

But when she pulled open the front door, it wasn't a journalist she saw standing on her doorstep. It was Bella.

'What the hell?' Clodagh said. 'How did you get into the garden?'

'I remembered you had a gate at the back,' Bella said. 'The one that leads onto the downs. When I saw those creeps outside, I came around the back. I didn't want to give you a fright like the last time, so I knocked on the front door. You haven't forgotten we'd arranged to meet up, had you?'

Of course. Coffee and a catch-up.

'Completely slipped my mind,' Clodagh said. 'But you know what? It's bloody good to see you. Come in.'

'It's good to see you too.' Bella smiled. 'I tried calling earlier, to check you were still okay to meet, but I kept getting your voicemail.'

'It's turned off,' Clodagh said. 'Too many phone calls from journalists.'

'Have the police been in touch yet?' Bella asked. Then, when Clodagh nodded, 'Us too. They turned up on our doorstep first thing. I can't take it in, Clodagh. First Nick, now Tara.'

'Come on,' Clodagh said. 'I'll make coffee and we can sit in the garden and have a proper chat.'

It was a grey day. Clouds and humidity had replaced the warm sunshine they'd been enjoying for most of the summer. But it was still better being outside than stuck in the house with the walls closing in on her.

'This coffee is amazing,' Bella said, after Clodagh handed her a mug of the special coffee Adam ordered online. 'You're not having any?'

'I'll stick to water, I think.' Clodagh held up the glass she'd brought out for herself. 'I'm not feeling too good.'

'I'm not surprised,' Bella said. 'It's the shock. I thought I was going to faint when I heard she was dead. The police wouldn't tell us how she died. They kept saying it was too early to give details. She was so fragile, part of me wonders if it all got too much for her and she took her own life. But then there's another part of me that keeps thinking, what if she was killed too? Because it's impossible to have any real perspective on anything after what happened to Nick.'

Clodagh shifted in her chair, knowing she'd have to tell Bella sooner or later.

'She was killed, Bella.'

'The police told you that?'

'They didn't have to. It was me who found her body.'

'Oh God.' Bella put a hand over her mouth. 'Clodagh, I don't know what to say. How awful for you. Are you okay? Sorry, stupid question. How could you be okay? But I don't understand. The police said she'd been found in her apartment.'

'I went to see her yesterday,' Clodagh said. 'But by the time I got to her apartment, she was already dead.'

'I see,' Bella said, after a moment. 'If you don't mind me asking, why did you go to see her? I didn't think you guys were particularly close.'

Clodagh's insides tensed. She didn't want to talk about what had happened yesterday. It was still too raw: the fear and the shock and the utter disbelief that another one of their group had been murdered.

'We weren't. Tara called me yesterday and left a message. Said she needed to see me urgently. I tried calling her back but she didn't pick up, so I went to see her.'

'You went all the way to London because she wasn't answering her phone?' Bella said. 'Isn't that a bit extreme?'

'Probably,' Clodagh said. 'Part of me wishes I hadn't gone. But then another part of me keeps thinking what if I hadn't? How long would she have been there before someone found her?'

'Doesn't bear thinking about,' Bella said. 'So… you know how she died?'

'She… I think she was stabbed.'

It was an effort to force the words out, but she somehow managed.

'It was horrible, Bella.'

'I'm sure it was,' Bella said. 'I know this is probably a stupid question, but is there anything I can do for you? I mean, shit, Clodagh, first Nick and now Tara. How are you coping?'

'I don't know that I am,' Clodagh said. 'I can't stop thinking about them both. And wondering if I'd got to London a little earlier yesterday, maybe Tara would still be alive.'

'You can't think like that. Besides, if you'd got there earlier, who's to say you wouldn't have been killed too?'

Clodagh shivered. She hadn't thought about that.

'She called Simon too,' Bella said. 'Practically accused him of killing Nick. He was pretty upset afterwards. Maybe it's better you didn't get to speak to her. What did she say in her message?'

'Just that she needed to speak to me, and it was urgent.'

'Isn't that the same thing Nick said in his text on Saturday?'

A puff of wind sent the clouds scurrying across the sky and suddenly the sun was out, turning the world lighter and brighter. The exact opposite of how Clodagh was feeling right now.

'Something like that,' she said.

'And you really have no idea what either of them wanted to talk with you about?'

'None.' Clodagh lifted her glass and drank some water to avoid Bella's gaze.

'Isn't it driving you crazy, not knowing?'

It wasn't driving Clodagh crazy because she already knew. Although this wasn't something she could share with Bella.

'It doesn't matter,' she said. 'Whatever they wanted to talk to me about, it had nothing to do with why they were killed.'

'Of course not.' Bella smiled, but Clodagh couldn't bring herself to smile back.

'The police asked us about Ivan as well,' Bella said. 'Apparently they don't know where he is. I told them they should ask you. That you know him better than any of us.'

'I thought I did,' Clodagh said, 'but he hasn't been picking up my calls or replying to any of the messages I've left him. I wish I knew where he was. I'm worried about him.'

'Simon thinks he might have killed Nick.'

'Ivan?' Clodagh stared at Bella. 'Jesus, you're serious, aren't you?'

'I know he's your friend,' Bella said. 'But the fact is, somebody at that hotel killed Nick. Simon and I have been trying to work out who might have had a motive. And no one had more of a motive than Ivan.'

'Because of what happened with the restaurant?' Clodagh said. 'That was ages ago.'

'Two months. Hardly ages. Ivan told me about it on Saturday night. So he was definitely still angry about it.'

'What did he say?'

'That Nick had promised him a job in his new restaurant,' Bella said. 'The one he opened in Brighton last September. According to Ivan, Nick got him to do loads of work helping to get the restaurant opened, all on the promise that Ivan would get the head chef's job. Except at the last minute, Nick changed his mind and said there'd never been any job offer.'

'That's right,' Clodagh said. 'It was a really shitty thing to do.'

She could feel the burn of anger as she recalled the dejected look on Ivan's face when he'd finally got through to Nick on the phone. She'd encouraged Ivan to make the call. Sitting close enough so she could hear Nick's voice down the line, telling Ivan he was grateful for all his help but he had never promised Ivan a job, because the last time he'd checked, Ivan had never worked in a Michelin starred kitchen before, and surely Ivan knew that Nick only ever hired chefs with that sort of experience? And then Nick had laughed, long and hard, as if the very idea of hiring Ivan was a joke.

And Ivan – brave, funny, clever Ivan who'd already been through so much – had laughed right back and said, sure Nick, no problem, but maybe you keep me in your mind if there is any other work I can do?

And Nick, the bastard, had said, I wouldn't hold your hopes up, Ivan.

'Nick made out it was all a big misunderstanding,' Clodagh said. 'But that's not what happened.'

'You sure about that?'

'Positive.'

The first few months after the crash had been a blur. Trauma and grief made any sort of normal life impossible. Hospital appointments, funerals, incessant coverage of the crash in the media, anger and shock and outrage at the scale of the tragedy. Somehow, through all of that, Adam had brought them together – the survivors and the families of those who had died. Creating a space for them to gather and start the slow process of accepting what had happened. He'd brought in counsellors, experts in grief and PTSD, and started the fight for compensation and made sure that every single person affected by the crash of flight 975 got as much support – financial, emotional and anything else – as they needed.

It was during that time that Clodagh had become friends with Ivan. Now, she could barely remember there'd been a time when he wasn't her friend. It felt as if they'd always been like this, although she knew there must have been a 'getting to know each other' phase. But if there was, that had passed so quickly and become a friendship as strong and solid as any she'd ever known.

'I've always felt Ivan blamed me for the crash,' Bella said.

Panic fluttered in Clodagh's chest. She should have known Bella would bring this up. The one thing Clodagh couldn't talk about. Not now, not ever. She willed herself to calm.

'No,' she said. 'That's absolutely not true, Bella. Ivan never thought badly of you because of the crash. How could he? If Gary was drinking before flying the plane that's down to him and no one else.'

'That's what Simon says. We talked about Gary a lot when we first got together. It sounds odd, I know, talking about my ex-husband with my new boyfriend, but weirdly it's one of the things that brought us closer.'

Clodagh was tired of talking about the crash. Endless conversations with endless different people about what might have happened to cause Gary to drink alcohol that day. She couldn't blame Bella for wanting to understand it, either. Bella hadn't been on the plane but there was no denying she'd been badly affected by what had happened.

'The press claimed the divorce was my decision.' Bella put her hand on Clodagh's arm. 'But that wasn't true. I loved Gary. It broke my heart when he told me he didn't want to be married to me any longer. Did you know that, Clodagh?'

Clodagh couldn't answer. The last time Bella had touched her arm like that, it had triggered the start of a memory. The same thing was happening now, except this time the memory was stronger. She remembered standing in the Ladies' toilet at Heraklion airport, her reflection in the mirror staring out at her, white face and wild eyes.

'Are you okay?' Bella asked.

'I don't know.' Clodagh frowned. 'I've remembered something, but I don't know what it means.'

It was the first time she'd remembered anything from the airport. Which meant her memory was finally coming back. All the effort she'd put into remembering was paying off.

'Do that again,' she said.

'What?'

'Put your hand on my arm and lean towards me as if you're going to say something.'

Bella frowned, but did what Clodagh asked her and this time the memory expanded. Clodagh saw herself, standing at the sink, splashing cold water on her face. Her hands, her whole body, shaking with rage. Behind her, the sound of a toilet flushing, a cubicle door opening and… Nothing.

Clodagh shook Bella's hand off her arm and rubbed her face. Whatever had happened at the airport, it had happened there in the Ladies' toilet. Someone else had been in there with her. But no matter how hard she tried, she couldn't remember who that was.

Twenty-six

Day Six

Rachel was lying on her back on a sun-drenched beach, her eyes closed as she listened to the soft sound of waves rustling over the white sand. A cool breeze whispered against her warm skin. She couldn't see the cocktail on the table beside her, but she knew it was there. Just as she knew Grace was lying on the other sunbed, a straw hat covering her face and a book on the ground beside her. Rachel reached out to take Grace's hand, when a loud, clanging sound broke through the peace. Her eyes shot open. Instead of white sand and turquoise ocean, all she could see were dark shapes and the white glare of a light. Gradually, she realised the light was her phone screen, which lit up when her alarm went off. Groaning, she leaned over, switched off the alarm and slumped back onto her pillow. The details of the dream had already faded, replaced by a rush of thoughts about what lay ahead of her today.

She was alone in the bed. Grace must have got up earlier, without Rachel hearing her. She would be out for her morning run before the day got too hot. With a bit of luck, they'd have time to grab breakfast together before Rachel had to leave for work. But by the time Rachel was showered and dressed, Grace still wasn't back. Which meant she'd gone on one of her long runs and might be out for another hour. Disappointed, Rachel sent a text, telling Grace she loved her and promising to be home in time for dinner. After that, she hung around the house for another half hour, just in case. But Grace didn't come home and, eventually, Rachel had to give up waiting and go to work.

She'd sent a message out yesterday afternoon, telling everyone working on the investigation to be ready with their updates for the morning briefing. At eight o'clock, she was standing at the front of the Major Incident Room, facing everyone who'd been brought in to assist with the case. This included a number of detectives, the uniformed officers responsible for different parts of the investigation – house to house (H2H), exhibits, family liaison, disclosure, interviews, HOLMES, and the Intelligence Development Officer (IDO), a selection of uniformed officers and PCSOs.

Rachel started the meeting by giving a summary of where they'd got to so far on the joint murder investigations.

'For now, London is still leading on Tara Coleman's murder. We're working on the assumption there's a link between the two murders. But until we know this for certain, we need to consider all other possibilities as well.'

She didn't mention her frustration at having to liaise with another force. As far as she was concerned, the two murders were clearly connected and it made sense for them to be part of a single investigation, led by East Sussex. Unfortunately, her attempts to take control had got her nowhere so far. Her only hope was that Sharon might pull some strings to make it happen. But if her meeting with Sharon later this morning didn't go well, there was every chance Rachel would be taken off the investigation entirely.

She pointed at the timeline on the interactive board.

'Which is why, for now, I'm including key elements of Tara's murder here. Ade is liaising closely with our colleagues in London, and we've agreed to share as much information as we can with each other. Unfortunately for us, Tara had a party at her apartment two weeks ago. Most of the people who were at the villa were also at that party. That means their DNA will have already been in the apartment, which buggers up the investigation into Tara's killing. However, there is something we can work with. Most of you will remember a few strands of hair were found on Nick Gilbert's jacket. Unfortunately, we weren't able to get any DNA from these. However, several strands of hair were also found on Tara's body. One of these has the root attached, so it's suitable for nuclear DNA testing. The hair is long, so it probably belongs to a woman. And we know the woman isn't Tara, because the hair is too long to be hers. Of course, we won't know until it's been tested.'

A hand shot up from the back of the room. Sam Latimer.

'Sam?'

'If the hair isn't Tara's, does this mean our killer's a woman?'

'Possibly,' Rachel said. 'But there could be all sorts of other reasons hair was on the victim's clothing. Humans shed on average 100 head hairs every day. Realistically, that hair could be from anyone. We don't know how the killer got in and out of Tara's building, but CSI found an open fire escape door on the ground floor. It's possible they used that.'

Someone's phone started to ring.

'Sorry,' Sam stood up, his phone in hand. 'Border Force, I've been expecting this.'

As he left the room to take the call, Rachel went around the room, getting updates from different people and allocating tasks for the rest of the day. She was just finishing up when Sam appeared back in the room, grinning like a little kid who'd been given free run of a sweet store.

'Robbie Fuson took a ferry from Portsmouth to Bilbao on the twenty-fourth of April this year,' he said. 'He hired a car at Bilbao and handed it back into the same rental company three days later at Malaga.'

'Where his mother lives.' Rachel beamed back. 'Good work, Sam. Can we get onto the local police and get them to pay the mother another visit? See what she says this time about her son's whereabouts.'

'I'm on it.' Sam already had his phone to his ear as he left the room again.

'Right then,' Rachel said, looking around at the others. 'This is an excellent step forward, people. We'll meet back here again at six p.m. In the meantime, get to work.'

She glanced at her watch. She had one minute before she was due to meet with Sharon. Grabbing her laptop off her desk, she left the room and walked along the corridor to her boss's office.

The meeting with Sharon went better than Rachel could have expected. When she had finished giving her update, Sharon sat back, crossed her hands behind her head and stared at Rachel for five long seconds before speaking.

'Your first case as SIO, isn't it?'

'That's right.' Rachel licked her lips, waiting for the inevitable criticism.

'I'm impressed.'

Rachel might have imagined it, but she thought she saw the flicker of a smile at the corners of Sharon's mouth.

'You're doing a good job, Rachel. Just one question for you. How do you feel about London leading the investigation into the Coleman murder?'

'Not too happy about it, if I'm honest.' Rachel decided it was better to be straight about how she felt, even if it wasn't what Sharon wanted to hear.

'Would you like to expand on that?'

'It just feels wrong,' Rachel said. 'There's clearly a link between both murders. And a strong possibility both victims were killed by the same person. In my opinion it makes more sense to bring them together under a single investigation.'

'And that should be here in Sussex, you think?'

'Yes.'

There was a moment's silence. Not long, but enough for Rachel to wonder if she'd been foolish to tell Sharon what she really thought. But then Sharon laughed.

'I agree. As it happens, so does the Chief Constable. In fact, she's already been on to London and got them to see sense. The investigation into Tara Coleman's murder is being passed to us. Which means you're now leading on both investigations. You think you're up to that?'

'Absolutely,' Rachel said. Her head felt light, as if it was about to float away from the rest of her body. She couldn't decide if she was terrified or delighted. Either way, she wasn't able to hold back the big grin she could feel spreading across her face.

'Good.' Sharon grinned back at her. 'I went out on a limb to get you this, Lewis. Make sure you don't mess it up. Now get out of here. You've got a double murder to solve.'

Twenty-seven

A pack of reporters had congregated outside the entrance to Adam Murray's house. They crowded around Rachel's car, flashes of light blinding her as she pulled up outside the gates.

'Bloody vermin,' Ade said. 'Disgusting the way the paparazzi treat people. No amount of fame or fortune would make it worth having that lot following you around all the time. The gates are locked, Rach. How are we going to get past this lot?'

'You'll need to jump out and ring the buzzer,' Rachel said.

Ade unbuckled her seatbelt and got out of the car, batting cameramen out of way. Rachel watched her press the intercom buzzer then speak to whoever had answered. A moment later, she turned around and nodded at Rachel. The gates started to slide open and Rachel pressed her foot on the accelerator. Ade stayed outside, making sure none of the 'vermin' followed them into the garden.

A discreet wooden sign informed Rachel the property was called Glebe House. She had a vague memory that the word 'glebe' meant 'parsonage', although this house seemed too big to have ever been a parsonage. It was a stunning, detached property in its own grounds with unobstructed views of the South Downs from every side of the building. Rachel was no expert, but she guessed the house had to be at least 300 years old. It was the sort of properly she would love to live in one day but could only ever dream of owning.

'Wow,' Ade said, joining her at the front door. 'Maybe it's worth putting up with all that press intrusion, after all. This is one fancy place.'

Adam Murray wasn't pleased to see them. He did his best to hide it, but Rachel wasn't fooled. She'd caught the look of intense irritation on his face when he'd first opened the door.

'Detectives,' he said, giving them a smile that was as big as it was fake. 'To what do I owe the pleasure?'

'Can we come in for a few minutes?' Rachel said. 'We'd like to ask you a few questions about Tara Coleman.'

Now that she was officially in charge of the case, she'd made it her priority to speak with everyone who'd been at the villa the previous weekend. One of those people had killed Nick Gilbert. Rachel knew it was possible Tara had been murdered by someone else but, for now, she was working on the assumption that – at the very least – the two murders were connected.

Adam hesitated, just for a moment, before inviting them in.

'Would you like something to drink?' he asked, closing the front door. 'I've just made a fresh pot of coffee. Ethiopian Yirgacheffe Chelelektu. Are you a coffee connoisseur, by any chance?'

'Not really,' Rachel said.

'Me, I'm more of a Diet Coke girl,' Ade said. 'You don't have any of that, I'm guessing?'

'I'm afraid not. Although, I'd urge you to try some coffee. It really is excellent.'

Rachel suspected he was trying to intimidate them, but she let it pass for two reasons. One, she'd been around too long to let a pretentious twat like Adam Murray make her feel inferior. And two, the smell of coffee as they followed him through the big hallway into a light, airy kitchen, made her inclined to overlook his twattiness. For now, at least.

'You have a beautiful house,' Ade said.

'Thank you.' Adam smiled. 'Vivienne and I moved in here shortly after we married. She wanted a place in the country, an escape from London. We found Glebe House after a few weeks and knew right away it was perfect. Here.' He poured coffee from a metal cafetiere that looked suspiciously like one Rachel had seen for fifty quid in Waitrose a while back. 'I think you might like this.'

Rachel took the mug he held out for her, breathing in the rich and slightly citrusy aroma of the coffee.

'Wild Ethiopian beans.' He smiled at Ade. 'You sure I can't tempt you?'

'I'm good, thanks,' Ade said.

'Your loss. The beans are hand-picked and washed at the Chelelektu washing station for processing. They're... oh, Christ, I'm sorry. I sound like an absolute dick, don't I?'

'A little bit,' Rachel said, smiling to take the sting out of her words.

Adam nodded at her mug. 'Maybe you'll forgive me when you try that.'

The coffee, when she sipped it, was like no coffee she'd ever tasted before. Fruity, with an undercurrent of caramel and a rich, smooth coffee flavour that made her want to keep drinking it all afternoon.

'It's good,' she conceded. Then, thinking of Grace who was far more sophisticated in all things than Rachel, 'Where do you get this?'

He told her the name of a website and, when he offered to text her the link, she accepted. When her phone pinged a moment later, she was already imagining Grace's surprise when Rachel served up a cup of coffee that tasted nothing like the standard beans they bought in Aldi each week.

'We need to speak to you about Tara,' Ade said.

'Of course.' Adam looked suitably distressed. Although if he was embarrassed to be showing such enthusiasm for coffee so soon after a second survivor's body had been found murdered, he did a good job of hiding it. 'The whole thing is a nightmare. Clodagh has been hit particularly hard, as you can imagine. She's not here at the moment, if you were hoping to speak to her. She's gone for a walk. Sorry. I'm talking too much, aren't I? The truth is, detectives, I'm struggling to understand why this is happening. We're a community, you see. The survivors and the families of those poor people who died, we share a common bond that's brought us together. It's inconceivable to imagine one of us is a murderer.'

'From what we've heard,' Ade said, 'a lot of that sense of community is thanks to you.'

'It's kind of you to say so, but it's not true. I helped set up the foundation, and of course I've used my little bit of celebrity to leverage as much support for us as possible. But that community spirit is down to every one of us who has been involved in the foundation and the work we do. I've seen people make friendships and support each other to work through their grief and rebuild their lives together.'

'People like Simon and Bella?' Rachel said.

'Exactly! They both lost so much, especially Bella, but they've also managed to find the courage – and believe me, it takes courage – to fall in love again. I was so happy when I found out they'd got engaged.'

'Bella's husband was the pilot,' Ade said, 'is that right?'

'He was her ex-husband by then,' Adam said. 'Although that didn't stop the press hounding her in the weeks and months following the crash. They were appalling. I still don't know how she got through it without completely breaking down.'

'Simon told us that Bella wasn't entitled to any of the compensation money,' Rachel said. 'That must have felt like a double blow to her, after everything else she'd been through.'

'It was tough,' Adam said. 'If it had been down to me, I'd have made some provision for Bella. I tried my hardest to fight for that, but the decision was out of my hands. There was nothing I could do.'

'I'd like to know more about the foundation,' Ade said. 'How you set it up, how it's funded and what you do?'

'Sure.' Adam leaned forward, his face animated as he reeled off a spiel he'd obviously given many times before.

'The idea came to me in the first few months after the crash. It was clear that so many of us were devasted and struggling to come to terms with what had happened. I realised our voices were more powerful if we came together. So I looked into what I could do to support everyone and make sure we all got the help we needed to cope with what had happened to us. I created the foundation in Vivienne's memory, setting it up as a charity. You may not realise this but creating a charity from scratch takes a lot of time and effort. I had to write a plausible business plan, set out our aims and put together a board of trustees. The airline was very supportive, as you can imagine, and made several significant donations in the early days. At first, the foundation was focused solely on supporting all those affected by the 975 disaster. As we've grown, we now work with victims of all sorts of disasters. We also do consultancy work, advising other people who are thinking of setting up charities.'

'And funding?' Ade asked.

'A mix of donations and lottery,' Adam said. 'The airline continues to be a significant donor, but we also work with lots of companies connected with the aviation industry. Corporate Social Responsibility is a big thing in business these days. The organisations we partner with raise significant funds for the foundation. It's been a huge challenge, but I'd say we've been pretty successful to date. I'm certainly very proud of what we've achieved.'

'I assume Robbie played a key role over the years?' Rachel said.

'Absolutely.'

'Did you know we've found him?' Ade said.

Adam's face paled.

'Excuse me?'

'Robbie,' Ade said. 'He's been in Spain all this time. Hiding out at his mother's.'

They'd got confirmation on the drive over here. Sam had called with an update. The Malaga police had gone back to Robbie's mother and told her they had proof her son was in Spain. She'd broken down and admitted lying when they'd first spoken to her. She claimed that, after leaving the UK, Robbie had wanted to get away from everything for a while. After Nick's murder, he'd been worried about being hounded by the press, so he'd asked his mother not to tell anyone where he was.

'How do you know?' Adam said. 'I mean, wow. It's great he's okay. Has he said anything about why he disappeared?'

He seemed visibly shaken, which was a reaction Rachel hadn't expected.

'Are you okay?' she said.

'Yes.' He drank some coffee. 'Relieved, I think. I hadn't realised how worried I've been. Now I know he's okay, well, it's a weight off my mind.'

'You're sure that's all it is?' Ade asked.

'Of course.' He gave them both another smile. 'It's great news. I can't wait to tell Clodagh.'

'Where were you on Wednesday afternoon?' Rachel said, hoping to catch him off guard with the sudden change of topic.

'Wednesday? I have no... oh I see. The day Tara was killed. I've completely forgotten my manners as well. Please, let's sit down and then I'll answer whatever questions you've got for me. I have nothing to hide, you know.'

He pulled out one of the chairs at the delightfully shabby chic kitchen table, gesturing for Rachel and Ade to do the same. Rachel suspected his little speech was an attempt to stall for time while he got his story straight, but she sat down anyway.

'Wednesday,' she reminded him.

'I had a meeting in London in the afternoon,' he said. 'I'm about to launch my own TV show. It's very exciting and, at this stage, it involves a lot of meetings with the TV production company. The show's called *Murray's Hour*. A chat show format, but with just one guest each week. It will have a lot of depth, quite different to so much of the fluff that's on TV these days. I'll be speaking to people who've overcome different challenges, looking at the skills that make us resilient and keep us going during the toughest of times. In that sense, it will be an extension of my writing and the other work I do. But this way, I get to reach a far wider audience.'

If it wasn't for the coffee, Rachel was pretty sure she'd have nodded off by now. Biting back the urge to tell him she didn't give one damn about his TV show, she cut him off with another question:

'Anything else?'

'Let me see. I got a mid-morning train to London because I was planning to find a coffee shop and get some writing done before my meeting.'

'So that's all you did before your meetings?'

'Not exactly.' He took a sip of his coffee, pausing before answering her question. 'I got a text from a friend while I was still on the train. He said he needed to see me. We arranged to meet for coffee before my meeting.'

'Can you tell me the name of this friend?'

'Keith Mason. He's one of the people the foundation was set up to support. Poor man lost his entire family in the crash. He hasn't been able to move past what happened. At the time, he was working as an orthopaedic surgeon. He hasn't worked a day since. I doubt he'll ever work again. He spent the first four years drowning his sorrows. At the end of last year, I managed to get him into rehab. It's helped a bit, I think, but he still needs a huge amount of support.'

'I didn't realise the support you offered was so hands on,' Ade said.

'I'm not that close with everyone,' Adam said. 'But Keith needs me. I don't feel as if I have a choice.'

'He'd be happy to confirm he was with you on Wednesday morning?' Rachel said.

'I'm sure he would, yes.' Adam stood up, picked his phone off the granite worktop, scrolled through it and handed it to Rachel. 'Look, here's the text he sent me.'

Sure enough, there was a text sent from Keith Mason at 11:25 a.m. on Wednesday.

> Not doing great today, Adam. Any chance I could take you up on that offer to meet for a coffee?

'We met at the cafe in St James' Park,' Adam said. 'It was a beautiful day and I thought it would be good for Keith to get some sunshine.'

'And after that?' Ade said.

'I went to my meeting with the TV production company, had dinner with Jake and Felicity. Then went back to my hotel. Clodagh turned up about midnight and told me about Tara. She was in a terrible state.'

'Where's the TV company based?' Ade asked.

'Soho. I can give you the address. The meeting was at three o'clock so I had a bit of time after I left Keith. I walked up through Trafalgar Square and spent a very pleasant hour browsing the bookshops on Charing Cross Road before my meeting.'

'That's it?' Ade said.

'I think so.' Adam frowned. 'Well, there is one other thing, actually. I'm sorry, I've no idea how I forgot. Tara called me.'

'Really?' Ade asked, doing a good job of sounding surprised although both she and Rachel already knew this. Charing Cross had sent Tara's phone records over earlier. She'd made a series of phone calls the day she was killed, including one to Adam Murray at eleven fifty-five that morning.

'I didn't speak to her,' Adam said. 'She left me a voicemail. She sounded pretty upset, actually. She wanted to know if I'd had any information on how the investigation was going. Apparently, she'd called you lot several times but no one had called her back.'

'You didn't call her back?' Rachel asked.

'I never got around to it.'

'Adam?'

Clodagh's voice, behind her, made Rachel jump.

'You're back.' Adam stood up and walked across to kiss Clodagh's cheek. 'How was your walk?'

'Fine.'

She didn't look fine, Rachel thought. She looked done in. Dark rings under her eyes, skin so white it was almost translucent.

'What were you saying about Tara?' Clodagh asked, looking from Rachel to Adam.

'Adam was telling me about Tara's phone call to him on Wednesday,' Rachel said.

Clodagh frowned.

'What phone call?'

Clearly, Adam hadn't bothered telling his girlfriend about the phone call. Which made Rachel very keen to find out why he'd kept that information to himself.

Twenty-eight

Clodagh saw the flare of anger on Adam's face when she asked him about Tara. Right now, she didn't care. She thought back to Wednesday night, turning up at his hotel. The opened bottle of wine, the weird way he'd been acting. She felt scared, suddenly, as she tried to understand why he hadn't told her.

'You didn't say anything about a phone call.'

She could feel the two detectives watching her and knew she needed to be careful about what she said. But she was angry with Adam for not telling her everything. And, just like her sister, Clodagh was reckless when she was angry.

Adam held his hands up defensively.

'You were upset. The only thing I was thinking about was making sure you were okay. Besides, the phone call wasn't important. I didn't even speak to her. She left me a message asking if I knew how the police investigation was going. That's all.'

'She called you too, didn't she?' Ade said, looking at Clodagh. 'I know you've already spoken to the police in London about that. But the investigation has been officially passed over to us now. So maybe you could tell us about that phone call?'

Clodagh felt like crying. The last thing in the world she wanted was to go through all that again. But Ade

Benjamin was smiling expectantly at her and she knew she didn't have a choice.

'I didn't speak to her,' she said, pulling out a chair and sitting down.

'Here.' Adam poured some coffee into a mug and passed it to her.

She lifted the mug to her mouth, savouring the rich smell of the freshly ground beans, before remembering she shouldn't drink it. Putting the cup down, she noticed Rachel Lewis watching her closely but, thankfully, Rachel didn't say anything.

'She left me a message,' Clodagh said. 'Said she needed to speak to me. I tried calling her back but kept getting her voicemail.'

'So you went all the way to London to find out why she wanted to speak to you?' Rachel said. 'Why would you do that?'

'I was worried.'

Rachel stared, waiting for Clodagh to say something else.

'Look, I know it sounds like an overreaction, but you've got to understand I wasn't thinking rationally. Nick had just been killed and when I couldn't get through to Tara, I kept thinking what if something had happened to her as well?'

'Turns out your instinct was right,' Ade said.

When Clodagh didn't reply, Rachel pushed her chair back and stood up. 'We'd better get going and leave you to enjoy the rest of your day. Thank you both for your time. And thanks for the coffee recommendation, Adam. I may have to buy some for myself.'

At the kitchen door, Rachel turned back and looked at Clodagh.

'I almost forgot, have you had any luck tracking down Ivan Babić?'

'I didn't know I was meant to be tracking him down,' Clodagh said.

She wanted them to stop asking questions and leave.

'I thought you and he were quite close.'

'Ivan's probably the person I'm closest to of all the survivors.'

'Closer than you are to Adam?'

'Adam wasn't on the plane.'

God damn Rachel Lewis and her piercing eyes that seemed to look right inside your head. Well good luck looking inside my head, Clodagh thought. It's a mess in there.

'You met him while you were on holiday in Crete?'

'No.' Clodagh shook her head. 'How could I have? Crete's a big island. Ivan was staying somewhere in the south. I was in Analipsi in the north.'

'Of course.' Rachel snapped her fingers. 'It was Robbie he met in Crete, not you.'

'Robbie?' Clodagh frowned. 'I don't think so. Ivan didn't know any of us before the crash.'

'He knew Robbie,' Rachel said. 'I'm surprised you don't know. If you're such good friends, why do you think he would have kept that information from you?'

Clodagh looked at Adam.

'Did Robbie ever say anything to you about meeting Ivan in Crete?'

'Nothing,' Adam said. 'As far as I know, Robbie had gone to Crete by himself. He never mentioned being there with someone else. And certainly never let on he was there with Ivan.'

Something shifted inside Clodagh. For a moment, she thought it was the baby, before she remembered she was too early in her pregnancy for that. Ivan had told her he'd been working in Crete at the time of the crash. He'd been coming to London for a sightseeing holiday.

She'd spoken with him at length about Robbie over the past few months, speculating where he'd gone and why he'd left without saying goodbye to anyone. In all those conversations, Ivan hadn't once given Clodagh the slightest hint that he'd ever known Robbie before the crash. He'd lied to her. And now he'd disappeared so Clodagh couldn't even ask him why.

Twenty-nine

Day Seven

Clodagh was in the spare bedroom, looking out of the window. Adam was sitting in the garden with Jake and his tiresome girlfriend, Felicity. Clodagh had excused herself twenty minutes ago on the pretence she wanted to get the room set up for their guests. The truth was, she'd needed to get away. It was still early, six thirty or thereabouts, and Jake was well on his way to getting drunk. Clodagh didn't like the man when he was sober and found him insufferable when he was drinking. She couldn't believe Adam hadn't cancelled this visit. The last thing she felt like was socialising, especially with Jake bloody Harris. But Adam had insisted, said Jake and Felicity were looking forward to getting out of London. When Clodagh pointed out they'd spent the previous weekend in a luxury villa by the sea, Adam had frowned and reminded her that the weekend had ended in tragedy.

As she watched, Jake lifted the bottle of rosé and refilled his glass. Adam said something. Clodagh hoped that maybe he was pointing out to Jake there were two other people whose glasses were also empty. But Jake threw back his head and roared with laughter, so she guessed Adam had said something else entirely.

She'd lain awake most of last night, unable to sleep as she wavered between anger at Ivan for lying to her, and fear for his safety. She'd tried calling him again after the detectives left yesterday afternoon, but she'd got his voicemail. Just like every other time she'd called him. And when she'd spoken with Adam about it, he'd dismissed her concerns, telling her Ivan would show up when he was ready.

Turning away from the window, Clodagh looked around the room, making sure everything was in order for their guests. She didn't like Jake or Felicity, but she'd grown up in a house where you couldn't do enough for people who came to stay. It wasn't a habit she could shake off now.

Walking in here earlier had triggered a wave of nostalgia. This was the room she used to stay in when she'd come to visit Vivienne and Adam. In many ways, she preferred it to the master bedroom she now shared with Adam. It was a bright and airy room with views over the garden to the countryside beyond. Rolling green hills and ancient woodland spread out in every direction, as far as the eye could see. There was no en suite bathroom here, which was why it wasn't classed as the master bedroom. But in a house with three upstairs bathrooms, Clodagh didn't really see how that was a problem.

She had forgotten to leave towels out. As she crossed the room to get some from the wardrobe where she kept the guest towels, one of the floorboards wobbled beneath her foot. Strange, she thought, pressing her foot down on the loose floorboard. She knew Vivienne had spent a lot of money restoring the floorboards throughout the house; stripping them back, varnishing them and ensuring they were properly sealed to keep the rooms warm in winter.

She rocked her foot back and forth, feeling the floorboard wobble, as if it was about to spring out.

When they were growing up in Dublin, Clodagh and Vivienne had lived in a Georgian townhouse in the city centre. There had been an attic room, at the top of the house, which their parents had turned into a playroom. The room didn't have a carpet. Their mother had scattered some old rugs on the exposed floorboards, instead. Some of the floorboards had been loose, just like this one, and the sisters had used the space beneath as their secret hiding place.

She'd spent so many happy times in that room, with Vivienne and their friends. As the girls grew older, the room changed from a playroom to a place they could hide away from their parents. It was where they had their sleepovers, hiding illicit bottles of cider and packets of cigarettes beneath the floorboards.

The need to find a reconnection with those happy days was powerful. Before she knew what she was doing, Clodagh crouched down and started feeling along the edge of the floorboard. There it was. A narrow space between this floorboard and the one beside it. Manoeuvring her finger into the gap, she was able to lift the piece of wood and feel around in the space beneath it. She hadn't expected to find anything, so she could barely believe it when her fingers brushed a small object lying on the plaster surface below. She pulled it out and looked at it, her brain gradually registering that the object in her hand was a USB memory stick.

The layers of dirt on the stick indicated it had been lying, undisturbed, for a long time. It could easily have been there for five years, or longer. She knew it might not have belonged to Vivienne, but she needed to check.

Standing up, she replaced the loose floorboard and left the room, closing the door quietly behind her. Back in her own bedroom, she inserted the stick into the USB port on her laptop. She opened Windows Explorer, expecting to see the USB listed, but it wasn't there. Frowning, she took it out and reinserted it. Again, nothing happened. Then, down in the bottom right-hand corner of her screen, she noticed a message:

USB device not recognised.

Swearing under her breath, Clodagh sat back, trying to work out what to do. There had to be a way to fix it. She went onto the internet, looking for a solution, but there were too many options and her brain couldn't cope with the amount of information. There were plenty of laptop repair shops in Brighton. The next time she went there, she'd take the memory stick with her and see if the people in the shop could help. Until then, there was nothing else she could do. She removed the memory stick and put it in the drawer by her bed before going back downstairs.

In the kitchen, she got a glass of water and was about to go outside when she heard Jake's voice and froze.

'I remember having a conversation with Shelly about it,' he was saying. 'She said Gary was this big, fun-loving personality but the day of the crash he was acting really weirdly. She said he was upset, like he'd just had some really bad news.'

'Stop it!'

Three faces turned to look at her.

'What's the matter?' Jake said. 'It's not a secret that something was off that day. Why else would he get pissed before he flew that plane? See, what I'm wondering is this. What if it's connected?'

Clodagh looked at Adam and saw he was uncomfortable with the way the conversation was going. She waited for him to tell Jake how insensitive he was being but, true to form, Adam let Jake carry on talking.

'Ooh,' Felicity said, joining in, 'maybe someone spiked his drink and Nick was killed because he worked out who it was? They were friends, right? So maybe Nick knew what had happened but he never told anyone.'

Clodagh felt nauseous and dizzy. Scared she was going to throw up or faint, she pulled out a chair and sat down. Even though the last thing she wanted to do was sit out here with the rest of them.

'Are you okay?' Adam asked. 'You look really pale.'

Clodagh took a sip of water before slamming the glass down on the table. 'Hardly a surprise. Can you imagine what it's like, listening to all of you talking about the crash as if it's a TV drama and you're trying to work out the plot? None of you were there that day, so none of you can understand what it was like. How fucking terrible and terrifying and utterly devastating it is to be involved in something like that.'

'We get it,' Jake said. 'Course we do. But you've got to accept that people are going to be talking about it, Clodagh. I mean, no one knows how Gary got away with flying that plane while under the influence. I reckon it was vodka. Most other drinks, they make your breath stink. Not vodka, though.' He winked at Felicity. 'Might have to start drinking it myself the next time you have a go at me for drinking.'

'Let's talk about something else,' Adam said. 'Felicity, why don't you tell us how your audition for *Love Hotel* went?'

As Felicity prattled on about some pointless reality TV show she'd auditioned for, Clodagh's mind travelled back to the day of the crash. The memory was clearer now. Just a tiny sliver of a bigger picture, but it was a start. Standing at the sink in the Ladies' toilet, splashing cold water on her hot face. Cheeks burning because she was angry. The sound of a toilet flushing, then a cubicle door opening. And nothing after that.

Her glass was empty. She stood up to get more water, ignoring Jake's request to bring out another bottle of wine. While she refilled her glass, she focused on that memory, searching the dark empty spaces of her brain for what had come before. At first, it was the same as always. No matter how hard she tried, the memories wouldn't come. And then, just as she was about to give up, it happened. A single memory. On its own, it didn't make much sense but she already knew it was important.

Being single is your choice.

Vivienne's voice, dismissive and mocking, the way she could be when someone dared to criticise her.

You've chosen the moral high ground instead of happiness.

'Clodagh?'

She might have remembered more, but Adam had come into the kitchen, his voice dragging her back from the past.

'Give me a second,' she said. But it was too late. The rest of the memory wasn't there. All she had was that moment: Vivienne's mocking voice and the rage inside her, ready to explode.

Thirty

'This thing is becoming bigger than we'd anticipated, wouldn't you say?'

Sharon took a swig of coffee and continued speaking without waiting for Ade or Rachel to answer. Which Rachel, certainly, had no intention of doing. She'd worked with Sharon Spalding long enough to know that her boss only ever asked questions that were rhetorical. Because when you went through life believing you knew more about everything than everyone else around you, there was never a need for any other sorts of questions.

'First we have Nick Gilbert,' Sharon said. 'Murdered on the private beach of the Blue Dolphin, a fancy seafront villa in Seaford. Which in itself is a bit of a PR disaster for our local tourism industry, but we'll park that particular piece of shit for now. A few days later, the woman Gilbert was dating is also killed. Her body discovered by the same person who discovered her boyfriend's body.

'Meanwhile, this whole story has the tabloid editors rubbing their hands in glee. Because not only was Nick Gilbert a celebrity chef who had achieved quite an impressive level of fame, considering the fact he was remarkably talentless and without charm, he also happened to be one of only eight people to survive a plane crash at Gatwick airport five years earlier. Add to this, one of our suspects is Adam Murray, also in the public eye because of some maudlin memoir he's written about his wife, a famous actress who died in the crash.'

'And the work he's done for the Vivienne Kinsella Foundation,' Ade said.

'Indeed.' Sharon rewarded the interruption with a smile in Ade's direction. Even though Rachel was pretty sure that's not the reaction she would have got if she'd dared speak up when Sharon was in full flow.

'It's good news we've managed to track down Robbie Fuson,' Sharon continued. 'Although I can tell you both now, I'm not buying his story about buggering off to Spain for no reason except he wanted a break.'

Sharon glowered at her two subordinates, sitting on the opposite side of the table.

'I invited you in this evening to get an update on your investigation and hear your thoughts on how close we are to a conviction. Believe me, there are many other ways I'd rather spend my Saturday than sitting here looking at both of you. But as you can imagine, there's a lot of pressure from above to get this tied up as quickly as possible. I've promised the boss we'll have a substantial update for her by Tuesday morning. I assume that won't be problematic?'

How substantial was 'substantial', Rachel wanted to ask. Instead, she returned Sharon's smile and said, 'I think we can manage that.'

'Good. In that case, perhaps you'd both like to share your thinking to date? Who are our main suspects? How close are we to getting a conviction?'

'Hair samples from both bodies have been sent for testing,' Rachel said. 'Lots of fingerprints in Tara's apartment, but none matching any of our suspects. Apart from Clodagh's on the door, but we already know she found the body. Her train got into London at 3:55 p.m. We've got

CCTV footage of her coming through the ticket barriers. Pathologist thinks Tara was killed earlier than that, so we know Clodagh's not the killer. The floor in Tara's apartment is tiled. No carpet. CSI found the outline of several shoes on the tiles. Some are Tara's, it's not clear where the others came from. The floor hadn't been cleaned in several weeks so it was pretty dirty, which hasn't helped. We're still checking CCTV from the area around the apartment building. So far, Clodagh's the only one of our suspects we've picked up.

'We know Adam Murray met someone for coffee in St James's Park on Wednesday morning. His alibi has confirmed he was with Adam until just after midday. Adam had a meeting with his TV company at 3 p.m. He says he browsed some bookshops until then.'

'What about Simon and his wife?' Sharon asked.

'We interviewed Simon on Wednesday afternoon,' Ade said. 'It's possible he could have got to London and back prior to that. But he swears that the first time he left his house that day was when he came here for his interview. We've spoken to his neighbours and none of them remember seeing him leaving the house in the morning. But he could have slipped out without being noticed. Bella's work has a security system and we've already checked that. She entered the building at eight a.m. Wednesday morning and didn't leave again until eight p.m. that evening.'

'A long day,' Sharon said.

Something snagged at the back of Rachel's mind when Sharon said this. But she couldn't focus on it now, because Sharon was looking at her expectantly.

'She's a computer technician at Max-Roysten,' Rachel said. 'They're rolling out a new IT system and she's putting in a lot of long hours, apparently.'

'Ivan Babić?' Sharon asked.

'Still no sign of him,' Ade said. 'As far as we know, he hasn't left the country. There's no record of him going through any border controls.'

'Well that's something, I suppose. Anything else?'

'Right now,' Rachel said, deciding she might as well go for it, 'my gut is telling me there's something dodgy going on with Adam Murray's foundation.'

Sharon's right eyebrow shot up, while her left remained exactly as it was.

'Your gut, Rachel? Since when did we run a police investigation based on our feelings? I know we're all meant to be woke these days, but I'd like to think our investigations are still based on good old-fashioned police work. Or have I missed the memo that says we need to start feeling instead of thinking?'

'It's more than a feeling,' Rachel said. 'I spoke to Robbie Fuson this morning. He's hiding something. So is Adam Murray.'

'Hiding what?'

'The real reason Robbie walked away from the foundation,' Rachel said. 'Something happened but, for some reason, both Adam and Robbie are trying to keep it hidden. I think Ivan Babić might be connected to it all and that's why he's disappeared.'

'Well, you'd better make it your business to find out,' Sharon said. 'The clock's ticking on this one.'

Not for the first time, Rachel wished Ed was here. He had a way of handling Sharon that she had no hope of mastering. In the past, Ed had led these meetings with their boss. Rachel had only chipped in when necessary, happy to let Ed do most of the talking. Ed, who would have told her she was right to trust her instinct but would never have been stupid enough to use the word 'gut' in Sharon's presence.

'We need to look at Clodagh Kinsella again,' Sharon said. 'She discovered both bodies and, right before they were killed, both victims contacted her to say they needed to speak to her. You already told me you think she's hiding something, Rachel. I want you to find out what that is. Go back and check the timings again for when she arrived at London Bridge the day Tara was killed. If we can get Clodagh near Tara's apartment at the time of death, then we've got the start of a good case.'

Rachel didn't chip in to say that her gut was also telling her – loudly and repeatedly – that Clodagh wasn't their killer. She knew Ade had her doubts too, but she was glad, for Ade's sake, that she had also chosen not to share these doubts with the boss.

'The problem is,' Sharon said, 'I can't see her being physically capable of overpowering Nick Gilbert and moving his body after he'd been killed. Clodagh's... what? Five three at the most? And skinny as a rake to boot. What is it with these men who like their trophy wives without any flesh on their bones? No. Don't answer that. I already know the answer. They're scared of a real woman, that's what it is. Scared of breasts and flesh and all the things that make women so bloody brilliant.' Sharon crossed her arms over her own substantial breasts. 'Anyway, my point is this. If Clodagh killed Nick, she didn't do it by herself.'

Rachel was about to ask if Sharon thought Adam could be their killer, when the mobile phone on Sharon's desk started to ring. Answering the call, Sharon listened to the speaker at the other end, a smile playing at the corners of her mouth.

'Sounds wonderful, darling. I'll be with you in half an hour.'

Hanging up, she rubbed her hands together.

'Sorry to break up our little party, but there's a hot tub and a bottle of Moët waiting for me back at home. You two can scoot away for now. I'm treating myself to a long weekend, so I'll see you back here on Tuesday morning.'

Outside the office, Rachel breathed a sigh of relief.

'Thank goodness that's over,' she said.

'She's not that bad,' Ade said. 'You just need to know how to handle her.'

'And how's that?'

'You act like you're scared of her,' Ade said.

'I wonder why.'

'She can see it and she feeds off it,' Ade said. 'It's like a game to her. And that is not a game you want to get caught up in, Rach.'

The fact that her much younger partner was right did nothing to improve Rachel's mood. She felt the way she always felt after an encounter with her boss, useless and incompetent. Somehow, Ed and Ade had a way of letting the worst of Sharon wash over them without leaving a mark. Unlike Rachel, who absorbed every barb and snide remark, taking it all too personally. In Sharon's own words, Rachel would have to 'grow a pair' if she was to have any chance of clambering up the slippery, predominantly male, career ladder within the Sussex Police Force.

Thirty-one

Day Eight

Clodagh swam across the still sea, her mind clear of everything except the sensation of being here, in the water. The flashes of sunlight captured in the drops of sea that splashed through the air as she moved; the blue sky above her and the cool water all around her. When her muscles grew tired, she rolled over onto her back and floated, the sun warm on her face, her body loose and relaxed. It was easy, here on the water, to push the events of last week to the furthest corner of her mind. But she couldn't stay here forever. Sooner or later, she would have to go back onto the beach, get dressed, go back home and face real life once more.

The others had all been in bed when she left. She'd sneaked out of the house, through the back gate to avoid the journalists, and walked into the village where she'd called a taxi to take her to the beach. She'd been here for two hours so far, putting off going home for as long as possible. Yesterday evening had been excruciating as Jake had got progressively drunker and more offensive. Clodagh didn't particularly like Felicity, but she had no idea how the woman put up with such a boor of a man.

Eventually, when she couldn't put it off any longer, she got dressed and ordered a taxi. Wanting to bypass the paparazzi again, she asked the driver to drop her in the village. From here, she followed the path through the woods to the gate at the back of the house.

'Clodagh!' Jake's voice greeted her as she entered the garden. 'We thought you'd done a runner.'

He was at the table in the garden with Felicity. A selection of mugs and yesterday's newspapers lay scattered around them.

'You missed my special scrambled eggs,' Jake said, standing up and planting a wet kiss on her cheek before she could stop him. He reeked of last night's booze, the stink lingering after he'd pulled away.

'Adam's in the kitchen tidying up,' Jake said, pressing a glass of sparkling water into Clodagh's hand. 'Why don't you go in and let him know you're safe? He's been worrying about you.'

He took her elbow and manoeuvred her through the open doorway into the kitchen, patting her arm before leaving her alone with Adam.

'You're back, then.' Adam looked up from loading the dishwasher, his face pinched and white. 'Where have you been?'

'I went to the beach,' Clodagh said, wondering why she felt the need to defend herself. 'I felt like a swim and you were all still asleep.'

'You could have sent me a text or something,' Adam said. 'I was worried about you.'

'Sorry,' she said, even though she wasn't sure what she was apologising for. 'You want a hand tidying up?'

'It's fine,' Adam said. 'You sit down and chill out.'

He crossed the kitchen and put his arms around her.

'I know last night wasn't easy for you. Thank you for putting up with us all. I owe you one.'

She let her body relax into his, wishing they could spend the day alone. She still hadn't told him about the pregnancy. Maybe she'd do that later, after Jake and Felicity had gone home. No matter how hard she tried, she couldn't imagine that this time next year, she would be a mother. The idea excited and terrified her. Most of the time, she was doing her best not to think of it at all. Very soon, she'd have to start making some big decisions – like whether she was going to continue living with Adam or not. And, if they didn't stay together, she would have to come up with some sort of plan for where she was going to live and what she was going to do with the rest of her life.

'Are you okay?' Adam asked, his breath warm against the top of her head.

'I am now,' she said. 'You were right about last night. It wasn't much fun. At least they're going home today.'

'Not until after lunch, I'm afraid. We're going for a walk and I've booked a table at the Plough after that.'

Clodagh groaned.

'You're right, Adam. You really do owe me.'

The next few hours were painless enough. Clodagh always loved getting out for a walk and, once Felicity stopped going on about her struggling acting career, she was actually quite good company.

Adam had booked an outside table at the pub and they sat in the glorious sunshine, taking in the views across the rolling hills of the South Downs. Jake drank a bottle of rosé over lunch. By the time they'd finished eating, he was slurring his words.

'At least he'll fall asleep in the car,' Felicity said, as the men went to the bar to order more drinks. 'Which is better than putting up with his nonsense the whole way back to London.'

'Let's hope it has the same effect on Adam,' Clodagh said. Adam hadn't drunk as much wine as Jake but he was quite tipsy as well. She had no intention of telling him about the baby while he was in this state. Hopefully he would sober up in time for them to talk later.

'It's so lovely here,' Felicity said. 'You're lucky to live in such a beautiful place.'

Clodagh couldn't disagree. Streaks of golden sunshine criss-crossed the yellow grass in the field behind the pub, and long shadows stretched across the garden to the trees at the end.

'More wine,' Jake boomed, coming back outside. 'Who's for a top-up?'

He refilled his own glass and put the bottle on the table. Not even bothering, Clodagh noted sourly, to see if anyone else might like some too. The man was a pig.

'To you.' Jake tilted his glass in Adam's direction, before taking a drink. 'And your career in TV.' He winked at Clodagh. 'This new show is going to be huge. I hope you're ready for it.'

'It's not going to affect me very much,' Clodagh said.

'That's where you're wrong.' Jake wagged his finger at her, in that patronising way of his. 'The press are going to be almost as interested in you as Adam. Sister of the famous Vivienne Kinsella, now living with her husband. It's a tabloid editor's wet dream.'

'Jesus, Jake.' Adam shook his head. 'Do you always have to be so crude?'

'She ought to know what to expect,' Jake said. 'It'll be worse if they find out it was Clodagh who discovered the two bodies. You think the cops will manage to keep that information from them?'

'The cops?' Clodagh said.

'Pigs, fuzz, whatever you want to call them.' Jake waved his hand in the air, dismissively. 'You reckon that chubby detective is up to leading a case like this? I tried to have a chat with her the other day, I wanted her to do something about all the press intrusion. Stupid bint made it clear she wasn't going to help. She needs to pull her finger out and get this mess sorted out ASAP. Because the longer this business drags on, the more problematic it'll be for us.'

'Problematic how?' Clodagh had curled her hands into fists, digging her fingernails into her palms to stop herself shouting at him to get the fuck out of her life forever.

'You serious?' Jake scowled at her. 'This whole mess is bad for us, Clodagh. Adam here is on the brink of the biggest moment in his career. If that woman can't clear this up quickly, there's a real risk Trident will pull out of the deal. If that happens, we are royally stuffed, my dear.'

'No you're not,' Clodagh said. 'Even if the TV show doesn't happen, Adam has already made more money than most people could ever dream of. He'll carry on writing his books and doing his talks. Life will go on for us. Unlike Nick and Tara. Whether you like it or not, what happened to them isn't just some little problem for you or Adam. Someone killed them. Probably someone we know. And finding out who did that, and why they did it, might take time but so what? Isn't it more important that the police find the killer than what this might mean for some stupid TV show?'

'You think it's stupid?' Jake laughed, a low, nasty sound. 'Well isn't that something? Your boyfriend's career's just a joke to you now, is that it?'

'That's enough, Jake.' Adam spoke calmly but Clodagh heard the edge of anger in his voice. She hoped Jake had heard it too. 'Clodagh's right. It doesn't matter if this messes up our plans for the show.'

'That's not what you said earlier this week,' Jake said. 'The last time we spoke, I got the distinct impression you were extremely concerned about the impact all of this was going to have on the deal with Trident.'

'I was wrong,' Adam said. 'I've been wrong about a whole load of stuff recently.'

Clodagh wanted to ask what he meant by that, but she wasn't about to do that in front of Jake.

'Robbie wasn't your fault,' Jake said.

'Robbie?' Clodagh looked from Adam to Jake, then back at Adam again. 'What does he mean by that, Adam?'

'Nothing.'

'Bullshit.' A flare of anger rose up inside her. 'What the hell is wrong with you both? You're like a pair of stupid kids with your secrets and your plotting. Tell me what Jake is talking about, or I swear to God I will pack my bags and never come back.'

Something came up behind the anger now. Fear. Because the last Clodagh had heard, Adam didn't know why Robbie had stepped down from the charity.

'What happened with Robbie?' she said.

'You know what happened,' Jake said. 'He stepped down from his role and disappeared.'

'No,' Clodagh said. 'There's more to it than that. What is it you're not telling me? Adam? Talk to me.'

'There's nothing to say,' Adam said, but he wouldn't look at her when he spoke and she knew he was lying.

Clodagh stood up, unable to bear being with them a moment longer.

‘Hey,’ Adam said, as she walked off. ‘Where are you going?’

‘As far away from here as I can.’ She looked at Felicity. ‘Good luck getting home with him. I don’t envy you.’

She heard Adam shouting at her to come back, but she didn’t turn around. She barely knew who he was these days, she realised. He had lied about the argument he’d had with Nick, he hadn’t told her that Tara had called him the day she was killed, and he sure as hell wasn’t telling her the full story about why Robbie Fuson had disappeared.

Thirty-two

Grace and Rachel were heading out for a walk when the phone call came through.

'Sorry,' Rachel said, pulling the phone out of her bag. 'I've got to take this. It's work.'

'I thought today was your day off?' Grace's voice made it clear she didn't approve of this last-minute interruption to their plans.

Rachel didn't bother explaining that there was no such thing as a day off during a murder investigation. She was officially not working today, but she had told Ade to call her immediately if any new information came in.

'Ivan Babić called the station this morning asking to speak to you,' Ade said. 'I've told him it will have to be an under caution interview. He's agreed to that.'

'Any idea where he's been for the last week?'

'Staying with friends in Chichester, apparently. I've arranged to meet him at the Custody Suite at Brighton an hour from now. Duty solicitor's on his way over and I'm about to head across. I can get Sam to do it with me if you can't come in.'

'No, it's fine.' Rachel kept her eyes averted from Grace, not wanting to see the expression on her face as she told Ade she'd be into work within an hour. 'The sooner we get this over and done with the better.'

'Don't tell me,' Grace said, as Rachel hung up. 'You've got to go into work.'

'I'm sorry,' Rachel said, although her apology did nothing to shift the look of irritation on Grace's face. A look, Rachel realised, she was seeing more and more these days. 'You know how much I'd been looking forward to spending some time together.'

'I don't know that, actually.'

'What do you mean? Grace, I love you. Obviously I'd rather be with you instead of going into work. But something's come up and I don't have a choice.'

Grace sighed.

'I understand that, Rachel. But it's not easy always taking second place to your job. How would you feel if I kept cancelling our plans at the last moment because of work commitments?'

Rachel didn't point out that their jobs were so different that was unlikely to happen. Grace designed her own clothes and sold them from her shop in Lewes, which focused exclusively on clothes made by local fashion designers.

'I'd probably feel the same way,' Rachel said, choosing a more diplomatic response. 'And if I could get out of this, I would.'

'What's happened?'

'One of our key suspects has been missing all week. He's turned up at the station this morning, saying he wants to talk to me.'

Grace's expression softened.

'Who am I to stand in the way of justice? At least let me make you some tea and a sandwich before you go. It's Sunday. The canteen at work won't be open and all the sandwich shops will be closed. If I don't make you something decent you'll end up eating a processed sandwich from the Co-op.' Grace was already walking towards the kitchen and Rachel had to bite back a stab of selfish impatience. She was keen to get going right away, but it would be churlish to refuse Grace's offer. Especially when Grace herself was being anything but churlish.

'I'll make a sandwich for Ade too,' Grace said. 'She's pescatarian, right? I'll do a tuna sandwich for her, and chicken for you.'

Grace looked over her shoulder, smiling. In that moment, Rachel wanted nothing more than to grab hold of this amazing woman and never let her go. She followed Grace into the kitchen and wrapped her arms around her.

'You're incredible,' she said, 'I hope you know that.'

'I do.' Grace kissed her. For a moment, the two women melted into each other until Rachel reluctantly pulled back.

'I really wish I could stay here with you.'

'No you don't.' Grace smacked Rachel's arm, smiling. 'You can't wait to get into work and find out where that suspect of yours has been hiding all week. In fact, right now you're wishing I hadn't suggested making sandwiches so you could already be on the road.'

'That's not true.'

'Oh, I think it is. I know you better than you realise, Lewis. You'd do well not to forget that.'

Forty minutes later, Rachel and Ade were sitting across from Ivan Babić and the duty solicitor in one of the special interview rooms in the Custody Suite at Brighton. He was looking decidedly less chirpy than the last time she'd spoken to him. Last Sunday, despite expressing his shock at Nick's murder, Ivan hadn't seemed too affected by the incident. Today, his demeanour was subdued and anxious.

'Where the hell have you been, Ivan?' Rachel asked, once she'd set the tape up and recorded the time, date and the names of the people in the room.

'I was staying with friends in Chichester,' he said. 'I woke up Monday morning and knew I couldn't face work. So I called in sick, packed my bags and off I went.'

'We've been trying to contact you all week,' Rachel said. 'Why didn't you return any of our calls?'

'I forgot to take my phone.'

'You really expect us to believe that?'

'What can I say?' Ivan shrugged. 'It's the truth.'

Rachel didn't believe him, but she knew there was no point trying to prove it. If they needed to, they could track the mobile signal and find out exactly where his phone had been this last week. For now, she had more important questions to ask him.

'What about when you heard that Tara had been killed?' she asked. 'Surely that would have made you want to call one of your friends and find out what was happening?'

'I already told you,' he said. 'I didn't have my phone and all my numbers are on that.'

'There are plenty of other ways to contact people,' Ade said. 'If you'd wanted to get in touch with Clodagh or one of the others, you could have done it through social media.'

'I went to Chichester to get away, not to speak to people.'

'Where were you on Wednesday?' Rachel asked.

'The day Tara was killed? I was in Chichester.'

'Is there anyone who can confirm that?'

'Sure. I spent most of the day in a gay bar called The Box. You can ask the barman, Mikey.'

'They'll have CCTV as well,' Rachel said. 'If you're lying we'll be able to find out pretty quickly.'

'I'm not lying,' Ivan said. 'You can check all the cameras you want to. You'll see I was falling around drunk most of that day. Most other days during the week as well.'

'I can understand the need to get away,' Ade said, softly. 'It must feel a little too much sometimes, being part of that group of people.'

'I care for all of them,' Ivan said, 'but you are right. There are times when things get too intense and I can't stand it. After Nicky was killed, I knew there would be so much gossip and talk and going back over everything that had happened. I couldn't stand to be part of it so I ran away.' He gave a sad smile. 'Running away is something I am very good at.'

'So you haven't spoken to any of the other survivors during the last few days?' Ade said.

Ivan hesitated, as if he suspected she might be trying to catch him out. But he must have decided she was on the level, because after a moment he shook his head.

'None of them.'

'Not even Robbie?' Ade said.

Ivan had been slumped down in his chair but, at the mention of Robbie's name, he straightened up, his body tense, like an animal sensing danger.

'Why would I speak to Robbie?'

'Because he's your friend,' Rachel said. 'We know that immediately prior to the Air Euro crash, Robbie went on holiday to the same village you were living in. What happened? Did you guys hook up while you were there? Is that why you came back to England with him? And while you're giving me the answers to those questions, you can tell me why none of the other survivors – not even your good friend Clodagh – knew about the two of you.'

'There is no me and Robbie,' Ivan said. 'And I promise you, we are not friends.'

'I don't believe you.'

The duty solicitor scowled at Rachel.

'I hope you have something to back this up, detective?'

'It's okay,' Ivan said quietly. 'I am telling the truth. It was a holiday romance, nothing more than that. At the end of it, he asked me to come to London with him and I thought why the hell not? I'd already been in Crete for six months and I was ready to visit somewhere new. I had never been to London. I thought maybe I'd spend a week with Robbie then move on somewhere else. I never intended it to be serious. He wasn't my type. Too self-obsessed and stuck up.

'But after the crash, he acted like we were already a couple. He tried to get me to move into his house, he told me he loved me and I was the best thing that had ever happened to him. And I swear to you that the more he spoke this crazy stuff, the more I knew I'd made a mistake ever coming to England with him in the first place. In the end, we had a huge row and I told him I didn't want to see him again. He was angry and upset. It was horrible, but I thought it's okay because I won't see him any more. But of course I did, because we had the investigation and there were meetings with lawyers and then Adam started organising events for all the people affected by the crash. Robbie called me before the first meeting and told me he didn't want anyone to know about us.'

'Why would he do that?' Ade asked.

'I think he was embarrassed. By then, he had started working with Adam to set up the foundation. I think he wanted to start from fresh, without people talking about him behind his back.'

'But you were on the plane together,' Ade said. 'Surely people would have seen you?'

'Most of the people who saw us are dead,' Ivan said. 'Even if anyone remembered us, they would have assumed we were just sitting together. No big deal.'

'So you did what he asked,' Ade said.

'Of course. It was a relief, if I'm honest. I wanted to forget all about it just as much as he did.'

Rachel pretended to straighten the papers on her desk, as she thought about what to ask next.

'Except neither of you really forgot about it,' she said, 'did you?'

'I don't understand,' Ivan said.

'I think you understand perfectly.' Rachel smiled. 'Two days ago, we managed to find Robbie. He's been in Spain all this time, living with his mother. But you don't need me to tell you this, because you already know.'

Ivan opened his mouth to speak, but she held her hand up.

'Before you say anything, let me finish. The Spanish police spoke to Robbie on Saturday. I think he called you after that to tell you we'd found him. You can deny it if you want to, but we can always check your phone records. It would be better if you simply told us the truth.'

'You're right,' Ivan said, after a moment. 'I've known all along that Robbie was in Spain.'

'Why didn't you tell anyone? Adam and the others have been worried about him.'

Ivan looked at his solicitor.

'Do I have to answer that?'

'No. Detectives, unless you can prove that Robbie Fuson being in Spain has anything to do with your murder investigation, my client won't be answering any further questions about his relationship with Mr Fuson.'

Rachel had been a detective long enough to know a dead end when she hit one. She could, if she really wanted to, continue to push Ivan about why he hadn't told anyone that Robbie was in Spain. But the solicitor was right. For now, Rachel couldn't see how Robbie's disappearing act had anything to do with why Nick Gilbert and Tara Coleman had been murdered.

Thirty-three

After she left the pub, Clodagh went back to the house, grabbed some water and headed up the downs. She walked for hours, not wanting to return home until she was certain Jake and Felicity had gone. She did a circular walk, starting at the house and crossing over the downs to Rodmell, the beautiful village where Virginia and Leonard Woolf had lived. At the river Ouse, where the author had tragically taken her own life, Clodagh sat on the grass and took a moment to enjoy the simple pleasure of sitting by water on a warm summer's day. The sky was blue and cloudless, light reflecting off the river as it made its journey south towards Newhaven where it flowed into the English Channel. Soothed by the beautiful setting, the storm of emotions raging through her gradually abated.

She hadn't expected to fall in love with Sussex. When she first moved here from London, she missed the city. She still did, some days. But there was something about this place that tugged at her, made her feel grounded in a way she hadn't for a long time. The soft curves of the South Downs, the white chalk cliffs, the grey-stoned shingle beaches and the strange stillness of the little country churchyards with their Commonwealth graves and squat, flint-stoned churches. She couldn't imagine ever not wanting to live here.

She lay on her back, her face turned towards the sun and closed her eyes. As her body relaxed, she became aware of the different sounds around her. The whooshing of feathers on air when a bird flew past, the gurgling of the river and the whispering sound of the soft breeze as it rustled through the reeds on the banks of the river. All of it brutally interrupted when her phone started to ring.

She sat up and looked at the screen. If it was Adam she wasn't going to answer. But it wasn't Adam calling her.

'Hey, lady. You have been missing me?'

Clodagh took two deep breaths before answering.

'Where are you?'

'Back home in Worthing. You want to come and visit? I am bored out of my head today. There's nothing to do, and I spent most of my day at the police station answering their stupid questions. Now, I am alone and I'm twiddling my fingers wondering how to spend the rest of the day without going crazy out of my head. And then I think, I know what I'll do. I'll call my good friend Clodagh and tell her she needs to come and see me. So, you'll come?'

'Why didn't you tell me you knew Robbie before the crash?'

'Ah lady, that is a long story and not one to have over the phone. It's why I need to see you.'

'I can't come today,' she said. 'It's too late and I've got something I need to do here. Where have you been, Ivan? I've been worried sick about you. You can't just disappear like that and not reply to my texts or phone calls.'

'Ah, but I am back now and desperate to see my favourite Irish girl. If you can't do today, how about tomorrow?'

'Maybe.'

'Maybe means yes. You can come to Worthing?'

'What time?'

'The afternoon. I'm going out tonight and will need my beauty sleep tomorrow morning.'

'And when I see you, you'll tell me what's been going on with you?'

'Cross my heart and hope to die.'

She told him she'd text him to tell him what time she would be arriving in Worthing. When she hung up, her heart felt lighter. She'd spent most of this week worrying about him. At least now, she knew he was okay. And hopefully tomorrow she would get to the bottom of why he'd lied to her.

It was getting dark by the time she arrived back at the house. She checked the driveway before going inside, relieved when she saw Felicity's car was no longer there. With Jake and Felicity out of the way, she could finally sit down and have a proper chat with Adam. She hated when they argued and she was sure, now they'd both had some time to cool down, they would be able to work things out.

'Hello?' she opened the front door and stepped inside.

No answer from Adam.

Taking off her trainers and putting them on the rack the way Adam liked, she went into the kitchen. There was no sign of him in here, either. She checked the time. Almost eight o'clock. She felt the first trickle of fear then. Images of Nick and Tara blasted through her brain and she couldn't get rid of them.

She went around the house, searching each room, terrified of what she might find. But there was no Adam anywhere. She thought back to earlier, trying to remember if he'd said anything about going up to London this evening. No. He didn't have any meetings in London tomorrow until the afternoon. They'd spoken about it and had planned to go for a walk together in the morning before he got the train to London. So where the hell was he?

She tried calling him but his phone was either switched off or he was somewhere without a signal, because her calls went straight to voicemail. By nine thirty, there was still no sign of him and Clodagh was growing increasingly frantic. Not knowing what else to do, she found the business card she'd been given by DI Lewis and called the mobile number written on that.

'It's Clodagh Kinsella,' she said, when the detective answered. 'I'm sorry to call so late, but I'm worried about Adam. I don't know where he is.'

'Okay,' Rachel said. 'I'm sure there's nothing to worry about, but I can understand it must be hard not to after everything that's happened. When was the last time you saw him?'

'Around lunchtime today,' Clodagh said. 'We had a row.'

'Ah, I see.'

'No, you don't see. I was the one who walked off, not Adam. I was angry so I went for a walk to get away from him. Well, not just him. Jake too. But when I came back earlier this evening, Adam wasn't here.'

'What about Jake?'

'He's not here, either. Nor is Felicity. They stayed here last night and were due to go back to London later today.'

'Is it possible Adam went with them?'

'Maybe.' Clodagh hadn't thought of that. Because surely, if Adam had decided to go to London, he'd have left her a note or sent her a text. It would be too cruel to leave without telling her, especially given what had happened over the last week.

'You've tried calling Adam, I assume?'

'I keep getting his voicemail. I've left a message but, so far, he hasn't called me back.'

'What about Jake? Can you call him and ask if he knows where Adam might be?'

'Good idea,' Clodagh said. 'I'll do that right away.'

'Let me know how you get on,' Rachel said. 'If Jake doesn't know where Adam is, I'll come over right away.'

'Thank you,' Clodagh said. 'I really appreciate it.'

As she dialled Jake's number, she ran back upstairs to the bedroom. Adam always used the same Samsonite suitcase for his overnight trips. If he was in London, the suitcase would be with him.

'Clodagh?' Felicity's voice, not Jake's. Because Jake was probably sleeping off all the alcohol he'd consumed this weekend, Clodagh realised.

'Hi Felicity, I'm really sorry to bother you. I'm trying to get hold of Adam. I don't suppose you know where he is?'

'I told him he should let you know,' Felicity said. 'I would have called you myself, but I don't have your number and Jake's phone has a security code so I couldn't call you from that.'

While she was speaking, Clodagh pulled open Adam's wardrobe. Sure enough, the suitcase was gone.

'Where is he?' she said.

'He came back to London with us. He was pretty upset after you left. He insisted we go straight back to the house so he could pack. He said he wanted to be gone before you came home so he wouldn't have to see you.'

Clodagh thanked Felicity and ended the call. She sat on the bed, a feeling of intense sadness washing through her, as she stared at the empty space in the wardrobe where Adam's suitcase should have been.

Thirty-four

Day Nine

When Clodagh woke up the following morning, she still hadn't heard from Adam. Normally, when he was away from her he sent regular texts, asking how she was. So far, she hadn't heard a word since she'd left him at the pub yesterday afternoon. She kept going back over the argument, trying to work out what she'd done that could have made him angry enough to go to London without telling her. Several times, she'd almost called him to apologise for walking out during lunch. Each time, she'd stopped herself. She'd had every right to be annoyed and if Adam didn't like that, then that was his problem.

After lunch, she got the train to Worthing. Ivan was waiting on the other side of the ticket barrier when her train pulled into the station. As she walked towards him, she felt nervous and excited, pleased to see him but worried about what she was going to find out about him.

'You're late,' he said, grabbing her into a big, Ivan bearhug that filled her with warmth and left her gasping for air.

'Blame Southern Rail,' she said, extracting herself from his arms.

'But late is better than never at all.' He beamed down at her and she was so glad to see him she knew she'd already forgiven him for lying to her.

'I've missed you,' she said.

'Of course you have. Now, let's get out of here and go for drinks. We can go to the beach. There's no sunshine today, which is good because you know how much I hate the sunshine. It's too hot and it causes cancer of the skin. I don't understand this devotion people have to a big ball of fire in the sky. It makes no sense to me.'

He continued speaking as he linked arms with Clodagh and led her through the town centre to the beach. There were several bars near the seafront and Ivan insisted on checking each one thoroughly before he finally selected one to his liking.

'Last month I slept with the guy working there.' He pointed to one of the bars he'd just rejected. 'The most boring person I've ever met. This place is better because the staff here don't know me. I'll let you get the drinks, lady, while I find us a table.'

Obediently, Clodagh went to the bar and ordered a pint of lager and a glass of water.

'You're not drinking?' Ivan asked, as she put the drinks down on the table he had selected. 'What is wrong with you? Are you sick? Oh shit, no. I can see it in your face. You are pregnant. How long? Poor darling, you're pregnant and you're not happy about it. Not one little bit. Come on, lady. Sit down and tell me why this makes you unhappy. A baby is a blessing. Or maybe it isn't. How would I know? Either way, you have choices, yes? If you don't want this baby, you don't have to have it. That's why we have abortion. So that women who don't want to have children aren't forced to do it. Your tummy is not even showing yet, so you have plenty time to make your mind up. This is not a big problem, lady. I promise you.'

When Clodagh tried to speak, she started crying instead. Big, gulping sobs that were as much about Nick and Tara and Simon and Bella and everyone else who had ever died or lost someone they loved, as they were about her pregnancy. Beside her, Ivan patiently sipped his pint and waited for her to pull herself together.

'Sorry,' she said, when she was finally able to get a word out. 'It's been one hell of a week, you know?'

'That's what you call an understatement, no?'

Clodagh snorted.

'I suppose so. Oh God, Ivan. How did you guess? I haven't told a soul yet. Not even Adam knows. But all you have to do is take one look at me and you guessed right away. How are you able to do that?'

'My sister, Lucija, she has three children. Each time she got pregnant she looked just like you in the early days.'

'How do I look exactly?'

'Haunted.' Ivan took a self-satisfied sip of lager, clearly pleased with himself.

'Two people I know have died this week,' Clodagh said. 'I discovered both bodies. Don't you think that's why I look haunted?'

'No.' Ivan shook his head. 'You look haunted because of the pregnancy. Unless you're now going to pretend to me that I'm wrong? Which would be a lie, and I don't like it when my friends lie to me.'

'That's a bit rich.'

He scowled at her.

'What do you mean?'

'You know exactly what I mean.'

'Maybe.' He drank some more beer. 'But we won't talk about that yet. First, you must tell me about your baby and what you are planning to do.'

Baby. Clodagh felt a mix of emotions when he said the word. Fear, anxiety. Something else, too. Hope. She'd spent the last few days convincing herself the collection of cells inside her womb were something tiny that she could get rid of whenever she wanted. Except she already knew that wasn't what she wanted.

'I'm going to keep it.'

Ivan nodded, as if he'd already worked that out. Sometimes, Clodagh thought, he seemed to know her better than she knew herself.

'I would do the same.' He grinned. 'Although I'm pretty sure getting pregnant isn't something I'll ever need to worry about. Of course you'll keep it. After so much loss, how could you do anything else?'

And there it was. The reason she'd known all along she would keep this baby. Because these cells inside her already had parts of her dead family in them. This person, whoever she or he became, might look like her mother, have her father's quirky sense of humour or her sister's sharp tongue. Clodagh was being given back something she thought she'd lost forever. She couldn't pass up a gift like that.

She looked out at the sea, grey and solid today, and thought about what brilliant grandparents her mother and father would have been. And she remembered the promise she'd made in the dark months following the crash. She'd promised she would be grateful for every single day of life she was given, that she would never take anything for granted ever again. She would do this for her dead family who'd had that privilege taken from them too early.

She'd spectacularly failed to deliver on that promise. When she'd moved in with Adam, all she'd wanted was consistency and predictability. She'd made the safest choice she possibly could. But life was, by its very nature, messy and unpredictable. Living it to the full meant taking risks. It was time to start taking those risks. Not just for herself, but for this person she hadn't yet met but she knew would change her life forever.

She looked at Ivan.

'Why did you lie to me?'

He took another sip from his glass before answering.

'I didn't plan on lying,' he said. 'Especially not to you.'

'What happened?'

He looked at her for a long time without answering.

'If I said I would rather not speak about it, how would that be?'

'I'm not sure,' she said honestly.

'Even if I swear to you, on my poor sick mother's life, that whatever happened between me and Robbie, it is over and is has nothing to do with these two murders?'

'I can't make you tell me something you don't want to,' Clodagh said. 'I wouldn't want to do that. But friends tell each other stuff, even sometimes stuff they don't want to talk about. I thought we were friends?'

'Oh we are. You are my closest friend in the entire universe, lady.'

'So what's going on with you?' Clodagh said. 'First you disappear without telling me where you've gone, and then I have to find out from the police that you and Robbie are much closer than I ever realised.'

'I left because I'm very good at running away when things get difficult.' Ivan smiled. 'It's my superpower. But I came back because you are my friend and I don't want to lose you.'

'And Robbie?'

'Robbie is nothing. We had a fling on holiday. It didn't work out and he got upset. That's it.'

Clodagh knew there was more, but she wasn't going to push him if he didn't want to talk about it.

'You know, if it wasn't for you,' Ivan said. 'I don't think I'd have got through that first year.'

'Really?'

'You remember that first meeting we had?'

Three months after the crash, Adam had arranged a series of meetings just for the survivors. The first time they'd all been together since that terrible day.

'I almost didn't go,' Ivan said. 'In that first year, especially, I was struggling so badly with my mental health and my anxiety. There were many times I thought about ending my life, because it seemed so much better than forcing myself to keep going day after day after day.'

This was so unlike the version of Ivan that Clodagh had in her head, she didn't know what to say.

'There was a couple sitting directly in front of me on the plane,' Ivan said. 'I remember they were so excited about coming to London. Izabella and Georgy. I overheard her speaking and realised she was Croatian so I introduced myself. She told me Georgy was her fiancé and they were going to London for his cousin's wedding.

'Afterwards, I couldn't stop thinking about them. I read everything I could about them, trying to understand how they died while I had somehow survived. Izabella was twenty-three years old. She came from Rijeka, a city I know very well. She was her parents' only child. Georgy was a philosophy student from Chania. He had three sisters and a brother. He met Izabella when she came to Crete for a holiday with her friends the previous summer.

They fell in love and she had moved to Crete so they could be together.'

Clodagh knew the couple he was talking about. Izabella Bošnjak and Georgy Doukas. The names of those who had died were burned onto her brain, impossible to forget. Those poor souls whose screams still invaded her dreams, night after night, year after miserable year.

'I had a problem with crying,' Ivan said. 'For the first year after the crash, I would cry like a baby for no reason. When I started crying, I couldn't stop. I never knew what would trigger me. It could be anything. One day I went to the shop and they had no garlic. I cried for twenty-four hours straight after that. Because of garlic. What do you think of that? No, don't answer. The thing is, the day we all met up I was very, very tired of crying. I did not want to cry in front of all you people, because others had suffered and lost much more than I had. It felt selfish and wrong of me to cry. But even though it wasn't what I wanted, I could feel it building up in me. And then you came over and sat down beside me and started speaking and, somehow, you made me feel better.'

'Really? What did I say?'

Ivan smiled.

'You told me your memory was gone but your sense of taste had survived and you had never seen a shirt as ugly as the one I was wearing that day.'

Clodagh put a hand over her mouth.

'I really said that?'

'You sure did. It made me laugh. I'd started to think I might never laugh again. And right then I thought, this is someone I want to get to know better.'

He drained his glass and stood up. 'I am going to buy another pint of lager, because Homer Simpson was right when he said alcohol is the answer to all of life's problems.'

'He also said it was the cause, didn't he?'

But Ivan had already disappeared into the bar. While she waited, Clodagh took her phone out and typed Georgy and Izabella's names into her internet browser. Here on the beach, the internet was slow and it took a moment for their photos to appear. When they'd finally loaded, she saw a couple in their early twenties, arms around each other, laughing into the camera. She searched their faces, not sure what she was looking for but wanting something so desperately her chest ached from the longing. But whatever she was looking for, it wasn't there. After a moment, she put the phone away again, and looked at the sea, trying to empty her mind of everything but the sound of the waves crunching over the shingle.

Thirty-five

Adam was at home when Clodagh got back from Worthing, full of apologies for leaving yesterday without telling her where he'd gone.

'I've been under a huge amount of pressure,' he said. 'And something snapped yesterday when you walked out on me. I was so angry, I couldn't think straight. I knew I didn't want another row, but I knew the mood I was in that's what would happen. So I packed my bag and asked Felicity to drive me to London.'

'You switched your phone off,' Clodagh said. 'I had no idea where you were. Don't you think I've been through enough this last week without spending a night worrying about you? It was such a selfish thing to do, Adam.'

'I know. It was appalling and I'm so sorry. You got my messages today, didn't you?'

She'd been so angry she'd switched her phone off soon after breakfast. When she'd switched it back on after she'd left Ivan, she'd had ten new text messages and eight new voice messages. All from Adam.

'A load of messages doesn't make everything okay,' she said.

'I know. Let me make it up to you? I picked up some food at Borough Market earlier. I'm hoping you'll let me cook dinner and we can have a proper chat. I know it was difficult at the weekend with Jake and Felicity. I'm sorry about that too. You were completely right. I should have cancelled them. I wasn't thinking.'

He sounded sincere and Clodagh decided it was easier to let it go instead of forcing another argument. She was willing to accept that he'd acted out of character and he wouldn't pull a stunt like that again.

'Let's both agree to put yesterday behind us,' she said.

'Oh, thank goodness.' He pulled her close and wrapped his arms around her. 'You've no idea how pleased I am to hear that. Now tell me, how was your day? Where have you been this afternoon?'

'I went to see Ivan.'

'He's back then?' Adam stepped back and looked down at her. 'Where's he been hiding all this time then?'

'Visiting friends apparently,' Clodagh said. Then, not wanting to talk about Ivan, 'You look tired, Adam. Why don't you let me cook for a change?'

'You know it's easier when I do it. Remember the pesto you tried to make?'

Two months ago and he was still talking about it, she thought with a stab of irritation. She'd attempted to make homemade pesto sauce and completely forgotten to add the basil, one of the key ingredients.

'Fine, then,' she said, too tired to argue any further. 'You cook. But first you need to tell me the truth about Robbie.'

'I know.'

'Why did he step down from the foundation?'

'Because I didn't give him any choice,' Adam said. 'Five months ago, we were audited by the Charity Commission. It's something we're obliged to do and I've never worried about it. I had complete faith in Robbie. But this year, the audit questioned some payments made. There was an invoice that had been paid twice and some gift aid claims that we couldn't immediately reconcile. When I asked Robbie about it, he reassured me there was nothing to worry about and he would sort it out. And he did. He rectified all the queries and the Charity Commission was satisfied. But I wasn't. I went back over the accounts since we'd started. I discovered Robbie had been stealing from the foundation for years.'

Several questions crowded around Clodagh's mind. She picked the most obvious one and asked that first.

'Why?'

All the survivors, including Clodagh and Robbie, had received substantial compensation payouts from the airline company after the crash.

'It took three years for all the money to come through,' Adam said. 'When I confronted him, he said he'd planned to pay it back as soon as he could. But by the time he got the money, he was already in over his head. He'd stolen more than he could ever pay back. It's my fault. I wasn't vigilant enough. I assumed Robbie cared about our work as much as I do. Turns out, all he cared about was lining his own pockets.'

Adam explained how, when he'd discovered what Robbie had been doing, he'd told him that he wasn't to have any further contact with Adam, the charity or any of the other survivors.

'He agreed to all of it. I said we'd tell people he'd stepped down for personal reasons. And I warned him if he ever tried to contact any member of the group, I would tell the police what he'd done. I think he knew he was lucky I'd decided not to take it any further.'

'But he committed a serious crime,' Clodagh said. 'How could you not tell the police about it? Think of all those people who've donated money over the years. And what about the victims' families? That money was for them, not Robbie.'

'I couldn't risk it,' Adam said. 'If we went public, it would destroy our reputation.'

'The foundation's reputation or your own?'

Clodagh's chest ached with disappointment and regret. This person talking to her was so different from the Adam she'd fallen in love with. The decision he'd made, to protect his reputation instead of doing the right thing, was unforgivable.

'You don't understand, Clodagh. This isn't about me. It's about doing what's right for all the people the foundation has worked so hard to help. If word gets out about what Robbie's done, people will stop donating. How will that help anyone?'

She didn't answer, because she didn't trust herself to speak without screaming. Whatever he said, she knew the decision not to go to the police was as much about protecting Adam as it was about looking out for anyone else. The other thing she knew, which made this whole situation even worse, was that Jake Harris had played a key part in the decision to cover up Robbie's crime.

'It's easy for you,' Adam said, his voice hardening. 'You don't have to make difficult decisions like this. You, and everyone else, get the benefits from the foundation's work without having to do anything. But I've worked my guts out to get us to where we are today. I've dedicated my life to doing everything I can for all the people whose lives were devastated by that terrible tragedy. I will not let one person's bad decision-making ruin all of that.'

'What if it turns out that Robbie's the murderer?'

'Don't be ridiculous.'

'You think I'm the one who's being ridiculous? You and Robbie had a huge falling out. You cut him off from the charity and all of the people he's got to know over the last few years. Is that not a good enough reason for revenge?'

'If he was out to get revenge,' Adam said, 'he would have killed me, not Nick and Tara. Besides, he's in Spain not the UK. He took the money and ran. Literally. He's used our money to buy his little bolthole in Andalucía, leaving me to clear up the mess he's left behind.'

Clodagh stood up, needing to put some distance between them.

'I'm going upstairs,' she said. 'I can't be with you right now. I'll sleep in the spare room tonight.'

'Clodagh, don't be like that,' Adam called after her. 'Please come back so we can talk about it.'

It occurred to her that this was the second time she'd walked away from him in as many days. She knew that didn't bode well for the future of their relationship, but the alternative – to go back into the kitchen and listen to his excuses – wasn't an option. It was still early, not yet eight o'clock. Too early to go to bed, but she didn't know what else to do.

She brushed her teeth before going into the spare bedroom. Crossing the floor, she felt the loose floorboard move beneath her foot, and remembered the USB drive, still sitting in the drawer by her bed. She thought about going into the bedroom and bringing it in here, but realised she was being paranoid. Whatever she thought of Adam, he wasn't the sort of person to look through Clodagh's things behind her back.

She got undressed and climbed into bed. There was a book on the bedside table, a crime novel by a writer

Clodagh had never heard of. Felicity or Jake must have been reading it and left it here by mistake. Clodagh picked up the book and tried reading it, but her mind kept drifting. After she'd read the same page several times, and still couldn't remember what was on it, she put the book down again.

It was impossible to concentrate when all she could think about was Adam. He'd lied to her. Three months pretending he didn't know why Robbie had left the foundation. It made her wonder what else he might have lied about too.

Thirty-six

Rachel sat opposite Ade in the beer garden of the Swan and took a long sip of lager.

'God, I needed that.' She nodded at Ade's glass of Sauvignon Blanc. 'How's the wine?'

'Great. I'm planning on having several more before the end of the night.' Ade nodded over at the bar, where Sam was standing with a group of other detectives. 'I'm feeling lucky tonight, Rach.'

'Well be careful,' Rachel said. 'It's never a good idea to mix work and private life.'

'I'm always careful. Besides, after all that driving earlier, I deserve to let my hair down a bit.'

They'd spent the morning in London, speaking to the financial director of Nick's restaurant chain. Stephanie Kelly had confirmed what Ade and Rachel already knew. Nick's business was in trouble. The last restaurant he'd opened was losing money at a pace that wasn't sustainable, Stephanie had explained. More than once, she'd urged Nick to slow down.

'He needed to focus on improving the restaurants we already had,' she'd said. 'Not opening any more. But he wouldn't listen. He had a few big successes and he let that go to his head. Thought he had the Midas touch when it came to the restaurant industry. But there's no such thing in this business. His restaurants had got some shitty reviews lately. We were haemorrhaging money. It was a disaster.'

After coming back from London, Rachel and Ade had spent the afternoon going back over all the evidence they'd gathered on both murders, looking for something that would push the investigation forward. The hair samples from Tara's dress they'd sent off for analysis had come back. They weren't a match for any of the people who'd been at the villa. Which either meant the killer was not part of the group at the villa or, the hair sample was unconnected with Tara's murder. Rachel still had a pair of officers trawling through the CCTV footage in the area around Tara's apartment building. So far, they hadn't found anything that helped identify Tara's killer.

'I've been thinking,' Ade said.

'Uh-oh.'

'Ha, very funny. Hear me out first before you mock, Rach. I'd like to go back and look at what each of the survivors was doing in the lead-up to the crash. It's like – how can I explain it? – like there's a piece missing, you know? Robbie and Ivan met on holiday, yet for some reason they kept this secret from the others. Then there's Clodagh and Nick. There's something she's not telling us about that holiday. I don't care what she says, I don't believe it's a coincidence she ended up staying at the same resort as Nick.'

'We've already been over this,' Rachel said. 'If they were seeing each other, why would they keep it a secret? They were both single back then. They would have had no reason to hide their relationship.'

'What if it was Vivienne?' Ade said. 'She would have known Nick too. Her and Clodagh used to eat at his restaurant together. If she was having an affair, she'd have wanted that kept quiet, right?'

Rachel took another sip of her drink as she considered this.

'That would mean her marriage to Adam wasn't the perfect union he's always claimed it was.'

'You think he made it up?' Ade said.

'I'm not sure. I bought his book when it first came out. Dreadful rubbish. Couldn't get past the first few chapters. Now I know why. Because he was describing a fairy tale, wasn't he?'

'What do you mean?'

'It's so obvious,' Rachel said, 'I don't know why it's taken me this long to work it out. Adam and Vivienne. It's probably not relevant to the investigation. Except it shows Adam Murray up as a liar. But people tell lies all the time. It doesn't make them murderers.'

'You do know I've no idea what you're on about?'

'Sorry.' Rachel smiled. 'The first chapter of Adam's book is all about how perfect his marriage was. It's nauseating. And it's a lie. I love my wife. I think she's the most remarkable, beautiful woman I've ever met. I know, deep inside me, that if I wasn't with Grace I wouldn't be with anyone else. Before I met her, I never believed in the idea of having a soulmate. But that's exactly what she is. My soulmate. I love her, and I will never stop loving her. Even if I went home tonight and she said she wanted a divorce, I would continue to love her for the rest of my life. I know how pathetically romantic that sounds, but it's true.'

'So you're saying… What?' Ade frowned. 'That it's okay for you to have a soulmate, but not Adam Murray?'

'No.' Rachel shook her head. 'I'm saying that even when someone is your soulmate, marriage is still hard work. I'm sure it helped that Vivienne and Adam had money. She was loaded, right? But even with lots of money, all relationships have their ups and downs. It's no secret that Vivienne Kinsella was quite a tricky personality. They must have had rows and arguments and times when they wanted to throttle each other. Just like every other couple in the world. Yet none of that is ever mentioned. His so-called memoir is nothing of the sort. It's a work of fiction.'

'Let me think this one through,' Ade said. 'You're saying Vivienne Kinsella was having an affair, and her husband knew about it but after she died he lied about the state of their marriage. Why would he do that?'

'Look at how successful he's been,' Rachel said. 'Before his wife died, he was a struggling writer. These days he's a celebrity about to launch his own TV show. There are a lot of people who'd think that's worth lying about.'

'Even if what you're saying is true,' Ade said. 'How is it relevant to this investigation?'

'Let's assume for a second that Adam lied,' Rachel said. 'And let's also assume that Vivienne and Nick were having an affair. We know Nick was drunk and obnoxious the night he was killed. What if he decided to tell Adam about the affair?'

'And Adam flipped and killed him.' Ade nodded. 'It's possible. Although it doesn't explain why Nick kept quiet about the affair for so long. I mean, if he didn't say anything for five years why say something now?'

'He was having money problems,' Rachel said. 'Maybe he threatened to blackmail Adam, expose his marriage as a sham unless Adam gave him some money.'

Ade drained her glass of wine and stood up.

'I'll look into it first thing tomorrow. See what I can find out.' She nodded at Rachel's glass. 'You ready for another?'

'Go on then.' As Rachel drank some more of her lager, another thought occurred to her. 'Sharon asked us to do a bit more digging into Clodagh. Can I leave that to you too?'

'Sure thing.'

'In fact,' Rachel said. 'Take another look at all of them. See what you can find about their time in Crete, up to and including the day of the crash. Take another look at Nick's friends too – Gary and the other two. Get Sam to help you.'

'I guess I'd better go and tell him now.' Ade smiled. 'Let him know he needs to get an early night. See you later, Rach.'

'What about my drink?' Rachel called, but it was pointless. Ade was already gone, moving across the beer garden with the speed and focus of a wild animal getting ready to pounce on its prey.

Thirty-seven

Day Ten

The following morning, Clodagh woke with a sense of purpose she hadn't felt for a while. She wasn't going to sit back and wait for things to happen. She was going to speak with Adam and tell him he didn't have a choice: either he called the police and told them about Robbie, or she would do it. But when she went downstairs, instead of finding Adam there was a handwritten note on the kitchen table informing her he'd gone for a bike ride and would be out for most of the day. Which, Clodagh realised with a stab of irritation, was his way of avoiding another difficult conversation.

Not prepared to sit around all day waiting for him to come home, she called Ivan and asked if he wanted to meet up later. He told her he was working this morning but he'd be free from lunchtime. They arranged to meet later that afternoon at his home in Worthing.

Clodagh was walking down the hill to the train station on the outskirts of the village, when she got a phone call from her neurologist, Charlie Simpson.

'Thanks for calling me back,' Clodagh said. She'd called Charlie's office the other day, left a message with his secretary saying she needed to speak to him.

'I've been following the news,' Charlie said. 'This can't be an easy time for you. How are you holding up?'

'Not too bad, considering.'

'We're not due another check-up until October,' Charlie said. 'Has something specific happened that's worrying you? Apart from the rather obvious fact that two people close to you have been killed.'

'I remembered something that happened at the airport,' Clodagh said. 'But it's a single memory that has no context. I want to know what I can do to remember the rest of it.'

'We've spoken about this,' Charlie said. 'It's not something you can force. You need to find a way of accepting some of those memories may never come back, Clodagh.'

'They're the final hours I spent with my sister before she died. It seems too cruel that I'll never remember what that was like.'

'It is cruel,' Charlie said. 'I wish there was something I could tell you that would make it less so. But there isn't.'

'What if I've forgotten something important?' Clodagh said.

'Like what?'

'Two people who were on the plane with me have been killed. Maybe they were killed because of something that happened that day.'

'Have you spoken about this with Rapinder?' Charlie asked, referring to the counsellor Clodagh had been seeing before she left London.

'I don't see her any more,' Clodagh said.

'Well maybe you should schedule some sessions. It sounds like you're giving too much weight to a few lost hours. I know it's difficult not being able to remember everything that happened that day, but it's like I've said before, it would be far healthier to accept your situation instead of trying to force your brain to do something it can't do. Being involved in a plane crash is a uniquely horrific and traumatic experience. There's a reason your brain has shut down those memories. It's trying to protect you.'

'If that's the case, why do I still dream about it?'

'I'm a neurologist,' Charlie said. 'Not a psychologist. That's why you need to speak to Rapinder. I really think you should give her a call.'

Clodagh promised she would call her counsellor, although she had no intention of doing that any time soon. Her problem wasn't an inability to accept the inevitable; it was an inability to remember. The last thing she needed was someone else telling her that acceptance was her only option.

She arrived at Worthing an hour before she was due at Ivan's, which meant she had time for a swim in the sea first. The sunny weather meant lots of people had had the same idea. The seafront was buzzing. Families on holiday, day trippers down from London, groups of teenagers and elderly couples strolling slowly along the promenade. All of them taking advantage of the endless miles of beach that never seemed busy, no matter how many people were around.

Clodagh had come prepared, wearing her swimsuit under her dress. She walked to the area east of the pier, with its imposing town houses and the East Beach studios. This area, home for Worthing's growing community of artists and craftspeople, was her favourite part of the town.

Walking down to the beach, she pulled the dress over her head and, leaving her bag, shoes and dress on the shingle, she ran over the stones and into the sea. A brief shock of cold before her body adjusted and then she was swimming through the glass-flat water.

She had always loved swimming. As she'd gradually recovered from the crash, swimming had become an important part of her recovery. After moving to Sussex, she discovered that swimming in the sea was far better than any pool. There was something about the colours – the sharpness of the blue sea and sky against the white and grey shingle beach, the way the drops of water caught the light as she swam through it – that made this place feel magical.

Later, she lay on the beach, drying in the sun and wondering what she'd do this evening if Adam still refused to tell the police about Robbie. She couldn't stay with him if he didn't do what was right. Maybe this latest revelation was the trigger she needed to move on. The problem was, she didn't know where or what she was meant to move on *to.* Her old life in London was finished. She hadn't worked since the crash. Her friends and colleagues had all moved forward with their lives, while Clodagh had remained stuck in this limbo.

She couldn't stay in Bramhurst if she split up with Adam. The village was tiny and the prospect of bumping into him each time she went outside wasn't an option. The coast was where she felt most at home these days. Maybe that was the answer. She could buy a little place in Worthing and raise her baby by the sea. The more she thought about it, the idea of setting up home here, with Ivan close by, started to feel less like an idea and more like a plan.

Ivan lived in a small, terraced cottage on a quiet street close to the beach. When Clodagh rang his doorbell, there was no answer. She pulled out her phone to call him, when she noticed the front door was slightly ajar. Pushing it open wider, she stepped into his hallway and called his name. Nothing. The sitting room door, on her left, was closed. She could see down the hallway into the tiny kitchen at the back of the house. There was no one in there, either.

But she could hear voices coming from upstairs. As she climbed the stairs, the voices became clearer. A man and a woman, something strangely familiar about the woman's voice.

There were three doors at the top of the stairs. The bathroom door and the door to the spare bedroom were both open. But the door to Ivan's room, at the end of the corridor, was closed. The voices were coming from there.

She moved down the corridor, the woman's voice growing clearer as Clodagh drew nearer to the closed door. Fear caught at the back of her throat. It was like being back in Tara's apartment building. Walking along a corridor, knowing something bad was waiting for her on the other side of that closed door. The urge to turn around and run away was powerful, but nothing compared to the need to get into that room.

She twisted the handle and pushed open the door. The woman was still speaking. The lilting rhythms of her voice as familiar as when Clodagh had last heard her speak, over five years ago. She stepped into the room and there she was, on the other side of the room, every detail of her face as perfect and full of life as Clodagh remembered it. Her dead sister, Vivienne.

Thirty-eight

Clodagh didn't know how long she'd been standing there, before she was able to speak. The shock of seeing her sister's face, and hearing her voice, had sent her mind spinning out of control. Different explanations came and went, nonc of them making any sense. Time travel, insanity, an alternative universe. Extracts from old episodes of Doctor Who, a programme she and Vivienne had both loved. Until suddenly, through the haze of confusion, she understood.

Vivienne wasn't actually here, in the room. She was on the large flatscreen TV that occupied most of one wall in the small bedroom. Gradually, Clodagh realised she recognised the film too. *Second Chances*, a below average rom-com that had been more successful than it deserved to be.

It was Vivienne's last film before she'd turned her back on acting to marry Adam. Why had she done that? The question had never occurred to Clodagh before. Now it had, she couldn't stop thinking about it. Vivienne had worked hard for her success. She'd loved the lifestyle that being rich and famous brought her. Yet she'd given it all up. For what? No matter how much Vivienne had loved Adam, no one had forced her to choose between him and her career. If she'd wanted to, she could have had both. Or so Clodagh had always assumed.

'What are you doing standing inside my bedroom? Are trying to give me a heart attack?'

Ivan's voice made her jump. She swung around and saw him standing at the top of the stairs, frowning as he looked at her.

'Ivan...' She gestured to the TV screen in the bedroom.

'Ah yes.' He grimaced. 'Not a good movie, I'm afraid. I started to watch it, but after half an hour I became so bored I went to the shop to buy chocolate. Because chocolate is the only thing that works when I am feeling the way I feel today. Well, chocolate or wine. But I decided that to drink wine would not be a good idea, because wine will make me drunk and tomorrow I will have a hangover, which will make me feel worse than I already feel. Plus, you cannot drink because of the baby and drinking wine by myself is not fun.' He held up two bars of Toblerone. 'So I chose chocolate instead. I didn't mean to be rude about the film, by the way. But really it's stupid. She is supposed to want to give that guy a second chance when he's such a dick. He's not even good looking. If he was, then maybe I could understand.'

'Ivan, please stop talking.'

Thankfully, he shut his mouth.

'Why were you watching that film?'

'I wanted to see what all the fuss was about.'

'Excuse me?'

'Vivienne. Everyone always says she was so beautiful and such a talented actress and her death was so tragic. As if it is sadder that she died than everyone else who died because she was famous and they were not. It's true, she was a very good actress, even if that movie is not so good. And yes, she was beautiful. But more beautiful than you?

No. I don't think that and I hope you don't think it, either. You look tired. Is everything okay?'

'I'm not sure. I need to talk to someone.'

'Well then, you came to the right place. But not up here. My bedroom is very untidy. We'll drink tea in the garden and eat chocolate and you can tell Uncle Ivan what has put that worry frown on your pretty face. Come.'

They sat in his courtyard garden, drinking the herbal tea he insisted on making 'because caffeine is not good for the baby' and eating chunks of Toblerone, while Clodagh told him about Robbie stealing money from the charity. When she'd finished speaking, Ivan was unnaturally quiet.

'You knew?' she asked incredulously.

'No.' He shook his head. 'I did not know about the money. I swear to you. But I knew Robbie was in trouble. He came to see me before he left. He told me he needed to get away. He said he was leaving the following day and he wouldn't be coming back. He'd had enough of life in England, he said. He was moving to Spain, and he wanted me to come with him. He begged me and it was difficult to say no because he was in such a strange mood.'

'Is that why you disappeared last week?' Clodagh said. 'Because you knew the police would ask questions about where he was and you didn't want to tell them?'

Ivan broke off another chunk of Toblerone and put it in his mouth.

'Maybe,' he said eventually.

'Maybe nothing. Ivan, I'm getting sick of people bull-shitting me. What else are you not telling me?'

'I knew he was running away from something,' Ivan said. 'I didn't buy his bullshit about being sick of life in England. But when I pushed him to tell me the truth, he shut down. After Nicky died, I called Robbie to tell him what had happened. I didn't want him to hear about it from anyone else. And he begged me not to tell the police where he was. I didn't want to lie so I thought it would be easier if I hid for a little while. I have a friend who runs a bar in Chichester, so I went to stay with him for a few days until things calmed down.'

'Except they didn't calm down,' Clodagh said.

'Robbie called me on Sunday morning,' Ivan said. 'He was upset because the police had tracked him down. He thought I'd told them where he was. It wasn't me, but that didn't stop him shouting at me as if I had betrayed him. The phone call made me angry so I decided to come back and tell the police everything I knew.'

'I wish you'd told me,' Clodagh said.

'Yes.' Ivan smiled. 'Me too, lady.'

'You think I should tell the police?' she asked.

'Of course,' Ivan said. 'What Robbie did is terrible. But before you do that, you need to ask yourself a question. Are you using this as an excuse to have an argument with Adam so you can break up with him? Or are you doing it because you really think it's the right thing to do?'

'Because it's the right thing to do,' Clodagh said. 'How can you even ask that question?'

'You've told him about the baby?'

'Not yet. I haven't had a chance.'

'I think that is probably nonsense,' Ivan said.

'And I think you should stop sticking your nose into my business.'

'If you don't want my nose in your business, why did you come here today?'

Good point. Clodagh broke off some more Toblerone and chewed it angrily.

'Lady, listen to me. That baby in your tummy isn't going to go away. You are very soon going to have to make some important decisions. You can't make those decisions without speaking to Adam. Tell me I'm wrong and I will close my mouth and not say another word to you about your business.'

'You're not wrong,' Clodagh said. 'Unfortunately.'

'So, what are you going to do?'

'Tell him, I guess.' Clodagh groaned. 'Oh God. Why is being a grown-up so bloody difficult?'

'Well, you know that the alternative to being a grown-up is a lot worse. The sooner you speak to Adam, the better. Then you'll be able to make plans. What about a doctor? Have you seen one yet? You'll need a midwife and proper care during your pregnancy. This is a very special time for you and your little baby.'

A seagull swooped down and landed on the garden wall. He stared at Ivan and Clodagh for a few seconds, before opening his beak and screeching furiously at them.

'That bastard is here all the time,' Ivan said. 'He hates me. I want to hate him back, but it is impossible to hate a bird with that much attitude. If he was a man, I'd be in love with him.'

'How do you know it's the same bird each time?'

'Look at him! He's completely unique. I would recognise him anywhere.'

Clodagh didn't believe that, but she liked the idea of a stroppy seagull keeping an eye on her friend so she stayed quiet.

'I remember seeing you at the airport,' Ivan said suddenly. 'That bird has reminded me. You were very angry with somebody.'

'Who?' Clodagh put her cup down on the table, her heart pounding. The memory of the rage she'd felt that day came back to her. A burning anger as she'd stared at her reflection in the Ladies' toilets.

'I don't know,' Ivan said. 'I saw you as you approached the boarding desk. I was waiting the other side to go outside onto plane. You came charging down the corridor like a woman being chased by fire. And your face was red and scrunched up like you wanted to kill somebody.'

You should never have married him.

'Vivienne,' she said. 'I was angry with Vivienne.'

The knowledge was like a light coming on inside her head. She could picture, in vivid detail, the incident Ivan was describing. The final boarding call had been announced. Clodagh was running, scared she'd miss the plane. Vivienne was running behind her, calling Clodagh's name. Clodagh remembered swinging around to tell Vivienne to go away and leave her alone, and saying those words:

You should never have married him.

An idea was starting to form. A slow understanding of why she'd said that to her sister. Other memories from the holiday all coming together to tell a very different story of what had happened that week in Crete.

She'd spent most of the holiday by herself. Vivienne always had an excuse for not joining her – claiming she preferred to eat in the hotel restaurant instead of the beachside taverna, or telling Clodagh she was too tired to come for a walk or go for a swim in the clear blue sea. Heaping lies upon lies, knowing she'd get away with it because she always did.

Since her sister's death, Clodagh had pushed the difficult aspects of her sister's personality to the back of her mind. But sitting here in Ivan's garden with the warm sun on her face and the white seagull staring down at her, Clodagh let herself remember. The truth was Vivienne had been a consummate liar who had never thought twice about hiding the truth to get what she wanted.

Thirty-nine

By the time Clodagh got back home, it was after seven in the evening. As she walked into the house, she was assailed by the smell of sizzling meat and spices. Adam was clearly back from his bike ride.

'There you are,' he said, coming out of the kitchen to greet her. 'I was starting to think I'd be eating dinner by myself.'

'Sorry,' she said, kicking off her sandals. 'I didn't mean to be home so late.'

'You could have called,' he said, crossing the hallway to pick up her sandals and put them on the shoe rack before she had a chance to do it herself. 'It's difficult cooking when I don't know what time you'll be back.'

'I didn't know you'd be back,' she said, biting down her irritation as she watched him lining up all the shoes.

'I only went out for a cycle,' he said. 'I've been home for ages. I was hoping to have a proper chat this afternoon, but you weren't here.'

She walked into the kitchen to get a glass of water. The heavy scent of cooked meat was stronger in here. She would have preferred a salad, but she could see from the array of dishes on the hob that Adam had clearly gone to a lot of effort. It seemed rude to tell him she didn't want to eat what he'd cooked.

'Lamb kebabs and a Greek salad, with homemade pitta bread. I was starting to worry the lamb would be over-cooked, but you've arrived home just in time. I've set the table in the garden if you want to go outside and sit down.'

'You don't need a hand in the kitchen?'

'It's all under control.' He smiled, and her frustration started to fade.

They had to find a better way to be together. The stress and anxiety they were both feeling was placing enormous pressure on their relationship.

'Adam, we need to talk.'

'I know. But let's do it over dinner, okay? Go and sit down. I'll pour a glass of wine and bring it out to you.'

'No wine for me,' she said, 'it's too hot. I'll get some water instead.'

He frowned but didn't say anything. She wondered if he had already guessed she was pregnant. She'd never been a heavy drinker, but she normally had a glass of wine with her evening meal. The idea that he'd worked it out but hadn't pushed her to talk about it until she was ready, was sweet.

Despite her reservations about eating meat the food was amazing. As it always was when Adam cooked. Clodagh knew he preferred his own cooking to the meals she prepared and, although this sometimes irritated her, mostly she was happy to let him take control of what they ate. The days he wasn't in London, he spent hours in the kitchen preparing delicious, complicated meals that Clodagh could never imagine making herself. Eating them was another matter. She didn't have weighing scales but she guessed she must have put on at least half a stone since moving in with him. If she wasn't careful, she would be the size of a house by the time she was nine months pregnant.

'I wanted to apologise,' Adam said, as they ate. 'You were completely right about Robbie. I should have told the police as soon as I found out Nick had been murdered.'

'You mean that?'

Relief washed through her. She had been dreading revisiting this and having another row.

'The truth is, I've known all along I needed to tell them. Hearing you say the same thing last night put me on the defensive. You made me realise what an ass I'd been. I was angry with myself so I lashed out at you instead. Do you think you can forgive me?'

'Of course,' Clodagh said. 'What happened with Robbie must have been terrible for you. I just wish you'd spoken to me about it, Adam.'

Her mind jumped back to three months earlier, when she'd first started to question whether moving here had been the right thing to do. Almost overnight, Adam became secretive and tetchy, showing a side of himself she'd never seen before and wasn't sure she liked. It was good to finally understand there'd been a reason for his strange behaviour. Although she didn't like the idea that he'd been hiding such a big secret from her. She might not be a world expert on romance, but she knew enough to understand that wasn't how a relationship was meant to work.

'I should have told you what was going on,' Adam said. 'But at the time, my head was all over the place. I felt betrayed by what Robbie had done and confused about the best way to deal with it. I didn't want to involve you in something so horrible. I was trying to protect you, that's all.'

'I've told you a thousand times, I don't need protecting.'

'I can't help it,' he said. 'You're so important to me, the thought of anything bad ever happening to you… I can't bear to think about it. Maybe losing Viv has made me like this. Whatever's behind it, I know I can be a little over-protective but it's only because I love you so very much.'

The food, which had tasted delicious a moment ago, had lost all taste. Clodagh forced down the piece of lamb in her mouth and put down her knife and fork. She had to tell him now that she was having doubts.

'And because I love you,' Adam continued before she could speak. 'I did what you wanted me to. I called Rachel Lewis earlier and told her the real reason Robbie had left.'

'You did? Oh, Adam, that's brilliant. Well done.'

'I should have done it ages ago. Thanks for making me see sense.'

'Does Jake know you've spoken to the police?'

'I haven't told him yet. He's not going to be happy about it. But I don't care. I feel a whole lot better having got it off my chest. In fact, it's made me realise what a distance it's put between you and me. When I was out on the bike, I was reflecting on how I've behaved these last three months. I haven't been myself recently. But I promise that's going to change, Clodagh. Do you think you can give me another chance? Please?'

'I can try,' she said, 'but Adam, we can only be together if you're honest with me. No more secrets, okay?'

'No more secrets, I promise.'

She opened her mouth to tell him about the baby. At the same moment, Adam's phone started to ring. It was inside, on the kitchen table, and he jumped up to answer it.

'I'm expecting a call from Boris, the show's producer. I sent him my outline for the first six episodes earlier today. I'm keen to hear his feedback.'

Clodagh's mouth snapped shut and she nodded for him to go ahead. After he left, she started to tidy away the plates and cutlery. When she went inside, she could hear Adam in the front hall, talking.

'Well you need to sort it, Jake. That's what I'm paying you to do, isn't it?'

She thought about going to check he was okay, then decided against it. He was more than capable of dealing with Jake and probably wouldn't want her interfering. Adam's iPad was on the kitchen worktop. When Clodagh had finished putting everything away, she picked it up and carried it outside. Adam kept a list of his favourite recipes on the iPad. She decided she was going to choose one of those and tell him she was cooking tomorrow evening.

She entered the passcode into the device and the screen lit up. She'd expected to see a recipe for lamb kebabs. Instead, there was a map on the screen with a series of dotted lines showing a route along the map. It took Clodagh a full five seconds to realise the map was of Worthing, and the dotted line tracked the route she'd taken earlier today from the train station to the seafront and, after that, to Ivan's house.

'What are you doing with that?'

Adam was standing in front of her, his body blocking out the sun so the garden suddenly felt dark and cold.

'You're spying on me?' she said.

'Not spying.' He grabbed the iPad from her. 'Making sure you're okay. I installed an app on your new phone so I'd know where you were if you ever got lost.'

'When the hell have I got lost?'

She stood up and took several steps back, putting distance between them.

'Clodagh, I don't think you realise what it's like living with someone with your problems. I do my best to protect you and second guess what you've forgotten or mislaid, but it's bloody hard work. Every single time you leave the house, I worry you're going to get lost and forget where you are. I haven't said anything because I didn't want you to know how worried I've been.'

'Bullshit. Putting that on my phone and not telling me? That's not about looking after me. That's about control, Adam.'

'How can you say that? You know you mean the world to me. I care about you, that's all. Maybe I care too much, but that's hardly a crime, is it?'

She felt sick.

Adam took a step towards her, but she held her hand up.

'Don't come near me.'

'You're being ridiculous.' He sounded irritated. As if she was at fault, she thought bitterly. 'It's not like I installed some secret spyware. Location tracker apps are really common. And let's face it, you haven't exactly been honest about what you've been up to, have you?'

'What's that supposed to mean?'

'Last week. You told me you were here all day. But that was a lie, because you'd spent the afternoon in Brighton. Why on earth would you lie about something like that?'

'It's none of your business where I go during the day.'

Adam threw his hands in the air.

'You know what, Clodagh? I don't have time for this shit now. That was Jake on the phone. The TV company is worried about how this business with the murders is going to affect the show's ratings. If the police don't find the killer soon, this is going to seriously damage me. I could really do with a bit of support at the moment, but I guess that's too much to expect.'

'I've always supported your career,' she said.

'Oh sure. Like the other week when Jake wanted you to come on TV with me? You think that's showing support? Well let me tell you, Clodagh. Your idea of what support looks like and mine are two very different things.'

He started to walk back into the house and she put her hand out to stop him.

'We're not finished talking, Adam.'

'Oh I think we are.'

He pushed her away from him, so hard she staggered back, hitting her hip against the table.

She thought he'd apologise. Instead, he kept walking, as if he hadn't even noticed that he'd hurt her. As she stood in the garden, shaking from head to toe, she heard his phone ringing again.

'Boris,' Adam said, his voice jovial and loud. 'How the hell are you?'

She watched him as he moved around the kitchen, pouring himself a glass of wine and laughing at something Boris said. He must have sensed she was watching him, because he glanced out at her, raised his glass and smiled. Acting for all the world as if everything was fine between them.

Forty

Day Eleven

Wednesday morning, eight thirty. Rachel stood at the front of the Major Incident Room for the morning briefing. This was a chance for everyone involved in the investigation to gather and update the team on their progress, before Rachel allocated tasks for the day ahead.

'Ivan Babić's alibi stands for the time of Tara Coleman's murder,' she said, skimming the notes on her laptop. 'So we can rule him out as a suspect for now.'

A young female officer whose name Rachel could never remember, and was too embarrassed now to ask for again, put her hand up.

'Is he still a suspect for the other murder?'

'He is,' Rachel said, 'although I'm still thinking we're most likely looking for one killer, not two.'

'Is it possible someone's killing off the survivors, one by one?' someone piped up from the back of the room.

'The purpose of this meeting isn't to sit around speculating,' Rachel said. 'We deal with the facts. And right now, the facts we know are this:

'Nick and Tara were both murdered. Any of the people at the villa the night Nick was killed is a suspect for his murder. With the exception of Shelly Clarkson, who left before the murder happened. Shelly also has an iron-clad alibi for when Tara was killed. Ivan Babić and Bella Gilbert too. Ivan was in a bar in Chichester, Bella was at work.

'A forensic analysis of hair samples left at both crime scenes hasn't given us anything we can work on. So our focus for the moment is twofold: checking CCTV footage and ANPR records, and doing a bit more digging into the survivors' backgrounds. We know that Nick was staying at the same resort in Crete as Clodagh and Vivienne. I don't think that's a coincidence, so I want to know why he was there and how well he knew the two sisters. Ade, anything on that yet?'

'I've spoken to Nick's parents,' Ade said, 'and some of the people he was working with back then. They've all said he had plenty of girlfriends, none of them serious. But one person, the restaurant manager at the time of the crash, says Nick had been seeing someone and it seemed to be the real deal. He also said Nick was very secretive about the relationship. Which was very out of character, apparently.'

'We need to find out who she was,' Rachel said. 'If Nick and Vivienne were having an affair, and Adam found out about it, we've got a clear motive.' She looked around the room, her eyes landing on Sam Latimer.

'Sam, anything new on Clodagh?'

'At the time of the crash, she was working as a lawyer in the City,' Sam said. 'I've spoken to her boss from those days. Says Clodagh was hard working, good at her job, popular. She was very private about her famous sister, apparently. The boss got the impression Clodagh and Vivienne weren't that close.'

'What were they doing going on holiday together if they weren't that close?' Rachel said.

'I asked the same question,' Sam said. 'Her boss didn't know. I managed to track down an ex-boyfriend as well. Shane Cross. He was going out with Clodagh until about a year before the crash. He says she left him because she'd met someone else.'

'Who?' Rachel asked.

'Cross couldn't give me a name,' Sam said. 'Just that she started dating some guy who he heard was already married.'

'What if it was Adam Murray?' Rachel said, testing the theory to see what the other people in the room thought about it.

'I don't think so,' Sam said.

'Why not?' Rachel asked.

'Because he never stops going on about how perfect his marriage was,' Sam said. 'He's built his entire career on it.'

'So what would happen,' Rachel said, 'if someone discovered the marriage wasn't as perfect as Murray claimed it was? Worse, what if they found out that Adam Murray was having an affair with his wife's sister?'

'Doesn't make sense,' Sam said. 'I mean, the man was married to Vivienne Kinsella. You ask me, I can't see him risking his marriage to shag the sister. Who, by the way, is pretty enough but not a superstar like Vivenne was.'

'Well then,' Rachel said, after a moment. 'I'm glad no one's asking you. I know you think it's impossible that a man could have an affair when he's married to a famous actress, but let's at least explore the possibility instead of discounting it out of hand. As soon as we're finished here, I want you to get back onto the ex-boyfriend and ask him what he thinks.'

'I've started looking at the rest of the people Nick went to Crete with,' Ade said. 'His three friends – Gary Wakefield, Josh Ward and Owen Williams.'

'And?'

'Josh and Owen were both happily married, as far as I can tell. Nothing to indicate either of them might be having an affair. Gary was divorced, as we know. I spoke to a guy at Air Investigations who was involved in the crash enquiry. His story backs up what Shelly Clarkson told us. There was a ten-hour delay on the way back because of a technical problem with the plane. During that time, the original captain fell ill with food poisoning. So the airline asked Gary to step in. Somehow, he managed to get on the plane without any of the other staff realising he'd been drinking.'

'Any hint of something going on between him and Vivienne Kinsella?' Rachel asked.

'Nothing.'

Rachel sighed. It felt as if they were going round in circles, instead of moving forward.

'If Vivienne was having an affair,' she said, 'it would be good to get some proof. But I don't want us focusing on that at the exclusion of other things. I also need you to speak to the guys looking through the CCTV footage near Tara's apartment building. Ask them how much longer they're going to take.'

Rachel spent the next twenty minutes allocating tasks and deadlines for when things needed to be done. When she was finished, she thanked everyone for their time and told them she'd see them at tomorrow morning's briefing. After that, she connected her laptop into one of the docking stations and started going through her emails.

She'd been working for the best part of an hour when Sam came bouncing up to her, with all the enthusiasm of an over-excited Labrador.

'You were right, Rachel,' he said, coming to a halt in front of them. 'I managed to get through to Shane Cross. Clodagh and Adam go way back. They've been friends since uni days, apparently. Early on in her relationship with Cross, she admitted that she'd been head over heels with Adam Murray for years. Cross said Clodagh never really forgave Vivienne for marrying him.'

'It still doesn't mean Clodagh and Adam had an affair,' Ade said.

'I know that,' Rachel said. 'But it's worth asking them about it, don't you think? Sam, you okay to see if we can get the two of them in for an interview over the next day or so?'

'Sure thing.'

'Good.' Rachel nodded. 'And maybe we can get you sitting in on the interviews as well.'

He looked so happy to be included, Rachel almost forgave him for his misogynistic comments earlier. Almost, but not quite. Because Sam Latimer might be sex on legs, but he was also an arrogant little shit who needed taking down a peg or two.

Forty-one

Rain poured from the sky as Clodagh hurried through the North Laine in Brighton. By the time she found the coffee shop where she'd arranged to meet Bella she was soaked through. Shaking the water off her, she looked around.

'Clodagh! Over here.'

Bella was sitting at a table near the back, half hidden in the shadows. Clodagh weaved her way through the tiny space, shivering. The cool air and dim lighting meant this was probably a great escape from the heat on a sunny day. Today, it felt bleak and unwelcoming.

'I ordered you a cappuccino. Hope that's okay?'

'Thanks.' Clodagh sat down and slid the cup towards her, breathing in the rich aroma of freshly brewed coffee.

'The coffee's great here,' Bella said. 'That's why I chose it. I'm glad you called. I'm not doing great today.'

'You and me both.'

The truth was, she'd barely slept. For the rest of the evening, Adam had acted as if everything was fine between them. He'd drunk more wine and talked incessantly about his concerns over the future of his TV show. He hadn't seemed to notice that Clodagh barely contributed to the conversation, at most giving monosyllabic answers when he asked her a direct question. When he finally stood up and said he was going to bed, she'd smiled and told him she'd be right up. And then she'd waited downstairs for two hours until she was certain he'd be asleep when she went up.

This morning, she'd got up while he was still asleep and left him a note saying she was going to Brighton for a day's shopping and wouldn't be back until later. Before leaving the house, she went online and followed the instructions for erasing the location tracker app from her phone. She'd called Bella on the train and asked if she was free to meet. Bella couldn't meet until the afternoon, which meant Clodagh had spent most of the day wandering around Brighton, trying to stay out of the rain.

'Has something happened?' Bella asked now.

'I had a row with Adam yesterday. I'm upset, that's all.'

Clodagh lifted her cup, was about to take a sip of the coffee when she remembered and put the cup down again.

'It's a bit hot,' she said, when she caught Bella looking at her.

'No.' Bella frowned. 'It's more than that. I know you, Clodagh. You're a coffee fiend. There's no way that coffee's too hot. It's been sitting there for five minutes, at least. And the last time I was at your house? You weren't drinking coffee then, either.'

'I'm pregnant.'

The words were out before she could stop them. The sudden urge to share her good news, especially now when she was feeling so low, had taken her by surprise.

'Oh.'

'It's a bit of a shock,' Clodagh said. 'I mean, we hadn't even been trying for a baby. I've been taking the pill but I missed a few days over the last couple of months. I didn't think it would make much difference, but I was clearly wrong about that.'

She stopped speaking, aware that Bella's reaction wasn't what she'd expected. Then she realised.

'Shit, Bella. I'm sorry. I should have thought before I opened my big mouth.'

'It's okay,' Bella said, clearly not meaning it. Her face was pale and there was a haunted look in her eyes that Clodagh had never seen before.

Clodagh reached out and took Bella's hand.

'I know how hard you and Gary tried for a baby,' she said, recalling the many times Bella had spoken her about her failed IVF attempts before the break-up of her marriage. 'I didn't realise it was something that still bothered you.'

'It will never stop bothering me,' Bella said, pulling her hand away. 'But I've reached a place of acceptance, I guess. Being with Simon helps. Unlike Gary, Simon's never wanted kids so he doesn't see it as some big failure that I'm not able to get pregnant.'

'It's not a failure,' Clodagh said.

'Easy for you to say.' Bella gave a small smile. 'Don't worry. I'm well past the stage of not being able to be happy for my friends when it happens to them. And I'm happy for you. Truly I am. If you're sure it's what you want?'

'I wasn't sure,' Clodagh said, 'not at first. But I've come around to the idea now.'

After last night, she was also starting to wonder if she'd be bringing this baby up by herself.

'Well, we could all do with some good news at the moment. I can't think of anything more exciting than my friend having a baby. Congratulations, Clodagh. I really mean it.'

'Thank you. Anyway, enough about me. How's Simon doing?'

'Not good, if I'm honest. He's in a very dark place and I don't know what I can do to help him. Nick's death hit him really hard. He's trying to be there for his parents, too. Which is adding to the pressure at the moment. They keep asking him to go over everything that happened on Saturday night. I swear, Clodagh, they're acting as if they think Simon could have prevented what happened. It's awful.'

'They're grieving too, remember?' Clodagh said. 'We both know people react differently to grief. The sooner the police find out who killed Nick, the better. Until then, it's difficult to know who to trust, isn't it?'

'Not for me,' Bella said. 'I trust you and Simon. No one else.'

What about Adam? Clodagh wanted to ask but decided not to because she wasn't sure she would like Bella's answer. And right now, she wasn't sure herself how she felt about Adam. His recent angry outbursts had left her wondering what had happened to the man she'd fallen in love with.

'The police haven't released his body yet,' Bella said. 'So we can't even start planning his funeral. I think if we could do that, it would help his parents. Give them something to focus on.'

'Is there anything I can do?'

'No.' Bella smiled. 'But thank you for the offer. When you called earlier, you said you wanted a favour. What do you need?'

'This.' Clodagh opened her bag and took out the memory stick.

She'd decided to find out what was on it. If it had belonged to Vivienne, then she'd hidden it for a reason. Clodagh was hoping whatever was on the stick might help her remember why she'd rowed with Vivienne at the airport.

'A memory stick?' Bella frowned. 'Don't tell me you're using this to back up your files. Haven't you heard of the cloud?'

'I think it was Vivienne's. The problem is, I have no idea what's on it. It doesn't work with my laptop. I called a computer repair shop but they said they couldn't help. And then I remembered you work with computers. So I thought you might be able to help.'

'If it belonged to Vivienne,' Bella said, 'there might be private stuff on there. Things she wouldn't like to you see.'

'I know that.'

'So why not leave it alone?'

'If I tell you, do you swear it won't go any further?'

'Cross my heart.'

'I've got no proof of this,' Clodagh said. 'Not yet. But I've started to wonder if maybe Vivienne was having an affair.'

'Wow,' Bella said, after a moment. 'You know what this means, don't you? If your sister was seeing someone else, then Adam's built his whole career on a lie.'

'That's why you can't say a word,' Clodagh said. 'It's too important. Besides, I might be completely wrong.'

'And if you find something on this memory stick that proves she was having an affair,' Bella said. 'What then?'

'I'm not sure. But I know something happened at the airport the day of the crash. I was angry with Vivienne, but I can't remember why. I'm hoping whatever's on that stick might help me remember.'

'When I said I wanted to know why Gary was drinking that day,' Bella said, 'you told me to let it go. Said I could drive myself crazy trying to work it out. I'm tempted to give you similar advice.'

'I've never been very good at taking my own advice,' Clodagh said.

She thought Bella was going to say no. But after a moment, Bella reached across the table and took the memory stick.

'I'll take a look as soon as I can. But don't blame me if I find something you didn't want to see, okay?'

Clodagh nodded. She was fine with that. Whatever Bella discovered, it was better to know the truth.

Forty-two

It had stopped raining by the time Clodagh left the coffee shop. She said goodbye to Bella and walked up Queen's Road to the train station. The journey back home seemed to take forever. By the time she'd got off the train at Bramhurst, she was ready to collapse onto the sofa and watch crap TV for the rest of the day. Adam was in London today; she wasn't expecting him home until later this evening. But when she got back home, he was already there, sitting at the kitchen table with a face like thunder.

'What the hell is going on with you, Clodagh?' he asked, his voice low and angry. 'I've tried to call you countless times. You've been ignoring my calls on purpose, haven't you? And don't think I haven't noticed that you've deleted the app. What have you been doing that's so secret I'm not allowed to know about it?'

'I wasn't ignoring your calls,' Clodagh said, bristling at his tone. 'Not that it's any of your business.'

'Is that what you've been doing?' he said. 'Waiting until I've gone to London so you can sneak around behind my back?'

'I haven't been sneaking around behind your back.'

'Bullshit!' He stood up and took a step towards her. For one terrible moment, she thought he was going to hit her.

'Jesus Christ.' He shook his head. 'There's no need to look so bloody scared. I've been worried sick, that's all.

I came home so we could spend some time together. I called you on the way back, but you didn't pick up. Since then, I've been sitting here waiting for you to come home. Praying nothing bad had happened to you.'

'How dare you talk to me like that?' Clodagh said. 'I'm entitled to a life of my own, whether you like it or not. Being your girlfriend isn't enough for me. Not anymore.'

'You blame me for the fact you're not working?' The anger was back in his voice. 'You haven't made any effort to find work since we got together. You haven't written a CV or put any thought into what you might like to do. Instead, you spend your days sitting around feeling sorry for yourself and being jealous of me because I happen to have a job that I love.'

'I am not jealous of you.'

'Oh I think you are. You're bored and unhappy. You think I don't notice how miserable you are? I've tried everything I can to make you happy, but nothing's good enough for you, is it? The harder I try, the more you shut me out. But I keep trying because I love you and I'm scared of losing you.'

'You're right,' Clodagh said. 'I am bored and unhappy. That's not your fault. It's mine. I should have done something about it ages ago. But I wanted so badly for this to work out…'

'It still can work out,' Adam said. 'You just need to try a bit harder, that's all.'

'No.' Clodagh shook her head. 'I'm done trying. I don't want to be with you. There's nothing you can say or do that will make me change my mind. We're finished.'

Adam started to say something, but she didn't wait around to hear it. Outside, it had stopped raining and the sun had come out. Tiny drops of rain hung from the leaves and branches of the trees that lined the driveway, twinkling and glistening in the sunlight. At the gates, she checked the road for any journalists that might still be lurking near the entrance. She hadn't seen any in a few days but knew better than to assume they'd gone for good. When she was sure there was no one around, Clodagh pulled out her phone, switched it on and called a taxi. There was only one place in the world she wanted to be right now, and it wasn't here with Adam.

An hour later, she was sitting at the table in Ivan's small kitchen while he bustled around, putting biscuits onto a plate that he placed in front of her alongside a mug of milky tea.

'Sugar and tea are good for shock,' he said. 'I don't know what's happened but you're very pale. Like you've seen a ghost. So, you drink your tea and eat some chocolate biscuits. After that, if you want to tell Uncle Ivan what's going on you can tell me. If you don't want to say anything, that's fine too. It's up to you.'

'I've left Adam.'

The whole way over here, she'd wondered if she'd made a mistake. Now, saying the words out loud, she knew she'd done the right thing. She took a sip of her tea, strong and sweet and just what she needed.

'So what happens now?'

'I don't know.' Clodagh smiled. 'But I'll work it out. I've been putting off making a decision. Now I have, it feels liberating. These last few weeks, there have been times I've felt frightened of him. I don't want to be with a man who makes me feel like that.'

'Does he know about the baby?'

'Not yet.' Clodagh reached for one of the biscuits. She couldn't remember the last time she'd eaten and suddenly felt ravenous. 'I'll tell him when he's calmed down a bit.'

'He's not calm about you leaving?'

'I don't think so.'

'I didn't know you'd been feeling scared,' Ivan said. 'Why didn't you say something?'

'Because I kept thinking it would pass or I was overreacting.'

'Well it sounds to me as if you've done the right thing. No one should ever make you feel like that. And you have your faults, lady, but being a drama queen is not one of them. If you were scared, then there is a good reason for that.'

'Thanks, Ivan. I feel relieved, more than anything, that I had the guts to walk away. I thought it would be harder than this.'

'It doesn't feel difficult because you know it's right. You're also on your third chocolate biscuit which makes me think you must be hungry. I have no food in the house. Let's go out. We can walk to the chip shop.'

They ate their fish and chips on the beach, watching the night creep in across the pale pink sky.

'You could move in with me,' Ivan said. 'We could split the rent and I could help you take care of the baby after it's born.'

Clodagh tried to imagine herself and her child living in Ivan's tiny little house and knew that was never going to happen.

'A single mother and her child would put quite a strain on your social life,' she said.

'That's a good point,' Ivan said, 'but if you don't stay with me, what will you do?'

'I've already told you, I don't have any plans at the moment.'

'Well I'll help you make a plan. You're not thinking of going back to Ireland, I hope?'

'Would you mind if I did?'

'Would I mind? Lady, I would be devastated. Besides, it wouldn't be fair on your baby.'

'Why is that?'

'Number one, because Adam is the baby's father even if you and he are no longer a couple. Adam deserves the chance to be part of his child's life, assuming he first of all works on his anger issues so he is not scaring people any more. If you move to Ireland you're taking that choice away from him.'

'What's number two?'

'Me.' Ivan thumped his chest. 'I am number two. This baby will need strong role models in its life. People like me who can guide them through their difficult teenage years and be there for them when you are being a pain in the backside and your poor kid needs an adult outside the family to talk to. This baby will not have any aunties or uncles. So that is who I will be: your baby's Uncle Ivan. It's so obviously the right thing that you cannot argue with me.'

Hot tears pricked Clodagh's eyes. Ivan was right. Her baby needed him. So did the baby's mother. She hadn't realised, until now, how scared she'd been of doing this alone. But with Ivan in her life, she would never be alone.

'Thank you, Ivan.'

'You're very welcome.' He put his arm around her shoulder and pulled her into a warm hug. 'You're going to be okay, lady. I promise.'

Forty-three

Day Twelve

That night, in Ivan's tiny spare bedroom, Clodagh slept better than she had any night since discovering Nick's body. She woke the next morning feeling refreshed and ready to start planning for her new life. When she went downstairs, she found a note from Ivan in the kitchen:

> *Gone to work. Help yourself to anything you can find. See you later. Uncle I x*

Clodagh had just made herself a cup of tea and was sitting down to drink it when the doorbell rang. She knew who it was before she opened the door and saw Adam standing outside.

'Can we talk, Clodagh?'

'How did you know I was here?'

'Where else would you be?'

'I don't want to talk,' she said. 'I want you to go.'

'I promise I'm not here to shout or beg you to come back if that's not what you want,' he said. 'I just want a chance to try to understand what I've done wrong.'

He looked as if he'd aged ten years overnight, and she couldn't help feeling sorry for him.

'If you don't understand,' she said, 'then there's no point talking.'

‘You’re right. I know I messed up. I lied to you and I’ve been moody and difficult to live with. I wish I could go back and change how I’ve been. I’m sorry, Clodagh.’

‘It’s not just the lying,’ she said. ‘You’ve been controlling me, Adam. It’s not right.’

‘I know. And I’d like a chance to explain if you’d let me?’

‘No matter what you say to me, it’s not going to change my mind.’

‘I respect that,’ Adam said. ‘If you’ve made your mind up, I promise I’m not going to try to make you change it back.’

‘Okay,’ she said, after a moment. ‘But not here. Let’s go for a walk. Give me a second to grab my bag.’

Her bag was on the small table in the hall. She picked it up, pausing to look at her reflection in the mirror over the table. In contrast to Adam, she looked rested and more relaxed than she had in weeks. Because she’d finally found the courage to do the right thing.

They walked to the beach, crossing the shingle and walking along the sandy section that only appeared when the tide was out.

‘I’ve been a complete dick recently,’ Adam said. ‘I’m not surprised you’ve had enough. The thing is, Clodagh, I haven’t been entirely honest with you.’

‘I’m not sure I want to hear what else you’ve been lying to me about.’

‘Please.’ He grabbed her arm. ‘This is important.’

His grip was too tight; fingers digging into her flesh. A stab of fear pierced her chest. They had walked beyond the town and there was no one else about. He could do anything to her out here and no one would ever know about it.

'I'm in trouble, Clodagh. The TV show has been axed. The producers aren't willing to go ahead until the killer's been found and charged. That's why I was back early yesterday. I'd gone to London for one last-ditch attempt to get them to change their mind. They wouldn't budge. No one wants to work with me with this cloud hanging over our heads.'

'You're hurting me,' she said. 'You need to let go of my arm.'

He looked down, as if he hadn't realised he was holding her.

'Sorry.' He dropped his hand and took a step back. 'All the way home yesterday, I'd been thinking of how I was going to tell you. When you weren't there, I started to panic that I was going to lose you along with everything else.'

'You haven't lost everything else,' she said. 'It's one TV programme, Adam. So what?'

'It's not just that. My publisher isn't returning any of my calls or emails. I'm due to renew my contract next month. I don't think that's going to happen. My next three live events have been cancelled. Everything I've worked so hard for; it's all crumbling down around me. I'm scared.'

He looked wretched, but that wasn't her problem any longer.

'Things will work out,' she said. 'I'm sure they will.'

'You really think so?'

'Adam, you need to take a good look at yourself. You already have so much. If your work dries up for a bit, it's not the end of the world. Take a break, relax and make the most of it. Who knows? If you stopped chasing so hard after the next thing, you might start to work out what it is you really want from life.'

'I hate to say this,' he said, after a moment, 'but you talk a whole lot of sense sometimes, you know that?'

'I know.'

'I really think we could give things another go,' he said. 'We've got something special here, Clodagh. I don't want to lose it.'

'Don't say that. Please. You promised you wouldn't try to get me to change my mind.'

She didn't want to be alone with him, out here on a desolate stretch of beach with no one else around.

'Come on,' she said. 'Let's head back.'

She thought he was going to refuse, but after a moment he sighed.

'Okay. If that's what you want.'

Back at the busy part of the beach, he insisted on ordering food and hot drinks from the cafe.

'It's the least I can do,' he said, 'after all I've put you through.'

She didn't want to sit and eat with him, but it seemed churlish to refuse so she told him she'd have a bacon sandwich and some tea.

'You can stay at the house,' Adam said, as they sat at one of the outside tables with their food and drinks. 'I'll give you as much space as you need.'

'Thanks, but I don't think it's a good idea.'

He would be in her space all the time, checking if she was okay and doing everything he could to get her to change her mind.

'Well at least let me drive you back home so you can pick up some of your stuff,' Adam said. 'You left last night without anything.'

'I'm not sure,' she said. 'Wouldn't it be better if I come over when you're not there?'

'I'm meeting Jake for lunch.' Adam looked at his watch. 'He's getting the train to Lewes. We're going to make a plan for getting my career back on track. I've worked too hard to give up without a fight.'

He was choosing to put his efforts into saving his career, over trying to win her back. It was exactly what Clodagh needed to hear.

'You know what, Adam? A lift back would be great. Thank you.'

They were in the car, driving back to Bramhurst, when her phone rang.

'I see you've finally remembered to charge it up,' Adam said. 'Miracles really do happen.'

'Smart arse.'

She took the phone out of her bag and saw Bella's name on the screen.

'I've managed to get into the files on the memory stick,' Bella said, when Clodagh answered. 'You need to see them right away.'

'It's not a good time right now,' Clodagh said, glancing at Adam.

He was looking straight in front of him, at the road ahead, but she couldn't be sure he wasn't listening to the conversation.

'When is a good time then?'

'I'm not sure,' Clodagh said. 'I'll call you in a bit, okay?'

Bella started to say something else, but Clodagh cut her off.

'Everything okay?' Adam asked as Clodagh switched her phone off and put it back in her bag.

'It's just Bella. She's having a hard time with Simon at the moment.'

'You sure that's all it was?'

'What else would it be?' Clodagh said.

'I don't know. You two seem to have grown very close these last few weeks, that's all.'

For a moment, she wondered what he suspected she'd been doing. Before she realised it didn't matter. They weren't a couple now and she didn't have to explain her actions to him if she didn't want to.

Forty-four

At the house, they said an awkward goodbye before Adam left Clodagh to pack up her things while he went to meet Jake off the train at Lewes. It was harder than she'd imagined, walking around the house they'd shared together, packing her clothes and the few other belongings she had. She'd been happy when she first moved here. It had felt like a dream come true, finally getting together with Adam. But like all dreams, it didn't last. No matter how hard this was, the alternative would be harder over time. They weren't right for each other.

She had just finished packing when the front doorbell rang. Looking out of the window, she recognised Bella's car parked in the driveway. She ran down the stairs and opened the front door.

'I'm sorry,' she said. 'I meant to call you back, but other stuff got in the way.'

'Is Adam here?' Bella said. 'His car's not in the driveway so I assume he's out?'

'He's gone to meet Jake,' Clodagh said. 'Why?'

'Because I don't think he should be here when you see this.' Bella held up the memory stick. 'Mind if I come inside?'

'Do you want a coffee or anything?' Clodagh asked.

'I'd rather get this over and done with,' Bella said. 'Where's your laptop?'

'Upstairs in my room. This way.'

Halfway up the stairs, Clodagh stopped and turned around to look at Bella.

'You're scaring me,' she said. 'Can't you tell me what you found first?'

'I'd rather not. I'm sorry, Clodagh. You'll understand when you see what's on the stick.'

Something dark in Bella's face, anger maybe, underpinned by gleam in her eyes that looked like giddy excitement. Guilt tugged at the back of Clodagh's mind, mingled with the fear of anyone – especially Bella – finding out what she'd done.

'Is it me?' she asked.

'Of course not.' Bella frowned. 'Why would you say that?'

'It doesn't matter. Let's just get this over and done with.'

In the bedroom, she took her laptop out of the suitcase and put it on the table by the window.

'Are you going away somewhere?' Bella asked.

'Adam and I are breaking up.' Clodagh motioned at the laptop. 'Will the memory stick work on this now?'

'It should do,' Bella said, inserting the memory stick into the laptop's USB port. 'I'll need your password.'

'DublinBay,' Clodagh said. 'All one word. Capital D and B. Not very original but easy to remember.'

'Here it is.' Bella slid the laptop across the table. 'I'm sorry, Clodagh. I really am.'

Clodagh sat down, looked at the screen. There were five files in a folder labelled 'Adam'. Four Word documents and one image file. The name of each document followed the same format: a surname and the name of a newspaper. Clodagh recognised one of the surnames, *McLean*. The tabloid journalist who'd been harassing her recently. She clicked on the first file, waited for it to open. It was a draft of an email, she realised, addressed to a journalist at *The Sun* newspaper. She had to read it twice before the meaning sunk in. When she was finished, she opened the next document. Another draft email. She read this one and moved onto the next.

When she'd finished reading all four documents, she opened the image file.

At first, she didn't know what she was looking at. A white expanse of skin, four purple elongated circles. Bruises. She was looking at a wrist with a ring of bruises around it.

Her mouth was dry. She tried swallowing, but it made no difference. The feelings of confusion and horror mixed with an aching nostalgia to hear her sister's voice one final time. Not her voice when she was acting, because Clodagh could hear that anytime she wanted by watching one of Vivienne's films, but her real voice. Because Clodagh knew, if she could just speak to Vivienne, there'd be a logical explanation for what she was looking at.

'I don't understand.' She pushed the laptop away and stood up, unable to bear sitting there a second longer. 'Those emails, what she's written, it's not true. It can't be.'

Words from the emails jumped around inside her head. *Abusive. Coercive control. Violence.* The image of the wrist was stuck to the inside of her eyes. Not just any wrist, her sister's wrist.

'I know it's a shock,' Bella said, 'that's why I drove over. Because I needed to know if you were okay. Men like that don't change overnight. Is that why you've decided to leave him? Because he's been doing it to you too?'

'No.' Clodagh's stomach twisted, the bitter taste of bile at the back of her throat. 'We don't even know Vivienne wrote those emails.'

But the words rang false and she didn't blame Bella for the pitying way she was looking at her. Like Clodagh was a poor, deluded fool. She tried to remember if there'd been any signs, going back over the times she'd met Vivienne during that period. There'd been an underlying restlessness, maybe. A few times Vivienne had drunk too much. But neither of those things were unusual and Clodagh had barely given them a second thought.

'You think she was planning to leave him?' Bella said.

'I don't know.'

She couldn't sort through the different thoughts, all jostling for attention but none of them making any sense.

'Have you got somewhere to stay?' Bella asked.

'I'm sorry, Bella. I don't think I can talk about this now. I need some time to process what's on those files.'

'I'm not going anywhere,' Bella said. 'I'm staying right here. What if Adam comes back? I can't leave you alone with him. Not now we both know what he's really like. You're pregnant. What if he does something to hurt you and the baby?'

'I'm not going to be alone,' Clodagh said, thinking quickly. 'Ivan is on his way over. I spoke to him just before we arrived. He's picking me up to save me having to get a taxi.'

'Cancel him,' Bella said. 'Come and stay with me instead.'

'It's too late,' Clodagh said. 'He'll be here any second.'

'I thought we were friends,' Bella said. 'But it seems you only want to be my friend when it suits you. Fine then. I know when I'm not wanted.'

'Don't be like that,' Clodagh said. 'Please, Bella.'

'It's okay. You don't want me here. I get it. I'll see you around, Clodagh. And the next time you want help with something, how about you ask Ivan, not me? He's the only one of us you really care about.'

Her words were so unexpected that Clodagh didn't know how to respond. So she said nothing, simply watched as Bella left the room and clattered down the stairs. A few seconds later, Clodagh heard Bella's car starting up outside and she turned her attention back to the laptop. She felt bad for upsetting Bella but couldn't worry about that right now.

As her fingers moved across the keyboard, she noticed her hands were shaking. This time, as she looked at the files on the memory stick, her initial repulsion and disbelief was replaced by a burning anger that grew inside her the more she read. She put her hand on her stomach, thinking of the little life growing inside there. She'd assumed Adam would be part of that life. Not any longer. She was going to go somewhere far away, where Adam would never find them. She was glad now she hadn't told him about the pregnancy. He didn't deserve to be a father, and she'd do everything she could to make sure he never was.

She opened the image file again. Her sister's wrist. White skin and purple bruises. Three words beneath: *My anniversary present.*

Clodagh couldn't stop looking at it. Her brain whirling as she thought of the different ways she'd make Adam pay for what he'd done. She was so caught up in her thoughts that she didn't hear the car pulling up in the driveway, or the front door opening. And she was completely unaware of the sound of footsteps crossing the hall and coming up the stairs. She only realised there was someone else in the house, was when she heard Adam's voice, right behind her.

'Where the hell did you get that?'

Forty-five

Clodagh slammed the laptop shut, stood up and turned to face him.

'What are you doing back so early?' she said.

'There's a problem with the trains. Jake can't get to Lewes so we've rescheduled for another day.' Adam nodded at the laptop. 'What's going on, Clodagh?'

'You tell me.' She crossed her arms, waited for him to say something that would explain the unexplainable. 'You knew about it, didn't you? Because you didn't ask me what I was reading. You asked me where I got it.'

She watched his face while he tried to formulate an answer. She saw anger and fear, but not surprise. *He knows.* The knowledge winded her. She didn't know what she'd expected, but not this.

'It's true then.' Her voice sounded like a stranger's. She waited for the rush of emotions to come – fear and grief and anger – but nothing happened. She didn't feel anything at all. Shock had left her numb. Shock at what he'd done and how well he'd hidden his real self from her. Shock at her own stupidity for not seeing what had been happening in her sister's marriage.

'No. I didn't do those things that she's written there. I loved Vivienne. I'd never have hurt her. Even after what she did, I still loved her. How pathetic is that?'

The words on the memory stick filled every corner of Clodagh's mind. Four emails, all documenting a cycle of abuse and control over the two years of Vivienne's marriage. All carried out by someone Clodagh had loved. She had shared a bed and a life with Adam, had sex with him. Her skin crawled with revulsion.

He took a step towards her and she put her hand up.

'Don't you dare come near me.'

'Clodagh, listen to me. Please. Vivienne made that stuff up.'

'You're a liar.'

He was standing too close. The stink of his body clogging the inside of her mouth and nose. She knew the smell would never leave her. No matter how much distance she put between them, it would always be here, clinging to her, reminding her of who he was and what he'd done.

'She was the liar,' he said. 'She twisted things and ruined things and only ever cared about herself. You want to know why she did that to her wrist? Because she wanted a divorce. She was having an affair, and she wanted out of this marriage. But first, she had to make sure I didn't get a penny of her precious money. Even though I was her husband and I was entitled to it. She couldn't stand to let that happen, so she found a way to get what she wanted without having to give me anything.'

Clodagh took a step back, shaking her head. This wasn't happening. He was a psychopath. He'd told the whole world how perfect his marriage was. He'd written a book about it and given talks and he'd lied, over and over and over, so what made him think he'd believe her now?

'I'm telling the truth.' He grabbed her arm, pulled her towards him. 'You know better than anyone that your precious sister wasn't as perfect as she wanted people to think she was.'

'What's that supposed to mean?' She knew she should be trying to get away from him, but anger was making her reckless. She wanted to confront him and make him admit to what he'd done.

'She was selfish and devious and would do anything to get her own way. And you want to know the worst of it, Clodagh? She was all those things and I still loved her. I would have done anything for her, but that wasn't enough. I wasn't enough. I did everything I could to keep our marriage together, but Vivienne never cared about me. She never cared about you, either. The only person your sister ever gave a damn about was herself.'

'How can you say that?' Clodagh screamed. 'She's dead and you think it's okay to talk about her that way?'

'At least I'm being honest,' Adam said. 'You should try it sometime. You've put her on this pedestal, as if she was some sort of saint, while you've conveniently forgotten what an absolute bitch she'd been to you over the years.'

'You have the cheek to talk to me about honesty? You're the one who's built an entire career on your so-called perfect marriage, when all the time she was planning to leave you and you knew about it.' She stopped speaking, as something else hit her. 'When did she tell you she wanted a divorce?'

'The morning she went to Crete. She called me from the airport. She didn't even have the guts to tell me to my face. She waited until there was nothing I could do about it.'

'Because she was scared of how you'd react,' Clodagh said.

'No. Because she was a coward. She didn't want to have to explain herself. That would have been too much like hard work. You know what she was like. She always wanted to get her own way without having to deal with the fallout of her actions.'

It was true, but Clodagh didn't want to think about that now.

'I don't want to hear any more,' she said.

'Well you don't have a choice. You've seen Vivienne's version of events, now you're going to hear mine. When she called to tell me she wanted a divorce, Vivienne told me she'd sent me an email explaining her reasons. These documents were attached to the email, along with that dreadful photo. She said if I didn't agree to the divorce on her terms, she would send them out to the journalists whose names were in the emails. I already knew, by then, that she'd stopped loving me. But I never imagined – not even for a second – that she'd stoop to something like that. She told me she wanted me gone from the house by the time she came back from Crete. If I didn't do what she wanted, she would destroy me. She did those bruises to herself, Clodagh. You want to know how I know that? Because I needed to see how she'd done it. Look.'

He let her go of her arm and jerked back, away from her. He put his right hand over his left wrist and twisted the skin, his face grimacing in pain.

'Stop it,' Clodagh said. 'Please.'

The room felt as if it was tilting, as if the whole house was sliding into the ground. Everything Adam had written and said about his marriage was a lie. How could he expect her to believe him about this when he'd lied about so much else?

'She was having an affair,' he said. 'That's why she wanted a divorce.'

'It must have been very convenient for you when she died.'

'You think I wanted that? Jesus, Clodagh. Is that what you think of me? No matter what Vivienne had done, I was heartbroken when she died.'

She didn't believe him. She'd never believe another word that came out of his mouth.

'After the crash, I thought that was the end of it. She was dead and it was awful, I knew I had to make something positive out of such a terrible mess. That's why I wrote the book. It was my way of remembering what things had been like when we first met. Before she destroyed everything. It never occurred to me there might come a time when someone would want to ruin it all for me.'

'What are you talking about?'

Something cold crawled up from the pit of her stomach, filling her chest and clogging the back of her throat.

'Nick.'

'What about him?'

But she already knew. Nick and Vivienne. It had always been there, hiding in the corners of her mind, waiting for the right moment.

'I thought you must have been in on it,' Adam said. 'It's been haunting me, ever since I found out, wondering how much you knew and why you'd never told me. When she went to Crete with you, I really believed it was so you both could spend time together. But when Nick told me that she'd gone there to be with him, I assumed you must have known all along and decided not to say anything. I thought you'd been trying to protect me.'

It all made sense now. Those times in Crete, when Vivienne was nowhere to be found; coming back hours later with all sorts of pathetic excuses; choosing to eat in the hotel every evening instead of wanting to explore some of the local restaurants.

'I never knew who it was,' Adam said. 'Five years, Nick kept it a secret. Until that night at the hotel. He was trying to persuade me to invest in his latest venture, a chain of upmarket fast food restaurants. I told him I wasn't interested, and he turned nasty. Threatened to tell everyone the sort of man I really was. When I asked him what he was talking about, he told me he'd seen the photo. I knew there was only one reason that was possible. He was the person Vivienne had been seeing behind my back.'

'You told me the row was about me,' Clodagh said. 'You deliberately chose a lie that would humiliate me and make me feel inferior.'

She needed to get out of here, into the clear air where she could breathe and think clearly. But when she tried to get past Adam, he grabbed her, holding tight so she couldn't move.

'Where are you going?'

'Anywhere that's far away from you.'

Her phone was on the table by the laptop. She tried to reach past him to pick it up, but he got there first, sweeping the phone onto the floor. Out of reach.

'You can't tell anyone about this, Clodagh. If it gets out, it will ruin me.'

'Is that why you killed Nick? Because of the risk to your precious career? Well you know what? Your whole career is fake. Everything about you is a lie.'

'I didn't kill him. But I was glad when I heard he was dead. He was a bastard. You should have seen him when he told me. He loved every second of it.'

Clodagh tried to pull free, but his grip was too tight.

'Let me go, Adam. I'm warning you.'

'Not until you've calmed down.' He shook her so hard her teeth rattled. 'I need to know you're not going to do something stupid just because you're angry and upset. Think about what it will do to me if I lose everything now. I know I lied about my marriage, but I've already paid for that. I lost my wife that day. I don't deserve to lose anything else.'

He pushed his face close to hers as he was speaking. Too close. She could smell the coffee on his breath and feel the heat of his anger on her skin. Again, she tried to pull free but all it did was make him squeeze tighter.

'You're hurting me.'

'I can't let you leave. Not like this.'

The fear and the anger took over and she opened her mouth to scream. But he clamped a hand over her mouth, blocking out the sound. She tried to wriggle free, but he twisted her around, one hand over her face, the other squeezed tight around her middle. Too tight. There was a baby in there. He could hurt it. Or worse. She should have told him she was pregnant. If he knew, he'd be more careful. But it was too late now, because she couldn't speak. His hand was still on her face, his fingers digging into her cheeks, the pressure of his palm making it impossible to speak or breathe.

As the blood roared inside her head, and her lungs screamed for air and her heart beat too hard and too fast, all she could think of was the tiny person growing inside her who would never get to see a sunrise or swim in the cool, clear ocean or experience love or sadness or loss or any of the other millions of tiny things that made up a person's life.

Forty-six

Rachel swivelled her chair around so she was no longer looking at her computer screen.

'Ade, the day Tara was killed, she called everyone who'd been at the villa the night Nick was killed except Bella. Why not?'

'Maybe she didn't think Bella could have had anything to do with Nick's death?' Ade said.

'Maybe.' Rachel wasn't convinced. They were missing something. What the hell was it? She ran back over everything she'd learned since the moment she'd stood on the beach at Seaford looking at Nick Gilbert's dead body. There had been sixteen people at the villa that weekend. Ten guests and six members of staff. Two of the guests were now dead.

Rachel's mind fast-forwarded through the investigation, trying to identify what she'd missed.

'Do you remember our meeting with Sharon last Saturday?' she asked.

'Sure,' Ade said. 'What about it?'

'Sharon said something that I meant to think about later but I never did. And now I can't remember what it was.'

Rachel glanced at the clock on the wall. It was almost five o'clock. She'd been working since six thirty this morning. The long hours were taking their toll.

She was tired and hungry. The pressure to find the killer before anyone else died was building as each day passed. Tomorrow morning, she had another meeting with Sharon that she was nowhere near prepared for. Sharon would be looking for results and progress. All Rachel would be able to offer was a big pile of nothing.

'Sam,' she called across the room. 'Any update on when we're getting Adam and Clodagh in for their next interviews?'

'I've left messages for both of them,' Sam said. 'So far, neither of them have called me back.'

'And you haven't bothered to chase them?'

Sam shook his head and Rachel had a sudden, shocking, urge to punch his handsome, smug face.

'Well try again,' she said. 'And keep trying until you get through to them. Jesus, Sam. This is important.'

'Sorry,' he mumbled, looking crestfallen.

Good, Rachel thought meanly. A bit of humility wouldn't do him any harm.

'Come on,' she said to Ade. 'Let's go and get something to drink. I need to move.'

She marched along the corridor to the vending machine.

'How can you drink that stuff?' Ade asked, as Rachel selected a black coffee. 'It tastes like pee.'

'I wouldn't know,' Rachel said. 'Never having tasted pee, myself.'

'I haven't tasted it either,' Ade said. 'Obviously. But I imagine it tastes pretty much like that.'

Rachel took a sip of the drink and admitted to herself that Ade had a point.

'You still think Clodagh and Adam were seeing each other before the crash?' Ade asked.

'It would explain why Clodagh's been holding out on us,' Rachel said. 'Except something about it doesn't feel right. I mean, do we really believe that Vivienne was having an affair with Nick Gilbert and, at the same time, her sister was sleeping with her husband?' She threw her cup into the bin. 'Remind me never to drink that stuff again, would you?'

Just then, Sam Latimer came through the double doors at the far end of the corridor and hurried towards them.

'Rachel we've got something,' he said, breathlessly. 'A phone call's come through. Someone responding to the media appeal. A guy called,' Sam paused to check his phone, 'Jamie Fitzgerald. He's a barman at a pub called the Founders Arms.'

The name was familiar, although Rachel wasn't able to place it until Sam told her where it was.

'It's in London,' he said, 'right by Tara Coleman's apartment block.'

'Of course.' Rachel looked at Ade. 'We grabbed a coffee there after the first time we went to see Tara.'

'Jamie Fitzgerald saw the police appeal on TV yesterday evening,' Sam said. 'He says he remembers serving Adam Murray the day of the murder.'

'You sure about that?' Rachel said.

'Positive.' Sam beamed. 'He wasn't a hundred per cent sure so he went back and checked through the pub's CCTV from that day. He's going to email it through, and we'll need to arrange for someone to go and pick up the tape itself.'

Sam waved his phone in front of Rachel's face.

'The email's already come through. You want to take a look?'

He pressed a few buttons on his phone, before handing it to Rachel. As she looked at the screen, Ade and Sam crowded close. Normally, she would have told them to give her some space but she was too excited to do anything except watch the black and white video playing on Sam's phone.

The camera was placed behind the bar, giving a clear shot of anyone walking in or out of the pub. The time was displayed in small digits on the bottom right-hand side of the screen. At 12:45 p.m. exactly, the pub door opened and a man came into the bar. His features were blurred at first, but as he moved closer to the bar they came into clear focus. And Sam was right, there was no doubt about it. The man ordering a glass of wine from the barman, at the same time as he'd claimed he was browsing the bookshops on Charing Cross Road, was Adam Murray.

'He told us he went from St James's Park to Charing Cross Road,' Rachel said. 'And straight to his meeting after that. The bastard lied to us.'

It took all of Rachel's self-control not to grab Sam Latimer's pretty face and give it a kiss. Instead she grinned at him and Ade.

'Which one of you fancies a trip to Bramhurst then? I'd say it's time we took Murray in for questioning.'

Forty-seven

Adam killed Nick. And Tara, although Clodagh didn't know why she'd had to die as well. The father of the child she was carrying was a monster. She went back over all the years she'd known him, searching for clues, but there was nothing. How could you know someone as long as she'd known Adam without realising who he really was? A sociopath. A psychopath. A killer.

She'd thought he was going to kill her too. But he'd dragged her in here instead, to the tiny storeroom beside the spare bedroom and locked her in. After he'd gone, she begged him to let her out, banging on the door until her hands bruised; screaming until her throat was raw. But he hadn't let her out and now she didn't want him to come back. Because when he did, he would kill her too.

She had to get out of here before that happened. She stood up, pacing the small room, trying to think. Pushing down the panic, the fear that no one would ever find her and she'd remain trapped here, dying of dehydration or a heart attack or starvation. Her stomach hurt from where he'd held her too tight. She didn't want to think about the damage he might have caused, but her mind kept picturing the baby – dead inside her.

'Stop!'

The sound of her own voice was enough to bring her back. She looked around the room, searching for a way out. There was a tiny window that she'd already tried to open but it was sealed shut. Even if it wasn't, it was too small to wriggle through. And she was on the top floor of a three-storey house with nothing but a sheer drop the other side. Which meant she needed to find something to break down the door. But the only things in here were replacement parts for the shower they'd installed recently, a pile of dust-covered books and a broken printer.

She'd thought about breaking the glass in the window – using the printer or her elbow or the shiny new shower head – and shouting for help. But who would hear her? This room was at the back of the house, overlooking the garden with thick trees bordering the perimeter, creating a private, secluded space. She could shout forever and no one would hear her.

She jumped up and banged on the door again.

'Adam,' she shouted. 'We need to talk.'

Silence.

She pictured him sitting on the other side of the door, listening. Waiting to kill her. Or downstairs, in the kitchen, sharpening a knife.

No. She couldn't think like that.

'I'm pregnant,' she screamed.

She held her breath, waiting, but nothing happened.

'Did you hear me, Adam? I'm having a baby. Your baby. You're going to be a father.'

More silence. Then, when she was about to give up, the stairs creaked as someone walked up them.

'I've made an appointment with the doctor. I was going to tell you about the baby after that. I didn't want to jinx it by telling you too early. I've been sitting here thinking about what you said and I can see now that you're right. No one needs to know about Vivienne and Nick. It would risk our child's future and I can't do that. Your career, all your success, that's what will allow us to give this child the life they deserve. The one you never had when you were growing up.'

She stopped talking. She thought she'd said too much, but then she heard more footsteps, getting closer now.

'Is it true?'

His voice made her jump. He was too close. Right there, on the other side of the door. The thought terrified her.

'Yes, it's true. We're having a baby, Adam.'

He wouldn't kill her if he knew she was carrying his child. She had to believe that, or she wouldn't have the strength to face him when he opened the door.

'I didn't kill anyone,' he said.

'I know you didn't.' She hoped she sounded sincere enough to convince him.

'You mean that?'

'I really do.'

'How do I know you're not telling me what I want to hear,' he said, 'just so I'll let you out?'

'I wouldn't lie about being pregnant.'

'And you swear, on the baby's life, that you won't tell anyone that Vivienne wanted a divorce?'

'I swear.' She crossed her fingers, hoping it was enough to ward off any bad luck.

'Okay.'

She wanted to whoop and cheer. Instead, she whispered her thanks and stood back so he could open the door. She heard the clink of metal as he put the key into the lock. And right then, the doorbell rang.

'Who the hell is that?' Adam muttered.

'It doesn't matter,' Clodagh said. 'Whoever it is, they'll go away. Please, Adam. Let me out?'

But he was already walking away. She could hear his footsteps as he hurried down the stairs, leaving her trapped inside the tiny room.

'Adam!' She banged on the door, but he didn't answer.

The doorbell rang again. She waited for him to open the door, straining her ears for the sound of voices but nothing happened. And then she heard a noise she recognised: the creak of the bifold doors in the kitchen sliding open. She ran to the window, climbed on top of the broken printer so she could see through the glass. At first, she didn't see anyone. Then a figure appeared. Adam. Running across the lawn towards the gate at the end of the garden. When he reached the gate, he pulled it open and kept running, disappearing into the woods.

–

'Doesn't look like there's anyone home,' Sam said.

Ade had offered to stay at the station, giving Sam the opportunity to come to Bramhurst with Rachel.

'What's his car doing in the driveway then?' Rachel said, pressing the doorbell again.

'They could have gone for a walk,' Sam said. 'Or taken a taxi somewhere, or they've more than likely got several cars. Either way, I'd say we're wasting our time here, Rach.'

Rachel wanted to tell him his observations and advice were remarkably unhelpful but she managed to keep her mouth shut.

'Let's take a look around the back,' she said. 'Just in case.'

They walked around the house, peering through the windows of each room, searching for any sign of life.

'Told you,' Sam said, as they reached the back of the house. 'This place is empty.'

The house had been extended to accommodate a big, modern kitchen with doors leading onto the garden. The kitchen was empty but there was a gap where one of the doors hadn't been closed properly. Looking around, Rachel noticed a wooden gate at the end of the garden, leading into the wood behind the house. The gate was also open. Nudging Sam, she pointed to the gate, gesturing for him to get down there and take a look.

As he hurried across the perfectly manicured lawn, Rachel slid open the door and stepped inside the house. She stood in the kitchen, holding her breath, listening. When she didn't hear anything, she moved slowly through the downstairs rooms. She could feel her heart, beating hard and fast, as she searched each room. Every time she pushed open another door, she expected to find either a dead body or a killer. When she reached the bottom of the stairs, she looked up through the house. Two floors above her. A lot more rooms to search. And still no sign of Sam.

She walked back to the open kitchen doors, scanning the woods at the back of the house. She couldn't see anything, but that didn't mean there was no one out there. She needed to decide the best course of action: go and check if Sam was okay or search the rest of the house first.

A sudden sound from inside the house made the decision easy. She swung around, creeping through the kitchen and into the hallway, where she stopped and listened. There it was again. Banging. She stood stock still, trying to work out where the noise was coming from. It was coming from upstairs. Someone, or something, was up there.

It could be a trap, but she had to check it out. Two people already dead; she would do whatever it took to prevent a third murder. She moved carefully up the stairs, testing each step with her foot before stepping on it, trying to avoid creaking floorboards. When she reached the second floor, she realised the noise was coming from the floor above. She could hear a woman's voice now, too.

'Help! Let me out.'

'I'm coming.' Rachel ran up the final flight of steps.

'Hello?'

'In here.'

A room at the end of the landing. The door shut.

'Clodagh?' Rachel said. 'Is that you?'

'Oh. thank God,' Clodagh said, from behind the closed door.

With a rush of relief, Rachel realised Clodagh sounded okay. Which meant she'd got here in time.

'Adam's locked me in,' Clodagh said. 'I'm trapped. You need to get me out before he comes back. It's him. He's the killer.'

Forty-eight

Rachel had managed to kick the door down and get Clodagh out of the room. When Clodagh told her she needed to get to hospital, Rachel had driven her to the Accident and Emergency department at Brighton General Hospital. Three hours later, Clodagh's stomach had been scanned and she had a black and white print-out of the eleven-week-old foetus growing inside her.

Rachel had sat with her the whole time, holding Clodagh's hand and reassuring her the baby was going to be okay. After the scan, she insisted on taking Clodagh to the hospital canteen, where she made her drink a mug of sweet, milky tea. Sam Latimer had called one of his colleagues to pick him up from Bramhurst, taking the USB stick with him in a plastic evidence bag.

'A baby,' Rachel said, 'how exciting, Clodagh.'

'Not so exciting knowing the father's a psychopath,' Clodagh said.

'We still don't know for sure that Adam's the killer.'

'But you think he is?'

'It's starting to look that way,' Rachel said. 'But whatever happens with Adam, you can't let that stop you enjoying your pregnancy. Having a baby is such a special time. I hope you can find a way of celebrating this new phase of your life.'

'Do you have children?'

It occurred to Clodagh that she knew so little about this woman who had spent the last weeks investigating every aspect of Clodagh's life.

'Not yet.' Rachel smiled. 'I hope to one day.' Then, steering the conversation back to Clodagh, 'Is there somewhere else you can stay tonight? I don't think it's a good idea to go back to the house.'

'I'd already moved out,' Clodagh said. 'I'm staying with Ivan.'

She was exhausted. And scared. Her mind kept taking her back to that moment when Adam held her, his arm across her stomach, his hand over her face. She never wanted to see him again.

'You've no idea where Adam could have gone?' Rachel asked.

'Jake's the only person I can think of,' Clodagh said. 'He'd do anything to protect Adam's career.'

'We'll send someone around to Jake's house and office,' Rachel said.

Clodagh covered her stomach with her hand. As if a hand was enough to protect a tiny baby from a psychopathic serial killer. She wondered if evil was genetic. If it was, what did that mean for this child she was carrying?

'There's something else I wanted to ask you,' Rachel said. 'When I spoke to Adam and Robbie, they both claimed Robbie left the foundation because he needed a break. But I couldn't shake off the feeling there was more to it than that. I don't suppose you could shed any light on why Robbie left?'

Something heavy lodged in Clodagh's chest.

'I thought Adam told you.'

'About what?'

'He found out Robbie was stealing from the foundation. He'd been doing it for years, apparently. Adam confronted him and told him he had to step down immediately.'

'He didn't go to the police?'

Clodagh shook her head, relieved when her phone started ringing and she had an excuse to stop answering Rachel's questions. Seeing Bella's name on the screen, she diverted the call. But when it started ringing again a few seconds later, she excused herself and went outside the canteen to take the call.

'I'm so sorry about earlier,' Bella said. 'I don't know what got into me, Clodagh. I've spent the last hour trying to pluck up the courage to call you. I don't want to hassle you, but I need to know you're okay?'

'I am now.'

'What do you mean?' Bella said. 'Has something happened?'

'You could say that. Listen Bella, I can't say too much. I'm with Rachel Lewis, right now. It was Adam.'

'What was Adam?'

'All of it. He's the killer. He's disappeared, but the police are looking for him. They'll find him too. He can't hide for ever. In the meantime, I'm going to go back to Ivan's and get some rest.'

'You can't do that. Ivan's house is the first place Adam will go looking for you.'

Clodagh opened her eyes, scanning the hospital corridor, suddenly afraid Adam was going to appear. Bella was right. Adam had gone straight to Ivan's house this morning. There was nothing stopping him doing the same thing again.

'You can stay with us,' Bella said. 'There's a sofa bed in the sitting room.'

'That's kind,' Clodagh said. 'But I don't want to put you out. I can easily book into a hotel.'

The truth was, she couldn't bear the idea of staying with them, having to fend off Simon's questions all evening.

'There's no need for that,' Bella said. 'Seriously. You can come over right away.'

'No.' Clodagh spoke more sharply than she intended. 'Sorry. I really appreciate your kindness, Bella. But I need to be by myself tonight.'

There was silence at the other end and Clodagh thought, at first, she'd managed to offend Bella yet again.

'I understand,' Bella said. 'It's just that you've been such a good friend to me. I want to be there for you too. How about this? Why don't you book a hotel in Brighton and we can meet up tomorrow? That way, I can check for myself that you're really okay.'

'That sounds perfect,' Clodagh said, relieved. 'Thank you.'

'Try the Lancaster,' Bella said. 'It's meant to be really lovely. Good value for money too. Although I know that's not an issue for you.'

'It will be from now on. I'll call them right away.'

'And I'll see you tomorrow,' Bella said. 'Until then, stay safe, okay?'

Forty-nine

Day Thirteen

Clodagh was with Bella, walking through the Lanes on Wednesday afternoon, when the call came through.

'That was Rachel Lewis,' she said, hanging up. 'They've found Adam. He's been arrested and is being held in custody.'

'Phew.' Bella gave Clodagh a quick hug. 'That's good news, isn't it?'

'I suppose so.'

The truth was, she didn't know how she felt. Adam had been a part of her life for thirteen years. He'd been her friend, her brother-in-law, then her boyfriend. She had never once, in all those years, considered he might be capable of murder.

'Where did they find him?' Bella asked.

'He handed himself in,' Clodagh said. 'He stayed with Jake last night, then travelled down to Lewes earlier today, walked into the police station and asked for Rachel.'

'It's over then,' Bella said. 'We can stop being scared and suspicious of everyone. They've caught the killer.'

At the end of the street, one of the bars had set up an outside barbeque. The stink of charred meat hung in the air, choking Clodagh when she breathed in. Her stomach contracted; heat spread from her chest, sweat breaking out across her face and trickling down her back. There were too many people all around her, bodies pushing into her. Voices and laughter; music pumping from the bars and shops; seagulls screeching overhead. She needed to get out of here.

'Come on.' Bella's voice cut through the noise, as she took Clodagh's arm. 'You look done in. Let's go back to your hotel and grab your bags. After that, I'm going to drive you home.'

'I'll be fine in a few minutes,' Clodagh said. 'It's the shock, that's all.'

'I know,' Bella said. 'It's going to take time for it all to sink in. You've been so good to me over the years, Clodagh. Now it's my turn to do the same for you.'

Except it wasn't the same. The only reason Clodagh had gone out of her way to help Bella was to alleviate her own guilt. Not that it had helped. Because no matter how much she did, it would never make up for the fact that she had ruined Bella's life.

The next few hours passed in a blur. Packing her bags, checking out of the hotel, sitting in the car while Bella drove her home. At one point, Bella had switched the radio on. But when the news came on and Adam's arrest was the first story, she'd switched it off again and the rest of the journey had passed in silence.

It was early evening by the time they got back to Bramhurst. Clodagh got out of the car and looked up at the empty house, wondering if this was a good idea. She wasn't sure she felt ready to be back here so soon.

'It'll be easier once you get inside,' Bella said, lifting Clodagh's bag from the boot of the car. 'You've got a key?'

Clodagh found her front door key and, somehow, managed to put it in the lock and open the door. Taking a deep breath, she stepped inside the house and was immediately assailed by memories. All the times she'd stayed here when Vivienne was still alive, sharing meals with her sister and her new husband, trying her hardest to be happy for them despite the bitter jealousy she'd thought she might never get past. Then later, once she'd accepted the marriage, there'd been happier times, sharing a bottle of Prosecco in the garden with Vivienne while Adam cooked dinner. Waking up in the spare bedroom and looking out over the downs, thinking how lucky her sister was to live somewhere so beautiful. Never once imagining that she, too, would live here one day. And alongside all of this, she remembered as well how happy she'd been when she first got together with Adam.

'How could I have missed it?' she said.

'What do you mean?'

'Adam. No matter how hard I try, I can't imagine him doing those things.'

'Clodagh, you saw what Vivienne wrote. You know what he's capable of.'

The problem was Clodagh knew what Vivienne had been capable of too.

'I'm so tired,' she said. 'I don't know what to think, any more.'

'I do understand, you know.' Bella took a step towards her, put her hand on Clodagh's arm. 'It's a terrible shock when you realise the person you've been with isn't who you think they are. But I promise, the sooner you accept it, the easier it will be.'

Clodagh had read all about the five stages of grief and recognised that she was deep into the first stage: denial.

'I'll feel better after a good night's sleep,' she said. 'My head feels as if it's going to explode with all the different thoughts swirling around in there.'

'I'm going to stay the night,' Bella said.

'You really don't have to do that.'

'I do, actually. You're in no fit state to be by yourself. I wouldn't be able to relax if I left you alone. I'm not giving you any choice in the matter.'

'What about Simon?'

'Simon will understand. Why don't you go upstairs, have a bath while I cook dinner?'

Clodagh knew she should tell Bella to go home, that she'd be fine by herself. But when she opened her mouth to speak, she burst into tears instead.

'I'm sorry,' she said, using her sleeve to rub the tears away. A pointless activity because no matter how often she wiped her face, more tears kept coming. 'I'm so sorry.'

'Hey.' Bella put an arm around Clodagh's shoulders and gave her a hug. 'There's no need to apologise. You're not the one who's done something wrong, are you?'

Two hours later, Clodagh was sitting across the table from Bella finishing off a plate of chicken curry.

'I had no idea I was so hungry,' she said, using a piece of naan bread to wipe the sauce off her plate.

'When did you last eat?' Bella asked.

'Yesterday morning, I think.' Clodagh took a sip of water to cool the burning sensation on her tongue. The curry Bella had made was delicious but had a strong chilli spice to it that Clodagh wasn't used to.

'No wonder you're hungry, then. I'm glad you enjoyed it. Simon loves curry so I've got a few recipes I can cobble together quite quickly. It helped that you had all the ingredients here already.'

'That's down to Adam,' Clodagh said. 'The kitchen is his domain, not mine.'

She put the unfinished piece of bread on her plate, suddenly feeling sick.

'Have you spoken to Simon this evening?' she asked, keen to move the subject away from Adam.

'He called earlier,' Bella said, 'while you were in the bath. He says he's missing me. Then again, that's what he always says.'

'What do you mean?'

'I mean,' Bella put her elbows on the table and leaned forward. Something about the way she looked at Clodagh, her blue eyes staring intently, triggered a memory. 'It's what men always say, isn't it? That they love us and they miss us. But it's all bullshit. The only people they really care about is themselves.'

'I thought you were happy with Simon.'

Clodagh tried to focus on the memory but it kept slipping in and out of focus, just like Bella herself. She was still leaning forward, but her features were blurring and multiplying until Clodagh could see several Bellas, all looking at her with an identical expression on their faces. Clodagh recognised the expression, but it took a moment to find the right word to describe it. When she did, she sat back so suddenly she knocked over the glass of water on the table in front of her.

Anger.

Clodagh wanted to ask what had made Bella so angry, but she couldn't get her mouth to work properly. Besides, Bella was speaking again, her voice low and hard, her eyes boring into Clodagh like she could see inside Clodagh's head.

'Simon's no different to any other man. They're all liars, in one way or another. And you know something, Clodagh? The only way to deal with a liar is to play them at their own game.'

Suddenly the memory was there, so fully formed it was impossible to believe Clodagh could ever have forgotten it.

Fifty

'I'm telling you, whoever killed those people it wasn't me.'

Rachel had to hand it to Adam Murray. If nothing else, the man was consistent. He'd spent the last two hours trying to convince her he wasn't a killer. So far, most of the evidence against him was circumstantial. They knew he'd had a row with Nick Gilbert, but that didn't prove he'd killed Nick. A witness could confirm Adam was near Tara's apartment the day she was killed but, again, that didn't mean he was the person who'd ended her life so brutally. There was the USB stick, of course, but that showed he had been a controlling and abusive husband; not a murderer.

Unless Rachel could get him to admit something during the interview, she would be forced to let him go. The situation wasn't helped by the niggling voice at the back of her head that told her Adam was telling the truth. She had to remind herself, more than once, that this was a man for whom fabricating stories was something of an art form.

So far, Murray had admitted lying to a number of things. The myth he'd created about his 'perfect marriage', the reason Robbie Fuson had walked away from the foundation, and the row Adam had had with Nick the night he was murdered.

'The problem is,' Rachel said, 'you've lied about so much that it's difficult to believe anything you tell us.'

'I know that.' Adam wrung his hands together, looking as if he was on the verge of crying. 'I realise how badly I've messed up and I can't blame you for not trusting me. But the only reason I didn't tell you everything about my row with Nick was to protect my reputation. If the truth about my marriage got out, it could destroy me. It's why I didn't tell you why Robbie stepped down from the foundation. I was trying to protect the work we do, not destroy it. Don't you see?'

'I would have thought,' Rachel said, 'being accused of multiple murders is a pretty good way to destroy your reputation.'

Adam's solicitor, a stuffed-up git in a suit, cleared his throat.

'Could we stick to the facts, detective?'

'If you didn't kill those people,' Ade said, 'who do you think did?'

'I have no idea. I genuinely can't think of anyone. If there was anything I could tell you, don't you think I'd do that?'

'Were you planning to kill Clodagh as well?' Rachel said.

'What?' Adam looked and sounded suitably horrified. Again, Rachel had to remind herself he was an accomplished liar. 'Of course not. I love Clodagh. I'd never do anything to hurt her.'

'You assaulted her and locked her in a room,' Ade said.

'I shouldn't have done that. I was panicking. I didn't know what I was doing.'

'What about the documents Clodagh found, alleging you assaulted her sister?' Rachel asked.

Adam put his head in his hands.

'I didn't do those things to Vivienne. She made it up because she wanted a divorce.'

'Bullshit.' Rachel slammed her hand on the table, making Adam and his brief jump. 'You cannot sit here and tell us all this crap and expect us to believe it. No matter what way you look at things, you have lied repeatedly. Which means you're now in a situation where no one's going to believe a word you say. You've told me how important your reputation is to you. Well, I'm afraid to tell you that reputation is ruined. And the only person to blame for that is you. Your lies have caught up with you, and now you're going to have to deal with the consequences of everything you've done.'

She stood up.

'Interview terminated at,' she glanced at the clock on the wall, '5:45 p.m.'

Outside the interview room, she leaned against the wall taking some deep breaths, waiting for the rush of anger to pass.

'You okay, Rach?' Ade asked.

'I'm angry he didn't tell us the truth earlier,' Rachel said. 'All that time we wasted and the killer was there in front of us. How could I have missed it?'

'We still don't know for sure he's the killer.'

'You think we've called this wrong?'

'I guess not.' Ade sighed. 'He's got a motive for killing Nick. Tara too, if she knew about Vivienne and Nick. He's got no alibi for either of the murders.'

'Okay.' Rachel nodded, her mind made up. Sod that voice inside her head. Her first case as SIO and she was almost ready to nail someone for the two murders. This was what she'd worked so hard for these last few weeks, sacrificing time with Grace and any prospect of a social life to get to this moment. She wasn't going to let her own self-doubts get in the way. She'd come too far for that.

'Let's call everyone together, go back over every single piece of evidence against Adam Murray until we've found a way to make it stack up. I'm not going back into that interview room until I'm ready to charge him.'

After talking things through with the team and assigning actions, Rachel sat down at her laptop to start pulling together all the information she needed to charge Adam Murray with two counts of murder. She put her headphones on. Playing music helped her concentrate and, right now, she needed to block out the sounds around her. Every conversation was a distraction, sending her thoughts off in other directions, away from Adam Murray.

She'd been working for over an hour, when she felt someone tapping her shoulder. Pulling off her headphones, she looked around and saw Ade standing behind her.

'Is it urgent?' Rachel said. 'Because if it isn't, I'd rather wait till later.'

'I think you need to hear this,' Ade said. 'See, I sat in that interview and I couldn't shake off the feeling that Adam Murray's telling the truth. I don't think he's our killer, Rach.'

'Feelings aren't enough,' Rachel said, 'you know that, Ade.'

'I know.' Ade beamed. 'Which is why I've taken another look back over the records from the original investigation into the crash. You're not going to believe what I've just found.'

Fifty-one

The day of the crash

Clodagh was shaking from head to toe. Rage tore through her, as she realised why she'd spent so much time by herself on this holiday. Vivienne was having an affair. With sleazy Nick Gilbert. All those times she'd disappeared, pretending she'd gone for a walk or been to the shops or had simply been by the pool and somehow Clodagh had missed her. Lies. This holiday had never been about Clodagh and Vivienne. It had been arranged so that Vivienne could spend time with him.

'Clodagh, wait!' Vivienne was hurrying after her, across the airport terminal.

'Leave me alone,' Clodagh hissed.

'No. I need you to understand.' Vivienne tried to grab her arm, but Clodagh shook her off.

'Nick Gilbert?' Clodagh said. 'Jesus, Vivienne. I thought you had taste.'

'He makes me happy, Clodagh. I'd almost forgotten what it was like to feel happy.'

'How long?' Clodagh said. Then, when Vivienne didn't answer, 'Oh no. This is my fault, isn't it? I took you to his restaurant and introduced you to him. Was that when it started? Did you slip him your telephone number that night? Actually, you know what? I don't care how it started. What about Adam? He doesn't deserve this.'

'Adam doesn't care about me,' Vivienne said. 'He only ever cared about being with me because of who I am and the lifestyle I could offer him.'

'Stop it!' Clodagh said. 'You lied to me. You said this holiday was about us spending time together. You said it was a coincidence that Nick and Gary were at the same resort. But it was just an excuse for you to be with him.'

'That's not true,' Vivienne said. 'If I wanted to be alone with Nick, we'd have gone away just the two of us.'

'Bullshit. You needed me with you so that Adam wouldn't suspect anything. So you planned to be in Crete the same week Nick was going to be here with his friends. You knew what it would do to me, but you went ahead and arranged it anyway.'

'Being single is your choice,' Vivienne said. 'You've chosen the moral high ground instead of happiness.'

'I've already told you, I have too much self-respect to let a married man string me along.'

'He wasn't stringing you along,' Vivienne said. 'If you don't believe me, ask him yourself. Look. He's coming over.'

Clodagh turned to go, but it was too late. Gary was here, standing in front of her, smiling that sheepish smile she'd once found so hard to resist.

'I never meant to upset you by coming on this holiday, Clodagh. I should have stayed away, but when Nick said you were going to be here with Vivienne I couldn't resist the opportunity to see you again and explain.'

He was wearing his pilot's uniform, the same one he'd been wearing the night she first met him. She'd gone out with a group of friends to a wine bar near St Paul's cathedral. Several times, she'd noticed him, standing at the bar by himself. He kept looking over, smiling every time he caught her eye. At some point in the evening, she'd bumped into him on the way back from the toilets. They'd got talking and ended up going home together when the bar closed. She'd been seeing him for a month when he told her he was married. Somehow, he'd convinced her to stay, promising he was on the brink of getting a divorce. Six months later, when he still hadn't left his wife, Clodagh had told him it was over and she never wanted to see him again.

'You're flying today?' she said. 'I thought you were here on holiday.'

'The captain's got food poisoning,' Gary said. 'The airline have asked me to step in.'

Clodagh realised she didn't care. She didn't want to spend another second with him.

'Please, Clodagh,' he said. 'I've left Bella. I've wanted to tell you all week, but you haven't given me the chance. You've been doing everything you can to avoid me.'

'I came on this holiday to spend time with my sister,' Clodagh said. 'Not to listen to your pathetic excuses.'

'They're not excuses. My marriage is over. The divorce came through a few weeks ago.' He moved towards her but she stepped back, out of his reach.

'Leave me alone, Gary. I told you when we split up that I never wanted to see you again. You strung me along for too long, lying to me and making promises you had no intention of keeping. We're finished.'

She turned and walked away, ignoring his shouts as he called after her. She didn't know where she was going, just that she couldn't be anywhere near her sister or Gary. If she hadn't already checked her bags in, she would have left the airport altogether. She checked her flight time on the departures board. Two hours before take-off. She hadn't gone through security yet and decided to wait a while. There was less chance of bumping into Vivienne this side of the gates.

In the Ladies, she splashed cold water on her face, trying to calm the rage still burning inside her. Behind her, the sound of a toilet flushing, then a cubicle door opening.

'Are you okay?'

She looked up, saw a woman about her own age, standing at the next sink, staring at her.

'Not really.' Clodagh shook her head, drips of water splashing onto the mirror, blurring her reflection. 'I've had a row with someone and I don't think I'm ever going to be able to forgive them.'

'What did they do?'

'It was my sister,' Clodagh said. 'She lied about something important.'

'Well I know a thing or two about being lied to.' The woman leaned towards Clodagh, as she continued speaking. 'You know what I've worked out? The only way to deal with a liar is to play them at their own game.'

'I don't know if I can do that,' Clodagh said.

'You'd be surprised.' The woman smiled. 'You need to find the one thing that would hurt them most and make them think it's happened. That's what I'm about to do right now. Wish me luck.'

Fifty-two

'I don't understand,' Rachel said, looking again at the photo on Ade's computer screen. It was a screenshot from the security videos at the entrance to Heraklion airport. A random shot, one of hundreds, that Ade had spent the last hour looking through.

The image showed people entering and leaving the building. Ade had zoomed in on the face of one of them – a woman, late twenties to early thirties, walking out of the building. The angle of the camera gave a clear view of the woman's face, and there was no mistaking who she was.

'It's Bella,' Ade said. 'No doubt about it. I was trying to find an image with Gary in it. I thought if I could get some footage of him at the airport, it might help us understand why he'd been drinking. I don't know why, but I had this idea it might be important. So I started looking through the images from the airport, and I found this.'

'Why on earth was she there?' Rachel asked. 'More to the point, how did we not know this before now?'

'I've called the detective who led the crash investigation,' Ade said. 'He can't shed any light on what she was doing there.'

'I wonder why she's never mentioned it,' Rachel said.

'Maybe she has,' Ade said. 'Maybe everyone already knows she was there. Even if she was, it doesn't matter. It was her husband flying the plane that day, not her.'

Before Rachel could respond, Sam called from the other side of the room.

'We've got something from the ANPR the day Tara was killed. A car registered to Simon Gilbert on the M23, northbound, at 11:05 a.m. The same car is picked up again twenty minutes later on the A23 just south of Lewisham.'

'What about later in the day?' Rachel asked, her mind racing ahead as she tried to work out the implications of this new piece of information. 'He was here being interviewed from about 4:00 p.m. onwards. Which means he'd have to have left London about two hours earlier.'

'Nothing so far,' Sam said. 'But he could have come home a different way. I've checked reports for that evening. There was a crash on the M23 southbound, just after Junction 8. If Simon knew about that, he might have decided to take a different route on his way back.'

'Simon told us he was home all morning,' Rachel said, standing up and motioning for Ade to follow her. 'But we've only ever had his word for that.'

'Where does this leave things with Adam?' Ade said, hurrying after Rachel.

'I don't know,' Rachel said. 'But before we charge him with anything, I want to speak to Simon and find out why he lied to us.'

She walked along the corridor to the lifts, stabbing the button repeatedly with her finger until a lift arrived.

'You drive,' she said, as they left the building and made their way to the row of fleet cars. 'I need to think.'

In the car, Rachel put out a call for a squad car with two officers to meet her outside the Gilberts' house at Portslade.

'What if it was Bella driving the car?' she asked.

'Not possible,' Ade said. 'She was at work all day, remember?'

'I'd still like to speak to her.'

The sound of a phone ringing prevented Rachel from saying anything else.

'It'll be Sam,' Ade said, taking the phone from her jacket pocket and passing it to Rachel. 'He was going to check if there were any other cars registered to Simon and Bella. Can you speak to him?'

'Only one car registered in Simon Gilbert's name,' Sam said, when Rachel answered the phone. '2010 Vauxhall Corsa. Same car picked up by the ANPR. Nothing registered in Bella's name.'

'Which probably means they share the car,' Rachel said. 'Thanks, Sam. I want a warrant to search their house. Can you get that started? We'll focus on perverting the course of justice for now. I'll call Sharon, let her know what we'll need from her.'

Hanging up from Sam, Rachel passed the phone back to Ade and used her own phone to call Sharon.

'You're on the way there now?' Sharon asked, when Rachel had finished updating her.

'We're about fifteen minutes away, tops. I've asked Sam to start processing a warrant. It won't be ready by the time we get there, but we've got enough to arrest Simon and keep him until we can search the house. I've called for back-up to meet me there.'

'Good work,' Sharon said. 'I'll call Sam now, tell him to go through me with the warrant so I can fast-track it. Keep me updated, okay?'

Simon was alone when Rachel and Ade arrived at the house and seemed genuinely confused when Rachel informed him that he was under arrest.

'I don't understand,' he said, frowning. 'You think I killed my own brother?'

Rachel had expected him to put up a fight, but the only resistance he gave was to repeatedly ask why he was being arrested.

'Where's your wife?' she asked, as she led him outside to the squad car.

'You want to arrest Bella too?' Simon looked even more confused. 'What's happened? We haven't done anything wrong. Is it Adam? Has he put you up to this?'

'Tell me where I can find Bella,' Rachel said, shoving him into the back of the waiting squad car.

'She's at work,' Simon said. 'But she won't speak to you. She's in the middle of something important and can't be disturbed.'

Rachel shut the car door and told the two uniformed officers to take Simon to Brighton police station.

'Get him processed and start the clock,' she instructed. 'I'll be back as soon as I can to interview him.'

The entrance to Max-Roysten Pharmaceuticals was closed when Ade pulled up outside fifteen minutes later.

'Doesn't mean she's not in there,' Ade said. 'Makes sense they'd lock up at nights. I imagine a company like this would be a target for animal rights activists.'

'MRP prides themselves on not doing animal trials,' Rachel said, remembering the promotional videos she'd watched the last time she'd been here. She spotted an intercom system in the wall beside the gates. Jumping out, she pressed the button that – she hoped – would connect her with a real person inside the building.

'Hello?' A man's voice, low and gravelly. 'Who's there?'

'Police,' Rachel said, giving Ade the thumbs up. 'I need to urgently speak to one of your employees, Bella Gilbert.'

The man gave a wheezy laugh.

'You've come at the wrong time' he said. 'Nobody here in this big old building except me and the two guard dogs, Arthur and Martha. If you want to speak to any of the staff, you need to come back during the day.'

'How do I know you're telling the truth?'

'Hell. How do I know you're the police? You could be anyone, for all I know.'

'I've got ID. Look. This proves I am who I say I am.'

Rachel held her warrant card up to the camera and waited.

'Detective Inspector Lewis,' the man said. 'All right. Sorry about that. We get all sorts of crazies coming here stirring up trouble. My job is to make sure no one gets into this building unless we know they're not going to cause us any problems. You're welcome to come in and look for yourself, but I'm not lying to you when I tell you there's no one here.'

'We probably should come in and take a quick look, anyway,' Rachel said.

She got back in the car and waited for the gates to open. As Ade drove up towards the building, it was obvious that the security guard had been telling the truth. Apart from one light in the entrance lobby, the entire building was in darkness.

'No cars in the driveway,' Ade said. 'Which means if she's here, she didn't drive. You going to tell me what we're doing here, Rach? Because the way I see it, our two key suspects are Adam Murray and Simon Gilbert. And both of them are currently in police custody.'

Rachel didn't answer. She was remembering the first time they'd been here. Sitting outside in the warm sunshine with Bella Gilbert.

'She told us she has her lunch outside,' she said.

'Who told us that?'

'Bella,' Rachel said. 'The first time we were here. She said she eats her lunch outside. Every day, unless it's raining.'

'So?'

Up ahead, a broad, tall man came out of the building and started walking towards them. He raised his hand in greeting. Rachel was about to wave back, when her phone started ringing.

'Sam,' she said, putting the phone to her ear. 'Everything okay?'

'I found something,' Sam said. 'It may not be important, but I thought you should know.'

'Go on.'

'Do you remember Clodagh's ex-boyfriend said she left him for a married man? You thought it might have been Adam. I decided to do a bit more digging. Spoke to a few people she used to work with. They all swore blind the man she was seeing couldn't have been Adam.'

'And that's it?' Rachel said. 'That's what you called to tell me?'

'There's more. One of them, a woman called Cheryl, said she'd been with Clodagh the night she met her new fella. She didn't know much about him, but she remembered he was wearing a uniform. A pilot's uniform.'

Suddenly, the different pieces of information came together. With it, a lurch of real fear. Gary Wakefield had left his wife because he was seeing someone else. Clodagh and Gary had been on holiday in the same resort. And Bella had been at the airport the day of the crash.

'Turn around,' Rachel told Ade. 'Now! Clodagh's in danger. We need to get to Bramhurst right away.'

Ade hit the brakes and swung the car 180 degrees so it was facing the gates. As she screeched down the driveway, Rachel looked back, just in time to see the confused look on the security guard's face as the car turned into the road.

Fifty-three

'You were at the airport,' Clodagh said. The words came out slowly, because she was finding it difficult to speak. 'In the Ladies' toilets.'

She tried to think through the fog in her mind, but it was getting worse.

Bella had stood up and walked around the table so she was standing over her. Clodagh looked up, trying to focus. There was something wrong with Bella's face.

'I knew where he'd gone.' Bella's words sounded faint and far away. 'Same place they went every year. A boys' holiday. Except it wasn't just the boys, was it? You were there too. Although I didn't make the connection then. When I spoke to you in the toilets, I didn't have the slightest clue that you were the bitch who'd ruined my life.'

'But you were already divorced. What were you doing there?'

'I never wanted a divorce,' Bella said. 'He didn't give me any choice. I begged him to give our marriage another chance, but he said he couldn't do that because he didn't love me any longer. After the divorce, he cut off all contact. It was unbearably cruel. Can you imagine it? You dream of spending your entire life with someone and then they leave you and you're by yourself.

'I asked him if there was someone else, but he swore blind it wasn't that. And I believed him. Which made it worse, because I spent months blaming myself, trying to work out what I could have done differently. And then I bumped into an ex-girlfriend of Nick's and she told me the truth. She said Gary had fallen head over heels for some woman he'd met in a bar one night.'

She knew. The knowledge hit Clodagh like a punch in the stomach. She pushed her chair back, tried to stand up but her body refused to do what she needed it to.

'I didn't know,' she mumbled. 'Swear to God.'

'It was the final straw,' Bella continued, as if Clodagh hadn't spoken. 'I had to do something. I couldn't wait until he was back in the UK. I flew to Crete the night before he was due back. I found out when the Air Euro flight was due to leave and I waited for him at the airport. I knew it would be my best chance of finding him. It was crazy, I can see that now. But that's what he'd turned me into. A bitter, crazy woman who couldn't control what she was doing.'

Bella leaned down, her face so close her features blurred together. Clodagh smelled garlic and spices and felt warm, damp breath on her cheek. She tried to swing her head to one side but Bella was holding her face, making it impossible to move.

'He wanted children,' Bella said. 'Was desperate to be a father. That's the real reason he stopped loving me. Not because of some stupid slapper he had a fling with. We'd tried to get pregnant but nothing happened and, over time, it wore us down. That day at the airport, I found him and told him I'd discovered I was pregnant soon after he left me. I let him believe that maybe I still was. Then I looked him in the eye and told him I'd had an abortion.'

The only way to deal with a liar is to play them at their own game.

'I wanted him to see that actions have consequences. I thought he'd be devastated. But you know what he said? He said it was probably just as well, because he didn't think I'd cope very well as a single parent. That's when I did it, Clodagh. I asked him to go to the bar and get me a glass of water. And while he was gone, I emptied my vodka into his glass of juice. When he came back from the bar, he was so keen to get away from me that he drank the juice in one go and left. It was the last time I ever saw him.'

'But his blood alcohol…'

The investigation into the crash had concluded Gary had been drunk. Clodagh knew you didn't get drunk from a single shot of vodka.

'He must have gone to another bar and carried on drinking,' Bella said. 'He'd never been able to stop at one drink. It's why he rarely drank.'

It was Clodagh's fault, then. Bella would never have been driven to do something like that if Gary hadn't cheated on her. And the person he'd cheated with was Clodagh. She had stayed with him, even after she knew he had a wife. The fact that she'd left him eventually didn't change anything.

'I'm sorry.' It was all she could say and she knew it would never be enough.

'I spent so long thinking about her,' Bella said, 'wondering whether she was alive or if she'd been with him in Crete and died in the crash too. Hating her because, if she was still alive, she had the chance to grieve in private. While my face was splashed all over the front pages of every newspaper. It never occurred to me, not even for a second, that I already knew her.'

Clodagh was struggling to understand what Bella was trying to tell her. Bella's fingers were digging into the sides of Clodagh's face, hurting her. When she tried to twist free, Bella squeezed tighter.

'You think I'd have spent the last five years being your friend if I'd known?'

Suddenly, Clodagh understood. And with that knowledge came fear. Using every last remaining piece of energy, she pushed Bella away from her and stood up. The room swayed, and when she tried to walk towards the door, her legs gave way and she fell to the ground. She scrabbled forward, her only thought to get away before it was too late. Bella had killed Nick and Tara. And now she was here to kill Clodagh.

She grabbed hold of the table leg, trying to haul herself up so she could run. But Bella grabbed the back of her head, pulling her back, away from the table. She could hear screaming, realised the sound was coming from herself and wondered how she had the energy to make that noise.

'Shut up!' Bella smacked Clodagh's face, the sudden pain bringing a sharp focus.

'You killed Nick.'

'It was an accident.' Bella let her go and Clodagh slumped back on the ground. Her limbs were heavy and uncoordinated.

'He told me about you and Gary,' Bella said. 'That night at the villa. I didn't believe him at first. But the more he talked, I realised he was telling the truth. He thought it was funny. Kept laughing as if it was all one big joke. I couldn't stand it. I pushed him away from me and he fell forward. He was on his hands and knees, still laughing. I wanted him to shut up but he wouldn't.

I picked up a stone and I hit him, and I kept hitting him, again and again. And you want to know something, Clodagh? Nothing I've ever done before or after made me feel as good as I did in that moment.'

Clodagh was drifting. Watching her body, on the ground. Looking down as Bella rolled her onto her back, pushed up her sleeves and put Adam's Japanese chef's knife into Clodagh's hand. Bella wrapped Clodagh's clumsy fingers around the handle and sliced the blade into the white skin on the underside of her wrist. A sharp pain and the warm rush of blood, as Bella put the knife in Clodagh's other hand.

'You'll write a suicide note,' Bella said. 'Very kind of you to share the password for your laptop yesterday. You'll say that it was Adam who killed Nick and Tara. You didn't tell the police, because he threatened you and you're scared of him. But the guilt has got too much and you can't stay silent any longer. The police already have the USB stick. It won't take much to convince them Adam's been coercing you into keeping quiet.'

'No!' Clodagh shouted but made no sound. As the knife cut into her other wrist, she thought of her baby, the little life growing inside her, and knew she had to fight harder. But no matter how hard she tried she couldn't stop the blood flowing from her body. She felt the darkness before she saw it, creeping across the room, blocking out the kitchen and Bella's face, until all that was left was a pin prick of light. As that, too, disappeared, Clodagh imagined her baby, disappearing into the light and floating up and out of her body into the wide open sky, finally free.

Fifty-four

'Clodagh and Gary Wakefield were having an affair,' Rachel said, as the car sped along the A27 towards Bramhurst. 'That's why they were in the same resort together. I think that's why Bella went to Crete – to confront them.'

'Doesn't make sense.' Ade frowned. 'Clodagh went to Crete with her sister.'

'To the same resort that Nick and Gary and their friends went to every year.'

'Gary was divorced by then,' Ade said. 'If he was going out with Clodagh, why didn't they share a room? It wasn't like they'd have to hide the relationship. His divorce was finalised by then.'

'Maybe they'd split up and Clodagh went there to try to win him back,' Rachel said.

'If Bella's known about the affair all this time,' Ade said, 'why wait until now to do something about it? I don't see what any of that's got to do with Nick and Tara being killed.'

'We know Nick was in a foul mood the night he was killed,' Rachel said, thinking as she spoke. 'He was doing his best to cause trouble, stir things up. He was Gary's friend. What if he knew about Clodagh and Gary but never told anyone? Then that night, he finally told Bella the truth about her friend.'

'Why would he do that?'

'Because he wanted to hurt her?' Rachel said. 'Or to stir things up just for the sake of it. Who knows? But I realised something earlier. The Max-Roysten security system shows Bella being at work when Tara was killed. When we went there to talk to her, she said she eats her lunch outside every day. Yet on the day of the murder, there's nothing on the security system to show that she left the building. Why not? I think she sneaked out somehow, so she could drive to London. If she went through a fire escape, for example, it wouldn't show up on the security system because she wouldn't have left through the main barriers. She knew if we checked, the system would log her as being in the building all day.'

By now, Ade was in Bramhurst, driving down the narrow country road towards Glebe House. They were almost at the entrance when a car pulled out of the driveway. The driver barely stopped to check for traffic before turning into the road and speeding away. But in the brief moment before it pulled out, Rachel had caught a glimpse of the driver's face.

'It's Bella.' She opened the door and jumped out of the car. 'Go after her. And Ade, whatever you do, don't let her go.'

She slammed the door shut and raced towards the house, pulling her radio out and shouting instructions into it. Arranging for checkpoints to be set up on the roads around Bramhurst, giving a description of Bella Gilbert and details of the car she was driving. After that, calling for an ambulance and back-up to Glebe House.

The front door was locked. No response when Rachel rang the bell. She ran around the house, banging on the windows of each room as she passed, shouting out Clodagh's name, her sense of foreboding growing with every passing second. Her mind flashed back to yesterday afternoon, when she'd found Clodagh safe and well, hoping beyond hope she wouldn't find something different this time.

Like the rest of the house, the kitchen lights were all switched off. But the blue glow from an open laptop meant Rachel had a clearer view into this room than any of the others she'd looked into so far. A Smeg fridge; a range with some pots on it; a large island dominating the centre of the room; the laptop itself, on a long table close to the glass doors; something lying on the floor beneath it.

A sudden lurch of fear. Not something. A person. Clodagh. Poor, damaged, pregnant Clodagh; the outlines of her face captured in the glow of the laptop screen. Her features white and ghostly, her eyes closed, her body too still.

'Clodagh!' Rachel banged on the window. The body on the floor didn't move. She could see blood now, pooling on the ground around Clodagh. Rachel tried to break the glass with her elbow, then by throwing her body against it but it wouldn't break. She scanned the garden, looking for something she could use. A selection of garden furniture, most of it too heavy to lift. Down at the end, amongst the wildflowers, a single deck chair. She raced across the lawn, lifted the chair and carried it towards the house, folding it as she ran.

With a roar, Rachel lifted the chair over her head and charged, throwing the chair into the glass door with every ounce of strength she possessed. An almighty crashing sound shook the silence of the night and suddenly the door was gone and there was broken glass everywhere, on the floor and in her hair, tiny cuts breaking out on her face and arms. She ran inside, slipping and sliding on the shattered glass, and fell to the ground before the body, praying to any god up there who would listen, that she wasn't too late.

Fifty-five

'I never meant for all those people to die,' Bella said. 'But to imply it was my fault? That's bullshit. I only gave him one drink. He must have had more after he left me. If the airline had been doing their job properly, he'd have been breathalysed. But they don't do that, do they? Those budget airlines, it's all about cramming bodies onto the plane and getting as many flights in as they can. Besides, I'd never have spiked Gary's drink in the first place if he hadn't left me. If anyone's to blame for what happened, it's Clodagh Kinsella.'

She stopped speaking and looked defiantly at Rachel and Ade. So far, she hadn't shown one bit of remorse for her actions. Self-pity outweighing guilt all the way.

'Tell us what happened with Nick,' Rachel said.

'I've already advised my client that she doesn't need to say anything else at this stage,' Bella's solicitor said.

'And I've told you I want them to hear my side of the story,' Bella said. 'They need to know that none of this was my fault.'

'We know Nick upset a lot of people that night,' Ade said. 'I'm guessing he was pretty nasty to you too?'

'Do you know the worst of it?' Bella's voice rose as she spoke. 'He was talking about Clodagh, saying everyone thought she was this goody two shoes but it was all an act and no one knew what she was really like. I thought

Clodagh was my friend, so I stuck up for her. I told Nick he shouldn't say those things about her. That's when he told me. He thought it was funny. Kept laughing at how clever Gary had been, hiding the affair from me even during the divorce.'

'How did that make you feel?' Ade asked.

'Horrible.' Bella scowled. 'You have no idea how stressful it is when you're trying to conceive. We tried so hard, but nothing worked. By the end of it, we were flat broke and emotionally wrung out. That's the real reason Gary left me. I don't care what anyone thinks, he'd never have looked at that bitch if I'd been able to give him what he wanted.'

'I assume Nick knew all of this?' Ade said.

'That made it worse,' Bella said. 'He was Gary's best friend and he knew what we'd been through and yet there he was, laughing at me as if it was all one big joke.'

'Gosh.' Ade shook her head. 'No wonder you lost your temper.'

'I didn't mean to kill him. You can think what you like, but it was an accident. If he'd been just a little kinder, a little less of a bastard, I wouldn't have got so angry.'

From there, it was easy to get Bella to tell them exactly what had happened. As she told them how she'd hit Nick multiple times on the back of his head before rolling his body over onto his back, Rachel was struck once again by Bella's utter lack of remorse.

'Why do you think Nick never said anything about Clodagh and Gary before that night?' she asked, when Bella had finished speaking.

'Gary was his best friend,' Bella said. 'After the crash, Nick did all he could to try to defend Gary's reputation.

Right up to the outcome of the investigation, he kept insisting the crash wasn't Gary's fault.'

She paused, as if something had just occurred to her.

'The thing about Nick,' she said, 'he wasn't that bad before the crash. He was best man at our wedding. We were friends, the three of us. But the crash changed him. His career did brilliantly, but his personal life was a mess. He lost his three friends and I don't think he ever got over it.'

'What about his relationship with Tara?' Rachel asked, keen to move the interview along. They had Bella on record telling them she'd killed Nick. Now, they needed to get her admitting to Tara's murder as well. Once they had that, they'd have all the evidence they needed to prepare their case for the CPS.

'Tara was a user,' Bella said. 'She was only with Nick because he was rich and famous. If he'd been a nobody, she wouldn't have been seen dead with him.'

'Can you tell us what happened the day she died?' Ade said.

'She called Simon,' Bella said. 'Left a message telling him she knew who'd killed Nick and she was going to tell the police. It was all a bluff, but when he called me to tell me what she'd said I couldn't stop thinking about it.

'I've got a key to a door at the back of the building at work. I've had it for years, ever since I had to go in late one night. No one knows I still have it. I don't even know why I've kept it, except I've always liked the idea of being able to get in and out of the building without anyone knowing about it. The whole security at work's a bit Big Brother, you know?'

'So you drove to London?' Ade said.

'I only wanted to talk to her. Make sure she didn't actually know anything. She was drunk when I arrived. Staggering about the place and throwing accusations around. One minute she was accusing Adam of killing Nick, the next she was blaming Simon. Then she started on about Clodagh, and she said she had something important to tell me. Nick had told her about Gary and Clodagh a few weeks earlier. He'd sworn her to secrecy, but now he was dead she felt I ought to know. Well, I could hardly let her live after that.'

'Why not?' Rachel asked.

'Because I didn't want anyone to know, and Tara was a blabbermouth. There was no way she'd keep something like that to herself.'

'So you killed her,' Rachel said.

'I didn't have a choice.'

'How did you do it?' Ade asked.

Bella's solicitor started to speak, warning her not to say anything else, but she silenced him.

'She had a rack of knives in her kitchen,' she said. 'I took the biggest one before sitting beside her on the sofa. And then I just stuck it into her. It wasn't difficult. Strange, really, to think that killing someone could be that easy.'

'She was stabbed twice,' Ade said.

'Really?' Bella looked surprised. 'Maybe I stabbed her again. I really can't remember. Either way, it wasn't planned. She didn't give me any choice.'

'I think it was planned,' Rachel said. 'I think, by then, you'd already decided to kill Clodagh. You had to get Tara out of the way before you did that. Because if Clodagh was killed, Tara might tell people about Gary's affair. Thereby, implicating you in Clodagh's murder.'

'You make it sound as if I'm the villain here,' Bella said. 'Surely you can see that none of this was my fault? It's why I didn't want to go no comment. I wanted you to understand that I'm the victim here. Clodagh Kinsella ruined my life. She left me with nothing while she ended up with Adam in that big house, pregnant with a baby she didn't even want. You tell me what's fair about any of that.'

'You knew she was pregnant when you tried to kill her?' Rachel said.

Bella opened her mouth, then closed it again and looked at her solicitor.

'I think we'll go no comment from here,' the solicitor said. 'My client has been extremely co-operative, I'm sure you'd agree. I'd like to request a short break now, so I can talk to her in private.'

Rachel knew she didn't have to agree to the break, but she'd already got more information than she could have hoped for. In most cases, when they had amassed this much evidence against a suspect, the entire interview would have been no comment. Bella's insistence on trying to get the police to see things from her perspective had given Rachel a confession that would greatly assist the CPS's decision to prosecute.

'We can take a break,' she said. 'Before we do, just one more question. Bella, tell me this: did you know about Nick's affair with Vivienne Kinsella?'

Bella shook her head, looking sad.

'I had no idea. I thought he was my friend, you know? But he was only ever Gary's friend. Looking back now, I don't think Nick ever gave a damn about me. None of them did.'

After leaving the interview room, Rachel suggested to Ade that they go outside.

'I could do with some fresh air,' she said. 'I feel dirty after listening to all of that.'

They walked out of the Custody Suite into the bright sunshine of another hot summer's day. Rachel switched her phone on and checked for new messages.

'A text from Ivan Babić,' she said. 'Clodagh's coming out of hospital tomorrow.'

'That's great news,' Ade said. 'What about the baby?'

'He didn't say. I guess we'll just have to wait and see.'

'You saved her life,' Ade said. 'You do know that?'

'Only just. If we'd been a few minutes later, she'd have died.'

'But we weren't a few minutes later. Come on, Rach. I'm hanging out for a Diet Coke. Let's walk across to Tesco and get some chocolate and drinks. My treat.'

As they walked through the car park to the exit, a plane flew over the sky above them. Rachel turned her head, watching as the plane moved further away, gradually getting smaller, until there was nothing left except a trail of white against the clear, blue sky.

Epilogue

Five months later

New Year's Day. Bright sunshine reflected off the still sea. An icy breeze skimmed over the town and along the seafront. Clodagh walked as fast as her pregnancy bump would allow. Seven and a half months and she was already huge. She couldn't believe her stomach was capable of getting any bigger, although her midwife assured her that was a certainty.

She heard her phone ringing and answered it without checking the Caller ID, already knowing who it was going to be.

'Adam, happy new year.'

'Thanks. How are you guys doing?'

You guys. He'd taken to speaking about them as if the baby was already born. Something Clodagh found sweet and irritating in equal measure.

'We had an early night,' she said, patting her stomach. 'Although your son was clearly up for a party. There was a lot of kicking going on.'

'That's my boy.' Adam paused. 'Everything's okay, then?'

'Since yesterday when you asked me the same question? Yes, Adam. Everything's still okay. If it wasn't, you'd be the first person to know about it.'

'I know I'm fussing too much,' he said. 'But after everything that's happened, this baby feels like a gift. I spend most of my time petrified something's going to go wrong.'

'That must be lovely for Georgia.'

'She's pretty patient,' Adam said. 'Although I do drive her mad half the time.'

Adam had only been with his new girlfriend for three months, but it was clear to anyone with a pair of eyes that they were crazy about each other. Ironic, considering that a few months prior to that he'd thought Clodagh was his true love. Not that she cared. With a baby on the way, Adam was always going to be part of her life. But her old feelings for him were gone entirely. She understood, now, why he'd been so controlling. His troubled relationship with Vivienne had damaged him. But understanding and forgiving were two separate things; Clodagh would never completely forgive him for the lies he'd told or the ways he'd tried to manipulate her.

He'd met Georgia at a television awards ceremony. A former reality TV star, Georgia's celebrity status was rapidly fading by the time she and Adam got together. She seemed more than happy to take on her new role as supportive partner to her famous boyfriend. As well as being very lovely, Georgia didn't put up with any of Adam's nonsense. She'd only agreed to move in with him if he gave up alcohol and enrolled on an anger management course.

'I've been approached about writing a book,' Adam said, 'about the murders. Georgia says I need to speak to you first before agreeing to anything.'

'What would you do if I said I don't want you to do it?'

The cold had made the scars on her wrists sting. She didn't want to talk about this now and resented Adam for ruining what had been, until now, a perfect morning.

'If you really didn't want me to,' he said, after a moment, 'then I wouldn't do it. But please don't say no right away. So much has already been written about it, this would be a chance to set the record straight.'

'I almost died that night,' Clodagh said. 'I'm not sure how I feel about you writing about it, if I'm honest.'

Another few minutes and Rachel Lewis would have been too late to save her. Luckily, Rachel had got there in the nick of time. Not that Clodagh had known anything about it. The sleeping tablets that Bella had crushed into her curry had knocked her out. She'd woken in hospital the following day, confused and terrified for the baby growing inside her. Somehow, Patrick Richard Kinsella had survived and, if the scans were anything to go by, he was positively thriving.

She knew it was testing fate, naming the baby before he was born. But she was tired of worrying about what might happen. Far better, she'd decided, to live life without always expecting the worst. Which was why, after they'd discovered they were having a boy, she'd persuaded Adam they should choose names. Patrick, after Clodagh's father; Richard after Adam's dad. And Kinsella, because Clodagh had insisted that any child of hers would have her surname.

'At least think about it?' Adam said. 'Please?'

'Okay. But I'm not making any promises.'

'I understand. Thanks, Clodagh.'

She could see Ivan, now, walking towards her along the promenade. She said goodbye to Adam and hung up, waving to get Ivan's attention.

'Good morning to you, lady.' Ivan grabbed her and embraced her in a hug before patting her stomach. 'How is my little baby Pat? Has he been a good boy for his mamma?'

'The way he's kicking around at the moment,' Clodagh said, 'I think he's going to be a professional footballer.'

'I was a very good footballer at one time,' Ivan said. 'I will teach him when he is old enough.'

'You played football?' Clodagh asked, glancing at Ivan's stomach which was almost as big as her own.

'I'm a man of many secret talents, lady. Although today I do not feel so talented. I am very hungover.'

'What a surprise.'

The two friends linked arms and started walking.

'It is a surprise, actually. I didn't drink very much, but still I feel like shit. So, I have decided. From today Uncle Ivan will drink no more.'

'You think that's possible?'

'It is a new year, lady. The sun is shining and we are here, walking together along the seafront, sharing our stories like a pair of old lovers. Anything is possible on a day like this.'

Acknowledgements

First and foremost, thank you to my agent Laura Longrigg for helping to rebuild my writing career during a very difficult time in my life. Huge thanks to the wonderful team at Canelo and Canelo Crime: Louise Cullen and Francesca Riccardi – two women I cannot wait to share a drink (or two) with after lockdown; Nicola Piggott, Siân Heap, Claudine Sagoe and Deborah Blake.

Special mention to two people who shared their knowledge and expertise so generously while I was writing this book. Deborah Reade, thank you for all the brilliant and insightful advice on police procedure. And Steve Wood, a man with an encyclopaedic knowledge of all things aviation, who helped me so much in working out some of the finer plot details. Both of you were amazing and, as always, any mistakes are down to me.

Thank you also Nigel Adams for your generous advice. Unfortunately, the scene you advised on got cut in the edits but I'm still hugely grateful to you!

Love and hugs to my fellow crime writers Lorraine Mace, Marion Todd and Chris Curran – y'all know how much your support means to me.

Thank you to Chris Simmons from crimesquad.com – someone else I'm looking forward to catching up with over a drink sometime soon.

Thanks to all the bloggers, reviewers and readers who've said so many lovely things about my books and work so hard to promote authors. And finally, thank you to the brilliant admin team at UK Crime Book Club – you guys are the best!